MW00831303

He's a scribe lookir
and frustratingly attr̲.̲.̲.̲.̲

THE SEEKER

Summoned to the Gulf Coast of Louisiana, Rhys of Glast, Irin archivist and scribe of Istanbul, must convince a legendary Irina singer to trust him. His success could shift the balance of power all over the Irin world and give singers an important key to their past.

Meera didn't call for Rhys's help, and she doesn't need it. The scribe's mission is to bring more martial magic into the Irin world, while Meera has been looking for a path toward peace. She's convinced that some other motive is at work, and his stubborn arrogance doesn't pass for charm in her hallowed opinion.

Discovering ancient Irina magic should be something both scholars can agree on, but can these two rivals find any common ground? Neither Rhys nor Meera can ignore the simmering heat between them, but will attraction overcome the caution that has shaped both their lives?

THE SEEKER is the seventh book in the Irin Chronicles, a romantic contemporary fantasy series by Elizabeth Hunter, *USA Today* best-selling author of the Elemental Mysteries.

PRAISE FOR ELIZABETH HUNTER

Elizabeth Hunter's books are delicious and addicting, like the best kind of chocolate. She hooked me from the first page, and her stories just keep getting better and better. Paranormal romance fans won't want to miss this exciting author!

— THEA HARRISON, NYT BESTSELLING AUTHOR

Developing compelling and unforgettable characters is a real Hunter strength as she proves yet again with Kyra and Leo. Another amazing novel by a master storyteller!

— RT MAGAZINE

This book more than lived up to the expectations I had, in fact it blew them out of the water.

— THIS LITERARY LIFE

A towering work of romantic fantasy that will captivate the reader's mind and delight their heart. Elizabeth Hunter's ability to construct such a sumptuous narrative time and time again is nothing short of amazing.

— THE READER EATER

# THE SEEKER

## IRIN CHRONICLES BOOK SEVEN

## ELIZABETH HUNTER

*For my son*

*Light of my life.*
*Travel companion.*
*The ultimate adventurer.*
*I thank God every day I get to be your mom.*

# CHAPTER ONE

*Houston, Texas*

Rhys of Glast, only son of Edmund of Glast and Angharad the Sage, Irin scribe and archivist of Istanbul, was not impressed by the biscuits and gravy at the diner on Kirby Drive. The biscuits were passably flaky, but the gravy tasted too much of flour and was thick enough to stand a fork in. Fortunately, the chocolate cream pie had redeemed the meal.

The waitress walked around the counter and down to Rhys's booth with a steaming pot of coffee. "Warm-up?"

Rhys quickly put a hand over his mug, an edge of ash-black ink peeking from the long-sleeved linen shirt he wore. "Tea."

Her brown eyes widened. "Pardon me, sugar?"

"Tea," Rhys said again. "I'm drinking tea, not coffee."

She smiled. "That's right. Can I get you some more hot water?"

"Please. And another bag of tea."

"You got it." She walked away with a natural sway to her wide hips, dodging with practiced grace the server coming at her.

There were two waitresses working in the diner that night, the older black woman with greying hair and quick reflexes and a younger white woman Rhys suspected was just starting her job. She looked to the older woman almost constantly for cues and lingered at a table in the back corner near the toilets where a brown-haired young man smiled and flirted with her.

Rhys catalogued the diner in detail. Fading incandescent bulbs reflecting off dated gold-veined mirrors provided ample visibility of every angle in the restaurant. The red vinyl booths squeaked whenever patrons moved, and an old-fashioned bell over the door alerted him to any new entry.

In addition to the waitresses, there were seven other patrons. Three students who had taken over a round booth, a middle-aged couple who appeared to be quietly fighting, an older man lifting coffee to his mouth with shaking hands, and the Grigori flirting with the young waitress.

Rhys sipped his tea as he watched the Grigori. It was plain black tea, nothing like the symphony of teas he was accustomed to in Istanbul. There one could find tea blended with spices from all over the world in countless varieties and subtle variations. Love of tea had redeemed Istanbul for Rhys.

Pie was on its way to redeeming Houston.

The Grigori glanced at Rhys and opened his newspaper, pointedly ignoring the scribe who watched him. A newspaper meant the Grigori had to be over sixty, early middle age for one of the Fallen children. Though his face was young and attractive to the humans around him, he could pose a slight challenge if he chose to confront Rhys.

The air-conditioning blasted in the restaurant, even in the middle of the night, forcing the hot, wet air of the Bayou City to cold condensation that ran down the windows and scattered the light of the passing traffic on Kirby Drive.

The Grigori glanced up, then looked down again. Despite the air-conditioning, Rhys could see a gleam of perspiration at the man's temples.

Rhys of Glast had spent his formative years in the cool, rolling hills of Somerset in southern England, but for some reason known only to the Creator, his entire adult career had been spent in various places that baked and steamed.

Spain. Morocco. Istanbul.

And now he was being sent to New Orleans, Louisiana, by way of Houston, Texas.

Hot and hotter.

The waitress returned with a battered metal pot with a red-and-yellow packet wedged on the side. "You want another piece of pie?" She motioned to the near-empty plate. "Sure didn't seem like you liked the biscuits and gravy much."

"I didn't."

The woman didn't look offended; her pink-painted mouth turned up at the corner. "More pie, Mr. Bond?"

"I beg your pardon?"

The waitress glanced over her shoulder before she turned back to Rhys. "Fancy British guy eating pie and drinking tea at two in the morning on a Wednesday night? Sitting in the corner booth with one eye on the door and the other on that flirty fella in the booth by the bathroom?" She wrote something down on her order pad. "If I didn't know you weren't carrying, I'd be worried."

Rhys sat up straighter. "Not that you're wrong, but how do you know I'm not carrying a firearm?"

The tilted smile turned into a grin. "Sugar, I've been waiting tables in Texas for thirty-five years. I know when someone's got a gun."

"Fair enough." He made a mental note not to discount the waitress.

Rhys hadn't approached the Grigori by the toilets. He'd been drawn to the diner by the scent of sandalwood that followed the half-angelic creatures—sons of the Fallen always carried the distinctive scent—but so far the Grigori had done nothing but flirt, and that was built into its DNA. In the complicated times they lived in, that meant Rhys was forced to show restraint.

No longer could scribes hunt Grigori on sight. Though the Irin race was charged with protecting humanity from the offspring of fallen angels, recent revelations had turned black and white to countless shades of grey.

Some Grigori had wrested freedom from their Fallen fathers and conquered their predatory instincts. Many of those had turned those instincts to join the Irin in their quest to rid humanity of fallen angels. Some of their sisters, the *kareshta,* had mated with Irin scribes. Rhys's own brother-in-arms was mated to the sister of a Grigori the Istanbul scribes had once hunted.

It was all so complicated now.

"Has he done anything to concern you?" Rhys asked the waitress quietly. "The man by the bathrooms?"

"No." She lifted the empty pie plate. "Just sitting there reading his paper. He likes the blueberry and wears too much cologne. Not my type."

Rhys forced his eyes away from the Grigori. "Another piece of chocolate for me."

"Cook just put a black-bottomed pie in the case."

His mouth watered. "That sounds perfect."

"See?" She winked at him. "Knew you were my type."

Rhys couldn't help his smile.

"You be good," she said, walking back to the counter.

Rhys sometimes longed for the days when the borders between enemy and friend were clear. Only a few years ago, he could have stalked the creature waiting in the restaurant with a clean conscience; run him to ground, pierced his neck with the silver blades he had hidden, and watched Grigori dust rise to the heavens to face judgment.

*It is what they deserve,* a vengeful voice whispered inside him. *It was the Grigori who slew the Irina singers. It was the Grigori who tried to wipe out their race. It was the Grigori—*

No.

That wasn't their world anymore. Rhys dunked the teabag into the silver pot. That would never be their world again. Their world demanded forgiveness. It required reconciliation, both within their race between the Irin who hunted and the Irina who hid, and outside their race between the Irin and those Grigori who pursued a peaceful life.

So Rhys waited for his tea to steep.

And he watched.

———

AT FOUR IN THE MORNING, the air outside the diner was still muggy. Rhys toyed with the end of a cinnamon toothpick as he watched the entrance of the diner from the car he'd rented at the airport. His phone was on speaker, and his brother Maxim was speaking.

"The Houston scribe house and the New Orleans house are combined under one watcher. It's a situation that's persisted despite complaints from New Orleans, but the American Watchers' Council is unconvinced that New Orleans needs a stronger presence."

Rhys said, "It's a large tourist destination." Grigori liked to feed on tourists.

"True. But as far as anyone can tell, attacks are surprisingly low. Houston has more. Larger population, bigger house."

Rhys pulled the toothpick from between his lips. "Fallen presence?"

"The closest known Fallen stronghold is in Saint Louis. There are always minor angels about, but Bozidar is the closest known archangel, and he resides in and around Saint Louis. Prior to his arrival around two hundred years ago, there hadn't been a significant Fallen presence in North America for four hundred years because of the native Irin presence."

And by Irin presence, Max meant what their people had once been. Not the fractured and suspicious people they were now. The Irin of North America were legend in Rhys's world, vibrant and powerful societies of warrior scribes and singers descended from Uriel, the oldest and wisest of the Forgiven angels. Renowned for their long lives and prowess in battle, the largest group, the Uwachi Toma had routed the archangel Nalu and all his cadre eight hundred years before, leading to a golden age of Irin peace that lasted for roughly five hundred years.

But with European expansion into North America, new Fallen came, breaking the rule of the Uwachi Toma and their allies.

Rhys said, "North America didn't escape the Rending."

"Nowhere did," Max said. "But they had already been weakened by the American Revolutionary War. By the time the Rending happened, many Irin communities were already scattered, more stories than actual presence."

"So what you're saying is it's entirely possible this singer we're looking for was already in hiding and lived."

Maxim didn't respond. Rhys frowned and tore his eyes away from the diner entrance to make sure they still had a connection.

"Max? Are you there?"

"I am. According to Sari's contact, this Irina is definitely still living. And likely somewhere in Louisiana. If we can find her—"

"We might be one step closer to restoring Irina status."

Max said, "The Irina need to relearn martial magic if they want a chance at regaining their rightful place in Vienna."

The Rending, the massive global Grigori attack that had killed eighty percent of Irin women and children, hadn't happened out of nowhere. The Irina had spent centuries focusing on creative, artistic, and scientific magic, letting their focus drift to peaceful pursuits while Irin scribes gained more and more battle prowess. Battle had become men's work, far beneath more lofty Irina goals. It had left the singers vulnerable to attack.

Two hundred years after the Rending, most surviving Irina were still reluctant to leave the havens where they'd hidden. The Elder Council in Vienna was the governing body of the Irin people, financing the scribe houses and protecting the secrecy of the Irin race in the human world. Since the Rending, the council was made up of old men reluctant to part with their power.

The lack of Irina martial power was a constant and pressing concern for those working toward reform in their world. Though the Irina Council had reformed in Vienna, every day Irina still lived with the threat of Grigori attack looming over them and a lack of confidence from Irin scribes around the world.

Damien, his former watcher in Istanbul, and Sari, Damien's mate, had taken over the martial training academy in the Czech Republic. They were only one example of reformers desperate to rediscover the once-potent battle spells Irina had sung. Songs that had destroyed angels had been lost to time and the Rending.

Unlike the scribes' vast libraries and archives, Irina libraries existed only within singers. Librarians were knowledge in human form, walking encyclopedias of magic, able to recall complex spells from memories trained since birth. They did not write magic down, believing that the delivery and emotion behind oral preservation were as essential as the spells themselves.

It was a stubborn ideology that drove Rhys mad.

He was a scribe of Gabriel's blood, trained to preserve knowledge and copy any manuscript with precision, gifted in tattooing intricate magic on his body. Rhys's tattoos, his *talesm*, started on his left wrist, wrapped around his arm and up his shoulder, down his chest, torso, and right arm, covering his body from the tops of his thighs to his neck. Only the space over his heart was bare, waiting for the mating mark he was mostly convinced would never come.

His *talesm* were not only magical armor but personal history. Every scribe was trained to preserve knowledge for future Irin generations in the most efficient and sensible way: writing.

"So this woman"—Rhys adjusted his seat—"the singer we're looking for. Is she a librarian?"

"She's more valuable than a librarian."

"Right." Rhys rolled his eyes. At this point in their history, there was nothing more valuable than an Irina librarian.

"Rhys, Sari's contact believes she's found the Wolf."

"What wolf?"

"*The* Wolf."

Rhys blinked. "You can't be serious."

"I am."

"The Wolf and the Serpent were both killed in battle."

"No. Ulakabiche died in battle, but his sister didn't. Atawak-abiche lives. At least according to Sari's contact."

Rhys was skeptical. "And not once in nearly three hundred years has she revealed herself to her sisters?"

Max sighed. "Don't ask me. You're the archivist. That's why Damien sent you on this job instead of me and Renata. Sort out truth from legend, talk to this woman in New Orleans, and find out if the Wolf is still living. She and her brother were the most feared Irin warriors in North America. Atawakabiche's magic destroyed an archangel without the use of a heavenly blade. If she exists, she could change everything."

"Who is Sari's contact?" Rhys asked.

"An Irina named Meera."

"Meera? Who is she?"

"I don't know anything about her except that she'll meet you in New Orleans in three days. Go to Jackson Square on Saturday morning, and she'll find you."

Rhys groaned. "She wants to meet me among the heaviest tourist traffic in New Orleans on Saturday morning? Is she serious?"

"I don't make the decisions here, brother. I'm passing along information. Be there by nine."

"In the morning?" Rhys curled his lip. He was a night owl.

"Nine in the morning, my friend."

Rhys's eyes locked on the dark-haired man walking out of the diner with a woman on his arm. It was the Grigori and the young waitress. He opened his car door and spit the toothpick on the ground. "Max, I have to go. I'll call you when I get on the road."

"What are you doing?"

Rhys slid his hand into his pocket, his fingers curling around the hilt of a silver dagger. "Just a little hunting. No need to be alarmed."

"Be careful. The Houston house thinks you're a mild-mannered scholar on vacation."

"Of course I am," Rhys muttered. "Goodbye, Max."

He hung up before his brother could say another word. He tossed the phone in the passenger seat and closed the car door. The Grigori and the woman had disappeared to the back of the parking lot. Perhaps the Grigori had convinced the woman to give him a ride to a more secluded location where he could feed from her.

Grigori were soul hungry. Human mythology called them incubi or vampires. Even cannibals. They fed from the soul energy that all human beings possess, though most preferred women. Women they could lure with their looks and their scent. They were born predators, dark sons of heaven made to seduce and feed.

In a shadowed corner of the back parking lot, Rhys saw the Grigori pressing the woman against her car, kissing her neck as her head was thrown back. She was panting, her breasts heaving in a macabre imitation of pleasure. In reality, there could be no pleasure for her because the Grigori's bare hands were pressed to her stomach and back, his touch robbing the waitress of her will. She was putty in the creature's hands, willing to do anything he asked, his touch more effective than a drug.

Rhys approached quietly, but the Grigori sensed him. The creature spun, keeping one hand on the woman.

"You," he hissed.

"If you were smart," Rhys said, "you'd already be running."

The Grigori's eyes were cold and blank. No hint of conscience warmed them. "She wanted me. She said yes."

"She doesn't know what you are." Rhys glanced at the woman. Her eyes were closed. She was still panting. Her moans of pleasure scraped against his ears like nails on slate. "Get away from her."

The Grigori hesitated, his eyes narrowed in growing panic. Rhys noticed the second the man decided to run. He broke away from the woman and lunged to the left, dashing between cars as Rhys caught the human woman and laid her on the ground. Then he shot to his feet and ran after the man who was running toward Kirby Drive.

The older waitress walked out of the restaurant just as Rhys ran past.

"Your friend is in the back," he yelled. "She's hurt!"

Rhys left the humans and sprinted, waiting for the traffic to pass so he could follow the Grigori. Cars honked and drivers rolled down their windows to yell.

There.

Rhys caught a glimpse of the monster as he darted between two parked cars in a multistory parking garage. The Grigori might have been running to his own vehicle or simply trying to lose Rhys. Either way, it was going to die.

He paused when he entered the garage, brushing a thumb over the *talesm prim* on his left wrist and waiting for his senses to sharpen. In seconds, his eyes adjusted to the darkness, his heart rate steadied, and his ears picked up the footsteps running up the ramp and toward the roof. Rhys followed the sound, drawing the silver stiletto from its hidden sheath and gripping it tightly.

He reached the top of the garage and was barely breathing harder. The moon had disappeared behind a blue fog that drifted over the city, but yellow lights buzzed on the roof, casting strange overlapping shadows between the parked cars.

There were several rows, and Rhys walked among them deliberately, waiting for a sound, a scent, anything. He sorted through the acrid smells of burning sulfur, exhaust, and mold.

There.

A row of pickup trucks caught his eye, every one of them a potential hiding place for the Grigori.

"Who do you belong to?" Rhys asked. "Who commands you, Grigori?"

A creak near the blue truck.

Not the blue, the red.

"There are ways to live without killing," Rhys said.

A shuffle and a break in the silence. The Grigori took a running leap from the top of the parking garage to the office building on the other side of the alley.

"Are you joking?" Rhys grumbled. He hated to jump, and he didn't particularly like heights. "You fecking knob!" Rhys gritted his teeth and ran toward the edge, concentrating on the burst of magical energy as he leapt into the darkness.

A fall from four stories wouldn't kill him, but it would hurt like hell.

He landed and rolled on the gravel roof of the office building just as the Grigori slipped over the side. Rhys needed to get to the ground fast. He spotted a drainpipe and ran toward it, shimmying down the dirty pipe until he was close enough to fall. He ran around the corner of the building and saw the man dangle from the fire escape before he dropped.

Rhys grabbed him by the neck while he was still catching his balance and shoved him face-first against the brick wall of the office building.

The man was smaller than he'd appeared on the run. Rhys was tall, over six foot, with a runner's build and a long reach. The Grigori was far from bulky, but Rhys dwarfed him.

He gripped him by the neck. "Who do you belong to?"

The man's shoulders slumped. "Bozidar."

"The archangel?" Not likely. Bozidar's sons would have more natural magic than this.

The Grigori began to laugh. "Our fathers are waking, scribe. The Fallen have only been sleeping, resting in their victory. Now you've roused them."

"Have we?" Rhys leaned in. "I look forward to the fight."

The man laughed harder. "You have no idea! How many of your

women did we kill? How many of your men died of despair? The Irin are pathetically weak."

Rhys curled his lip. "You call me weak? How many unsuspecting women have you fed from like that waitress?"

The man froze. "Not enough." Then he turned and snapped his teeth at Rhys's left wrist in a last-ditch effort to damage the scribe's magic.

Without a second thought, Rhys plunged the silver stiletto into the base of the Grigori's neck and waited. Within seconds, the body began to shimmer and disintegrate. Rhys stepped back and wiped the dust from his blade before he returned it to the sheath, watching silently as dust rose through the heavy night sky, disappearing into the darkness and mist.

Under his breath, Rhys said a prayer. He'd slain a son of the angels. Fallen angels, yes. But the same blood ran in his veins. The same magic fueled him. Grigori were the dark shadow of the Irin. Without knowledge and training, scribes could turn feral too.

The lone Grigori had been no challenge, and Rhys felt no satisfaction in the kill, no sense of righteous anger or vengeance.

Bozidar.

The archangel from Saint Louis. It hadn't been the whole truth, but there had been a ring to it. Perhaps the young man had belonged to one of Bozidar's lesser Fallen allies. He'd report the incident to his watcher and let Malachi decide if he wanted to pass the information along.

After all, Rhys was nothing more than a visiting scholar from Istanbul.

---

RHYS SLEPT until noon the next day, waking only when the housekeeper tapped on his door. He'd checked in with a Spanish passport, so Rhys called out in Spanish, asking for a few minutes more. He threw off the sheet that covered him and took a moment to enjoy the cool breeze on his bare chest. He rubbed the unmarked skin over his heart, wondering for the thousandth time what it would feel like to put a needle into it.

His first marks had been made at the age of thirteen by his father, a stern man who impressed on Rhys the importance of history and legacy and tradition. Those *talesm* ran down his back, covering the magic his mother had spoken over him from the time of his birth.

*"When you find your mate, then you will know true wisdom."*

His parents still lived, still tended the library in Glast as every scribe in his family had done since the beginning of time. Rhys was a direct descendant of Gabriel's line in Glastonbury. His father had been the chief archivist as his grandfather had been. Rhys's children —if he ever had any—would be expected to follow in that line.

In the early days, the scribes in his family only took trained Irina librarians as mates, so the Great Library at Glast had been one of the rare joined archives of their race. Rhys's grandfather had met his *reshon* and broken that tradition, but no one had blamed him for it. A *reshon* was a rare and beautiful gift, the single perfect soul created by heaven to be your equal.

In his rare optimistic moments, Rhys hoped for a mate. A *reshon* was likely too much to ask. Of course, it wasn't easy finding any mate when eighty percent of the women in your race had been killed.

He hadn't given up hope. Not... entirely. After all, his brothers in Istanbul had found mates. Malachi, his new watcher, had mated with Ava, an American with unique Grigori blood. Leo had mated with Kyra, and Rhys was fairly sure Max and Renata were finally together, though the cagey Irina had led his brother on a fifteen-year chase.

There was hope. Possibly. If those bastards could find women to put up with them, there had to be someone who could keep his interest for more than a single conversation.

Rhys groaned and rolled out of bed. He could feel the onerous heat pressing against the windows and creeping under the door. He showered and threw on his spare change of clothes, unconcerned about covering his *talesm* that morning. Americans were easy about such things. Tattoos were so common now; he'd noticed professionals and grandmothers inked with them. The neat rows of intricate writing covering his arms were unlikely to raise more than casual interest.

He stood at the door of his motel room, enjoying the brief moment of being perspiration-free before he slid on his sunglasses and walked outside.

Ah yes. Covered in sweat again.

Walking quickly down the stairs, he found his compact blue rental car and threw his backpack in the passenger seat. Then he drove two blocks away and returned the car at the rental agency before he called for a taxi. He took that car to another hotel and walked from there to a national car rental.

If he was going to take a road trip, he wanted the right car, and it needed far better air-conditioning than the blue compact. He took off his sunglasses and scanned the lot.

A salesman walked up to him. "Can I help you, sir?"

Rhys spotted it, a silver Dodge Challenger with tan leather interior. "That one." He walked over to look inside.

Legroom. Glorious, glorious legroom.

"The Challenger?" The man appeared to be excited. "An excellent choice. It has—"

"Would it be possible to return it in New Orleans?"

"Yes, sir. There would be an additional charge."

"Not a problem."

He slid his sunglasses back on. Yes, this one would do nicely.

Within minutes, he was driving on Interstate 10, "Way Down We Go" blaring from the speakers, crossing the channel and heading east to New Orleans and a legend lost for three hundred years.

# CHAPTER TWO

Meera watched the Englishman from behind her sunglasses. She licked powdered sugar from her fingers as he wandered aimlessly around Jackson Square. He tried to avoid the crowds, but it was impossible. She knew he was looking for her, but… she didn't get beignets anywhere but Café Du Monde. They were sin in pastry form, and Meera believed in indulging.

"You're a mean woman." Zephirin reached for a beignet from the paper bag Meera carried.

They were sitting on a shaded bench in a corner of the square. Zep had patrolled all night with no Grigori spotted. Far from satisfied, it left the scribe edgy, like a tiger waiting to pounce. Lazy on the outside with all that coiled energy within. Meera offered him sugar to appease the beast.

"I'm not mean," she said. "Watching how someone navigates tourist traffic is very telling."

"So this is a test?"

"Yes."

"Look at this girl." He took a bite of the powdered doughnut. "She's so damn cute. Little bitty thing with all that hair and all those curves, that sweet face…"

"You know you love me."

"Poor scribe doesn't know what he's in for getting within reach of her claws."

Meera cocked her head. "I'm trying to decide if I'm insulted."

Zep smiled. "You're not."

"You're right; I'm not." She watched the man navigate through a crowd of Chinese tourists and claim the corner of a bench. Meera had a clear view of him from her shaded seat. His eyes were covered by dark aviator glasses, but she could see annoyance in the lines around his mouth.

She smiled. "This is so amusing."

"Why do I like you?" he said.

"Because I am delightful and dangerous."

Zep shook his head. "Yeah. You are."

Meera crossed her legs, the flowing coral dress she wore brushing her calves. The sensual brush of fabric and humid breeze off the river enveloped her, feeding her energy like the humans that surrounded them. She was enveloped by humanity, the scent of coffee and the sound of jazz musicians filling the air. Vendors and artists set up their tables, and shopkeepers were opening their doors.

It was all so *rich*. The first time she'd stepped into Jackson Square four years before, she'd been entranced. Everything about the old French city felt like an indulgence. It was a million miles from the quiet and ascetic compound where she'd lived for the first part of her life as the long-awaited heir of Anamitra, wisest of singers.

Meera closed her eyes and took off her sunglasses, letting the morning sun heat her gold-brown skin. "You didn't have to stay if you didn't want to watch me torment him."

He finished the beignet in two bites. "I came to protect this poor scribe from your wiles."

"My wiles?" She looked at him from the corner of her eye. "I never use my wiles on hapless scribes."

He muttered, "Not even when we want you to."

"You know, when I came to this country, I was told it was a place to be free. To break with traditions and push boundaries." She finished off her beignet and brushed her hands together before she put her sunglasses back on. "But every scribe I meet just wants to lure me into mating."

He crossed his arms, the black ink of his *talesm* swirling over light brown skin. "There something wrong with wanting a mate?"

She almost gave in. Almost. Zephirin was a very handsome man, an attractive blend of Native American, European, and African blood like so many Irin in this part of North America. In addition to his looks, Zep was kind, funny, and respectful. Her father even liked him. When Zep had first asked Meera out to dinner, she'd been tempted.

But only tempted.

Meera bumped his shoulder. "Don't be cross. I just got out of the haven. I don't know if mating is right for me."

"So only human dates until you figure it out?"

"None of your business." She nodded at the Englishman who was still sitting across the square. "He's handsome, isn't he?"

"You're asking me?"

"You have eyes, don't you?"

Zep squinted at the other scribe. "He's thin and pale and looks like a buzzkill. Like a cranky professor."

"According to my mother, his name is Rhys of Glast. He's a renowned archivist of Gabriel's direct line."

"That sounds... not fun at all."

Meera pursed her mouth. "I think he looks amusing. And he has beautiful hair." And lips, but she didn't mention that. In fact, Meera found the Englishman highly attractive, with a tall, lanky build that caught her eye and a wide, expressive mouth that hinted at sinful things. He had blue-black hair and pale skin, high cheekbones and a sharp jaw.

He looked... severe. But the mouth distracted her. She wanted to muss that dark hair and wrinkle his collar. Knowing he was a "renowned archivist" intrigued her and concerned her, all at the same time.

"He's pale as shit," Zep said. "Looks like he never leaves the library." He stretched his arm across the back of the bench, resting his skin against hers. It was a natural affection Meera had grown to enjoy.

"Well, he's here now," Meera said. "So clearly he leaves it sometimes. He's supposed to be brilliant with computers."

"That so?" Zep's interest was piqued. He had an interest in technology, though he was the only one in his scribe house who seemed attracted to it. He idly brushed a thumb over Meera's shoulder. "Are you going to keep him locked away while he's here?"

"Maybe." Meera relaxed at Zep's touch.

Casual affection between friends in the Irin world was valued and necessary. The contact allowed singers to release energy they gathered from spending time around humans and gave scribes a boost of power. They were people of community, never meant to be isolated or alone, a tricky proposition for someone like Meera who guarded her privacy fiercely.

She glanced back at the new scribe and her breath caught. "Oh, hello."

The scribe had his eyes locked on Meera. She felt… found. The corner of the man's beautiful mouth turned up.

*Got you.*

Meera could almost hear his voice in her mind. She cocked her head and met his gaze behind her dark glasses, resisting the urge to lower her shields. In a place like Jackson Square, she would be quickly overwhelmed by the soul voices that surrounded her. Though she had to admit she was curious.

*Who are you, Rhys of Glast?*

Meera felt Zep tense beside her, so she put a hand on his knee.

"His instincts are good," Zep said.

"Maybe not such a recluse after all." She patted his knee and stood, handing him the empty paper bag. "I should go. I've kept him waiting long enough."

"Want me to come with you?"

She shook her head. "Give me your card."

Zep reached in his back pocket and handed a business card over.

Meera tucked it in the pocket of her sundress. "I'll tell him to contact you when he gets a chance."

"Still guarding your secrets?" Zep looked up. "I'll find out eventually."

She laughed a little. "Not if I don't want you to."

"Go." He nodded at the scribe. "It looks like the professor is getting antsy."

---

SHE CROSSED THE SQUARE, watching the man's reaction as she approached. Meera knew she was an attractive woman. She was petite and rounder than was typical for Irina. Most Irina burned massive amounts of calories surviving in the human world. Their metabolisms were faster than humans.

Meera had been raised to have near-perfect control of her ability to read souls and ironclad control over her shields. It allowed her body to be a bit softer, which many considered an attractive trait in the Irin world. She was aware of the appeal and used it to her advantage whenever possible.

But she was stymied by Rhys. He didn't rise as she approached. He didn't offer any acknowledgment at all other than a gaze locked on her face.

Interesting.

"Rhys of Glast," she said.

"And you are Meera," he said. "That's all Sari told me. She didn't say you'd be with anyone."

"I wasn't planning to be. Zep just happened to be patrolling the

Quarter last night."

"Anything interesting?"

"You'd have to ask him." She handed over Zep's card. "He wants you to call him later. He's very friendly, but he's protective."

"Understood."

He was still sitting. Meera didn't know if he intended to be rude, but her father and mother would have found the man's lack of deference insulting.

As if reading her mind, he said, "I thought you'd had your fill of watching me. So it's my turn."

Meera cocked her head. "Are you always so easily perturbed?"

It was then that he rose, stepped toward her, and Meera felt the full effect of the scribe's physicality. It caused an intriguing curl of interest in her belly. This was no mere scholar. He moved with practiced grace and control, not like Zep's lazy tiger, more like a stalking leopard. He might be an archivist, but he was a warrior too.

"I don't like people," Rhys said.

Meera angled her head up to meet his eyes. She could see them faintly behind his sunglasses when he was close. They were thick-lashed, another fiendishly sensual detail in an otherwise impassive face.

"You'll like me." She gave him a smile she knew would show her dimples. "I'm delightful."

He reached up, his expression unchanging, and stroked a thumb over the corner of her mouth.

Her smile fell away. It was everything Meera could do not to shiver. "What do you—?"

"You had powdered sugar on your lip," he said. "It was distracting."

"The best things usually are."

He narrowed his eyes. "Sari didn't say what you do here in New Orleans. Are you attached to the scribe house?"

"They wish. My parents are in charge of a haven in this area. I'm sure you understand why I can't be more specific."

"So you moved to be close to them?"

"Hmmm." They still hadn't moved from the middle of the square. Meera could feel the morning sun on her shoulders. She didn't mind the warm weather—she relished it—but she could see Rhys beginning to sweat. "Should we move into the shade?"

Only a slight softening around his mouth told her he was grateful. He held out a hand, motioning toward the bench where she and Zep had been sitting, but it was already occupied. Zep had disappeared and more and more humans were pouring into the square.

"Hmm. I know a place that's quieter," she said. "Would you like to grab a coffee?"

"Tea," he said. "I drink tea."

"How English."

"Or Indian." He shrugged when she glanced over her shoulder. "I'm assuming from the accent."

"It would be a mistake to assume anything about me." Meera turned and walked into the oncoming tourist traffic. "But I do drink tea. Follow me."

———

THE COURTYARD of the hotel was quiet save for the trickle of a fountain. Though they were only steps from Bourbon Street, the stone walls enveloped them and kept the crowds and the heat at bay. It was one of Meera's favorite hidden spots in the French Quarter, an intensely crowded neighborhood filled with small private corners.

She adored it.

Rhys lifted a teapot delicately, his long fingers arranging the teacups just so before he poured. There was something highly attractive about a man who handled fine things with care.

"Do you take milk or sugar?" he asked.

"Neither, thank you. If they come back, I'll ask for honey."

He glanced up as he passed her a teacup. He'd taken off his

sunglasses as she had, but Meera could tell he was uncomfortable without them.

*Fuss, fuss, fuss.*

"You're very tidy." She cupped her chin and leaned her elbow on the table. "Aren't you? I'm betting your suitcase is strictly organized."

"I live in an old house with three couples and two unruly children." His mouth curved just a little. "I have to be tidy."

He liked the children even though they were "unruly." It was the first hint of softness she'd seen from him, and it made her like him more. But he avoided looking at her, choosing to glance around the courtyard and examine every person who came in sight. He was definitely a soldier. Zep and his brothers all acted the same.

But Zep and his brothers didn't avoid looking directly at her.

*Hmmmm.*

"Do I make you uncomfortable?" Many scribes were awkward around Irina, but he'd mentioned living with couples. Then again, perhaps he didn't approve of Irina living in the scribe house. Perhaps Rhys of Glast was one of those Irin who wanted to keep all Irina locked in the havens, only visiting to breed children or consult on ancient songs.

"You don't make me uncomfortable." He stirred his tea.

"Are you sure?"

"Not knowing who you are or what you do makes me uncomfortable. Why did Sari send me to you, and what do you know about Irina martial magic? What is your role?"

"Aren't you direct?" Her mother would have said rude. "In your world I don't have a role."

His gaze stopped wandering around the courtyard and locked on her. "In my world I live with three highly skilled singers who work with the scribes in our house in all manner of ways, from healing to patrolling to mental combat. So perhaps it's a mistake to assume anything about me either."

"Fair." What to give him? Just enough. "Like you, I am an

archivist."

"Do you have a specialty?"

*If only you knew...* "I'm currently focused on Irina magic in North America. Like many of the indigenous human languages in the western hemisphere, local Irina traditions are in danger of being lost. As an archivist, it is my job to study these traditions and preserve them."

"So you *are* a librarian."

She replied cautiously. "Of a specialized sort. I was told you were also an archivist, so I assume you understand."

"I think I'm starting to." He sat back and watched her.

Again, Meera had the distinct feeling of being stalked by a great cat. "As I'm sure you know, there are many singers like me around the world. What I do isn't unique." Best not to sound too humble. She didn't pull off humble well. "Though unlike some of my more traditional peers, I also utilize a limited amount of technology in my study and preservation."

"Technology?"

"Recording technology. Digital." She turned to look around the restaurant. "Where is our server? My tea is going cold."

Rhys blinked. "Are you saying you record Irina songs?"

"Only with permission." Meera was pleased by his surprise; she did hate being predictable. "Do you see our server?"

"Singers allow this?"

"When they trust me, they *sometimes* allow it." Her recordings numbered in the hundreds of hours at this point, but there was no reason for the scribe to know that. The files were safe, and the backup drive was impossible to hack. "I really would like to drink my tea."

"Have some sugar?" He passed her the caddy with tiny paper packets.

Meera made a face. "No, thank you."

"You're quite particular yourself. Do you have a geographic emphasis?"

"For honey?"

He frowned. "For your research."

"I've focused on the closest Irina communities, most of which are remnants. Communities along the Gulf of Mexico whose human blood came from Mississippian peoples."

"I don't know much about North American linguistic groups," Rhys said. "My training was in manuscripts from the British Isles, though I've been more focused on Western and Central Asian manuscripts since I've been in Istanbul."

"My training didn't match my current emphasis either." She smiled. "But I found the challenge refreshing. It's been too long that the Irina have neglected preservation in North America, though we excel in it other places."

"What is the scribe tradition like here?"

"You'd have to ask your brothers here, though there are no major libraries in this area that I know of. I believe the emphasis has traditionally been on *talesm* as a means of magical preservation rather than manuscripts." She'd been aching for months to talk with someone who would understand how interesting her findings were, but she still didn't trust him. Couldn't trust him. "But the Irina here were incredibly influential. Oral tradition surpassed written by far."

"It sounds fascinating. And very promising considering the current political environment."

"Yes." Meera forced herself to be pragmatic. "I don't want to understate the challenge. My work is often frustrating. Many rumors. Few certainties."

"And those rumors are where you heard about the Wolf?"

And the hunting leopard pounced.

Meera controlled her reaction. The scribe didn't need to know about the Wolf. Her work was knowledge that belonged only to the Irina. What would scribes do with singers' history? Write it in some dry scroll, convinced that the recording of a thing equaled its understanding?

No. Not with her research.

She set her cold tea to the side and leaned forward. "I love following stories like those of the Serpent and the Wolf. So fascinating, don't you think? They provide good context for academic exploration."

"Stories?" Rhys frowned. "I don't understand. You think the Serpent and the Wolf are *stories*?"

"Of course." She had to change the subject. "Like the wonderful legends surrounding Glast. I'm sure you know of them. How Gabriel planted the hawthorn tree and the great library grew from the roots—"

"I know the legends of Glast." His expression had annoyance written all over it. "Are you saying you *haven't* found evidence of the Wolf?"

Meera shrugged. "Can we define evidence? The hawthorn in the Glast legend, for instance—"

"Is a hawthorn tree," Rhys interrupted. "Only a story. A library can't be built from hawthorn wood."

"Why not? Is it not suitable for building? I don't know much about carpentry."

"No, it's a hardwood, but the trunk—" He shook his head. "Why are we talking about carpentry?"

"I don't know anything about it, but you seem to. Is it something you learned from your father or mother? I was never taught to work with my hands, and I think I should have been. It was a failing of my training." Meera ran a finger along the edge of her teacup. "I think some kind of art or craft should be part of a well-rounded education. I always had an interest in ceramic art, but I was never given instruction. I think that's a shame, don't you?"

Rhys blinked. "I… don't have an opinion on that."

"That surprises me. You strike me as the kind of person who has an opinion about everything."

"And you strike me as the type of person who likes to avoid questions." He swiped a hand over his forehead. "I was called here because there were reports that the Wolf had been found. If that's not the case, why did you summon me?"

"Do you think I summoned you?" She cocked her head. "That's interesting."

Rhys said. "Who then?"

Meera sighed. "You're very persistent, aren't you?"

"Very."

It hadn't been Meera who'd told Sari of Vestfold to send a nosy scribe. Meera had listened to the stories and rumors and told her mother of her suspicions, her mother had told her old friend Orsala, and Orsala had passed the information on to Sari, the granddaughter mated to the praetor of Mikael's line.

That tended to be the way information was passed between havens. The poor scribes just hadn't gotten used to it yet.

"I didn't summon you," she said. "I can't tell you who did."

"Can't or won't?"

"Won't."

Rhys sat back, crossing his arms over his chest, and Meera clinked a teaspoon against her delicate cup, hoping honey would magically appear before her tea went completely cold.

Alas, they had been forgotten. It might have been the stormy expression on Rhys's face that kept the servers away.

"You didn't summon me," he muttered. "But someone passed a message along to Sari. Someone she trusted."

"How much does Sari like you?" Meera picked up her teacup and sipped the cold, unsweetened tea. Then she set it down. Awful. "She might have simply enjoyed sending you on a chase."

"No… Well yes, she would enjoy that. But my watcher wouldn't be pleased to lose me for no good reason. So whoever told Sari must be someone connected to the havens."

"Why do the scribes have any interest in these legends? Don't you have enough killing magic of your own?"

"We don't need the magic; the Irina do."

"If you're so convinced of that, why don't you leave the gathering of that magic to singers?"

"Why shouldn't we help? Strong singers mean strong scribes."

"So this *is* about scribes."

"That's not what I meant." Rhys had moved from irritation and was headed toward angry. He leaned forward, his eyes narrowing. "Didn't you say you moved here to be close to your parents?"

She smiled calmly. "I didn't say that. That might have been another one of your assumptions."

"I don't think so."

*Danger, danger, danger.*

Meera's eyes rose to his and she set her cup down. "I think we need some new tea. This pot is cold. And honey."

He blinked. "Honey?"

"Yes. I told you I don't like sugar in my tea."

"Sugar is just as sweet."

"But it's not honey, is it?"

She'd rendered him speechless again. Rhys of Glast, imminent archivist, was staring at her with a mix of confusion, indignation, and fascination. Meera was extraordinarily pleased. It was the best reaction she could have hoped for.

"You want more tea?" he asked.

"Are you offering to get it?" Meera smiled. "Thank you."

Rhys sat back in his seat. "You won't tell me who summoned me here, you're dismissing the legends of the Serpent and the Wolf as simple stories, and you want more tea?"

"I absolutely want more tea. After all, you've barely touched yours, and I think you might still be a bit jet-lagged. Are you? I'm really thinking of you."

He stood. Opened his mouth. Closed it. Opened it again. "I'll... get more tea."

"Excellent. And Rhys?" She looked directly into his eyes.

"Yes?"

"There's nothing simple about stories."

# CHAPTER THREE

"The woman is maddening!" Rhys yelled into the phone. "I spent five hours with her today and received nothing except a tour of the French Quarter, a disjointed lecture on the different properties of honey, and more food than I usually eat in an entire day. In five hours!"

Damien coughed as if trying to suppress a laugh. Sari, as usual, suppressed nothing. They had Rhys on speakerphone, and Rhys could hear her laughter bounce off the stone walls of their castle in Rěkaves.

"Oh Rhys," she said. "I wish I could see your face. I've never met Meera in person, but I like her already."

"Who the hell is this woman?" Rhys asked. "Other than a demon in Irina clothing."

"Trust me," Sari said. "She's more than your equal in learning, but I can't share her secrets or I'd lose her trust, and I absolutely cannot do that. She's too important."

Important how? Rhys was mystified. Damien's mate wasn't awed by much.

"Besides, Rhys, why must you be so impatient?" Damien asked.

"It sounds like a pleasant afternoon. I've always wanted to visit New Orleans."

"So have I," Sari said. "The gardens. The music. The food. It sounds like you had a wonderful guide."

"Who told me nothing!" He resisted kicking the wall. "I had dozens of questions, and she managed to deflect every one. I would think I was getting somewhere, then she'd distract me by diverting the conversation to jazz musicians or azalea cultivation or different properties of American whiskey. Five hours with the woman and I know nothing more about the Wolf than when I arrived. I'm completely turned around."

"A woman has out-clevered Rhys?" Sari asked. "I never thought I'd live to see this moment, but if anyone could do it, it would be Meera."

"Indeed. An opponent with equal cunning," Damien said. "He'll either fall in love with her or murder her."

"I would not take that bet, my darling."

Rhys closed his eyes. "I'm glad you find all this so amusing. I don't like it here, and at this rate, I have no idea how long this mission will take." He was ignoring the crack about falling in love. Damien and Sari had reunited after a long estrangement. Mated pairs were notorious for thinking everyone wanted to be as they were.

"How can you not like New Orleans?" Sari asked. "It's probably warm. The temperature here dropped below freezing last night. In April! And it's supposed to rain later this week."

"Sounds lovely." Rhys sighed. He did miss gloomy weather. "It's humid and hot. When it rains, the streets flood and the mud smells."

He knew he was just griping.

"The mud smells?" Damien chuckled. "Rhys, you've only been there a few days. How is the woman supposed to trust you? Give it time. Get to know her."

"And that does not mean hack her computer or surveil her apartment," Sari said. "Try using charm."

Rhys curled his lip. "She's not interested in charm." Well, not unless she was charming *him*. And she had. He hated to admit it, but the woman was intriguing. She was curious. Bright. Brilliant, in fact. If he weren't on assignment, he would wander through her fascinating mind for hours. It was part of the reason it had been so easy for her to distract him.

Add to that the dark orange dress with the strap that fell down her shoulder, the shining black hair piled on her head in a tousled knot, the curve of her leg teasing him as she walked, and...

He was on assignment—an important assignment—and she was a subject to interview.

One that seemed solely focused on stymying him.

"Can you call someone?" he asked. "Sari, did you vouch for me? Can you—?"

"I have vouched for you," Sari said. "She wouldn't have even agreed to a meeting if I hadn't. But Meera keeps her own council. She's liable to take her time making up her mind."

"Honestly, what is the rush?" Damien asked. "This is a fact-finding mission. New Orleans doesn't have a Grigori problem."

"Yet." Rhys narrowed his eyes. "And has anyone asked why? Doesn't that seem suspicious to anyone else? The Grigori I killed in Houston mentioned Bozidar's name. Said the Fallen were rising."

Damien grunted. "Yes, they love saying things like that. Melo-dramatic, every one of them."

"I thought Bozidar was in Saint Louis."

"Originally he was in Chicago," Damien said. "You can ask Malachi about him. He was routed from Chicago and is currently in the Saint Louis area, but the scribe house there is secretive and quiet. Bozidar is smart. He doesn't cause enough trouble to attract attention from the council."

"Saint Louis"—Rhys mulled it over—"is also on the Mississippi River, isn't it?"

"It's a long way from Saint Louis to New Orleans, my friend."

"Maybe," Rhys said. "But I'm going to ask around. I'll try to contact this Zep person Meera mentioned. The one she was with in the square."

"I'll pass the word through official channels if that's what you're asking," Damien said. "Do you want to clue them in to why you're really there?"

"For now leave it as it was in Houston," he said. "I'm a visiting scholar, researching North American tattooing practices. They don't need to know I'm in contact with the haven here. They'll report any activity with Irina to the council in Vienna."

And right now the scribes' council didn't have the best interest of the Irina at heart. They were old and entrenched power brokers who were clinging to influence with every breath, not servants working for their people.

"Fine," Damien said. "Let us know if you need any more help."

"I'll try sending another message," Sari said. "But Rhys?"

"Yes?"

"Take a breath. Put up your feet. You've been working like a madman for five years now. Maybe it's time you let an attractive woman distract you."

"I didn't say she was attractive," Rhys snapped.

"Trust me," Damien said. "You did."

---

THE NEXT AFTERNOON, Rhys met Zephirin—Zep, as he introduced himself—at the entrance to Lafayette Cemetery No. 1 in the Garden District. The New Orleans scribe house was only a few blocks away, and Zep was keeping close to home that rainy morning, waiting for the sky to clear and the tourists to flood the French Quarter.

"They come here too," the young scribe explained. "But not as much this time of year. Parade season? It's a madhouse."

Stormy skies hung low over the strange hamlet of grey and black marble graves in various states of disrepair. Ferns and moss peeked from exposed stones while many graves bore fresh bouquets and evidence of care.

Rhys sidestepped a puddle that had formed in the middle of an alley between the graves. "But even with all the tourism, there are relatively few Grigori attacks?"

Zep glanced at him sideways. "There's more than what our watcher in Houston wants to acknowledge. We've been asking for additional men for years now—and a level of independence—but they're reluctant to send more."

"Do you know why?"

"No." Zep shrugged. "Some of the brothers here say pressure from the haven keeps scribe numbers low."

Rhys frowned. "You mean Meera's haven?"

"Nah." Zep hopped over a larger puddle. "She's never lived there. Doesn't claim it. Her parents are another story."

"They're the guardians, correct?"

"Indeed they are. About four years now."

"You've met them?" Rhys avoided the question of Meera for the moment. He'd noticed the scribe became closemouthed about the mysterious Irina, and Rhys didn't want to push his luck.

A man under an umbrella crossed the alley in the distance, side-stepping the growing puddles as rain continued to fall. He flashed across Rhys's line of sight, then disappeared behind another line of graves.

Zep continued. "I've met her daddy. Who is one scary fucker, I might add."

"How so?"

"You know the quiet type that sits in the corner and you barely notice 'em until they stand up and you realize just lookin' at 'em they could kill everyone in the room and not blink?"

Rhys chuckled quietly. "My former watcher is exactly like that."

"That's Meera's daddy. And I hear her mama is just the same."

"So Meera's parents are both warriors, but she became a librarian?" It was just another confusing facet to an already confusing singer.

"Meera's a softer type." Zep smiled. "She's plenty powerful, but I ain't ever seen her pick up a knife."

Zep's expression revealed his admiration, and Rhys felt an unexpectedly territorial objection to it.

"So she's soft," he challenged.

The other scribe narrowed his eyes. "Not soft. Just... not a soldier. She doesn't have to be. She's under our protection here."

"Of course." Rhys forced a smile. "It's clear she feels very safe here. She must live near the scribe house."

"She lives close enough. None of your business where she lives."

*You don't know any more than I do.* Rhys backed off. "I would never intrude on her. I'm simply curious. It's not typical for Irina to live independently."

Unless it was Renata or Ava or any number of the Irina Rhys knew. Opinions about Irina independence diverged wildly among younger scribes. Rhys hadn't managed to read Zep yet.

"There ain't much typical about Meera." Zep stepped to the side to let a couple of rain-soaked visitors with fresh flowers in hand pass them, wandering farther back into the graveyard. "She's unique."

*That's what I've heard.* Rhys said, "I look forward to consulting with her on my research. She's clearly a brilliant woman with a much deeper knowledge of the native Irin of this region than I have."

Zep smiled at Rhys again. "You know, I *am* from around here. Just sayin' if you're looking for local sources, I can hook you up."

Rhys had already guessed that from the scribe's accent. "Then I suppose I'll be interviewing you as well."

"But you gotta buy me dinner first," Zep said. "I ain't some cheap date."

"Done." Rhys's eyes watched the humans turn left at the end of the graveyard. "I'll even buy you a beer."

"Buy me dessert and I might make myself pretty." Zep glanced over his shoulder. "You see that other fellow exit yet?"

"No."

"This is a small graveyard," Zep murmured, "but it's full of corners that ain't so obvious."

"Did you see him carrying a camera or a backpack?"

"No. You?"

"Neither." If the man was a tourist, he'd have some kind of bag with him. Lafayette No. 1 was a walled graveyard with two entrances; Rhys had researched it prior to meeting Zep. "The Sixth Avenue entrance?"

"He mighta gone out there," Zep said. "But why cross the cemetery at all?"

"Visiting a relative?"

"Maybe. This is a working graveyard. It's possible."

Rhys brushed a thumb over his *talesm prim*, trying to enhance his senses and gauge the air, but all he perceived was the scent of rain and mud, moss and rot, and a hint of the lilies the humans had been carrying.

"Lily," Rhys said quietly. "I'll follow the humans."

"And I'll try to find our mysterious visitor." Zep turned left at the next corner.

Lafayette Cemetery No. 1 was laid out in four quadrants, each with alleys of trees and numerous graves, most of which were far taller than Rhys. He walked swiftly, following the scent of the lily blossoms and ignoring the wet splash of his boots through the mud. He trailed the scent to the back corner where the lilies were carefully placed on a ledge under a small mausoleum marked Dours. Half the plaque was covered in a volunteer fern that obscured the rest of the name, but the bright lilies remained, a token of care and remembrance.

The humans were nowhere in sight.

Rhys followed a pair of muddy footprints until they dead-ended in another puddle. He hopped across it and tuned his ears to the ambient noise.

The distant rumble of a streetcar on Saint Charles Avenue and passing traffic as it zipped through rain-soaked streets. A pair of laughing tourists on the other side of the wall, walking down the sidewalk on Prytania Street. Zep's furtive footfalls turned into a run.

Rhys changed direction and followed the sound.

He leapt over fallen stones and shuffled through narrow alleys between graves before he came to the far side of the deserted graveyard where he saw Zep standing over two limp figures as the man with the black umbrella parried with him.

Rhys ran toward them, only to see the Grigori spot him over Zep's shoulder and swing the umbrella in a final blow that knocked the young scribe on the temple. Zep spun around, clutching his temple.

"Down!" Rhys yelled, and Zep dropped to his knees in the mud. Rhys leapt over him to pursue the fleeing Grigori. "Get help!"

Rhys left Zep with the fallen humans and gave chase.

The Grigori was obviously more familiar with the cemetery than Rhys was. He ran straight toward the wall and, using the trees and fallen stones to brace himself, shimmied up and over the cemetery wall before Rhys could catch up. He followed the path of the Grigori, scraping his hands as he climbed and hoping no one noticed the soaked Englishman perched on the historic walls of the cemetery as he scanned the streets.

There.

The Grigori was running toward a dripping group of students with backpacks and plaid umbrellas who looked as if they were part of a tour. He shoved them out of the way, ignoring the indignant shouts and curses thrown at him, only to dodge a truck that nearly ran him over as he crossed the street.

Rhys followed him, running around the students and turning

left at the intersection. He paused, nearly cursing his luck when he thought he'd lost the Grigori.

Then he spotted a muddy, blood-tinged handprint on the corner of the yellow house.

He jumped the wrought iron fence and crouched down, listening for his quarry. He stayed low, ducking under the windows as he walked between the two brightly painted houses with rocking chairs on the porch. He could hear panting in the garden.

Rhys crept on silent feet, hoping the Grigori had given up or mistakenly believed he'd lost his pursuer. The man was sitting, hunched over, his head in his hands. He sat on a dripping wrought iron chair pulled away from a bistro table under a wisteria arbor in a shared garden between the two houses. The wall on either side was at least seven feet, covered in vines and fragrant with flowers.

"Are you going to kill me?"

Rhys froze.

"I can hear you," the Grigori said. "I'm not running. Are you going to kill me or not?"

"Do you want me to kill you?"

The man looked over his shoulder and frowned. "You're not one of the local scribes."

"No, I'm not."

"Why are you here?"

"Research."

The man's shoulders shook but his laughter was hollow. "A professor? That's who finally caught me?"

The walls were high but not insurmountable, especially for the Grigori who'd led Rhys on such a merry chase.

"Why aren't you running?" Rhys asked.

"I'm tired." The words were spoken in a growl. "I shouldn't have run in the graveyard. Should have let you kill me there. But I suppose running is instinct at this point. Fighting. Hunting."

The man finally looked up, and Rhys stopped dead in his tracks at the haunted expression. "Who are you?" he asked.

"A child of the devil. A killer. You know who I am, scribe. 'You're all the same.' Haven't I heard that from more than one of you?"

"Who is your father?"

The Grigori gave him half a smile. "You'll find out soon enough. It's coming."

*What is?* Rhys wanted to ask, but something in the wild and desolate expression in the man's eyes told him no straight answer would be forthcoming. "You're dying, aren't you?"

"Yes." The man rolled his neck and shrugged his shoulders. "I didn't want to fall to dust in my sleep. Figured I'd rather go out in a fight."

Rhys drew a silver dagger and glanced over his shoulders, but the windows of the two old houses were shuttered and no lights shone behind them. He walked slowly toward the Grigori, mindful of a trap, but the weariness of the man's expression was unmistakable.

Unless given new life by their sires, the natural life span of a Grigori was usually only around one hundred fifty years from their births. They didn't show signs of age or weakness. They simply turned off, like a light bulb burning out. This Grigori had reached the end of his life and felt his final hours approaching.

"Tell me who your sire is," Rhys said. "And I will kill you quickly. Don't tell me, and I'll give you pain. I won't kill you at all. I'll wait."

The man's eyes burned. "You wouldn't."

"I would."

The Grigori lunged toward Rhys in a burst of raw fury, but Rhys slipped to the side and locked the man in a headlock before he could get away. The Grigori's body twisted as his feet tried to find leverage in the slippery mud.

Rhys said, "I can wait like this a long time."

The Grigori turned and tried to sink his teeth into his arm, but Rhys knocked him with a blow to the temple, shoved him to the ground, and pressed his face into the mud.

He twisted the monster's head to the side. "This won't kill you, son of the Fallen. But tell me the devil who sired you, and I promise I'll give you a quick death."

"Dieudonné," the man spit out.

"Wrong," Rhys said. "There is no angel by that name in the Americas."

"And you know them all?" He cackled. "I promise *you don't.*"

Rhys shoved his face in the mud. "Try again."

He spit mud from his mouth. "Teodoros."

"No."

The man began to laugh, the sound tinged with hysteria. "He's the gift of the Creator, don't you know? The celestial father. The glorious one!"

"Is that what he told you?"

"We are the sons of heaven," the Grigori screamed, "not a mongrel race of supplicant dogs!"

Rhys was worried about attracting attention. He'd overpowered the Grigori, and he was fairly sure the houses were deserted, but the monster's voice was getting louder every time he responded. It was only a matter of time before someone braved the downpour to see what the commotion was.

"Tell me your father's name," Rhys said through gritted teeth. "Don't you want to die?"

"You pathetic eunuchs have to steal our women now." The creature couldn't stop laughing. "Steal ours because we killed all yours."

Rhys snapped. He pressed the Grigori's face into the mud and plunged the dagger into the man's spine. The body wavered beneath him before it dissolved.

*Enough.* Goading Rhys was one thing. Dredging up the horror of the Rending...

Rhys saw movement out of the corner of his eye. Zep was standing between the two houses, water dripping down his face, watching the Grigori's dust melt into the mud as the rain washed it away.

"Will his soul rise?" Zep asked.

"Yes." Rhys tried to wipe the rain from his eyes but only succeeded in smearing himself with more mud. "He'll face his judgment, brother."

Zep looked him up and down. "Come with me. You can clean up at the house. The humans were fine after a few minutes. You, I'm not so sure about."

———

RHYS SOUGHT anonymity on Frenchmen Street that night, sitting at a back corner table at a club, drinking a bottle of red wine as a man played piano and a woman sang about lost love. He'd showered, changed, and dried off, but he could still feel the grit of the Grigori's dust under his fingernails, still feel the mud caked into his palms as he held the man down.

*Dieudonné.*

*Teodoros.*

God's gift.

Which Fallen considered themselves the Creator's gift? It hadn't occurred to him during the struggle, but the answer was obvious. He went by various names, depending on geography. Darko. Boško. Dado.

*Bozidar.*

The divine gift of heaven.

He was an archangel with an inflated sense of purpose and an ego considered monumental, even by Fallen standards.

*"You'll find out soon enough. It's coming."*

There was always something coming. Some horrible threat. Some catastrophe.

*"You've been working like a madman for five years now. Maybe it's time you let an attractive woman distract you."*

He couldn't rest. He couldn't stop. Not when he'd been one of the survivors. Until the Irina regained everything they'd lost—until hope wasn't just a dream in their world—he couldn't be distracted.

Rhys felt a hand slide up his arm before someone sat across from him. He turned to protest the intrusion only to find Meera sitting across from him, her eyes locked on the singer at the front.

"I love her voice," Meera said. "She's a regular here."

"How did you find me?" *How did you know I wanted to be found?*

She turned to him with a raised eyebrow. "The city's not that big, Rhys."

He could only stare at her. He was worn out. Tired. He had the absurd instinct to lay his head on her breast, close his eyes, and sleep for hours.

He shoved the impulse aside. He barely knew the woman. She was beautiful, yes, but so were countless other women. There was nothing particularly compelling about Meera.

*Liar.*

There was something about her—a glow, a *depth*—that drew him in, and he had no idea why. He was past the reflexive awe at Irina presence. He'd lived with females of his race for years now.

It wasn't awe. It was… attraction.

As if she could read his thoughts, her mouth turned up at the corner in an impish smile. "Have you eaten?"

Rhys barked out a laugh. "No."

"Going without dinner is a crime in this city." Meera waved over a waitress. "If you're looking for comfort food, you can't go wrong with the red beans and rice."

He was in the mood to be coddled, and Meera seemed to be offering. "Why not?" he asked. "Sounds good."

"I heard you had a day today." Meera paused and gave the waitress their order. Red beans and rice for Rhys. Gumbo for her. Another glass for wine.

Rhys couldn't take his eyes off her. "Yes. I had a day."

## CHAPTER FOUR

Meera looked at him, the prowling cat lying in wait. From the moment she'd sat across from him, his eyes hadn't left her. His gaze raked her skin like claws teasing her flesh. It was unnerving. And… arousing.

"Do days like this happen to you often?" she asked. "I thought you were a scholar."

"I am."

A scholar with battle-hardened eyes. Meera saw the same shadows her own father bore. When Zep had called her that afternoon and told her they'd met a suicidal Grigori in the Garden District, Meera's heart had hurt. For the Grigori and for the scribe who had killed him.

Meera said, "I don't often meet scholars quite so good at hunting Grigori in my world."

"Sounds like a narrow world."

"Yes, it was." She poured water from the carafe at the table, ignoring the slight tremor in her hands. "Until recently."

His eyes sharpened. "So you did live in a haven once."

"Not a haven." Meera didn't know what had caused her to lower her guard. Maybe it was the darkness in the club or the music or the pained look in his eyes. She wanted to comfort him, and that was a dangerous impulse. "I've been asking about you." She glanced over at him. "Rhys of Glast, son of Edmund and Angharad the Sage, heir of Gabriel's library."

"I see I'm not the only scholar at the table." Rhys set down his drink and leaned toward her. "Why were you asking about me?"

"Because you've been asking about me."

"That's fair." The corner of his mouth turned up in a slight smile, and it was far more tempting than it should have been.

"Zep thinks you're here doing academic research. But I know..." She leaned forward. "...the scribes' council doesn't send scribes like you to do academic research."

"I am no errand boy for the council. If you asked about me, you know who sent me."

Sari of Vestfold, one of her mother's oldest friends and mate of Damien, praetor of Rěkaves and former Watcher of Istanbul. Damien came from a military tradition much like her father's, and Meera knew how that tradition engendered loyalty beyond politics.

According to her mother, Rhys's allegiance was to Damien and his current watcher in Istanbul, *not* the Elder Council. But Sari had also sent Rhys without telling him anything about who Meera was.

She didn't know what to think about that.

Rhys was staring at the singer on the stage, his wineglass dangling from graceful fingers. "So, my fellow scholar," he drawled, "which of the Fallen would refer to the Irin as a race of mongrel dogs?"

"Mongrel dogs? That's a new one." She tapped her lip. "Is this Fallen here in the Americas?"

Rhys nodded.

"Who has a healthy ego and no respect for the Forgiven?" Meera mused. "My guess would be Bozidar."

"Right in one." He lifted his wineglass. "You are as clever as they say."

"Do they say that? I'll have to thank them."

"You know you're clever."

"Do I?"

"I'd lose patience with you if you didn't. I'm not a patient man."

Meera let the matter drop. She knew the scribe wasn't the patient sort. His restless energy didn't fit with other academics she'd known. Was it the setting, the assignment... or was it her?

"Bozidar." She waited for the waitress to set down another glass. "Is that who he belonged to? The Grigori today?"

"I think so."

"Interesting."

Rhys poured a generous serving into Meera's glass. "Interesting is one word for it."

"He's been moving closer every year. Tiny steps, but consistent ones."

"Why aren't the scribe houses more concerned?"

She shrugged. "They judge Fallen presence by the number of Grigori attacks. They're old-fashioned that way."

"But not you."

"Oh, I'm very old-fashioned." She smiled. "About some things."

Bozidar didn't concern her. Maybe he should have, but Meera had dealt with Fallen antagonists her whole life. The heir of Anamitra had always been a target of the Fallen.

"Mongrel dogs," she murmured. "That's interesting."

"Why?"

"Because we are. Mongrels, anyway."

The flash of Rhys's eyes told her he didn't like the label.

She continued, "All but a few of us are an odd mixture of various angelic lines and human blood." She sipped the dry red wine, another new taste since leaving Udaipur. "The Grigori, in their own twisted way, are more purely angelic than we are."

"Do you think that makes them more powerful?"

"Yes and no. I do think it would give them some advantages if they knew what to do with it. And I think the prospect of that should terrify the Fallen."

"Free Grigori rising up in an army against the angels who made them?" Rhys made a face. "I was hopeful once. In my experience, free Grigori willing to discipline themselves are few and far between."

"But their numbers are growing every day," Meera said. "Free Grigori *and kareshta.* With every Fallen angel we send back to heaven, more Fallen children are free. Surely that is better than endless war."

"You're an idealist. Endless war is a reality. Even when we wish it wasn't."

Meera felt a twinge of disappointment. She had hoped—she didn't know why—that this scribe might have been different. That he might have seen clear to envisioning a third way beyond victory or defeat.

The waitress brought their food, and Meera kept Rhys company as he slowly peeled off the layers of the day. When his gaze grew heavy, she reached over and brushed his hand, offering him a taste of the energy she gathered in the club. By the time they'd finished the wine and the food, the shadows had lifted a little. His belly was full and his soul was a little lighter.

"Thank you." He rose when she did.

"For what?"

"You know."

They walked out of the club when the musicians changed. Rhys held the door as Meera wrapped a scarf around her shoulders. The clouds had come back and the air had chilled.

Rhys took a deep breath. "It smells like rain." His sensual lips spread into a wide smile. It was the first time Meera had seen him truly happy, and the effect was breathtaking.

She said, "You're handsome when you smile."

He blinked. "I'm not."

Meera laughed. "I don't think you get to decide if you're hand-some or not."

"You think I'm handsome?"

"I think… I like your smile. Anyone would like your smile. It's a nice smile."

His trapped her with his eyes. "I'm not asking about anyone."

Meera turned and started walking up Frenchmen Street, away from the entrance to the club and the inconvenient scholar with poetic lips.

"Meera!" Rhys called.

She stopped and turned. "Yes?"

Rhys opened his mouth. Frowned. "I should walk you home."

"No, you shouldn't. I don't want you to."

He looked around. "This neighborhood can be dangerous after dark."

"I know."

"But—"

"Rhys." She stepped toward him and let the magic rise in her voice. *"I'm fine.* Don't worry about me. Go home and sleep. You need to sleep."

He opened his mouth as if to argue, then he shook his head and cleared his throat. "I don't think—"

"I'm fine." Damn him, he was strong-minded. She wasn't surprised, but it was still irritating. "I'll see you in a few days."

"A few days?"

A jazz band started on the corner, distracting him, and Meera stepped into the shadows, whispering a spell to avert his gaze. While he'd be able to see her from the corner of his eye, he wouldn't be able to focus on her.

"Meera?" He looked away. Looked back. The annoyed expression had returned. "Damn it, woman."

She bit her lip to stop from laughing and slipped away while he was turning in the street. A crowd gathered around him, and Meera kept to the shadows, slipping out of sight while he was distracted. She worked her way away from the river and farther into the Faubourg Marigny, heading toward the shotgun house that was her home.

She stayed in the shadows, avoiding the drunks whose voices echoed in the quiet residential streets. Within three blocks, the music from Frenchmen died down and she walked in silence back to the alley that led to her garden.

As if he'd been waiting up for her, the dark angel stepped out of the shadows the minute Meera latched the garden gate.

"Vasu?" She sighed. It wasn't as if she hadn't been expecting it. It was out of character for him to stay away as long as he had. "What are you doing here?"

"What am I doing here?" The shadow compressed into a smaller form, and a little boy with gold eyes and dark hair stomped up to her, his hands fisted on his hips. "Why are *you* in America, Meera Bai?"

Meera walked over and sat on the porch steps, bracing her chin in her hand. "Don't be cross. And don't pout."

The child transformed into an eerily handsome young man with long black hair and a trimmed beard. His hair shone with reddish-gold stripes not unlike a tiger's coat, and the arms he crossed over his bare chest were covered in raised *talesm* the same golden ochre of his skin. Unlike Irin scribes, Vasu's magic was inherent. The spells were part of him, not tattooed on but rising from beneath the surface.

It was not an unfamiliar figure. Meera guessed this form was as close to his truest self as Vasu ever showed in human presence.

"I'm not pouting," he said.

"You are."

"The last time I saw you, you were in your aunt's compound *where you belong.*"

Parrying with Rhys had taken too much out of her. "It's not for you to say where I belong. And the last time you saw me was four years ago."

Vasu frowned. "No."

"Yes, Vasu. Four years. A lot has changed."

"I know. That's why you should be back in Udaipur."

"I have work to do here." *Knowledge to find. Peace to pursue.*

"Is four years a long time?" He cocked his head. "You don't look older. Are you going to get old like Anamitra? That was a choice, you know. I didn't approve of that."

The Fallen angel truly didn't understand time. Meera often wondered if Vasu still saw her as the child he'd played with so long ago within the fortress walls of Udaipur.

He'd speak of things a hundred years before as if they'd happened yesterday, and he'd speak of the morning as if eternity was contained within hours. Anamitra had told her once that Vasu was a child and an ancient contained in the same body.

"Can you just…?" Meera sighed. She was soul-deep exhausted from her time with Rhys, and she needed to drive to the haven in the morning. "I need to sleep."

Vasu crouched in front of her, unperturbed by silly human conventions like personal space. "You're tired?"

"I'm weary."

He touched her temple, and Meera felt the penetrating flood of his presence in the delicate touch. "You *are* weary. I'll stay."

"Not necessary."

He ignored her. Before she could register it, he had transformed again, this time into a large house cat with dense black fur and amber eyes. He waited at her door as Meera retrieved her key and opened the house before he slipped into the darkness.

As always when Vasu was nearby, Meera slept like a rock.

———

SHE STARTED EARLY the next morning, leaving the city before rush hour traffic started. Vasu had disappeared in the night. She might see him in an hour or it might be three years. Both were equally likely.

It was simply the way he was.

*"He's not like the others,"* Anamitra had told her when Vasu had

first appeared. *"He never will be. He was newly born when the angels fell. His home is earth, not heaven."*

For centuries, Vasu had a relationship with Meera's aunt. She couldn't say it was an alliance—that would imply Anamitra had some influence or sway over Vasu. It would be closer to say that Vasu considered Anamitra—and Meera by extension—a loved and familiar pet. An amusement and comfort. Anamitra kept Vasu's secrets... to an extent. And she never revealed her knowledge of him to any singer or scribe until Meera had been presented to her as an heir.

> *"Don't ever mistake Vasu for anything but what he is. He is an angel. He can be as terrible as he likes. He could take anything he wants. The power we cultivate with labor and study is as easy to him as breathing."*

Meera never forgot it. She never forgot anything Anamitra had told her. That was her gift and her curse. Her memory was a perfectly formed prism stretching back centuries, long before she'd been born. Anamitra had spent hundreds of years conveying the knowledge of Irina power and history to Meera before she'd surrendered to the heavens.

Anamitra's power belonged to Meera; one day she would pass it on to another. A daughter. A niece. A singer of her own blood. The heir of Meera Bai.

She felt the weight of history and legacy bearing down on her as she spotted the old house in Saint James Parish that sat in a bend of the river and marked the edge of haven land. For as long as anyone could remember, that house had existed. No one lived there but an old man who usually sat on the edge of a small dock, hanging a fishing line into the water. No matter what time of day she arrived, no matter what the weather, he always seemed to be sitting there. Something about the old man always struck Meera as odd, but no one, not her mother, her father, or any of the other Irin at the haven, could find anything unusual about him.

*There are mysteries and peculiarities everywhere,* she mused. *Not only in the Irin world.*

Mysteries like a scholar who moved like a warrior, or a singer who was friendly with an angel.

She turned off the main road and back into the twisting tracks leading to the back of the haven. Dense foliage grew thicker. Cypress and pine gave way to rolling lowlands filled with sugarcane where the air hung heavy and sweet. She turned left at the first live oak.

An alley of trees guarded the front of Havre Hélène, the great Creole house that past singers had saved from ruin, but the entrance Meera used came in from the farm. The property stretched south from the river, guarded by high fences and thick foliage cultivated by labor and strong earth magic. Sugar was what had run the plantation when it had belonged to humans. Sugar kept their new farm running still.

Meera felt the wards welcome her as she crossed the threshold of the haven. The old overseer's home had been ripped out when the land was bought, and a new guardhouse had been built in a style matching the house. A mated couple, both of her father's clan, lived in it now with their young child. When Meera had decided to leave India, her father, Maarut, had called them and they'd followed without question.

Because everything must be done without question.

"Meera Bai, you will be called. Abha is gone. Meera is your new name."

"Yes, Auntie."

"Anamitra is my name. Meera Bai is yours. Names are important, so we must use them."

"Yes, Anamitra."

"You have been chosen as my heir. Do you understand what that means? Your life is no longer your own. You belong to all the daughters of heaven."

"Yes, Auntie."

*"I am not Auntie."*
*"Yes, Anamitra."*

Meera drove slowly down the dirt road leading to the second largest home on the property. It had once belonged to the matriarch of the family, but that human was long dead and the rambling home had been turned into rooms for unmated singers.

When the plantation had been taken over nearly one hundred years before, it had been near ruin and the shacks that had been the slave quarters were crumbling and rotting.

The singers who first came had burned the remnants of the cottages, singing laments and prayers of healing for the human souls who had suffered, while digging deep to find the roots of family, strength, and survival they had sowed in the land.

The ruins became places for meditation and teaching, with gardens growing around them. The plantation that had once been a place of horrible pain became a farm where the vulnerable could find refuge and survivors could grow. New cottages were built for mated singers and the scribes who had fled with them from the Rending. Everyone worked together.

It was a self-sustained ecosystem now guarded by Patiala and Maarut, her own parents, who had taken over from the previous guardian and her mate.

When Meera had told her parents she wanted to leave the great library at Udaipur after Anamitra's death, they had thought she was joking. She was not.

*"Anamitra had no life outside this place. Her world was this compound."*

*"Your world is here as well. This is a center of learning. A safe place where singers can seek wisdom and healing. You know what happened when Anamitra left."*

*"I refuse to be bound by rules set in stone before I was born. If I carry this burden, I will decide how and where I carry it."*

*"The world needs Anamitra's heir."*

*"And they will have me. Eventually. But I have lived over two hundred years confined to this place. There are other wise singers in the Irin world. They can survive without me for a few years."*

Meera had moved without asking her parents—her first act of rebellion but not her last—and she'd chosen a place that had fascinated her for personal and academic reasons. As a child, she'd been enthralled by the legends and stories of the powerful singers across the sea. She'd listened to the songs that told about great battles, vast landscapes, prosperity, and centuries of peace.

When the opportunity had arisen to break free from the boundaries of her childhood, she grabbed it.

She parked the car behind the main house where her parents made their home. Her father oversaw the farm and organization of the compound. Her mother oversaw the security of the haven and communication with other guardians around the world.

In the history of unbreakable bonds, theirs was one of the most ironclad, all the more amazing to Meera because their mating had been strictly arranged by their families.

"Meera!" Patiala waved from the back porch and jogged down the steps. "I didn't know you'd be here so early." She hugged her daughter in a tight embrace. "Nanette is making lunch for us right now."

"That sounds amazing."

Patiala flashed a smile. "It's so good to see you."

"It's only been three weeks."

She was short, like Meera, but there was nothing soft about her. Her skin was darker than her daughter's, tanned from a love of the outdoors, and her loose cotton pants and shirt hid the lean muscles of a world-class archer. Meera's father might have looked more forbidding, but her mother was the force in the family.

Anamitra's niece had been trained early as an archivist, like all the singers in their family were, but it had become clear early on that Patiala took after her warrior father. It was only fitting that her mate came from the same clan of Tomir warriors pledged to guard the fortress in Udaipur.

Patiala had found a ready and welcoming home among them and astonished everyone when her child had been the one to exhibit the extraordinary magic necessary for Anamitra's heir.

"Your father is in the fields," Patiala said. "I think he was expecting you later as well."

"I wanted to beat the traffic."

Patiala laid her head on Meera's shoulder. "And how is my joy this morning? Your shoulders look heavy."

"They are." Meera glanced at her mother. "Maybe you can explain how a very persistent scribe who sees far more than he should has managed to find me all the way from Istanbul."

Patiala lifted her head. "Well, he arrived much more quickly than I'd anticipated."

---

"How could you tell him where I was?" Meera rubbed her temples, wishing Nanette's excellent gumbo and fresh trout could rid her of the headache that had started the minute she'd brought up Rhys of Glast. "You told him my name!"

"You can't remain completely anonymous," Patiala said. "I refuse to give you an assumed name when requesting advice from allies. We didn't specify which Meera you are, and clearly Orsala and Sari didn't tell him. There are lots of Meeras in the world. He has no way of knowing which one."

"Do not underestimate this man. When you told me he wanted to meet, I thought I was going to meet with a normal scholar who'd have a few questions and then be on his way when I didn't want to have dinner with him. This one is entirely too persistent. And too perceptive."

Maarut frowned. "You said you needed help. That you were certain Atawakabiche was living but that you needed help to find her. This man is a scholar of very good reputation, and he is trustworthy. And he's a warrior who fought in the Battle of Vienna. What is wrong with him?"

"When I said I needed help, I thought you'd send Roch to help me," Meera said, pointing at the fair-skinned man with sandy-blond hair sitting next to her father. "He's the one who's most familiar with the bayous."

"Roch can't leave the haven for that long," Patiala said. "Meera, you can't possibly think that's an option. What about this Zep that you've spoken of?"

She shook her head. "I don't want Zep knowing any more about me than he already does. He's a good soldier, and he'd report on me to his watcher without a second thought. The scribes in New Orleans don't know what my role is, and I don't want them to know. Plus I don't need Zep getting ideas because I confided in him. And he would. Roch wouldn't get ideas because he's already in love with Sabine."

"That I am," Roch said with a slight smile. "But you also know there's no way I can leave her here alone. She'd go off the rails if I disappeared."

Logically, Meera knew Roch was right, but it still annoyed her that the scribe was tied to the haven by a singer who wasn't even his mate.

Not that she wouldn't be if she was in her right mind. Roch was devoted to Sabine as deeply as Maarut was devoted to Patiala, but the singer's mind had been broken during the Rending, and all attempts at healing had failed.

"Roch, I would like you to ask around about increased Grigori activity. Rhys and Zep ran into a Grigori that led them to believe Bozidar might be making moves south."

"I can do that," Roch said. "I'll talk to some of the loners up the river. See what they have to say."

"So Rhys of Glast has already given you information about Fallen activity," Patiala said. "I consider that a positive sign. Don't you, Maarut?"

"Very positive."

Patiala said, "He sounds like a very bright young man."

Meera felt a headache brewing. "That has nothing to do with Atawakabiche or—"

"He will be an excellent collaborator." Patiala nodded decisively. "I've spoken to Sari about this. And Orsala. She has great respect for the young man. Not only is he highly learned and trustworthy, he uses the same kind of… machines you do. Computers and things."

Meera shook her head. "Computers and things?"

"I'm just saying he probably wouldn't think it was an abomination to record Irina magic," Patiala said. "Some might."

"You mean like you do?"

"Anamitra's legacy cannot be preserved on gigabytes!" Patiala waved her hand in a shooing gesture. "Or whatever it is you use to record them."

Her mother might have looked the same age as Meera, but they were generations apart regarding modern technology. Meera still had to help her mother use email. "Mata, it's not… Never mind." She turned to her father. "You haven't even met this man, but you're comfortable with him pestering me?"

Maarut narrowed his eyes. "I don't like any scribe pestering you. I'd rather we were back in Udaipur where we know what the dangers are."

"Father, please," Meera said. "We're not doing this again."

Her father flared his nostrils. "Yes, Meera Bai."

"Don't do that." She was still uncomfortable with the fact that, technically, her parents were under her authority now that Anamitra was gone.

She couldn't even have an old-fashioned argument with them anymore. In the end, it was their duty to submit to her wishes. She'd used that power to her advantage when it came time to move to the United States, but it still felt wrong and unnatural.

"I'll consider this Rhys," she said, relenting, "but I still want to have some time to get to know him. And Father, if you had time to visit the city and meet him, that would set me at ease."

Her father's expression softened. "I'd be happy to do that."

She quirked her mouth into a smile. "I know you're missing my pullout couch."

"I'll be sleeping on the porch if that couch is my only option," Maarut said. "Wooden boards are more comfortable than metal bars."

Roch and Patiala started laughing, but Meera caught the satis-fied glance that passed between her parents.

*What are you up to?*

---

"I DON'T LIKE IT."

Meera glanced over to see Vasu standing near the window in her room, staring out at the oak trees in the moonlight.

"Don't barge in on me, Vasu." Meera was reading in bed. "What if I were getting dressed?"

"I saw you born. I saw you take your first steps. I have seen your death." Vasu turned and cocked his head to the side, examining her. "But it embarrasses you to think I might see you without clothes?"

"Yes. You don't have rights to me or my body. Don't assume them just because you are an angel."

"And don't assume I would take them." He slumped into the corner chaise. "All my lovers came willingly to me. Not that you will ever be my lover. You are too important for that."

Meera frowned. "You have such a twisted sense of sexual rela-tionships."

"And you don't? Your first lover was chosen by your great-aunt to educate you in magical sexual practices. The humans you've chosen since—"

"I'm not discussing this with you." It struck Meera that Vasu knew more about her than any living being. Which was slightly depressing. Then again, she didn't have normal friends. She didn't have normal relationships. Not even her parents treated her as they would treat a typical daughter.

"The only slightly normal relationships I have," she mused, "are with people who don't know who I am. And… you."

"I know. You're very lucky." He lifted a lock of his hair and started braiding it. "I don't like it."

"Don't like what?"

"You. Here. Why did you leave the fortress?"

Meera took a moment to think before she responded. "I think it's because the only normal relationships I have are with people who don't know who I am and you."

"You can't have normal relationships. You're the heir of Anamitra. You will always be different."

"I can try."

"You need a mate." He continued braiding. "Anamitra was much happier once her parents chose a mate for her."

Meera knew Vasu was right. A mate would be her one true confidant, the person who would be wholly and completely her equal no matter what role she played in the Irin world.

And she knew that all she had to do was snap her fingers and her parents would choose a suitable scribe for her, as Anamitra's had chosen for her. They would mate. Their magic would bond. Their love would grow. She would probably be supremely happy.

She didn't want it.

"I want…" She set her book to the side. "I don't know what I want."

"That much is obvious." Vasu looked up. "The son of Glast visits you."

"Who? Rhys?" She frowned. "You know Rhys of Glast?"

Vasu looked up at the ceiling. "I don't know how to answer that."

"Try truthfully?"

"I know of him, but I would not call us friends. He's tried to kill me a number of times."

Meera's eyes went wide. "What?"

"He is always cross when I appear unannounced near Jaron's daughter."

"I have no idea what that means. Who is Jaron's daughter?"

"His watcher's mate."

Meera pressed her palms to her eyes. "Vasu. Just... stop. You're not making any sense."

"I don't know why not." He rose from the chair and crawled next to her in the four-poster bed. "The son of Glast belongs to the Istanbul house where Jaron's daughter is mated to the watcher. I told Jaron I would watch over her, and I do not break promises to friends."

"So you visit her."

"Obviously."

"And Rhys tried to kill you for that?"

"When I appear, he throws daggers at me." Vasu shrugged. "He never hits me. I think he enjoys being cross with me."

"Yes, I can actually see that." Her irritation fled. She usually couldn't stay mad at Vasu for long. "So you know Rhys of Glast. Do you think I should trust him?"

Vasu pursed his lips as he thought. "He is very loyal to his friends and far more intelligent than most warriors. He should be a sage, but he is like you."

"What does that mean?"

"He's avoiding his responsibilities."

"I'm not..." Meera sighed. "Okay, I *am* avoiding responsibilities, but only for a short time."

"He thinks the same." Vasu turned a thousand-yard stare toward her. "But like you, his future will not be what he expects."

"Will you stop speaking in riddles?"

"No," he said simply. "If I shared my true thoughts, you would go mad. Riddles and stories are the only way to convey truth to those locked in human minds."

She ignored the insult. Vasu was Vasu. "But you think I can trust Rhys?"

"Perhaps."

"Vasu!"

"You have to decide for yourself." His corporeal form started to dissolve. "It's not my job to solve your puzzles for you."

# CHAPTER FIVE

Rhys was sipping tea and waiting for breakfast in the courtyard of the hotel where Meera had taken him his first day in New Orleans. He had returned several times in the week since he'd been in the city. He liked the cool solitude of the courtyard and the tall, trickling fountain.

He didn't hear her enter the courtyard. He only saw her when she pulled back a wrought iron chair.

How did she keep sneaking up on him? And sneaking away? It had to be some kind of magic. His situational awareness was too keen for any other explanation.

Blasted woman.

"Do you mind if I join you?" She sat down before he could answer.

"Am I going to be able to stop you?" He set down the newspaper he'd been reading.

She was wearing a bright green sundress that morning and her hair was knotted on top of her head. A few errant curls fell to shoulders that looked like they'd had a few days of sun since the last time he'd seen her.

*Where have you been?*

*What have you been doing?*

*Who have you been doing it with?*

Asking any of those questions would be impertinent and frankly too revealing of how much he'd been thinking about her. "Good morning, Meera."

"I'm glad you came back here." Meera waved over a server. "They don't get as much business as some of the more obvious restaurants." She ordered coffee and pastry.

"I like it here." Rhys sipped his tea. "The kitchen is fast and the servers remain aloof."

"You like aloof servers?"

"Yes. This city is relentlessly friendly. It's exhausting."

Meera threw her head back and laughed. "Relentlessly friendly. Yes, that describes New Orleans quite well. I wouldn't call it exhausting though."

"That's your prerogative." He itched to tuck the fallen curls back into the knot she wore. As if that would contain her. "You've been gone for a few days."

"Yes, at the haven."

"Your parents' haven."

She smiled softly. "It doesn't belong to them. They only came here a few years ago."

"From where?"

Meera said, "Did you order breakfast? I think you're too thin. You must eat more. Surely I'm not the first person who's told you this. Isn't your mother alive? What about your sisters in Istanbul?"

He didn't give in to the subject change. "Why are you so cagey about who you are? I've told you my identity. I've been completely open with you, and yet you continue to evade any questions about who you are and what your qualifications might be. How am I supposed to trust you?"

"You're asking for *my* help," Meera said. "I'm not asking for yours, remember? I never called for you, so why is it my responsibility to make you trust me?"

He hated that her point had merit. The fact that she could so easily spar with him was both maddening and quickly nudging his preoccupation toward obsession.

*Who are you, Meera?*

The question had kept him up over half the previous night.

"Someone—someone who knows exactly who you are—called me. They asked me to come here."

"Yes." She pursed her lips. "Someone did. Without my knowledge."

"Who knows who you are? Your parents, of course. The ones who run the haven." He quickly ran through everything he knew about North American havens and who their guardians might be. It wasn't knowledge that was readily available to most scribes, but then Rhys wasn't most scribes.

"Did your parents come to this place for you? Where were you before?" Rhys sorted through bits of information, tossing one option to reexamine another, trying to piece the puzzle of her identity together in his mind.

Her accent was clearly Northern Indian. Who were Sari's contacts in Northern India? Whom did she trust? Only one person fit all the necessary criteria.

Oh. *Oh.*

"Patiala lives in India," he mused. "Patiala of Udaipur. More accurately, she *did* live in India."

Only a flicker in Meera's eyes gave her away.

"Patiala disappeared after the death of Anamitra," Rhys said. "Orsala told me they hadn't heard from her in years."

"Orsala of Vestfold? You know many people," Meera said. "Of course, the library of Glast is considered one of the greatest in Europe. I'm sure you've met hundreds of scribes and singers. Glast is the most prominent combined library still in existence, I believe."

Patiala. Northern India.

*Meera?*

Why hadn't he seen it before? Rhys's heart picked up. Not Meera. *Meera Bai.* "Glast is a great library," he said, "but it is nothing like the ancient library in Udaipur."

Heaven above, it was so obvious.

The server brought coffee, and Meera added cream before she responded. "Yes, the library of Udaipur is one of the greatest in the Irina world. But don't be so dismissive of Glast. Combined libraries are rare. Did you grow up there?"

Meera Bai. He was sitting across from Meera Bai.

Rhys refused to be distracted. "Udaipur is the singers' library, filled with the wisdom of millennia. Led by Anamitra, most ancient and wise of Irina."

Meera placed her cup carefully in the saucer. "Anamitra is dead."

"But her heir lives." Rhys could feel the rush of blood as his pulse pounded.

Gabriel's fist. Not *here*!

Not in this strange, hot backwater on the other side of the world. Why would she come here? Why would she live on her own in this place with so little protection? Why would she expose herself to danger? What could possibly be worth that kind of risk?

"Meera," he whispered. "Why are you here?"

She sipped her coffee. "I'm having breakfast with you."

"You know that's not what I mean."

"I've told you, I'm doing research into Irina—"

"Meera Bai."

She looked up with a level gaze. "Who?"

Chess matches with this woman would be epic.

*Naked chess would be better.*

Damn his libido. He didn't need to be distracted by that mental picture.

"Meera Bai was a sixteenth-century human mystic from

Rajasthan," Rhys said carefully, "who was so admired by the Irina that the wisest and most learned singer in all the Eastern world vowed she would name her heir after the woman, therefore giving her eternity, not only in the human world, but in the heavens."

A smile flirted around the corner of Meera's mouth. "What a beautiful story."

Rhys tapped the edge of his teacup. "Isn't it? And it's true. Every single word. You're Meera Bai. You're not a friend or associate of Patiala. You're her daughter, the heir of Anamitra."

"That is quite a leap. I'm flattered."

"It's not a leap. It's a theory supported by evidence. If Patiala called Sari with information, that information would be trusted immediately. Without question."

He waited for her to respond—to give him some kind of reaction—but she gave him nothing.

*Naked chess is a must.*

Focus.

"This is not a game," he whispered. "My mother knelt at the feet of Anamitra and begged for her training, and you are her heir. Your mother must have known that Sari and Damien would send me without thinking twice because if the *heir of Anamitra* had found the Wolf, then it meant the sage of Irina sages had found a reservoir of lost magic."

"A reservoir of lost magic?" Meera's eyebrows went up, but her placid smile stayed in place. "My goodness, the elder scribes would love to get their hands on that, wouldn't they?"

"Is that why you don't trust me?" His heart raced again. "Gabriel's bloody fist, I am not their lackey! *Why are you here?* Why are you alone? You have no protection—"

"I don't need protection."

"The scribe house in the city doesn't even know who you are."

"Don't they?" She leaned forward, and her mask of amused indifference slipped. "Well, I don't know *you*."

63

"I'm trying to change that."

"Why? So you can accumulate more magic like a greedy boy hoarding his toys?"

He set down his teacup before it cracked in his hand. "You're impossible."

"I could say the same about you."

How could Patiala allow it? How could Patiala's mate? Meera Bai's father was rumored to have come from the Tomir warriors, dedicated to protecting the wisdom of Udaipur. If Meera was the heir, she should be living in a fortress, surrounded by a hundred warriors who could protect her and the treasures in her mind.

Instead, she sat across from Rhys at a wrought iron bistro table, sipping her coffee while a fountain bubbled in the background, wearing a colorful dress and bangles on her wrists like she was an ordinary woman with not a care in the world.

*"Sounds like a narrow world."*

*"Yes, it was. Until recently."*

*"So you did live in a haven once."*

*"Not a haven."*

She had lived in a fortress.

His anger dimmed. Meera Bai had lived in the fortress of Udaipur and spent her entire life receiving the knowledge of the Forgiven and the histories of the Irina. Their magic. Their heartbreak. Their power and their struggle. She'd been protected and sheltered.

Hidden.

The child who would become the heir of Anamitra would have been kept from anything that could hurt her. Probably treated like an object of curiosity instead of a person. Awesome to everyone around her, including her family.

*"Not a haven."*

A prison.

Rhys spoke softly. "I have no interest in exposing you. I came to help."

"Then leave me alone." She stood, tossing a ten-dollar bill on the table. Her fingers were shaking. "Go back to Istanbul, Rhys. Go back to your books and your scrolls and leave me alone."

———

HE CALLED Damien as soon as he arrived back at the guest house.

"Rhys—?"

"Tell me what is going on. Do you know who this woman is? Why am I here? So I can find the Wolf? What the hell is really going on?"

Damien was quiet.

"Damien?"

"I've told you as much as I can tell you about Meera. And as far as I know, your assignment is exactly what was told to you: find the Wolf and record her magic in whatever way you can so it can be shared and spread to martial singers around the world."

Rhys tried not to grind his teeth. *How to get more information?*

"Okay, tell me about Patiala."

Damien released a breath. "She's a friend. One of Sari's closest friends, though they've never met in person. Patiala went into hiding with Anamitra for some time after the Rending. They weren't in Udaipur when the Grigori attacked, which is why the fortress was lightly guarded and so many singers were killed. Eventually they reemerged, and the library resumed its former activities, though Anamitra, her family, and the Tomir order never left its walls again. They weren't hidden like other havens were, but they as good as disappeared."

"And her mate?"

"Maarut of the Tomir. He wasn't drafted into the order. Like me, he is the heir of its commander."

"Mikael's line?"

"No. The Tomir descend directly from Uriel. Their *talesm* traditions are different than Mikael's, though no less martial. There are very few records of their battles because they don't fight many."

"With a reputation like they have, that's surprising."

"They have a different mindset. The Tomir believe that if a battle must be fought, a failure has already occurred. Though they never shrink from protecting those under their guard, they prefer to work in stealth, and negotiation is always their first tactic. Their relationship to the singers of Udaipur is long-standing."

"Bodyguards?"

"It's more than that. They are symbiotic, a hidden community within a hidden community. Very, very secretive. The Tomir don't train in Udaipur—their historical home is in Kashmir—but they all serve Udaipur for part of their life. It's considered a very high honor, and most of the singers of Udaipur take their mates from the Tomir scribes."

"Like Patiala and Maarut, Meera's parents."

"Yes. I'm fairly sure that Patiala and Maarut's mating was arranged, though Sari says they are completely devoted to each other. If you encounter Maarut, don't treat him like a warrior; he is a guardian. The Tomir revere Anamitra and her line. Their prime directive the past two thousand years has been her protection. And of course that protection would extend to her heir." Damien paused. "And... that's all I can tell you about that."

Translation: Sari is listening and I'm not allowed to spill any more secrets.

"Understood," Rhys said.

---

THE NEXT NIGHT, Rhys was tapping away on his laptop, answering email inquiries regarding the Istanbul library while he enjoyed the cool evening in the courtyard of the guesthouse. He'd just finished answering the last message when he sensed another scribe approaching.

The magic was strong and it was not familiar.

The scribe made no attempt to conceal his power, and his magic heralded his arrival like a forward guard sounding trumpets. Rhys felt it approaching from beyond the gate, and the two humans lingering in the courtyard moved away, back into the rooms that surrounded them, without a single word.

The scribe who walked into the courtyard was not only magically impressive but physically imposing. He was as tall as Rhys but broad at the shoulder with a heavy beard and long dark hair braided down his back. His *talesm* were wrought with immaculate precision on his forearms, neck, and collar, and Rhys knew a warrior of this man's power would likely have spells inked from his neck to his knees, if not farther down his legs.

Rhys met the man's eyes and didn't look away.

Seeing Maarut made Rhys twice as glad he'd already spoken to his watcher. If he hadn't known anything about the Tomir order, he would have assumed the scribe was coming to kill him, that was how intimidating the man felt. After all, if Rhys was right and Meera was the heir of Anamitra, he'd been badgering the woman with questions and intruding on her privacy.

The Tomir were charged with Meera's protection, and if Rhys's suspicions were correct, this particular warrior was Meera's father. But though Maarut's expression revealed nothing, his magic didn't feel aggressive. It announced his power and nothing more.

He sat across the table as Rhys shut the laptop and moved it to the side.

The imposing scribe nodded at the laptop. "My daughter likes this kind of technology as well."

"I can assume you're Meera's father?"

"You can."

"She was telling me she's been able to record some Irina songs."

A stern eyebrow rose. "Her mother does not approve."

"But Meera has a mind of her own."

A slight smile. "That she does."

"I am Rhys of Glast," he said. "Archivist of the Istanbul house, watched by Malachi and sent by Damien and Sari of Rěkaves. I came here to assist your daughter in any way she needs as our house was told that Atawakabiche, last leader of the Uwachi Toma, may be living. I wish to conceal nothing from you, your mate, or your daughter."

Maarut stared at Rhys with his arms crossed across his massive chest. "Are you always so formal?"

Rhys let out a breath. "No. But I spoke to Damien yesterday; he told me who you are. I think he was attempting to scare the arrogance out of me."

"Did it work?"

"According to my brothers, nothing will."

Maarut smiled. "We are not so formal here. In Udaipur, it was easy to follow protocol. Here, things are different. Life is softer."

"Is that why Meera likes it?"

"You'd have to ask her that question."

"I will."

"But will you listen?" Maarut asked. "That is the problem, you see. Too many in her life give deference, but they only pretend to listen."

"Who wouldn't listen to the heir of Anamitra?"

Maarut narrowed his eyes. "If the heir of Anamitra speaks, the whole world listens. But I am speaking of my daughter."

Rhys frowned. "With all respect, can we dispense with the subterfuge? I'm not trying to be invasive, but at this point I am quite sure that Meera *is* Meera Bai, the heir of Anamitra. You are her father, Maarut of the Tomir and mate of Patiala, who is a dear friend of Sari. I'm trying to help. I'm not here to expose you."

"You're young," Maarut said. "You will learn, or she will dismiss you."

"If Meera did not request help, then I'm quite certain Patiala did. I don't enjoy wasting time."

Maarut's friendly expression didn't waver. "You are impatient."

"Always."

"Acknowledging your faults doesn't excuse them, brother."

Rhys leaned forward. "I'm here to help. I promise that. If you're interested in that help, then let me assist you. If not, then I will leave."

"No, you won't. You're too much of a hunter. I can see it in your eyes. You're curious now. You won't be able to leave it alone." Maarut rose. "I will tell Patiala I have met you and share my impressions with her. You are correct. She is the one who called you."

"Why?" Rhys rose to look Maarut in the eye. "It's quite clear her daughter doesn't want me here."

"Mothers and daughters." Maarut gave an enormous shrug. "They are a mystery. Patiala will want to meet you."

What on earth? It was clear Maarut and Patiala weren't over-protective of Meera if they let her live in New Orleans on her own. Why did Meera's mother care whom she worked with?

"Do you at least know where Meera lives?"

The scent of Maarut's magic changed and an aggressive note filled the courtyard. He was no longer smiling. "Why do you ask?"

"Because the scribes at the house here have no idea. I have no idea. I'd like to be sure at least *someone* knows where she is living if there's a threat. She seems to have no sense of self-preservation at all."

Maarut's magic dropped back to an easy tenor. "You are... not what I expected. It's certainly not obvious what she was thinking, but this may work after all."

"You're being cryptic on purpose now."

"I know." Maarut gestured to Rhys's face. "I quite enjoy that tic you get near your eye. It's amusing."

"Maarut—"

"Don't worry. I know where Meera lives because I listen to her. But trust me, despite what her mother and you think, she has more of a sense of self-preservation than anyone you know. And plenty of ways to protect herself. Goodbye."

The scribe's magic eased to almost nothing. The essence of it dissipated, and the humans wandered back to the courtyard as Maarut left by the garden gate.

---

"You're right," Rhys said to Zep the following night. "Meera's father is… how did you put it? A scary fucker."

"Right?" Zep laughed. "I nearly pissed my pants the first time I met the man."

They were walking down Bourbon Street, but despite the hubbub and confusion, neither of them had sensed any Grigori. They'd caught the scent of sandalwood on one corner, but it had simply been a smoke shop, not any supernatural predators.

"You know," Zep continued, "I thought a warrior who'd follow his mate into a haven would be…"

"What?"

"I don't know." Zep shrugged. "A little softer? Wanting to hide away like that, abandon your house, you'd have to be a little softer, right?"

"Not if you had a mate or children to protect." *You immature idiot.*

Zep said, "I guess."

Rhys tried not to overreact. He'd run into Zep's attitude before, the idea that living in the scribe houses and fighting Grigori was somehow more important than guarding women and children.

"If I were running from Grigori and felt targeted as the Irina did," Rhys said, "I have a feeling I'd feel very safe with a scribe like Maarut protecting my haven. And trust me, Irina warriors are plenty scary on their own. We have more than one living in the Istanbul scribe house."

"I heard that." Zep smiled. "I'd like to see a few more here. See a few more kickass ladies."

*I'm sure you would.*

"And Meera's dad? He's all right. If I had a daughter, I'd be protective too."

Rhys stopped dead in his tracks on the sidewalk. A tourist bumped into his shoulder and cursed under his breath, but Rhys didn't move.

*"If the heir of Anamitra speaks, the whole world listens. But I am speaking of my daughter."*

Gabriel's fist, he *was* an idiot. Maarut hadn't visited him the previous day because he'd been asking questions about the heir of Anamitra. He'd been questioning the man who was spending time with his *daughter.*

*"I know where Meera lives because I listen to her."*

He listened to his daughter, the woman behind the legacy. The woman who loved color and music and life beyond fortress walls. Rhys thought about where he'd run into Meera and where she'd found him. Thought about tiny clues she'd dropped and directions she looked when she wasn't paying attention to who was watching her.

Then he smiled. "Zep, you don't need me here do you?"

Zep shrugged. "Not if you've got things to do."

"I have an idea I want to check out. For... my research." Rhys turned around and started walking back toward Ursuline Avenue. "I'll see you. Call me if you need anything."

"Later."

Rhys didn't turn to look as Zep continued down Bourbon,

following the tourist traffic. He walked the opposite way, heading toward the Esplanade and the Faubourg Marigny. He was almost sure it was where Meera lived.

He ignored the annoying voice in his mind asking him why he needed to know where she lived.

*Naked chess.*

Not naked chess. This wasn't about his libido. It wasn't. Meera was living anonymously in a city that could be dangerous. She needed his protection.

Rhys crossed the Esplanade and turned right on Kerlerec Street before he cut across to Frenchmen. The music and the crowd wasn't as loud as Bourbon Street, but the street was filled with tourists. It was so packed he could hardly see anything.

The fourth time he was shoved off the sidewalk by a group of revelers, he nearly gave up. What had he been thinking? The city was small, but not that small. And he didn't know Meera that well. Just because he was drawn to this neighborhood didn't mean she was. He'd run into her because she was looking for him.

Rhys leaned against the wall near the Three Muses and listened to the singer who'd sung to him and Meera earlier in the week. He watched the crowds flow around him, his senses tuned to detect anything angelic.

Nothing.

Then he remembered the way Meera had concealed herself in shadow and wondered if she was watching him in that moment. He could feel a faint prickle on his neck. Was it his own imagination or something else?

*Where are you, Meera Bai?*

He wandered over to the art market and walked through stalls selling everything from wire sculptures to earrings made of spoons. There were delicately painted teacups, screen-printed T-shirts, and watercolors of the city.

*She likes this. She likes life and color and variety. She likes the chaos and humanity.*

Her life had probably been ordered beyond what he could imagine. While his own schooling had been more rigorous than most young scribes, Rhys had also been a boy who grew up with a class of other small troublemakers around him. He'd acted out and been punished harshly, but he'd acted out. He'd had his rebellion.

*This place is hers.*

The thought made Rhys smile. He left the art market and wandered back up Frenchmen Street, heading toward the sound of trumpet and clarinet. A jazz band was playing on the corner, and tourists crowded around them, shouting encouragement and tossing coins and dollars in the bucket they passed.

A red flash from the corner of his eye made him turn, but it was a human woman in a bright red dress. She looked nothing like Meera, but she was short and laughing on the arm of a man who led her away from the crowd.

Just a man?

Rhys followed them for a block until they turned into a club and he was sure it was nothing more than a human couple out for a date.

He was paranoid, seeing threats where none existed. He'd been in unfamiliar territory for too long without a mission he could sink his teeth into. He had no direction, no goal, no—

Sandalwood in the air.

His heart leapt at the scent of Grigori drifting from the shadows. Rhys turned and followed the trail down an alley and toward a residential area.

The Grigori was walking alone, his hands in his pockets. He didn't appear to be hunting, but he did look like he was searching for something. He was a handsome man with light brown skin and dark curly hair that reminded Rhys of the Grigori in Istanbul. He was of medium height and build. Like all Grigori, humans would have found him attractive.

The Grigori had been on Frenchmen; why hadn't he taken a human?

A faint hope sprang up in Rhys's chest that this was a free Grigori. Perhaps this man was the reason New Orleans was mostly free of attacks. Maybe there were free Grigori in the city who had claimed the space for their brothers and had forced the Fallen sons to run.

The strange Grigori stopped in the middle of the road, shook his head, then turned a different direction. Walked down another alley, then back again.

What was going on?

Rhys followed the Grigori north and east of Frenchmen, deeper into the Marigny. The man stopped and closed his eyes.

A homeless man on the corner shouted at him. "Hey buddy, you got a buck?"

The Grigori turned and stared at the man. "What did you say to me?" His voice dripped with disdain.

"Just asking for a buck, man."

The Grigori stared at the human and walked over, drawing a hand from his pocket. Rhys was expecting a dollar to emerge, not a stiletto.

"Stop!" he shouted, but it was too late. The knife plunged into the human's neck. The man seized, his arms and legs flailing before he went suddenly limp.

The Grigori didn't even turn. He took off jogging back toward Frenchmen Street.

No!

Rhys ran over and bent down to the human, but the human was dead, his blood pouring into the gutter where the Grigori's blade had slit his throat.

Rhys took off after the murderer. He touched his *talesm prim* as he ran down the road, following the man into the shadows and activating the magic that acted like living armor. The Grigori was fast, but Rhys was faster. He leapt over a garden fence and through a backyard, following the scent. He could see the Grigori in the distance. The man was standing frozen in the middle of a residential street, then he walked into another alley as if he was in a trance.

Rhys silently followed.

The alley was bound by a brick house on one side and darkened garden gates on the other. The Grigori walked to a gate and paused. He pressed his hands to the gate and fell to his knees just as the gate creaked open.

Meera stood in the gate, the bloody Grigori fallen at her feet.

# CHAPTER SIX

*A*nother one had found her.

Before Meera could register the weeping Grigori at her feet, a deadly figure flew from the darkness and pulled the man away.

"Rhys?"

He pushed the Grigori up against the brick wall and pulled his dagger on the struggling man.

Meera shouted, "No!"

Her words rang hollow in the dark alley. Rhys plunged his silver knife into the back of the Grigori's neck. The man's back arched before he fell to the ground; his body curled into a fetal position before it began to dissolve.

Rhys turned back to her. "Meera?"

"Why did you do that?" She felt the tears welling in her eyes. Angry tears. "He wasn't attacking me."

The scribe stepped closer. "How did he know where you live?"

She shook her head and felt the tears hot on her cheeks. "You didn't have to do that. He wouldn't have hurt me."

Rhys raised his hands. They were covered in blood. "He murdered a harmless man in front of me. The human asked him for a dollar and instead got a knife to the throat, so tell me again, Meera, *how did he know where you live?"*

She slumped against the gate. "They find me. They always have. But I can send them away. All I have to do is talk to them and they leave me alone." She turned and walked back into her garden, ignoring the scribe who followed her.

Meera's heart hurt. She could still feel the torment of the Fallen son who had found her. He'd been young. Sometimes she could ease their emptiness. Sometimes she could give them peace. She would touch them and whisper a spell, easing some of the relentless soul hunger that plagued all their kind. Most of them never returned.

She heard the gate close behind her and Rhys's footsteps on the path. He strode past her, walking toward the house.

"Stay back," he ordered.

"There's no one else here," she said woodenly. "Just me."

He ignored her, walked up the steps and through the kitchen door. Meera followed him into the cozy house that had become her refuge. Rhys kept his dagger drawn as he swept through the kitchen and past the antiques and eclectic collection of furniture in the living room, his head swinging every direction.

Despite his size and speed, he didn't make a sound. His magic permeated the air, drawing up the dark hair on her arms and making her skin prickle.

"Rhys, there's no one here."

He acted as if he didn't hear her, poking his head in the bathroom before he walked through her bedroom, scanned it quickly, and went back to her office. It was the room that faced the street, the front of the shotgun house lovingly restored by her human landlord who lived next door.

Meera followed the intruder who was violating every inch of her private retreat. He stood before the shuttered front windows as a car drove by, the shadows cut by lines of yellow light.

She stared at him. "I told you. There's no one here but me."

"And me."

Seeing him in her office, surrounded by her carefully collected books and art, turned sorrow and confusion into anger. He'd brought blood and violence to her door, killed a man who needed help. He'd been hounding her, asking intrusive questions, relentlessly searching to unveil her secrets.

Meera had had enough. "Get out of my house."

"Did you hear me? That Grigori killed a man in front of me."

"I heard you." The thought of the dead human made her sick, just like all the violence that soaked their world, but Rhys's actions had only caused more violence. He healed nothing. "Get out."

He stepped away from the windows and his eyes drank her in. It was a shadow, just a glimpse, of the hunger she'd felt from the Grigori.

"Meera." His voice was rough.

She'd been ready for a night in. She was wearing loose cotton pants and a tank top. Her hair was pulled into a bun, and she wore no makeup or jewelry. She felt exposed, stripped of the practiced frivolity she'd worn in his presence.

There was an open bottle of wine in the kitchen and étouffée cooking on the stove. While it was cooking, she'd been ravenous. Now the air smelled of spice and blood. She wasn't hungry anymore. It would likely be days before she felt like eating again.

Rhys stepped closer. "I did what I was trained to do."

"I know."

"He was a murderer. He would have hurt you."

"No." She shook her head. "He wouldn't have."

"What do you mean, they find you, Meera? Does your father know about this? Your mother?"

"Get out." She stepped away from the doorway and pointed to the kitchen. "I want you to leave. Now."

"What is going on?"

He didn't move, and he did not obey her. Meera Bai, the heir of

Anamitra, had utter control in all things, but the arrogance of this scribe threatened to rouse her temper past restraint.

*How dare you?* she wanted to yell. *Do you know who I am?*

He did. That was the problem.

Meera raised her eyes and lifted her chin. "Shall I make you leave?" She whispered ancient words under her breath, letting the scribe feel a taste of her power. "You won't like me if I do."

His fair skin turned paler, and Meera knew he was feeling the effects of her power. Pain. Nausea. If he didn't leave her presence, he'd soon be sick.

The arrogant expression fell away from his face. Rhys put a hand on the doorway to brace himself and bent toward her. "Nice trick."

"Don't ever underestimate me."

"I've never done that," he said through gritted teeth, "you infuriating woman."

"I'm not the one intruding on your privacy. I've asked you to leave three times."

"Do you want me to apologize for killing that man? I won't do it."

"Why am I not surprised?"

He grunted in pain when she whispered another spell.

"He killed that man without hesitation. I needed to make sure you were safe."

*You stubborn ass.*

"Do I look vulnerable, Rhys?" She leaned closer. "Do you really think he could have withstood the amount of pain you're in right now?"

Rhys pressed his eyes closed, steadying himself. In any other circumstance, Meera would be impressed by how he withstood magic that brought most men to their knees. But all she could think about was Grigori dust at her gate and the smell of blood in the air.

"I am not trying to intrude on your privacy," he said. "I could have found you if I'd tried."

"I'm sure you think that."

"I know it." He stepped closer despite the obvious pain he was in. "I know who you are, but don't underestimate me. You don't know who I am."

Rhys was so close Meera could feel the heat from his skin. His nose started to bleed, and Meera whispered a spell to ease some of the pain.

She didn't want his blood on her floor.

"I know who you are, Rhys of Glast," she said. "You're like all the others."

"If you really think that, then you haven't been paying attention."

*Haven't I?*

Some deeper instinct pricked her mind, and Meera lifted her shields for a split second before she slammed them down. It wasn't fast enough to shut out the bell-like clarity of his soul voice.

No. *No no no no no.*

It couldn't be. It was a trick of her mind brought on by an emotionally trying night. That was all. Meera wouldn't meet his eyes, so she looked at the lean muscle that crossed his chest. The black-inked *talesm* scribed over his shoulders were just visible under the white cotton shirt he wore.

"I'm leaving now." Rhys straightened his hunched shoulders. "Call me if anyone else comes."

"You're the last person I would ever call for help, you stubborn, intrusive *ass*. If you tell anyone where I live—"

He walked toward the door. "I have no interest in telling anyone where you live. I'm not generous enough for that. And I won't return, not until you invite me."

*Not if you were the last scribe on earth.*

As if reading her thoughts, Rhys turned. His nose had started bleeding again. "You *will* invite me."

---

HER HOUSE FELT empty after he left, even though he'd only been there for a few minutes. The scribe's presence lingered like the spices from the étouffée she threw in the trash. The scent of his magic haunted her senses, but it was more than that.

The bell-like timbre of his soul voice had shaken Meera to her core.

*"You must take a mate, Meera Bai, for there is no better protection and counsel than a scribe bonded to you by magic. He will be your one true confidant in the world and your most fervent ally. If you are fortunate as I was, love will be your companion, but do not look for a* reshon. *That blessing is not for those who hold the memory of our people. To take a* reshon *means to have your very soul linked to another, and your soul must be only yours, for it is the one thing you will ever truly own. The heir of Anamitra does not belong to herself but to all the Irina and those yet to come."*

The memory of her great-aunt's words came to her as they always did, with utter clarity, as if the old singer was still sitting next to her in the gardens of Udaipur. The fountains trickled in the background, the palms rustled in the arid breeze, and Anamitra's ageless voice filled her mind.

Most Irin people thought Anamitra had stopped her longevity spells when her mate was lost, but Meera knew the truth. She could only stop her longevity spells once a suitable heir had been born.

By tradition, the keeper of memories would come from Anamitra's own blood. Unfortunately, Anamitra only had one child, a son who had not lived to maturity. But her niece had given birth to a daughter, and that daughter had shown the power of memory before she could speak.

Meera had been given to Anamitra as her heir. Her birth name, forgotten. She became Meera Bai, heir of Anamitra, keeper of heaven's songs, living archive of Irina memory and magic. Her rooms were moved to Anamitra's wing of the fortress, and every moment was spent with the old singer as her great-aunt began lessons that would last two hundred years and occupy every moment of Meera's life.

She was a walking repository of Irina memory, a library that lived and breathed, a counselor to kings and queens. As seers saw into the future, Meera could delve into the past, magically accessing the trove of memory Anamitra had woven into her mind.

*"Your soul must be only yours, for it is the one thing you will ever truly own."*

Anamitra had waited hundreds of years for an heir. She could never allow her life to end because of love. Never would she allow her legacy to fade because her heart was wounded. From the time Meera understood the bond of mates, Anamitra had made it clear that a *reshon* was a dangerous indulgence Meera was not allowed to have.

Which meant the sound of Rhys's soul voice *might* make him the most dangerous man she had ever met.

Vasu appeared next to her in his adult form. "You are troubled."

"Yes."

"Because of the scribe?" Vasu cocked his head and took the pan Meera was washing. He tugged it from her and set it on the tile counter. "Shall I remove him?"

Meera picked up the pan and reached for a towel to dry it. "No, Vasu. Don't kill him."

"I could take him back to Istanbul."

A knot of inevitable dread sat in her belly. "He would come back."

"Then I shall kill him if he displeases you."

"No." She dried off the pan and hung it on the hook above the counter. "Did my aunt let you kill people for her?"

"Sometimes."

Meera froze, but only for a heartbeat. No, that should not

surprise her. Though Anamitra was a scholar, she was also ruthless in protecting her family. If a human or Grigori had threatened her, she would have no qualms about allowing Vasu—with his inexplicable loyalty—dispatch him or her.

Her great-aunt would likely have approved Rhys's actions.

Vasu, bored by Meera's kitchen chores, sat on the table and put bare feet on her kitchen chair. "There is a dark shadow around you."

"The scribe killed a Grigori in front of me."

"Yes, I saw."

"That doesn't bother you?"

Vasu shrugged. "He wasn't one of mine."

"I thought you didn't have any children left."

"I have a few." His eyes drifted to the side. "Human women do not interest me any longer."

Meera cleared off the counter and hopped up, putting her at eye level with the fallen angel. "Did human women ever interest you? Really?"

The corner of Vasu's mouth turned up. "Oh yes."

"When you were young."

"Was I?" Vasu frowned. "Yes, I suppose."

"Were you ever a child?"

"Not as you think of one." He squinted at her. "Why are you asking about me? You know I don't like answering questions."

"I'm sad," she said. "Cheer me up."

"That scribe is connected to you."

Meera rolled her eyes. "That is not cheering me up."

"I can see it. There is a tie between you. Is he your mate?" Vasu stretched out a leg and tapped her foot with his own. "You are displeased by the question."

"I thought he was a scholar, a man in search of knowledge. But he killed that Grigori without hesitation."

"You judge others too harshly. The Grigori killed another.

Would you have a scholar ignore the mandate of the Creator? The Irin were left on this earth so they could protect humanity."

Meera couldn't respond to that because Vasu was right. She was just… tired. Tired of violence and war and the schemes of the powerful to obtain more power. She wanted to find another way. She wanted there to be a different solution.

"Wise Vasu," she started, "seeker of heaven's vision. May I ask you a question?"

Vasu's eyes lit up. He loved discussions like this. "Daughter of heaven, I am listening."

She asked, "Does one person's gain always mean another's loss?"

"In what way, Meera Bai?"

"Is power finite?"

"No, power is infinite."

"Then must there always be war?"

Vasu raised an eyebrow. "You should ask another question. Will there always be humanity?"

"Can humanity only exist with war?"

"War is about power," Vasu said. "Once there was balance, but humanity was not satisfied with that. Once a scale is tipped, it must always be in motion. To answer your first question, if a scale goes up, it must again go down."

Meera swung her legs. "So one person's gain must mean another's loss?"

"That is the way of power until there is balance again. You can strive for balance, but until both sides want to achieve it, it is only an idea."

"So if both sides want balance, then neither loses."

"But neither gains."

She smiled. "Or they gain together."

"You seek to remake the world."

"If both oxen pull together, then the field is plowed straight."

"But both must have the same goal." Vasu shook his head. "I thought Anamitra was ambitious, but you will surpass her."

"The Irin world has been at war since we were born. War with angels. War with Grigori. We will never win until we redefine what victory means."

"You're not going to like this," Vasu said. "But I'm going to tell you the truth and you must listen to me."

"What?"

"You need that scribe, Meera Bai. If you seek to redefine what power is, if you seek to change the paradigm, then he must be the one to help you."

"Why?" she asked. "What makes Rhys of Glast special? There are other scribes more powerful than him, I'm certain of it."

Vasu's eyes lit up. "Do you seek power? You, who wants to redefine what power means?"

Meera narrowed her eyes. She hated when Vasu made good points. "You're avoiding the question. Why Rhys?"

"He owns something more important than power. I have seen him with his brothers and working among those far stronger than he is. I have seen him with Fallen children and those weaker than he is. He does not seek the spotlight, nor is he ambitious for anything other than knowledge."

"I don't know about that."

"I have watched him," Vasu said. "You have not."

Meera sighed. "Fine. I can accept that you know him better than I do."

"Rhys of Glast has a willing and flexible mind. He will understand you like few others could. If you want to bring balance, you must have leverage your opponent understands. For the Irin, that means magic. Rhys knows that. If you truly want to bring change, he is the ally you want."

---

THREE DAYS HAD PASSED, but Meera hadn't heard from Rhys. She escaped New Orleans and went to the haven to think. If there was any place she felt restful, it was in her mother's home. Patiala might not have been the most maternal of Irina mothers, but with her, Meera always felt safe.

She sat on the porch, staring out at the swaying fields of sugarcane, and Patiala came to sit beside her.

"The fog comes on little fox feet," her mother said.

"I don't think that's how the poem goes." Meera smiled. "And I don't see any fog. Or any foxes."

Patiala shook her head, a frown marring the smooth skin on her forehead. "That's what Sabine was singing this morning. Over and over again. Roch was trying to calm her, but she refused his touch."

Meera didn't take her eyes from the cane fields. "Sabine is exactly as she has always been."

"No, she's not. She's growing worse, which means something might be coming. She may be an earth singer, but she has seer's blood too. It is my job to look for signs of trouble, and I believe this behavior is a sign. She keeps rambling about the man on the river."

"The old man?"

Patiala sighed. "We've investigated him too many times to count. There's nothing unusual about him. He has no criminal record. No secret life. There is no sense of magic about the place. It's her mania. It's getting worse. Last month she claimed wolves were in the sugarcane, so she couldn't do her chores."

Meera's heart sank. Was it too much to ask that this vibrant and colorful place remain an island of peace in their world? "I can't help her, Mother. I've given every healing song I know to Alosia, but none of them make a difference. What would you have me do?"

"You know what you need to do. Roch will not ask you, but I will. Find the Wolf. Search Sabine's memories and find her."

Meera turned to look at her mother. "Do you think I haven't tried? The woman's mind is broken; her memories are a maze. I'm convinced Sabine has seen the Wolf, but that means nothing. Not even Roch can make sense of Sabine's rambling, and he's the one who knows the bayous best. None of what she has told us makes sense."

"So talk to the scribe. The one from Istanbul."

First Vasu, now her mother. "What does he know about the Wolf that you or I don't? What does he know about the bayous that Roch doesn't?"

"Did I raise an arrogant woman?" Patiala pursed her lips. "Maybe he knows nothing, but he has eyes. He has a mind. And allies I trust say he has experience finding those who are hidden. Are you so impressed with your own understanding that you would refuse the help of another?"

Meera felt her mother's disapproval like a blow to her chest. "I'm not arrogant."

"You are so certain of your own knowledge that you will not ask for help, convinced that anyone outside your tiny circle of trust cannot be relied upon." Patiala rose to her full height and looked down at Meera. "It's not just Sabine, you know. Something is coming. I've seen too many heartbreaks to ignore this knot in my belly, so I called to my friend and asked her for a favor. I asked her to send an ally, and you refuse to work with him. This disappoints me."

Patiala walked into the house without another word, leaving Meera alone and bruised by her mother's displeasure.

---

THE NEXT MORNING Meera drove back to New Orleans. She gritted her teeth and called the number Rhys had given her.

He picked up in three rings. "Hello?"

"Bring your brain and your research to my place tonight," she said. "Seven o'clock. What do the Americans say? I'll show you mine if you show me yours."

"Done."

"And bring dinner too. You owe me étouffée. And an apology."

# CHAPTER SEVEN

A t seven o'clock that evening, Rhys knocked on Meera's door, a messenger bag slung over his shoulder and a bag from Fete au Fete in his hand. Meera opened the door wearing an outfit similar to the one she'd worn the last time he'd seen her. Her shoulders were tan, and she was wearing a bright coral tank top. Her hair was piled on top of her head in a disordered tumble of thick waves.

She scattered his senses without saying a word.

Rhys thrust the bag into her hands. "They didn't have crawfish étouffée," he said crossly. "I bought shrimp and grits and crawfish poutine. I hope that's acceptable."

Meera took the bag. "Thank you."

Neither of them moved.

"*Étouffée. And an apology.*"

He took a deep breath and reminded himself he had been an arse. He'd been high on adrenaline and magic, appalled that the Grigori had been drawn to Meera so precisely, and worried far more than he expected for someone who was, at best, an intriguing new colleague.

*Liar. You want to play naked chess with her.*

So he'd been an arse.

"I'm sorry I underestimated you," he said. "I won't do it again."

She started to say something, then stopped and took a breath. "Fine. Apology accepted."

"Good."

Neither of them moved.

Rhys glanced over his shoulder. "Your garden is lovely. Did you plant it?"

"No. I just enjoy it. My landlord takes care of it since both properties share the backyard." She pointed to the narrow shotgun-style house beside her own. "I do a little bit here and there."

Rhys nodded, having exhausted his capacity for small talk. He didn't want to eat. Didn't want to talk about gardens. He wanted to find out what Meera knew about the Wolf—

*And play naked chess.*

No. He had goals. Objectives for the evening. And the woman hadn't moved from the front door.

She looked down at the bag, then back to Rhys. "As you might have been able to tell the other night, I'm not accustomed to having other people here."

Her unexpected admission eased his nerves. "No one?"

"Sometimes my father visits. That's all. I invited my mother once, but she couldn't relax. She kept eyeing the house's exit points and muttering under her breath."

"I've met your father." *And your mother sounds equally terrifying.* Rhys didn't say that part.

Meera nodded. "Yes, he mentioned he'd met you."

"It was an interesting experience."

"He's an interesting man." She stood awkwardly in the doorway for another few seconds before she stepped aside. "Please come in."

"Thank you."

"Do you like beer?"

"I do."

"Have a seat." Meera put the food on the table, and Rhys sat down while she went to the refrigerator and pulled out two bottles.

The bubbly, confident woman he'd met on the streets of the French Quarter was gone. The comforting woman who'd read his mood and coddled him in the club on the night he'd killed the Grigori in the cemetery was also gone. Her silence annoyed him, and he couldn't understand why. He wasn't usually one for chatter.

*You like her chatter.*

"Meera, stop." Rhys caught her hand as she walked past him in the small kitchen.

She turned and her eyes were hot. "I didn't say you could touch me."

He dropped her hand. "I am sorry I intruded the other night, but I'm not sorry I killed that Grigori."

"I know you're not sorry."

"Why did you call me if you're only going to glare at me?"

Meera sighed and set the two beers on the table. "We need to work together. More than one person has... admonished me for refusing your help."

"I'm not going to admonish you. You're clearly very bright, and you know whether you need help or not. If I'm not needed—"

"You are."

The simple statement hit him like a punch to the chest.

*She's not talking about you, you idiot. She's talking about your brain.*

"If I'm needed, then I'm happy to help. I know what it is to be discreet. You don't have to worry about my spreading rumors or revealing private information to the council."

She busied herself taking boxes and cartons out of the bag. "I'm not worried about that."

"Then why—?"

"You know who I am." She opened the boxes of food and moved the empty bag to the counter. She still didn't look at him.

"Are we finally doing away with the subterfuge? Thank you. Yes, I know who you are. And?"

She said nothing.

Rhys grew irritated. "I'm not a mind reader, Meera. And I don't know why you find it so annoying that your secret identity has been revealed, but if you think I'm going to defer to you because you're the heir of Anamitra, then you've grossly misunderstood what kind of person I am. I don't bow, and I've been in the presence of elders and seers."

She didn't say anything, but she sat down at the table and crossed her arms, a smile touching the corner of her lips.

"You may have been raised like a princess—"

"Did you just call me a princess?"

"—but it's not my job to worship you. It's my job to find leverage for the Irina so they can force the old arseholes in Vienna to pay some bloody attention to them."

The smile touching her lips grew until she was once again the bright and alluring woman who had tormented him his first day in New Orleans. Her brilliant smile, combined with the vibrant orange hue against her skin and her sparkling brown eyes, dazzled Rhys and knocked down the indignant head of steam he'd been building. "What?"

Meera leaned forward and rested her chin in her palm. "I think I like you."

She wasn't flirting to distract him. They were beyond that now. Rhys didn't know quite how to react. He blinked and stammered. "Good. I mean… not that you have to like someone to work with them."

"True." She didn't look away.

"What?" He sighed. "What is it?"

"You *can* be an ass. You're cross. A bit surly. And very arrogant."

"You're the one who said you liked me."

"I do."

His body roused at the tone of her voice, but there was something else. A warmth in his chest he didn't want to identify. "So you're willing to—as you said on the phone—show me yours."

Her eyebrows went up. "I did say that, didn't I? How forward of me. You brought yours?"

Rhys tapped his messenger bag with the toe of his boot. "I brought everything."

"And you want me to show you mine?"

*Yes!*

He let the smile come. "I believe you're the one who made the proposition, darling."

"Did I, *darling*?" She pursed her lips. "I suppose I did. Though I'm not sure you're ready to see it all."

Wariness and animosity had fled. In their place a new awareness was growing along with the playfulness she'd teased him with since their first meeting. They had stripped away their disguises in more ways than one, and the exposure wasn't strained. It was freeing.

"I'm very difficult to shock." Rhys couldn't stop himself from provoking her. "Try me."

"I'm not trying to shock you, but it's rare that I reveal myself, especially to a stranger."

"Are we still strangers? I thought we'd become rather familiar."

*We could become more familiar. I would not object to that.*

Meera lifted a sweating beer bottle and reached across to the bottle opener mounted on the counter, revealing an enticing hint of cleavage. She cracked the bottle open and set it in front of Rhys before she opened the second and took a long drink. A bead of perspiration rolled from the bottle down her neck.

"Feed me," she said. "Then I'll show you what you want to see."

---

"The Uwachi Toma weren't the only Irin people on this continent, but they were the largest and most dominant group." Meera's hand hovered over a map of North America. "The Irin people in the East fled as soon as Norse humans arrived."

Rhys and Meera were in her office, a large map spread out on a library table in the center of the room.

"It's a big continent," he said.

"It is. There were Irin groups in the Great Plains and on the West Coast like the Dene Ghal, but they weren't as active or organized as those in this region. The only thing close were the Koconah Citlal in Central America." Meera rolled open another map on the table and placed small weighted bags at the corners. "The Irin from the East moved to the South. They integrated into the existing Irin communities here, which concentrated the population."

The new map was a closer detail of the Gulf Coast region. Rhys immediately spotted the precise writing in the margins where Meera had made notes. He leaned over to read a notation farther north on the Mississippi River. "The Uwachi Toma were a mound-building culture, correct?"

"Correct. First in the northern Mississippi Valley, then moving south and into the coastal regions. The Uwachi Toma—'people of the sun'—mostly came from Uriel's blood, though they looked outside their immediate area when they mated, so bloodlines became very mixed."

Rhys pulled a stool from under the table. "Uriel was known for keeping the peace and had very few enemies, even among the Fallen. He was also incredibly powerful."

Meera grabbed another stool and sat next to Rhys. "Which was why they had such an extended period of calm. There was one major battle that we have recorded songs for. The Pakup Kun—the red water—where the archangel Nalu and his sons attempted to eradicate the Uwachi Toma. They failed."

"According to written accounts I could find, Nalu failed because the Wolf slew him with her song." Rhys raised his eyebrows. "Her song alone. It's the only account of an angel being killed without a heavenly blade in Irin history. Do you understand why Sari and

Orsala went a little mad when your mother said she might be alive?"

Meera ignored the question. "That victory led to something of a golden age for the Irin in North America. There were roughly five hundred years of peace before new angels came with European colonists and there were further conflicts. But during that peace, Uwachi Toma culture thrived. We just don't have much record of it because written tradition wasn't as valued as oral."

"But you have some of the songs."

Meera smiled softly. "Pieces. I'm always looking for more."

Rhys was fascinated. "Social structure?"

"Matrilineal but surprisingly patriarchal for Irin people."

"Agricultural?"

"Their economic base mirrored the native people. They did farm, but they also hunted in the bayous. Fish, shellfish, and alligator mostly."

"Mound building…," Rhys muttered. "Did the native people in this region build mounds in the bayous? How is that possible? The bayous look like flooded forests."

"They are." Her face lit up. "But go deep enough and you'll find many, many shell mounds where small villages flourished. The Uwachi Toma lived all along the rivers and bayous here, most escaping notice by humans for years."

"Language?" Rhys asked.

"Various. Atawakabiche and her clan spoke an early dialect of the Natchez language. The pieces of songs and history I've been able to capture have been in the Old Language, of course, but I've also recorded stories from a few singers who spoke Tunican languages."

Rhys was watching Meera, not the map. She was pushing every scholarly button he had—Max would have called this a "nerd party"—but she was also pressing other, more personal buttons. Her mind was relentlessly fascinating. Her curiosity was such a mirror of his own, he didn't know quite how to react to her.

He said, "You studied this before you came to America."

"Yes." She rose and walked to the corner to open a drawer.

"That's all?"

She glanced over her shoulder. "What do you mean?"

"You're not going to tell me what drew your curiosity? You must have spent hundreds of years studying with your mentor. When did you have time to—"

"Three hundred ninety-five." She withdrew a map and walked back, still not looking at Rhys.

He blinked. "What?"

"I spent three hundred ninety-five years under Anamitra's tutelage."

"Studying Irina history?" Rhys couldn't even imagine. He'd thought a hundred years at the academy was grueling.

"Yes." She moved the weights and rolled up the previous map. "It's not as you imagine."

"How so?"

"Learning with Anamitra…" Meera gazed out the dark window as a car's headlights swung past. "It wasn't study. Not like the scribes think of it, anyway."

"But your life was not your own," Rhys said, suddenly understanding her fierce need for privacy. "Not until you came here."

"My life still isn't my own. That's not the way it works." She rolled the new map out, stopping when Rhys put a hand over hers.

The jolt of her energy made his heart race. She let out a long breath and closed her eyes as Rhys eased her fingers open and pressed her palm to his. Meera's shoulders relaxed. She rested her forehead in her other hand as Rhys let her magic flood his senses.

"What are you doing to me?" she whispered.

"You need this. Too long in isolation—"

"Causes a dangerous buildup of soul energy that can lead to anxiety, loss of focus, and in extreme cases, hallucinations."

"That's right." That wasn't why he was doing it. He just wanted to touch her. Wanted to ease some of the burden he saw in her eyes. "What happened in Udaipur? Why did you leave?"

She pulled her hand from his, breaking off the connection so abruptly Rhys felt as if something inside him had torn.

"This is where the Wolf lives." She spread the map and repositioned the weights. "Not that I have an exact location, of course."

HE FORCED himself back to the reason he'd come to New Orleans. "Why here?"

Meera pointed to a neat red dot that lay on a bend of the Mississippi River where the state of Mississippi butted into the state of Louisiana. "Because this is where the last major battle occurred, which was the battle that killed the Tattooed Serpent." She moved her finger southwest to the bend of another river. "This is the last-known sighting of the Wolf after her brother was killed."

"She could have traveled."

"And this…" Meera spread her hand over a large area of the map marked in green. "This is the Atchafalaya Swamp. Somewhere in here is where our sister Sabine was lost. And somewhere in here was where the Wolf found her."

THEY WERE SITTING in the living room across from each other, drinking red wine that Meera had opened after dinner.

"So Sabine," Rhys started. "She sounds… eccentric."

"Eccentric is one way of putting it." Meera tapped her finger on her wineglass. "She's wounded. It's nothing a healer can fix. Not by normal means. Alosia, the haven's healer, has tried. I've tried. Most of the time she is calm but erratic. She'll work in the fields for a few days but then she might try to cut someone with a cane knife. She'll say it was a joke later, but we all have our stories."

"She's dangerous."

"Yes." Meera shrugged. "She's not the only Irina with scars."

Rhys knew how true that was. "But you're certain she's met the Wolf?"

"From the bits and pieces I could pick from her memory, I'm certain of it."

He thought about everything Meera had told him, about the wounded singer running from the violence of the Rending. About the mysterious "fox woman" who found her and saved her in the swamps. About the disparate signs and clues Meera had already accumulated.

"So the Wolf saved Sabine and someone—we have to assume it was her—delivered Sabine to a haven after the danger had passed."

"Yes, to the haven that used to exist around Lafayette. It's gone now."

He waved a hand. "Immaterial. Other than that, no one has seen the Wolf for hundreds of years. Why?"

"She's powerful. A legend. If she's remained hidden for all this time, it must be her own choice."

Rhys wasn't terribly sympathetic to singers with vast amounts of knowledge they didn't want to share. In their world, knowledge wasn't to be hoarded. It was how they managed to survive.

"We need to find the Wolf," he said. "Tell me more about Sabine's mate, Roch."

"Not her mate. But he loves her completely."

"Who is he?"

"He's younger than Sabine—he was born in the Lafayette haven. Very smart. Very quiet. His parents were part of the Acadian-related Irin who came from the north a long time ago. Old Ones, some others call them. They lived in the bayous until the Rending."

"So Roch knows this area well." Rhys pointed to the map.

"He knows more than you," she said with a laugh.

"I know plenty." Rhys fought back a smile. "I just don't know much about swamp navigation."

"Clearly."

"And I may not know much about the Wolf. Yet." He reached for the wine bottle and refilled their glasses. "But I do know about finding people."

"This singer isn't going to show up on a database."

Rhys sighed. "Databases are only one of my tools. I was trained by my father, who was and remains the most tenacious librarian I know."

"A tenacious librarian?"

"The *most* tenacious." Rhys smiled. "And if there is anything a librarian prides himself on, it is finding information even if we have to hunt."

Meera smiled at him. "You like the hunt."

He licked a bead of wine from the edge of his glass. "The hunt is the fun part."

Meera shook her head. "Well, now that you have an idea of what we're looking for, I truly hope you can help. Sabine is impossible, but perhaps there is an avenue—"

"Would Roch help us?"

"Roch?" She looked up. "Why?"

"You said the Wolf helped Sabine once. She's old. Very powerful. Maybe she can help her again."

Meera looked skeptical.

"If we can convince Roch it will help Sabine, he'll help us find the Wolf. If he's Acadian, his people lived in the bayous for hundreds of years. He would know the stories. Know the storytellers."

"Probably. And?"

"Stories could be the key. Folktales. Legends." Rhys frowned. "Who lives in the swamp now?"

"Not many people. It's huge. The basin is over three thousand square miles. A lot of that space is uninhabitable to modern people."

He shrugged. "Good. That narrows down the pool of people who might have had contact with her. Not a bad thing."

"I'm not sure what you're getting at. I've interviewed many humans. Hunters. Guides. Residents. As many storytellers as I can find. As far as I can tell, no one has seen the Wolf or anything like the "fox woman" that Sabine describes. Did you see the drawings in my office? The Uwachi Toma had extensive tattooing, both scribes and singers. If a human or Irin saw the Wolf, she would be noticeable."

"I'm not talking about the Wolf." He shook his head. "No, she wouldn't be seen unless she wanted to be seen. I'm talking about Sabine. Stories about a lost woman. Stories about Sabine."

Meera frowned. "She was lost over two hundred years ago."

"I know."

"And humans don't live that long."

"But stories do," Rhys said. "I need to see her and talk with her, and then I need to do some research of my own in this swamp. It's very possible you were asking the wrong questions." He curled his lip. "There are going to be mosquitos the size of house cats, aren't there?"

"In the bayou? Probably." Meera looked skeptical. "You think I was asking the wrong questions?"

Rhys cocked his head. "How many people say no to you?"

Her dimple almost winked at him. "Not many."

"And no Irin, correct? Anyone who knows you gives you exactly what you want."

Meera frowned. "You make it sound like I'm a spoiled brat, and that's not—"

"No, you're not spoiled. You're too self-aware for that. But you've mostly dealt with Irin people in your life, people who were taught to deny you nothing."

"And?"

"You asked questions and humans gave you answers, correct?"

"Yes."

Rhys smiled. "Did you ever think they might have been lying to you?"

"Why would they lie? I was asking very mundane questions. I recorded notes. You're welcome to listen to them. They would have no reason to lie."

"Except that you're an outsider," Rhys said. "They don't know you. You talk differently. You look different. Maybe they're racist. Maybe they're bored. Maybe they simply don't want to give you what you want because they're contrary."

"So humans would lie to someone asking for information for... no reason at all?" She looked utterly confused. "That makes no sense."

"People often don't make sense. Human or Irin. They don't fit into formulas. They can be equally wonderful and awful, sometimes in the same day. I'll ask different questions, and I won't believe their words. I'll believe the look in their eyes and listen for what they're not saying."

She still looked uncertain.

"Think of it this way," Rhys said. "You've spent your life studying the past, but a very specific past. I've spent my life learning myriad ways to tease the past into the present because I don't have your magical ability or resources." He held up a hand when she started to speak. "You've done an extraordinary job with what you have. And I have no doubt you've been able to help Sabine more than any other singer, save perhaps the one who found her and saved her life."

"But?"

"But I'm here and I'm happy to help. You've seen all my research, most of which is only a prelude to what you've done. But I do have skills and resources. I've found people even angels were trying to hide. Let me find Atawakabiche."

A shadow passed behind Meera's intense gaze. "And then?"

Rhys took a deep breath. From her reaction the night he killed the Grigori soldier at her gate, he could guess what Meera's opinion was going to be, but he'd been up-front since the beginning. He didn't want to hide anything now.

"I think you're right. If she's in hiding now, it's because she doesn't want to be found. But we need balance in our world. We need the knowledge she holds. If she knows martial magic other Irina can use, I will ask her to share it, and I will then share it with our allies."

Meera set her wineglass down and walked into the kitchen.

Rhys rose and followed her. "I know you don't like that."

"I hate it." Meera was rinsing dishes and putting them in a rack on the counter. "How will bringing more war into the world—more violence and potential for violence—solve anything? We should be talking to the Grigori, free and bound."

"And how do you propose we do that?" Rhys crossed his arms over his chest. "Do you think they'll be content to meet us for tea and give up their hunting?"

"I can make them listen." She turned to face him. "Do you understand? I can *make them* listen to me."

The passion in her eyes softened his resolve. "I don't doubt that. But Meera, there is only one of you. There are so many of them. The Fallen rape and deceive women every day, each birthing sons and daughters who drain the life from them."

"I can stop them. We can stop them without killing." She stepped closer. "Tell me the truth, Rhys. How much of this war is still based in revenge for the Rending?"

The arrow hit pointed and deep. "Didn't Anamitra lose her own mate? I still have my parents. You still have yours. Do you know how rare that is?"

"I do know, and my heart aches with it. But we must be stronger than vengeance. When do we forgive? Most Grigori in the world today had nothing to do with the Rending." She cut her hand to the side. "The guilty are dead, Rhys. The victims are at peace. We have to move beyond this. We have to rise together."

Rhys spoke past the grief in his throat. "And how can we do that when our wounds are still bleeding? There is evil in the world; I have seen it with my own eyes. Should we battle the Fallen with an embrace?"

She frowned. "I know we cannot. That's not what I'm saying."

"I want peace as much as you do. I fight, Meera. Every day I am on watch for enemies who would kill the people I love. But I dream of a day when the most conflict I face is academic. When I can argue about points of study instead of survival strategies."

"You say you want peace." She spread her hands to the side. "But you work for war."

"I fight in a war that will lead to peace. Do you really think all the Fallen will just crawl away and give up their power without a fight?"

"No." A voice spoke from behind him.

Rhys spun around, drawing his throwing daggers from their hidden sheaths. He spotted Vasu and sent his daggers hurling toward the Fallen, but the angel blinked out of sight and the daggers embedded themselves in Meera's smooth green wall.

"Missed me again," the angel said from a perch on the counter.

Rhys reached for Meera, shoving her behind him before he drew two more daggers.

"Stop!" Meera yelled. "Stop putting holes in my house. Vasu, what are you doing here?"

Rhys turned on her. "You know him?"

She opened her mouth, but no sound came out.

"It's complicated," Vasu said. "Ava doesn't like it when you try to kill me, Librarian. She told you the last time."

Rhys pointed at Vasu. "You do not show up at the house and talk to the children without permission. She told you that, and you ignored her."

Vasu leaned back on the cabinets and stuck his lower lip out like a petulant child. "The children are amusing and enjoy my games."

"They don't know what you are," Rhys growled. "They don't know about your sneaking around, trying to—"

"What about you?" Vasu asked. "Why are you here with my

Meera? Did she ask for you to come? No, she did not. Her inter-fering parents asked for you. And they have ulterior motives. If she knew—"

"Everyone be quiet!" Meera stepped between Rhys and Vasu. "Are you..." Meera blinked. "How— I don't... I don't even want to know. Rhys, Vasu had a curious and respectful relationship with my great-aunt, and I've known him since I was a child. Vasu, I know my parents called for Rhys. I don't want to know what you think their motives were because it doesn't matter."

Rhys thought it did matter, but he shut up. He was taking perverse pleasure in seeing the small, curvy woman lecturing the fallen angel like he was an errant child.

"He's going to help us find the Wolf and help Sabine, and that is what matters. And I told you the other day that you were absolutely not allowed to interrupt me when I have company."

"This one already knows who I am because I have helped his friends."

"Help," Rhys said, "is very subjective when it comes to Vasu."

Vasu pouted. "I want to point out he knows who I am and he still threw daggers at me."

"And I'll throw them again the first chance I get."

"No you won't," Meera said. "Everyone calm down. Seriously, Vasu, why are you here?"

"Because you need to go to the haven," Vasu said. "Your father is going to call you in a minute."

The phone rang a second after he blinked out of sight.

# CHAPTER EIGHT

M eera clutched the steering wheel tighter the closer they got to the haven. It was against every instinct she owned to bring a stranger to that place, even if her parents had given Rhys permission to visit. In fact, they had insisted he come. Rhys had packed his things quickly, checked out of his guest house, and returned the car he'd rented that morning. They were on the way to the haven by nine o'clock.

Rhys was a calm, steady presence in the seat beside her. "You can explain your relationship with Vasu later. Tell me what to expect when we get there."

"Vasu is… complicated," Meera said, her nerves on edge. "Don't mention him to my parents. Anamitra and I are the only ones who interact with him. As for Sabine, Alosia sang her to sleep. I don't know what time she would have woken this morning, but she is usually up with the sun, like most of the haven. It's a working farm, so it runs on a very old-fashioned schedule."

"I understand."

"Sabine cycles in her episodes. When she descends like this, it's usually very predictable. She'll have a series of days with sullen behavior before she begins to be destructive in her cottage. We can't have any fire near her, because her magic is elemental. She can amplify fire."

"So she's an earth singer."

"Yes, which is why she is usually happiest working on the farm. The earth magic in the place is old and keeps her more stable."

"How often do these episodes come? How long do they last?"

"They come a few times a year. It seems to be related to seasonal change. Even though the seasons here are very subtle, they do exist. She spirals. She's destructive. She's remorseful. Then she has these startling hours of clarity on the upswing. Those moments are when I've been able to get the most information from her. For a day— sometimes only a few hours—you get a glimpse of who she must have been before the Rending. So if you want to question her, now is the right time to visit."

Meera could feel his compassion reaching for her. Rhys's blood might have come primarily from Gabriel, but there was a strong vein of Chamuel's power in his magic. Meera found herself wanting to curl up in his warmth and take a deep breath.

"Who was she before the Rending?" he asked.

"She's black Creole and still speaks mostly French. She understands English but turns her nose up at it. She's related to the Irin who originally owned the land where the haven is now. That family abandoned the farm after the Rending." Meera smiled. "Her family was very wealthy and was in charge of the trading house in New Orleans where Irin families sold their sugar before the Rending. They interacted freely with humans."

"Did they own slaves?" Rhys asked.

Her eyes went wide. "The Irin? Of course not."

"But the humans did."

Meera nodded. "There was a lot of debate among Irin elders about how to deal with humans who owned slaves. Older Irin and younger didn't agree. Human slavery was so common in the ancient world that many older Irin viewed it as a human sickness we had no hope of curing, so we should ignore it. Younger Irin saw things very differently. Of course, after the Rending happened, that topic became moot. The Irin who didn't flee became even more insular. They completely withdrew from the human world."

"But they came back. When?"

"The scribes trickled back from over the border in Texas. The Irina have never officially come back, but some Irina bought and restored the farm and the house in the nineteen sixties. It's been a haven ever since."

"Right under the noses of the scribes in Houston and New Orleans."

"There are wards," Meera said. "You'll feel them even with me singing us through. You won't remember exactly how we got to the farm. I can't do anything about that. It's my mother's magic."

"Is she the reason you can influence other's thoughts?" Rhys asked quietly. "Even those with angelic blood?"

She glanced at him nervously. She hadn't intended to let that ability slip. "It's not a popular power. I don't use it often."

"Except on Grigori," he said. "And anyone who gets too close." He cleared his throat. "Like, perhaps, scribes who innocently offer to walk you home at night?"

She looked at him from the corner of her eye. He appeared to be more amused than put out. "Point taken."

"At least tell me I'm not an easy mark."

"You?" She glanced over. "No, you have very good natural shields and a strong mind."

"Which you won't test again, because you won't be manipulating my mind. Ever." Rhys narrowed his eyes when he spotted the old house that marked the haven boundary. "What is that?"

"Just an old house. An old man lives there with his dog. Likes to fish."

"Are you sure?"

"Scribes are so suspicious." Meera spotted a palmetto tree that marked the beginning of the haven grounds. "We're almost there."

"Meera, that wasn't an— Oh heaven above." Rhys nearly doubled over as Meera began to sing.

She opened her mouth and let her magic fill the car, shielding Rhys as much as she could from the brutal supernatural fences her mother had erected around the haven.

"I'm almost afraid to meet your mother," Rhys forced through gritted teeth, "if this is a taste of her magic."

"She's very good," Meera said. "For a pacifist, I do not come from peaceable people."

"Do you take after your father?" Rhys grunted and put his head in his hands. "Headache."

Meera sang louder, weaving the magic around Rhys until she saw his shoulders relax. They were turning into the oak alley of the haven grounds. "Look up, Rhys. If you can."

He looked up and she saw the wonder even through the pain. The twisted, towering oaks rose on either side of them, gnarled guardians of the old Creole home. Bright blue and red trim made the yellow house glow in the diffused light of the morning, and birds called from every side.

"Welcome to Havre Hélène."

The wards eased off as soon as they passed the second oak, and Rhys sat back and rolled his window down. The cool morning air filled the car, suffused with the scent of jasmine and rich earth. It was long before cane harvest season, so Meera suspected they were turning the kitchen garden.

"Beautiful," Rhys said. "Not at all what I was expecting from a Southern plantation."

"Be careful with those expectations. This is Creole Louisiana. It's guaranteed to confound you."

---

MEERA PARKED AROUND BACK and immediately walked to Sabine's cottage where she could hear a ruckus. A window was broken and two silk-upholstered Louis XV chairs lay in the front garden. Her father was picking them up as Meera approached.

Maarut frowned. "I thought you were bringing the scribe?"

Meera stopped and looked over her shoulder, only to see Rhys in the distance, examining the current construction project behind the main house. Her parents were reconstructing the outdoor kitchen to be used communally.

"Rhys!" she called. "Be curious later."

"You know," Maarut said, "I thought he was like you, but I underestimated how right your mother would be. Don't tell her I said that."

"It shall never pass my lips." She squinted up at her father. "What do you mean, how right Mother would be?"

Maarut's face went blank. "Just that Sari and your mother thought the two of you would work well as… research partners."

Meera's eyes narrowed. She was sensing a hidden agenda. "Father."

"Yes?"

"Research partners?"

His eyes went round and innocent. "Of course."

"*Research* partners?"

"Yes, that is what I said." Maarut refused to look at her.

Oh no. Meera glanced at Rhys, who was ambling their direction, still stopping every now and then to examine a new thing or take a picture or type a note with his mobile phone. Then she looked back at her father. Then back to the house where she could see her mother on the back porch, watching all of them.

"She is trying to set me up with him!" Meera hissed at her father. "She's trying to matchmake, isn't she?"

The look on his face revealed everything. Her father might have been a stoic warrior to hundreds of Tomir warriors, but to his daughter, he was an open book.

"My Meera—"

"I told her she was not allowed to do this. I told her—"

"You can tell her whatever you want," Maarut said. "Do you really think she'll pay attention to you? Yes, she's part of your retinue, but she's also your mother. You're nearly four hundred years old, and she wants to see you settled. She wants grandchildren." He crossed his arms. "We had an arranged marriage, and look how happy we are."

"I am not you. This is not… six hundred years ago. I came here so I could—"

A shout from the cottage put their argument to rest. Meera shot her father one more dirty look over her shoulder before she rushed up the porch and into the fray of one of Sabine's "episodes."

"I hate you!" Sabine screamed in French. "You pig! Give me the wine bottle, for I will beat you with it. You cannot do this to me. Send for my carriage and leave me alone!"

"*Cher*, you know I can't do that," Roch replied in his smooth accent. "And I'm not going to give you a wine bottle. It's too early for wine. How about some lemonade? I made some fresh coffee and you only spilled a little bit, but we can get you something else if you don't want the coffee."

His tenderness stayed any lingering resentment Meera felt. She could see both the love and torment in the scribe's face.

Meera leaned against the doorjamb. "Good morning, Sabine."

Sabine looked her direction. "Who are you? Did we get a new servant? Who is *she*, Roch?"

"I'm your friend Meera, remember?" Meera felt Rhys at her back and reached behind to take his hand. "I brought a gentleman to call with me today. I hope you don't mind. Mother said you wanted me to come for breakfast."

Sabine's light brown cheeks blushed. "Meera, why didn't you tell me you were bringing a gentleman to visit?" She stopped struggling and turned in Roch's arms. It was as if a switch had flipped. She moved from anger to hospitality in a blink. "*Mon ange*, can we have one of the servants set up a table in the garden? We should make sure Meera's friend is welcome, and the garden is so nice right now."

"A beautiful idea," Roch said. "I'll ask Maarut for help, shall I? And I'll leave you with Meera to introduce you to her friend."

Sabine was wearing a silk robe over her nightgown that morning, and she clutched the robe together at her breast. "I'm so sorry. Let me go change my clothes." Her laugh lit up the sitting room. "I don't know why I'm still dressed for sleeping."

As soon as she retreated to the bedroom, Meera turned to Rhys. "She's a flirt and she loves compliments. I should have known bringing a handsome man to the house would help her mood."

The corner of his mouth turned up. "You think I'm handsome?"

Meera rolled her eyes. "False modesty is irritating, Rhys."

"So you do think I'm handsome. Good to know." He wandered over to look at a vintage gramophone in the corner. "Does it work?"

"It does, and she loves to dance."

Rhys flipped through the stack of records on the table beside the gramophone, picked one out, and put it carefully on the turntable before he cranked the lever to start the music.

Meera smiled at the cheerful tune that played. "What is it?"

"It's called 'Cuban Moon.'" He held out his hand. "How about you? Do you dance?"

The sight of him holding out his hand was tempting. He *was* handsome. Handsome, intelligent and—when he wanted to be— very charming. She liked his gruff moods and his relentless curiosity. She liked his intensity, even his arrogance.

*Then there was his voice...*

Meera remembered her mother's machinations. "Sorry. I've never danced to anything that sounds like this."

The bedroom door opened and Sabine emerged in a summer- yellow dress that reached her knees. "Oh, I love this song!" She glanced at Meera. "Don't you, Meera?"

"I don't know it." She moved to the window to track her father and Roch's progress. They were debating something in the garden with Roch looking overwhelmed and frustrated and Maarut looking like he was counseling the younger scribe. He had a hand on Roch's shoulder. The two chairs were upright, but nothing else had been moved.

"Sabine," Meera said in cheerful voice, "why don't you and Rhys dance?"

"Oh, I'm sure he wouldn't be interested in dancing with me." Sabine played the reluctant partner, but Meera could tell she wanted to dance with Rhys. "He's *your* friend."

"But we're here to visit you," Rhys said smoothly. "I'd be delighted if you danced with me, Miss Sabine." Rhys had slipped into French with ease. "We can show Meera what she's missing."

Sabine giggled, her energy buoyant. Rhys held out his hand and she went to him. They danced a fast-stepping number in the space where the breakfast area had once been before Sabine threw the table and two chairs out the front door. Roch and Maarut were turning the table upright from its precarious perch on the front porch as Rhys and Sabine danced and chatted about favorite songs and places to dance.

Rhys played along with the talk of balls and socials that must have happened before the Rending, exhibiting a light charm Meera had never seen from him before. Sabine spoke of humans long dead and a city that mostly existed in history books.

"So I said to the governor that he must not do it, but you know human men always ignore their women."

"Are you saying the governor ignored you entirely? How rude."

"Entirely! He sent troops to those people, and all because he was angry with the English." She spit out the word *English*. "Who likes the English, I ask?"

Rhys smiled. "I certainly don't."

"*Tout à fait*. But what do the native people have to do with it?"

"Nothing at all, I'm sure."

"Nothing," Sabine said firmly. "You are correct, nothing. But they sent the soldiers and..." A stricken look crossed Sabine's face. "No, that wasn't how it happened."

Meera moved closer, sensing a shift. "Sabine?"

She shook her head, frowning. "It wasn't humans, was it? It was our people they killed."

Rhys held Sabine lightly. The flirtatious woman had disappeared. Something dark swam behind her eyes.

"It wasn't them," she whispered. "It wasn't the humans who died."

Meera had witnessed this many times. The turn was coming. Sabine would cycle from anger to frivolity to mania rapidly, but then at some point—usually the third day of an episode—the melancholy would come. And with the melancholy came memory and grief.

Then... clarity.

Roch must have sensed Sabine's shift in mood, because he came running in the house just as she slumped against Rhys's chest.

"Roch?"

He grabbed her from Rhys's arms. "Come with me. I have you. Come now."

"Roch, they're all gone." The raw pain in Sabine's voice was enough to tear Meera in two. It was as if Sabine was remembering the death of her family for the first time, over and over again. "They're gone," she sobbed. "They're gone, and there is no one left. The house was burning and they were all gone."

"I know." He kissed the top of her head. "I know they're gone, but I'm here."

"Don't leave me." She gripped his shirt. "Don't ever leave me."

"I promise I won't."

Roch led a weeping Sabine into the bedroom while Rhys stood helpless, watching them from the center of the room as the gramophone switched to the next song. It was another fast dancing number, but there was no more joy in the cottage. Meera moved to the turntable and removed the record. Then she picked another from the table and put it on.

"Debussy," she said softly. "She likes this one when she's sad."

"What do we do? Are there spells you know? Have Roch and your father—"

"We wait."

"How?" He was incredulous. "She was in terrible pain. Surely there is something—"

"We have tried all the magic we know. And I know a lot. Some broken things cannot be mended, Rhys."

He shook his head. "That's not acceptable."

"Come with me." She took his hand and led him out to the garden. "We'll make some tea and wait for her in the garden."

———

THE WOMAN who emerged from the cottage looked older than Sabine usually did. She carried the weight of memory in her eyes. It was both painful and welcome. It likely wouldn't last long, but for the next few hours, maybe even a few days, Meera could see Sabine as a peer and a friend.

"Meera." Sabine sounded exhausted as she sat with Roch next to her. "Roch told me you were here with a friend."

"Thank you for seeing us," Meera said. "This is Rhys. He's an archivist from Istanbul."

"Istanbul." Her eyes lit up. "How exotic. I've never been out of Louisiana, though my father often talked about my going to Paris before he died. Have you been?"

Rhys nodded. "It's a beautiful city. You would love it."

Her smile was sad. "Roch said it wasn't so bad this time." She gripped Roch's hand like a lifeline. "Was he being honest or kind?"

"Honest," Meera said. "It wasn't so bad. Nothing broken."

Sabine looked at Rhys. "I can always depend on Meera to be honest. She's good at honesty. I hope you appreciate that."

"I do," Rhys said.

"You trying to say I lie to you?" Roch teased.

"No, but you're too kind." She squeezed his hand. "I saw the window. You should leave me. This isn't any kind of life for you, taking care of me like this."

He shook his head. "Only life I want."

Sabine closed her eyes and shook her head tightly.

"Stop," Roch said. "We're not talking about this right now. I think Meera has some ideas about finding her."

"Who?"

"The Wolf," Roch said. "Rhys is helping her."

Sabine frowned. "I thought he was coming to be her mate. Did I misunderstand what Patiala said?"

Rhys's eyebrows went nearly halfway up his forehead, but he said nothing.

"I must have misheard." Sabine laughed. "I'm sorry. This is awkward. My memory is so bad."

"It's fine," Meera said. Dammit. Now she'd have questions to answer later. "But Rhys does have some questions about the Wolf."

"She saved my life," Sabine said. "Most of the time I'm grateful, but not always. After the Grigori attacked, I ran from the city, but none of the villages I knew had anyone left alive. I'm sure you know why. I took a boat out to the bayou."

"What kind of boat?"

"A pirogue. What the fishermen use. I didn't know much about the swamp—I was raised in New Orleans—but I'd heard the older people talking and knew that there were still Irin in the swamps. I thought maybe…" Sabine shrugged. "It was probably a foolish idea, but what else was I to do? No one was left. I didn't fear death, I only feared being alone. If there were Irin anywhere, I was determined to find them."

"But you didn't," Rhys said.

"I did. But I found someone else first."

Meera offered, "The Wolf?"

"No." Sabine shook her head. "There was someone else."

Meera sat up straight. This was new information. "Who, Sabine?"

"Humans." The word came in a painful whisper. "Men. They were human and they took me farther into the swamp. I lost track of where I was. They put a gag in my mouth and they…" Tears rolled down her face. "They didn't know what I was. Eventually they took off the gag. The minute I could speak, I killed them, every one of them. I'm not sorry."

"Don't be sorry," Rhys said. "Don't ever be sorry."

"I'm not. But I was really lost then. I was in a shack in the bayou. A hunting shack, I think. Completely turned around. I knew the rivers a little, but nothing about the swamps. I took one of their boats and some supplies, but I wandered for days, singing out every night and hoping to hear something back. I think I went a little mad."

And then it had only gotten worse. Meera's heart hurt for Sabine, but other than the new information about abusive humans, there was no new information. Meera tried not to be frustrated, because it looked like this episode of clarity would pass with no new answers.

But then Meera hadn't counted on Rhys.

## CHAPTER NINE

"Give me your hand and close your eyes," Rhys said. "I want you to imagine yourself back in the bayou."

"When?"

"When you'd taken the boat and were searching. Just before the Wolf found you."

He leaned in and took Sabine's outstretched hand. This was a memory spell he could only use on other Irin. It didn't work on humans, and it didn't work on a reluctant subject, but Sabine was open to sharing. She'd shown no reluctance to answer their questions. He cradled her palm in his and spread her fingers, using his other hand to write a spell into her palm.

"Do you see yourself there?" he asked.

"Yes."

He touched his own *talesm prim,* activating the spells he'd written over his life. He searched for those his father taught him and those his mother helped him with. Angharad the Sage was known for her empathy, but when the subject was willing, she could extend that ability to all her senses, not only feelings. Rhys carried her blood, and his mother had taught him how to access the same power through written spells instead of spoken ones.

"Picture it in your mind," he said.

The memory that Rhys caught hints of wasn't clear in any sense, but it gave him impressions. Scents, mainly. Water carrying a faint essence of rotting wood and salt. Cypress and pine trees. He could hear the swishing sound of a tail moving in the water and a woman humming an indistinguishable tune.

His hands hurt. He'd blistered them poling through the water, ducking under branches, and following narrow pathways through the flooded forest. He was hungry. Desperately hungry.

He could hear birds in the distance, calling through the trees. A distinct bugle that cut through the dense tapestry of insects in the early morning fog.

"Rhys."

He blinked his eyes open, his finger still tracing the spell over Sabine's palm. Meera had her hand on his shoulder.

"Was I speaking?" he asked.

Meera looked confused. "Yes, in the Old Language."

"What did I say?"

"You were singing an Irina song. An old children's rhyme."

"Which one?" He tried to reorient himself from the vision. "It was likely what Sabine was singing or thinking in the memory just now."

Meera said, "*Anya niyah, mashak tamak.*"

Rhys drummed his fingers on his knee. "The boat rocks, pull to shore. I know that rhyme."

"We all do, don't we? It makes sense if Sabine was singing that," Meera said. "She was frightened and alone."

Sabine smiled. "Why would I sing a children's song?"

"You were a singer desperate for another one of your kind to find you," Rhys said. "Just because it's a nursery rhyme doesn't mean it's not powerful."

*Anya Niyah* was a simple song most Irin children were taught when they were small. But like all nursery rhymes, it had a hidden meaning.

*Anya niyah.* The boat is rocking. Things are unstable in the world. It was a plea and a prayer directed by children to the Creator when life was uncertain or they felt fear.

*Mashak tamak.* Pull to shore. Go home. Seek the familiar. The Creator responds to his children by leading them home.

But Irin adults knew that *mashak tamak* had another meaning as well. When a child who was singing it truly felt fear and need, it was a song of attraction. A simple magic that would pull an adult to them. It was a pull Rhys had felt himself.

"The Wolf found you because you called her," Rhys said, looking up. "You called out while you were going through the bayou." He squeezed Sabine's hand before he released it. "I have a sense of the place now. It's not clear, but it's more than I had before." He looked at Meera. "I need an audio file of birdcalls. I'm not familiar with the birds here. There was one in particular that was very distinctive."

She nodded. "I can't promise you they'll be helpful. There were birds around in the early nineteenth century that are probably extinct now."

"We can try."

Sabine and Roch stood and exchanged a look before Sabine spoke. "If you don't need us for anything else," she said, "I'd like to spend the rest of the day with Roch."

"Of course." Rhys stood with them. "You know... a simple mating ceremony doesn't take long. I know I don't know either of you well, but if you want to be together, this sickness shouldn't hold you back. And there are healing spells only a mate can sing."

Sabine gave him a sad smile. "You don't understand."

Rhys looked at Roch. "You're devoted to her and no one else. You are her other half whether she is in her right mind or not. If you could dream walk with her, it could center her, even when her mind is unwell." He looked at Sabine. "He won't leave you. Not ever. Whether you think you're the best for him or not. If you were sick in body, you wouldn't have these doubts. Being sick in the mind is no different."

Roch looked like he wanted to add something, but he didn't. Rhys saw him squeeze Sabine's hand tight before he nodded and pulled her away.

"*Anya niyah,*" Meera whispered behind him. "*Mashak tamak.*"

"Yes." When life was uncertain, as it was so often for the Irin, it was even more important to have people you could call your home. Rhys turned to her. "Will they listen to me?"

"I don't know. I've told them similar things, but they know I care for them. You're an objective observer. They might give more weight to your words."

He was frustrated that he couldn't do more. It was quite obvious to him that they were mates in every sense except formally.

Rhys held out his hand to Meera. "Will you show me Havre Hélène?"

She had the same look in her eye as she'd had when he'd asked her to dance. Desire and stubborn defiance. He didn't know what the latter was about, but the former was starting to become clear.

Meera was maddening and brilliant and confusing and enticing. She was untouchable and irresistible. Both his mind and body were attracted to her, but Rhys was starting to grasp a deeper truth.

With a woman like Meera—heir of a magical legacy or not—he might just fall in love.

---

THEY WALKED for an hour around the farm, Meera pointing out the different technical aspects of growing and processing sugarcane while Rhys listened. She managed to make anything interesting, just by her own passion and intellect.

"Is it very different here?" he asked. "From where you grew up?"

"Yes, very different. The weather, the people, the food. The closeness of the community here." She waved at two women walking to the house from the cane fields. "Everyone works together. There are fewer boundaries. Fewer set roles. And of course a lot fewer people. We have a cook and a healer and a forewoman for the farm. But if the cook is tired, then my father fills in. If Alosia wants to visit the city, another will tend to our wounds. It's very different in that sense."

"Udaipur was more formal."

"It *is* much more formal." She smiled. "I'll have to go back eventually. This is... kind of a vacation for me."

"A vacation to find a lost strain of Irina martial magic?"

She glanced at him sideways. "I want to find history. You're the one looking for war."

"I'm looking for knowledge, but only to share it with those who would bring balance."

Something about his words softened the firm set of her mouth.

"Balance," she said. "Yes, Vasu and I talk about balance."

"Now would be a good time to explain him."

Meera shrugged. "There is nothing to explain. He appeared to Anamitra when she was a child and followed her through her life. I wouldn't call him a friend or an ally, but... he's not an enemy either. He's not anything like other Fallen."

"That I can confirm." He glanced down and watched the light play in her hair as they walked under dappled shade. "And you've known him since you were a child?"

"As soon as I was given to Anamitra, Vasu appeared for a visit."

"*Given* to her?"

Meera raised her eyebrows. "Yes, of course. I was her heir."

"But your parents—"

"They were there. They have always been there. They were part of Anamitra's retinue and then became my retinue when Anamitra passed into the heavens."

Rhys paused under a spreading dogwood tree. "So your parents didn't raise you?"

"In a sense they did." A frown creased her forehead. "But it was mostly Anamitra and her servants."

Rhys didn't know what to say to that, but a part of him ached for her. "Were there other children?"

She shook her head. "Not that I was allowed to play with. But I had pets. Anamitra kept birds, and the Tomir warriors breed a wonderful line of taji dogs in Udaipur. They were my favorite."

Dogs and birds and a fortress of people guarding her.

"Don't try to make my childhood tragic, Rhys." Meera smiled at him. "It wasn't. It was very rich and very privileged, even if it was isolated. I had a wonderful life and I was surrounded by family. But I was raised for more than myself. The heir of Anamitra must return to Udaipur at some point, and she must make herself available to counsel any petitioners or scholars in need. That is how it must be, especially now that singers have returned to the Elder Council. They will need the wisdom that I carry."

"And you're content with this?"

She looked at him. "What about you? I know who you are too. Are you saying the great library of Glast doesn't call you?"

"No, it doesn't. I would be there if I wanted to be, but the work I'm doing in Istanbul is important. I want a stable and secure world for everyone, not just scribes. Singers deserve equal status in our world, and right now that means finding ways for them to defend themselves."

"Yes, defense. Not war."

"Sometimes war *is* defense."

"How?" Meera asked. "Why do we limit ourselves in this way? What use is language if we don't use it to communicate?"

"With our enemies?"

"With anyone." She paused. "Yes, our enemies. Yes, with free Grigori. Yes, with each other. I'm not just here looking for lost magic or dying languages. The Irin here found a peace that lasted for five hundred years. No other population of Irin on earth have matched that before or since. I'm looking for the Wolf, yes. But I'm also looking for peace."

He was staring at her and he couldn't look away. She wasn't just an idealist, she was a visionary.

*She'll either change the world or get herself killed.*

And there was no way in heaven or on earth that Rhys could walk away.

"Well, I don't know about finding peace," he said. "But I can help you find the Wolf. Istanbul can exist without me for a while."

"What about Glast?"

"There are many other scribes of Gabriel's line in Glast," he said. "They don't *need* me."

"But they want you, don't they?"

He glanced over his shoulder. "Well, I have been told I'm very handsome."

Meera laughed and walked past him. "I said handsome, not *very* handsome."

"The *very* was in your voice." He followed along the path behind her. "I could hear it. I'm very perceptive."

She laughed louder. "And very humble."

"Exceptionally humble, really. Very clever."

"Do continue." She waved her hand in royal fashion. "I need to know my new assistant's qualifications."

Assistant? Yes, he could be her assistant. Especially if he got to watch her walk ahead of him like this, her hips swaying beneath another bright summer dress. "I'm also very curious."

"And very persistent?"

"*Very* persistent." He caught up with her. "And very... attracted."

She stopped walking, but she didn't look at him.

"Meera," he said softly. "Surely you feel—"

"It's not a good idea, Rhys."

"Why? Because you don't have relationships with Irin men?"

"That's one of the reasons."

"So you've never experienced—"

"Don't assume." She turned and looked up at him. A hint of the mischievous woman he'd met in New Orleans had returned. "There are songs of sacred lovemaking that are taught only by the singers of Udaipur. Scrolls of magical congress preserved by the Tomir warriors." Her gaze was direct. "I am well-educated in *all* aspects of Irina history."

She walked away, leaving Rhys's mind reeling.

Scrolls of magical congress? He thought he'd read everything, but he hadn't read those. His mind was churning and his body was screaming for him to follow Meera.

*Tell me more.*

*Show me more.*

*Heaven above,* please *show me more.*

A loud bell rang at the main house, signaling the start of the midday meal.

---

ROCH AND SABINE hid themselves away for the rest of the day, but Roch found him the next morning before Rhys had found any tea.

"Yes?" He opened the door of the small guest cottage. "Oh, it's you. Good morning. Where can I find some damned tea?"

Roch smiled. "Main house will have it. Patiala only drinks tea, so there's always hot water on the stove."

"Good." Rhys scratched the stubble he been indulging for the past few days and squinted at the bright morning on the farm. Verdant lawn stretched to the cane fields, dotted by cottages and small garden plots. Smoke rose from the outdoor kitchen behind the house, and he could already hear hammers and saws going. The haven was a hive of activity.

"How many scribes live here?" he asked.

"A few." Roch shrugged. "Most of us came with our mothers or our mates. I was born at a different haven just north of here. My parents left a few year ago after the elder singers took seats on the council again, but I stayed."

"Because of Sabine."

Roch nodded.

"How is she this morning?"

"The same." Roch started walking away. "Come up to the library in the main house when you've found your tea. Patiala wants to meet you."

"Lovely." Rhys yawned and stretched his arms over his head, enjoying the soft morning breeze that rustled the cane in the distance. Birds sang from the oak trees, and he could hear laughter and music from different corners of the haven. He even caught a hint of Sabine's gramophone and wondered what Roch meant by "the same."

It wasn't his business. He should keep his nose out of it.

Meera's mother on the other hand...

*"I thought he was coming to be her mate. Did I misunderstand what Patiala said?"*

He hadn't missed Sabine's slip, and he hadn't dismissed it, even though Meera had sailed right past it as if nothing had been said. *Coming to be her mate?* It was an interesting twist to an already interesting situation. Maybe Patiala had intentions she hadn't told Meera. Maybe Meera wasn't keen on her mother's interference. Heaven knew Rhys could understand that.

He decided to shave. After all, this meeting might be far more interesting than he was expecting.

———

PATIALA OF UDAIPUR, niece of Anamitra and mother of Meera, was smaller than he'd imagined. Tiny, in fact. She was the same size as her daughter and appeared roughly the same age, but while Meera had soft curves he wanted to handle, Patiala had muscle intended to intimidate.

"So," she said from the head of the table, "tell me what you will do to further my daughter's research."

"I have some ideas having to do with a memory I was able to extract from Sabine yesterday. One of those ideas has to do with tracking avian populations in the Atchafalaya Basin where Meera believes the Wolf is living. Another has to do with tracking folklore among human populations."

Patiala's eyebrows went up. "You play no games, scribe."

"I have no interest in being reticent with information." Rhys glanced to a side door where Meera had just entered the library. "Your daughter is brilliant, and we'll find the Wolf faster if everyone is forthright and works together."

Patiala looked pointedly at Meera. "Indeed."

"Don't look at me that way. I've shared my information with Rhys," Meera took across the table from Rhys. "He's seen the research I've done so far."

"Most of what Meera has collected is important for preservation, but it's not geographically significant. If your haven desires to find Atawakabiche, I believe my tactics will do that most quickly. However, I'll need her help when we locate the singer."

"Why?"

"She's hidden herself for somewhere around three hundred years. She obviously doesn't want to be found. It's far more likely she'll speak to one of her sisters than to a scribe she doesn't know."

Patiala folded her hands under her chin. "And you're confident you can find her?"

Rhys recalled the feelings of desperation, hunger, and fear Sabine had passed to him with her memory. "I think if the Wolf truly believes we need her, we *will* find her."

"Interesting."

Patiala fell silent, and Rhys took the opportunity to drink his tea. It was a truly excellent Darjeeling that she'd poured for him and his first indication that Patiala might not hate him. He certainly couldn't tell from her expression. It wasn't often outside Turkey that Rhys found a tea enthusiast as passionate as he was, but this well-balanced blend from Nepal would send the tea blenders of Istanbul into raptures.

Patiala said, "I find your confidence reassuring, scribe. I was told you are a proud man."

"I am," Rhys said. "I am the best at what I do. I was born from a line of scribes who have been guarding Gabriel's library for thousands of years. I have no false modesty about my abilities." He kept his eyes locked on Patiala, absorbing the intense stare of the Irina singer and warrior without flinching. "But despite how my brothers joke, I am not arrogant. I can work well with others if they are equal to me."

Patiala turned to Meera. "I approve of him."

"Mata, don't start with this."

"You avoid this part of your life, *Abha*."

"Don't." Meera's expression hardened and she turned away from her mother. "Just don't."

Rhys knew he needed to tread carefully. He was getting a picture of what might have put the reluctant look in Meera's eyes when it came to a relationship with him, but assumptions were dangerous.

"I'm pleased and honored to work with your daughter." He directed his words to Patiala. "It's clear her work on language and cultural preservation is very important, and it will likely create a bridge for us with the Wolf. We are asking her for a favor, so Meera's work will assuage any suspicions Atawakabiche might have about us merely using her for her magic."

"Pragmatic too." Patiala sipped her tea. "But you do intend to record her martial magic if you are able."

"Absolutely. The singers in Vienna need it if they're ever to regain their leverage over the council and be seen as equals."

"I like your thinking," Patiala said. "Yes, equality is what we need."

"Equals in war," Meera said. "Equals in violence. Equals in destruction. This is the equality we strive for?"

"Equals in a language the scribes' council currently understands," Rhys said. "After the elder singers regain status, then we can work on changing hearts and minds."

Patiala set her tea down on the table. "I *really* approve of him."

"I wonder why," Meera muttered.

Before the conversation could get any more fraught for Rhys, he rose. "I hope you don't mind if I try to find Roch this morning. I'd like for him to be our guide, and I think I may have a way of convincing him."

"You are excused," Patiala said. "Thank you for your candor, Rhys of Glast."

"You're welcome." He turned to Meera, nodded, and walked out of the room, feeling like he'd just passed a test.

# CHAPTER TEN

"You think you have all the time in the world." Patiala set her teacup on the table and folded her hands. "But you do not. Every day we live in a world that is not our home. Every day the sons of the Fallen stalk us. This is a good man who is your equal. A man who would stimulate your mind and, if I am reading both of you correctly, every other part of you as well."

"Mata!"

"Why do you hate my counsel? Why do you rebel like this when I only want what is best for you?"

"Because everyone wants what is best for me!" Meera said. "Everyone thinks they know what I want. Everyone coddles me and guards me and sends for favors from the other side of the world so that I can meet a man *you think* is right for me!"

"He is right for you!"

"I want to decide that." She pointed at her chest. "I do. I didn't even get to pick my first lover. Everything in my life was prescribed. Everything."

Patiala said, "You had no complaints at the time, and Dalvir was a good friend."

"This is not about Dalvir." Meera closed her eyes and tried to banish the memory of her first lover from her mind. "It's not about that."

She would never forget his pure joy when he informed Meera that he'd found his *reshon* among the healing singers of Udaipur. They hadn't been lovers for over five years—her sexual education had been deemed complete after two—but she'd still felt fondness for him. More, she'd felt jealousy that she would never know the joy that Dalvir and Simrat shared.

She'd never know it because a mate would be picked for her, a mate who was not her *reshon* but a partner who couldn't threaten the higher calling of Anamitra's heir. A partner who would know his place.

"He's not who you think he is." Meera stared at the intricate pattern on the table linen. "He's not someone you can manipulate. Not even with good intentions."

"I know he's not," Patiala said. "He's a man with his own mind. That's why I like him for you. He will be a strong ally. Your best ally." Her mother shrugged. "And he comes from a very good family, but that is secondary."

Meera swallowed the bitterness in the back of her throat. "His voice…"

"What about his voice?"

Meera remained silent, staring at the intricate swirls of red and blue paisleys.

"What about his voice?" Patiala stood. "What are you talking about?"

Meera looked up and directly at her mother. "What if he is my *reshon*? Will you like him for me then?"

The quick play of emotions in her mother's eyes reminded Meera why she loved her parents so fiercely even when she didn't agree with them.

A quick flash of joy. Then worry. Then calculation. Joy again. Caution.

"How certain are you?" Patiala asked.

"I've only allowed myself small pieces. You know how ironclad my shields are. The fact that bits have slipped through tells you how strong his mind is. It's... different." Her heart rushed in excitement. "I've never heard anything like it. I want to wrap myself in it, if that makes any sense. But I know I can't. I know that's not for me."

"When you are mated," Patiala said quietly, "your partner's soul voice becomes your home. Your father may not be my *reshon*, but there is nothing that centers me like his voice. He is my steady place. My anchor. I want this for you because I know the burden of purpose you carry. I know you have been frustrated with my attempts to find you a mate, but you must understand my reasons."

"Anamitra—"

"Anamitra was an old and wise singer who loved you very much," Patiala said. "But she was not your mother."

"You know she warned against anything that could divide my loyalty."

"I know." Patiala sat. "I know she did."

"The idea of Rhys being more than other scribes—"

"Being your *reshon?*"

"*Don't* use that word," she said. "I don't know that. Neither do you. But it makes me wary. I don't like the idea of others deciding my fate, not even the Creator."

Patiala smiled. "Rebellious child."

"I'll take my rebellion where I can find it," Meera said. "We both know my life doesn't belong to me. Not really."

Her mother's smile turned sad. "When you are ready to step into your power, you will be revered by elders and rulers. Emperors will pay you tribute, and angels will tremble at your voice."

"There aren't many emperors left in the world."

"There will always be emperors," Patiala said, "even if they go by different names."

Meera held out her hand. Patiala stretched her arm out and linked their fingers together.

"When you were born," Patiala said, "I gave you the name Abha because you were the light of my life. I had been born to scholars, found my true path when I met Maarut as a warrior, but you were the light and joy of my life. And when you showed your gifts, I held on to that, even when your old name became a memory. I knew you were still my light. I knew my purpose to protect you as your mother only became a greater mission as part of your retinue. You have always been my purpose."

"Mata." Meera closed her eyes and held on to the warm glow of her mother's love.

"As your guardian, I must caution you away from any attachment that could divide your loyalties." Patiala squeezed Meera's hand. "But as your mother, I only feel joy that the Creator may have given you the gift of a mate designed by heaven just for you. No singer deserves that joy more."

"I don't know if that is what Rhys is. I haven't given him any encouragement."

"Truly?" Her mother's eyebrows went up. "That doesn't seem to affect the way he looks at you."

She looked up. "How does he look at me?"

"Like a hungry man. Hungry for your attention. Hungry for your words." She offered a wry smile. "And *very* hungry for your—"

"Don't." Meera held up a hand. "Please."

Patiala burst into laughter. "You are your father's daughter! When did I teach you to be so reserved?"

"You taught me to be the opposite," Meera said. "And embarrassed me at every turn."

"My poor shy daughter."

"Not shy. Simply not… rude."

"I will back off for now," Patiala said. "Because when you and this man go searching for the Wolf, you won't have any chaperones. We'll see what happens when you can't keep him at a distance."

As always, Meera was very afraid her mother was correct.

SHE FOUND Rhys in the guest cottage, his computer open on the small kitchen table and notebooks spread across the bed.

"I didn't wait for you," he said. "I've been researching historic birds of Southern Louisiana, and I believe the distinctive call I heard was the whooping crane."

"Is that helpful?" Meera sat in the other chair, watching him sort through his thoughts at lightning speed. "I don't know much about birds."

"The cranes were considered nearly extinct in the wild until recently, but there have been projects that tracked their historic range and new efforts to seed wild populations are following that." He didn't look up as he spoke, shuffling through a notebook with one hand while typing with the other. "I've found some research projects online that give some interesting clues about the areas where the cranes historically nested in the Atchafalaya Basin. It gives us a starting point."

"That's a good lead."

"Combine that with oral history reports—I want to focus on crying woman or ghost legends—and I believe we can narrow down the geographic area significantly. It's not as precise as wildlife mapping, but it's an avenue to explore."

There was something very seductive about watching a man work at a job he was passionate about, and Rhys had dived into the mystery of finding the Wolf headfirst.

*"Your soul must remain your own."*

She was fighting against herself. Part of her wanted to keep her distance—keep a sense of control over her heart—but the other parts...

She'd told her mother the truth: she didn't like the idea of a predetermined fate. Too much of her life was already predetermined.

But then there was Rhys.

Irritating, persistent, relentlessly curious Rhys with a soul voice that soothed her, a mind that called to her own, and a body that woke parts of her she kept under very strict control.

Desire equaled weakness, which was why she only took it in small doses. Doses she could handle. Men she could control.

She wouldn't be able to control him.

"Do you have any maps?" He gripped a fistful of hair as he clicked his keyboard, a frown wrinkling the space between his eyebrows. "I need a large map of the basin. Topographical if that's possible." He stood and looked around the cottage as if expecting a topographical map of Southern Louisiana to magically appear.

Meera rose and walked across the room. "I don't have a map."

"Damn."

She stepped in front of him and put her palms on his chest.

Rhys froze. "Meera?"

She could feel his heart beating under her right palm, the firm muscles of his chest rising and falling with his breath. He was warm and vibrant with energy. Heaven above, he made her *want*. She lifted her shields a fraction, just enough for the resonance of his soul voice to hum in the back of her mind.

She closed her eyes and let his voice fill her. The sun poured through the window, warming her skin as a breeze licked along her neck. She lifted her face and leaned into his voice and scent.

Rhys's lips touched Meera's, and he was the only thing.

The scribe's mouth was slow and deliberate. His hand came to the nape of her neck and pulled her closer. He placed a firm hand at the small of her back and pressed in. She was enveloped in his scent and touch and sound. The outside world dropped away, and she was transported to a place of sense and heat.

The slow glide of his mouth against hers didn't stop as he swung her around and pushed her against a wall. He reached down and wrapped an arm around her waist, lifting her so they were face-to-face. He held her with ease, angling his mouth to taste her more thoroughly.

For the first time in a very long time, Meera didn't think. She took. She took his hunger as her own, stretching into it as the magic twined between them, amplifying her need into his. It was a crescendo of senses. Rhys reached down and cupped her bottom, pressing her into his body as a low groan left her throat.

*There you are.*

The thought was unmistakable, thrilling, and alarming, like seeing the flash of a face familiar only in dreams.

*There you are.*

*Reshon.*

Meera tore her mouth away from Rhys's, her breath coming hard and fast. His eyes locked on her mouth, and she recognized the hunger her mother had spoken of. It was written across his flushed lips and the hard set of his jaw.

"I wasn't finished," he said roughly.

"I know." She pushed back and he lowered her to the ground. "We need to stop."

"Why?"

Meera blinked. "You know why."

He frowned and tore his gaze from her lips to look into her eyes. "I want you. That doesn't mean I'm going to let it interfere with this mission."

"Good." Meera's heart was racing. She felt split in two and exposed. "Good. I was…" She didn't know where to look, but it definitely wasn't a good idea to look at the arousal evident in Rhys's trousers. That gave her too many ideas. "I'm… going to—"

"What?"

Meera blinked. "I'm going to get you a map."

"A map?" He frowned. "Why?"

"Because you were just looking for one. A topographical map of the Atchafalaya Basin. It's an excellent idea. We definitely need one."

He looked around the cottage. "A topographical..." He looked back at her. "Right. A map. I needed a map before you..."

"I kissed you."

"Yes you did." His eyes turned from hunger to caution. "You said that wasn't a good idea."

"It's not." Meera walked to the door. "I just decided to do it anyway."

He caught her arm before she could walk out the door. "Is this lapse in judgment going to happen again?"

"I haven't decided yet."

"I'll take that as a yes."

"It wasn't intended to be." Damn it, why did she find him charming when he turned stubborn like this?

"I'm being presumptuous," he said. "Feel free to put me in my place. Use both hands if you like."

Meera didn't know whether to scowl or smile, so she tugged her arm away and walked out to the porch without saying a word. Rhys did not follow her.

"I'll take that as a yes too!" he shouted.

Meera ignored him and kept walking.

Impossible man.

---

MEERA PAGED through the maps desk in the library of the main house. The afternoon had heated up, and someone had opened the windows and hung damp sheets on the porch, allowing a cool breeze to waft through the house. The overhead lights and lamps were shut off; only the filtered light that trickled through the oaks illuminated the east side of the mansion where the library was situated.

Blue shadows in the corner coalesced into the shape of a slim, dusky-skinned girl with gold eyes and jet-black hair. "You can't deny it now. You're connected to the scribe."

Meera glanced up but quickly looked away from the perceptive amber gaze. "What are you doing here, Vasu? You know I don't like it when you come to the haven."

"That's why I took this form."

"You don't look like a harmless girl no matter how hard you try. If I saw you in a dark alley, I'd still run away."

"Don't you recognize me, Meera Bai?"

She looked up, and before her eyes, the girl aged until she'd become the mature woman Meera remembered from childhood with deep-set eyes and grooves where her mouth had laughed.

"Anamitra."

Vasu shrugged and the young visage of her great-aunt returned. "You didn't know her when she looked like this, but I did. You didn't see into her heart."

Meera sensed a trap, so she returned to shuffling through maps.

"Don't you want to know what was in her heart?" Vasu asked. He disappeared and reappeared in a blink, hovering over Meera's shoulder. "Aren't you curious?"

"Her heart isn't my business, Vasu. It wasn't when I was child, and it isn't now."

"She was your aunt. Your mentor."

"She was my teacher." Meera tried not to react to the now-familiar visage. She could see Anamitra in every line of Vasu's face now. The angel was doing it on purpose.

Vasu leaned in. "She would say she never met her *reshon*—that she wouldn't even want to—but that would be a lie."

Meera's stomach dropped.

"She wasn't mated yet, but he was. He was one of the Tomir warriors, a distant cousin of your father's. His mating had also been arranged, and he was well-pleased with it. To him, meeting his *reshon* was a chance event that changed nothing about his life. He was bound and loyal to his woman."

She couldn't not ask. "And my aunt?"

"She was furious."

Meera looked up in surprise. "Furious?"

The girl with Anamitra's face gave Meera a very Vasu smile. "Long before she met her mate, when Anamitra was a young singer first come into the fullness of her power, she became drunk upon it. She was the heir of heaven's wisdom. Kings and queens bowed to her counsel. Gold was placed at her feet. In Udaipur, her word was absolute."

"And she had no mate," Meera said.

"She had many lovers, as was her right. Men vied to be her beloved, and more than one family offered riches if she would mate with one of their sons. She was beautiful, powerful, and brilliant. She had everything she desired."

"Except..."

"This warrior. He wasn't hers. He could not be. Not even Anamitra could break the bond between mates. This Tomir warrior was the one thing that had ever been denied her, and because of that, he was the one thing she wanted above all else."

"What happened?"

Vasu shrugged. "Nothing. Maarut's father, your grandfather, saw that the presence of the scribe disconcerted your aunt and assigned the warrior to another post. Anamitra eventually consulted with her parents and her most trusted counselors to choose Firoz, your great-uncle. He was a scholar two hundred years her senior and considered a wise and mature choice. They mated and were wholly devoted to each other until Firoz was killed. I don't think Anamitra even considered another lover after Firoz returned to the heavens. She loved him very much."

*But he was not her* reshon.

"Why are you telling me this?" Meera asked.

"There is nothing that should keep you from what you want," Vasu said. "If you want the scribe as yours, take him. Anamitra told you a tale that she used to comfort herself. She once told me that if

Firoz had been her *reshon*, the pain of his death would have destroyed her."

"Wouldn't it have?"

Vasu cocked his head. "How many scribes and singers live beyond their *reshon*? Many. The Irin race wouldn't have survived if it weren't so. Anamitra told you the lie she made herself believe. There is nothing dangerous about your taking your *reshon* as your mate. Do you think the Creator makes mistakes?"

No, but she did think Vasu would manipulate her if it suited his purposes. It was possible the angel wanted what was best for Meera. Sometimes he was oddly benevolent. It was equally possible that distracting Meera by dangling a fond wish in front of her suited one of Vasu's twisted schemes and everything the angel had just told her was a lie.

"I'm going to check what you said," Meera told him. "I'm going to ask my father."

"Ask." Vasu shrugged. "He knows the truth. All the Tomir do."

"Fine."

"Good." Vasu stretched and turned into his more familiar self, complete with tiger-striped hair and bare skin.

"Clothes, Vasu."

He glanced down. "Oh." Vasu didn't rush to accommodate her wishes. "It's hot."

"You still need to wear clothes."

"Are you sure?"

She looked to the porch where a shadow passed. Someone was approaching the library. "Vasu, seriously," she hissed, "put some clothes on."

"Don't you want to—"

"Meera?" It was her father, standing at the door. "Did you need help finding something?"

Since her father hadn't gone silent in a killing rage, Meera guessed that Vasu had made himself scarce.

"I'm fine," she said. "Just looking for a topographical map of the Atchafalaya."

"You'll need to speak to Roch," Maarut said. "I believe he just checked out every map and guide for the basin we have."

"Roch?"

"Yes," her father said. "Didn't you hear? Rhys convinced him to act as your guide."

# CHAPTER ELEVEN

R hys kept his eyes on the road and tried not to notice Meera's gaze on him as he drove northwest toward the Atchafalaya Bird Research Center and Becki, the very nice avian biologist whom he'd been emailing the day before.

He tried to ignore her, but he felt her eyes on him, could almost hear her brilliant mind calculating. What? He couldn't say. He didn't know what Meera was thinking of him.

She was attracted to him, or she wouldn't have kissed him. He was certain of that.

Rhys was also fairly sure she didn't want to be attracted to him. It could have been a result of her own reluctance toward Irin men or because of too many interfering guardians. He couldn't imagine a life as prescribed as hers. She'd been raised for a very specific role, and he could tell her personality bucked against it even as she recognized the value of it.

*You could be her rebellion.*

It was a tempting thought, to be the wild fling of her "vacation" as she referred to her time in Louisiana. To be her rebellion would be to indulge her whims and explore his own. They could be lovers. There could be naked chess. She could tell him more about these scrolls of sacred congress, and he would be her very happy pupil. When they had tired of each other, they could part with burning memories and no regrets.

*You idiot. You'd never be satisfied with that.*

Rhys wasn't delusional enough to fool himself that way. He didn't want to be her rebellion. He wanted more. But *more* was complicated. Very complicated. More meant considering Meera as a potential mate and a move across the world. More meant navigating political spheres he'd left behind in England. More meant a life as the partner of one of the most prominent—and most targeted—singers in the Irin world.

If she even wanted that, which she probably didn't. He was being presumptuous even thinking that far ahead. Maybe she was only looking for a lover.

She probably didn't even want that.

"Am I losing the shine yet?"

"What?"

Roch was snoring in the back seat, and Meera's eyes were hidden behind dark shades, but he could still feel her gaze.

"This is why I don't tell people who I am," she said blithely. "One of the reasons anyway. It's always too much."

Heaven above, she was perceptive. "Nothing about you is too much."

Her lips twitched and she turned to face the highway. "That's kind."

"No, it's a fact."

"Rhys, you don't need to flatter—"

"I don't flatter. I don't flirt. I'm often a cranky arsehole, and I'm too impressed with my own opinion because I'm smarter than the vast majority of the world. That's a fact too."

She gave a sharp laugh. "No false modesty for you."

"So believe me when I say nothing about you is too much. You are exactly who you should be. And you're going to need every bit of stubbornness, caution, and vigilance when you take your place in the Irin world. I didn't understand it before; I'm starting to now."

Her voice was softer. "Thank you."

"As a point of curiosity, is that why your parents are trying to arrange a mating for you? To find a suitable candidate for the heir who'll understand the level of your responsibilities?"

She glanced into the back seat, but Roch was still sleeping. "Yes," she said quietly. "That's one reason."

"And they like me for that role?"

She winced. "I was hoping you hadn't caught that."

"I don't miss much."

"I know." She crossed her arms. "You came highly recommended as a scholar, which they knew I would prefer. They approve of your family because, while your mother didn't have the same role as Anamitra did—"

"She's still a sage. Elders come to her for council."

"Yes. And your father is not known to be a scribe whose ego competes with his mate's. You would understand my role and the role of my future mate better than most warriors."

"Except the Tomir." He felt a spike of jealousy. "The Tomir warriors are dedicated to you. They would do anything for you according to my research. You could have your pick of hundreds of highly trained scribes, any of whom would worship you."

Meera's lips turned to a hard line. "The Tomir are dedicated to the heir, not to me."

*"Who wouldn't listen to the heir of Anamitra?"*

*"If the heir of Anamitra speaks, the whole world listens. But I am speaking of my daughter."*

Rhys understood Maarut's words far better now. "You need a mate, not another member of your retinue."

Meera gave a sharp nod.

"I didn't mean to offend you."

"No, you meant to imply that I would want a servant instead of a partner for a mate. Who could possibly be offended by that?"

He smiled. "Never fear, princess, I speak fluent sarcasm."

"Princess?" She curled her lip. "Don't call me that."

The corner of his mouth turned up. "It's more than a bit accurate though, don't you think?"

"Rhys, I'm not some idle figurehead who—"

"Who said princesses are idle? Quite narrow-minded of you, Meera."

"Don't turn this around on me. You're the one trying to minimize—"

"Nothing." He saw the turnoff for the research center and moved to the right lane. "I'm making a joke."

"Is that what that was? I'll keep an eye out for them from now on." She cleared her throat. "And yes, my parents might have been considering you as a potential mate for me. They believe in arranged mating."

"*Might* have been? I think I'm still in the running." He tapped the steering wheel and muttered, "Fairly sure your mum approves of me." He couldn't stop the smug smile.

Meera continued speaking as if he'd said nothing. "Which of course means nothing to me. I make up my own mind about these matters, and right now our focus should be on finding Atawakabiche and healing Sabine, not my mating status."

"But you did kiss me."

Her lips twitched.

Rhys smiled. "And you're thinking about doing it again."

"Can we focus on this biologist, please?" She sounded flustered. "You said she had information that might narrow the search zone."

Rhys could live with flustered for a while.

"She tracks bird populations in the basin," he said, "so they have monitoring stations set up throughout the swamp. They're remotely operated, and all the recordings are stored here. I have a theory."

"Which is?"

He spotted a small brown sign for the center nearly hidden behind Spanish moss. "I'll explain after we see a map of the stations. I don't want my theory to influence your observations. We're almost there."

"Very well." She opened a small backpack and checked several notebooks she'd tucked inside. "I'll bring my notes if you don't mind. This is an avenue I hadn't considered before."

"Sounds like a good idea." He drove slowly down the narrowing road, watching for rough spots as Meera fussed with her backpack and checked the points on her pencils. "I think I might keep calling you princess."

"Please don't."

"I make no promises." He reached over to the back seat and slapped Roch's knee. "Wake up, Cajun. We need you to speak to your people so they don't feed us to the alligators."

Roch didn't open his eyes, but he was awake enough to flip Rhys off.

---

BECKI THE BIRD BIOLOGIST WAS, in a word, delightful. It was clear she didn't often come in contact with people as excited about bird population tracking as she was. Of course, she thought Rhys and Meera were visiting researchers from England and Roch was acting as their guide.

"As far as whooping cranes go, the wild population hasn't rebounded in the Atchafalaya." The petite Caucasian woman with a slight Cajun accent ushered Rhys, Meera, and Roch down a hall framed by pictures of researchers in various habitats. Becki was in a few of them, but there were also three men who appeared in many, along with large groups of what looked like community or volunteer groups.

"Where has it rebounded?" Rhys asked.

"Southwest Louisiana right now," Becki said. "The flock that's there is a result of a federal reintroduction program. Some success, but it's been limited. So while we occasionally get excited by a call that might be a whooping crane, for right now we're focused on monitoring other species."

Meera was looking at a picture of a large group in narrow boats and kayaks. "You do a lot of work with the local communities about cleaning the swamps?"

"The bayous are where there are more cleanup operations," Becki said. "Bayous and rivers have more open water, so they get more traffic from people. People equal trash."

"Indeed." Rhys stopped to examine one male researcher posing with a metallic-and-plastic contraption with antenna sticking up. "Is this one of the listening stations you utilize?"

Becki walked back to Rhys and nodded. "Sure is. We have these scattered all over the basin. They take weather readings, record birdcalls, and we're gradually setting all of them up with camera traps."

"How many?"

Becki blew out a measured breath. "We put a new one out every time we get funding. I'm not sure what the exact number currently is, but I can show you a map."

Rhys smiled. "That would be helpful. We're considering setting up a similar program in Yorkshire, and I'm specifically looking at what kind of coverage would be necessary."

She waved them toward a set of double doors. "Then come on back. I'll pull up a map."

Meera walked over to Rhys as Roch chatted with Becki about local news.

"I thought you'd identified the call you heard as a whooping crane," she said quietly.

"I did, but how sure are you that the Wolf is in the Atchafalaya?"

"Very sure."

"Then whooping cranes won't help. But seeing a map of their listening stations might."

"Why?"

Rhys lifted his chin toward the large computer monitor mounted on one wall. "Because we don't want to find things that exist. We want to look for things that don't."

"Come on over," Becki said. "Pull up a stool and I'll bring the map up." She pointed to the large television on the wall. "We just got this set up. I was working on my laptop for this kind of stuff a year ago. This makes the school kids much more excited."

Becki's desktop suddenly appeared on the monitor. She clicked on an icon in the bottom right corner and immediately a map popped up. Rhys only got a quick glance before the biologist clicked on one of the small yellow dots scattered over the satellite image.

"So this is a very active monitoring station. Woodpeckers love this area of the basin. We get lots of activity." She pointed at the screen. "Weather recordings are down on the left. Do you see?"

"Yes," Meera said. "How far back to they go?"

"The individual stations rewrite every forty-eight hours, but they back up to the server here every four unless we manually program them otherwise. So we have records of all these stations from the time they were put in. Temperature readings, humidity, rainfall. And then the birdcall recordings, which are all time-stamped."

"Fascinating," Rhys said. It was fascinating, but he didn't want to see how many downy woodpeckers made their home in Louisiana; he wanted to see that map again. "Can you pull it back to the larger map? Maybe give us an idea about the coverage? Ratio of land to listening stations, so to speak."

"Sure." Becki double-clicked on a window, closing it and bringing the larger map back up.

"Interesting." Rhys cocked his head, trying to make sense of the negative space he was seeing. "Can I see a satellite map overlay of this area?"

"Sure."

There it was.

Once the satellite image was up, Rhys could see the pattern. The yellow dots were fairly regularly placed along the major waterways in the area, but they avoided the small towns and hamlets tucked into the swamps. Rhys could see peaks of roofs through the trees, and boats on the water. In the denser parts of the uninhabited area, the bird researchers had set up listening stations at regular intervals to provide the most coverage. There were little yellow dots scattered all over the swamp.

Except for one area.

"This area here." Rhys pointed to the screen. "Is there a reason you don't have any listening stations there?"

Meera's eyes lit up, but she said nothing.

Becki frowned. "You know... I don't know. I don't know that area well, but it's possible we just haven't seen much activity there, so it's not a high priority. Or it might be really hard to get to. That's pretty dense forest right there."

*I bet it is.*

"Okay." He nodded. "That is very good to know."

Meera pulled out her notebook and jotted down numbers as Rhys made small talk to distract Becki and keep her from closing the map. He could feel Meera's excitement vibrating through the room.

"Would it be possible to get a printout of this map? Even just a rough one would give us some guideline about how many pieces of equipment we're going to need funding for."

"Of course." Becki turned back to her computer and clicked the Print icon in the corner. "Give me just a minute and you'll have it in your hands."

"Yes, yes, yes, yes, yes."

Rhys had never seen Meera do a happy dance before, but he immediately decided he wanted to see it again and as often as possible. Especially from the rear.

Roch grabbed the printout from Rhys's hand and turned it to the side. "Yeah, that narrows it down for sure. Every inch of that basin was covered except for this area. Some serious magic keeping them out. Did you notice that scientist didn't even question it? This singer is powerful." He pointed at a small town not far from the unscanned area. "I know this place. It's a hunting camp more than a town, but we'll be able to rent a boat there." He glanced at Rhys up and down. "Why don't you let me do that part?"

"I bow to your drawl and your plaid flannel wardrobe," Rhys said graciously. "How far is it?"

Roch shrugged. "A couple of hours."

"Why don't we try to find a hotel nearby? Meera and I will gather provisions while you secure a boat. We won't want to start until morning."

"Sounds like a plan, except we both need the same truck for that. I'll stay here until we get all the food, then I'll take off. We need any more camping gear?"

"No, but we probably need more bug spray." Rhys glanced over his shoulder. Meera was still dancing. "Do we have any kind of bucket shower for her?"

"Hell yeah, I got a camping shower. Nobody spends a week in the swamp without wanting to get clean, my friend."

"Good."

They drove together to Walmart where they bought the few miscellaneous things they hadn't brought from Havre Hélène, along with enough dried food to last a week and fishing gear for Rhys and Meera.

Roch dropped them off at the hotel before he took off to find a boat.

Meera turned to Rhys. "Do you like biscuits and gravy?"

"I don't like them, I love them."

She held out her hand. "Come with me."

---

RHYS LICKED HIS FINGERS. "I don't understand why this is so good."

"It's the flakiness of the biscuits, don't you think?"

"It can't be. I've had flaky pastry before. It's the gravy."

Meera shook her head. "We shall have to agree to disagree."

"How did you know about this place?" Rhys looked around at the tiny diner in the strip mall where Meera had led him. It was on the highway a few blocks from their hotel, and Rhys had been more than doubtful until he walked inside and smelled whatever was cooking in the kitchen.

"I was in Lafayette for research last year," she said. "Someone recommended this place—I can't remember who—but I came. I ate. The rest is history. You have to try the boudin after this."

"Good?"

"So good. The best I've had anywhere."

Rhys sat back and watched Meera devour her food. It was as delicious to watch her as it was to eat. She relished every bite. She smiled and hummed as she ate, chattering about the spices between long drinks of cold beer.

"What?" She paused. "Why are you staring at me?"

"Because you're... darling." *Did you actually say darling?*

She blinked. "What?" Meera frowned and set down her beer. "Is this a princess thing again, because I really don't appreciate—"

"Meera."

"What?"

*Don't do it. Don't lay yourself bare. Remember the baggage, Rhys. Remember your mission. Remember all the reasons you left England.*

Or... fuck it.

Rhys leaned forward. "You are darling. You're funny and beautiful and you shine so brightly I think I could watch you cut your toenails and still be fascinated. I want you. Very much. I want to learn more about you. I want to show you my favorite places. I want to know yours. I want to pick your mind about everything. And I want to absolutely ravish you."

Meera set down her beer. She opened her mouth, but she didn't say anything.

"And I think you're reluctant because you don't want to give in to your parents and their ideas about your future mate, but I know you're attracted to me. I know you are. You kissed me, not the other way round."

"You kissed me back," she said quietly.

"And I wanted to do more." He looked at her mouth. "I want to take your lower lip between my teeth and bite it. I want to get my mouth on your breasts, get my hands on your ass and just—"

Meera slapped a hand over his mouth. "We are in public," she hissed.

He grabbed her hand, turned her palm over, and sank his teeth into the soft swell of flesh at the base of her thumb. He bit down just hard enough to make Meera gasp, then he kissed the center of her palm and gripped her hand with his as he hooked her ankles between his under the table.

"My attraction to you has nothing to do with your role in the Irin hierarchy," Rhys said in a low voice. "It has nothing to do with the power you will have. I can't say it has nothing to do with your magic, because your magic is intoxicating to me and it's part of who you are. And I want who you are." He took a shuddering breath. "I want you... far more than is comfortable or well-mannered."

Her mouth was hanging open. "You bit me."

He shifted in his seat. "Yes. I like to bite you. Apparently." He was uncomfortably aroused just thinking about the other parts of her he wanted to bite. "Say something very boring."

"What?"

"Boring, Meera." He glared at her. "Otherwise walking to the car might be very awkward."

"Shall I start reciting from Chomsky's *Aspects of the Theory of Syntax*? I always found transformational grammar theory to be a mood killer in past relationships."

Rhys covered his eyes. "Gabriel's fist, that just made it worse."

"You are a very strange man."

Rhys's phone rang. "What?"

"Who pissed in your cornflakes, brother?" It was Roch. "Are you two back at the hotel?"

"No."

"Well, get back. I just talked to a local scribe. There's some Grigori in Lafayette, and we need to take care of them. Tonight."

## CHAPTER TWELVE

"How do we know they're not free Grigori?" Meera asked. "Just trying to live their lives quietly? You said they were living in the swamp. Do we know that they're hunting?"

Roch glanced over his shoulder as he drove. "This scribe isn't the kind to start shit for the sake of starting shit. He's a quiet guy. If he says they're a problem, they're a problem."

"So we're possibly killing a group of Grigori on the word of a single person?"

"Yeah, Meera, we are."

She stared at the passing green blur of the darkening bayou. "I don't agree with this."

Roch's voice was low. "This isn't something you have a say over."

*I should.* Meera pressed her mouth shut and tried to rein in the quiet rage that simmered in her chest. She knew Roch was correct. She knew that in matters of Grigori, not even elders were consulted in the field. Warriors had to make quick decisions to save lives. She even agreed with that philosophy. To a point. The Elder Council laid down protocols. The scribe houses followed them. It was the only way to retain any kind of order in their world.

Meera didn't deny that the Irin were at war, she just questioned the lack of any power other than a warrior's hand.

Rhys turned around and looked at her. "What would you do?"

"Roch is correct. I don't have a say."

"You do to me. What would you do?" He glanced at Roch. "Do you have a... method for talking to the Grigori that we should know about?"

It was clear from Rhys's expression that he hadn't forgotten what happened to the Grigori at Meera's house or the conversation they'd had after.

*Does Roch know?* his expression asked.

Meera shook her head. *No.*

"I would talk to them," she said. "Find out who they are. Find out who their father is and why they're living alone."

"They're living alone because it's easier to make their victims disappear that way," Roch said. "People go missing in the swamps. People aren't found. You pick up someone that no one is going to miss, they won't even leave a ripple in the water."

Meera turned her head. Roch would ignore her. She cared for Roch, but he was like most scribes, convinced that violence was the only way to deal with Grigori.

"What would you do?" Rhys asked again. "After you talked to them. What if they weren't free? What then? Would you kill them? You know the violence bound Grigori are capable of."

"I know."

"So...?"

Meera looked Rhys in the eye. "Keep Roch from killing them, and I'll show you what I would do."

He looked wary. "You expect me to let you get that close to these Grigori?"

"Yes." She kept her eyes on Rhys. Would he challenge her abilities?

"Roch"—Rhys didn't look away—"we're going to let Meera try talking to them."

"What?" Roch did not sound pleased. "You can't be serious. These aren't children or untried soldiers. The scribe who called me—"

"We'll be with her, and I've experienced a touch of her offensive magic," Rhys said, finally turning back to face the front. "I have confidence that she'll be able to deter them with us protecting her."

Roch's voice was a growl. "Someone put you in charge and I didn't hear about it?"

"Two votes against one," Meera said. "Give me a chance, Roch."

The scribe was silent. She could feel his ire radiating when she lowered her mental shields, though the smooth timbre of Rhys's soul voice mitigated the effect on her senses.

They turned off the paved road and rolled onto a smaller track. Roch touched his *talesm prim* and cut the lights in the car. The spells he'd scribed for night vision would be enough for him to navigate through the rougher terrain.

"How far?" Meera asked quietly.

"A few miles."

She could make them come to her. That would be better.

"Find an easily defensible position," she said, "and stop there."

Roch asked, "Why—?"

"Do it," Rhys said. "Trust me."

A few more turns and there was a wide spot in the road next to a clearing. The trees had been hacked back, and an old shack was crumbling to pieces on the edge of the woods.

Meera got out of the truck as soon as Roch stopped. A slow-moving creek flowed behind the shack, and the moon reflected off the water. She could hear night birds calling with the high screech of insects a constant cacophony in the darkness.

*Where are you?*

Meera opened her senses and tried to ignore the voices of the two men with her as they took veiled positions, Roch near the road and Rhys in the trees behind her. She could smell the bite of both their magic in the air. One by one, the birds left. The insects fell silent.

Predators were hunting in the forest.

With her shields down, Meera felt a tug in the pit of her belly. *Where are you?*

Coming closer.

She sat on a fallen log in the middle of the clearing and tucked her trouser legs into her socks to keep bugs and brambles away from her skin. The Grigori would be there shortly.

*How many?*

She held up a hand with three fingers when she caught a hint of their voices. She heard three. Four? No, just three. They were confused. Drawn to her. They were always drawn to her.

Anamitra told her it was the weight of memory that drew them. Grigori were empty creatures, children who had killed their own mothers with their birth. They were used or discarded by their Fallen fathers. They were empty inside, though not soulless. They were soul hungry.

And Meera carried the weight of a thousand generations.

*"They will always be drawn to you; that is why the Tomir were bound to the heir of heaven's wisdom so many centuries ago. The Grigori hunger for the souls of everything they have been denied. We are everything they need and yet cannot have."*

The Grigori could not have her. Or they could not have all of her. But perhaps just a little of heaven's light could be granted to them. Could make them see reason. After all, they were no different from the Irin. If Forgiven children were abandoned for a millennia, what would they become?

Closer. They were almost to the clearing. She couldn't feel Roch or Rhys in the trees, but she could hear them. Especially Rhys. The sound of his voice...

*I could become addicted to him.* Even the thought of never hearing it again made her stomach hurt. But he would leave eventually. His life wasn't with her. Even if he was interested in Meera as a lover, no one wanted the weight of responsibility that followed her position. Heaven knew she would never have chosen if for herself.

*"I want you far more than is comfortable or well-mannered."*

He didn't even know why he felt that way. Only an Irina knew when she found her *reshon*. There was no way for a scribe to know unless she told him. Rhys would never know what Meera heard from his soul unless she chose to reveal it.

The first Grigori entered the clearing from the shadowed alley of the road between the trees. He was young and beautiful, his dark brown skin glowing near blue in the full moon. He walked to Meera in a trance, but she didn't move from her spot on the fallen log.

"Who are you?" He fell to his knees a few yards from her. "You're Irina, aren't you?"

"Yes."

"Not like the others. You're more."

Meera's heart fell. "When have you met other Irina?"

"Our father caught one for us," he murmured, his eyes fixed on her face. "She fed three of us before she died."

Meera was sick to her stomach, but she didn't move. Didn't react.

Two identical Grigori entered from the road. They were the opposite in looks to their brother—their pale blond hair shone like silver—but their smell and energy was the same. They were three brothers, though they'd come from different human mothers.

Meera could feel Rhys and Roch's magic stirring the air, but the Grigori didn't notice. They were fixed on her. She drew them closer until all three were staring wordlessly at her.

She closed her eyes and reached into the well of power within her. *"Vashah ya."*

The Grigori surrendered their will to her. She could ask them to dance and they would dance. She could ask them to drown themselves in the river and they would do it. As long as their Fallen father remained at a distance, they belonged to her. Most Irina could only command this magic with skin contact.

Meera could control a crowd.

"Who is your father?" she asked them.

"Bozidar," they said in unison.

Sons of the most powerful Fallen in North America were hiding in a swamp in Louisiana?

"Why are you here?"

"He told us to come," one of the blond Grigori said. "We came."

"Why here?"

"There will be more." The other pale Grigori sat next to his brother. "He said there will be many more."

"More what?"

"Irina," they said in unison.

*They're going after the havens.* There was no way Rhys and Roch were letting these three Grigori leave the forest that night. She wouldn't have let them leave either. As much as she hated to admit defeat, she wasn't going to be able to turn any of these Grigori against their father. Their energy was ravenous, and she felt no light in them. The darkness enveloped them completely.

Meera's stomach twisted as she asked the next question. "How have you been feeding?"

"We find prostitutes," one of them said. "They come with us willingly."

*Not to die. Not to disappear.* Meera's heart ached, and she felt the tears on her cheeks. The shields she had lowered threatened to rise instinctually, but she forced them down even as the rasping soul voices of the men in front of her grew louder and louder.

"Don't cry," one of the Grigori said. "No one misses them."

"I do."

"Did we make you sad?" The first Grigori cocked his head. "I don't like that feeling."

"I know you don't."

"Make it stop."

Their voices were calm on the outside, but their interior voices grew louder every minute that passed. Meera pressed her fingers to her temples, raised her voice, and asked, "Is there anything else you want to know?"

Rhys stepped out from the trees. The Grigori didn't look at him. They were completely fixed on Meera. "Is Bozidar coming to New Orleans?"

"Is your father coming to you?" she asked.

Their eyes all lit up at once. "Is he?"

"They don't know," she said. "Is there anything else?"

"How many Fallen children are there in the swamp?" Roch asked as he walked from behind the tumbledown house. "How many others?"

Rhys and Roch moved closer, Rhys coming to stand behind her. Despite their proximity, the Grigori never looked at them and didn't seem to react at all.

Meera asked, "How many of your brothers are nearby?"

"There were seven of us, but the wolves came in the night and killed the others."

"The wolves?"

"She travels with wolves," the Grigori whispered. "There was no sound. None at all. Then they were dead."

*The Wolf.* Rhys's hand fell on her shoulder.

Roch asked, "How did they escape?"

Meera repeated the question.

"Water," one said. "We fell in the water and we couldn't hear what happened."

"Interesting," Rhys murmured.

Meera felt sick inside. She turned her head and pressed her cheek to Rhys's wrist. The growing cacophony in her head quieted instantly. She pressed her eyes closed and took a deep breath.

"Are you done?" she asked.

"I'm done," Roch said. "I don't think they know anything more."

"We'll finish them," Rhys said. "Meera, go back to the truck."

"No." She opened her eyes and locked eyes with the first Grigori who had knelt at her feet. "Do it."

The silver stilettos came out. The knives slid into the back of the Grigori's necks, piercing their spines. Meera kept her eyes on the Fallen child locked under her control. She felt the tug of his surprise when the knife touched his neck. His eyes widened. His mouth fell open. The silver pierced him.

The Grigori crumbled to the ground and began to dissolve before her eyes.

Meera ran to the edge of the trees and emptied her stomach over a palmetto. She was bent over, crying and sick, when the cool cloth landed on the back of her neck.

"Come here," Rhys said. "We had to do it. You know we did. They would have continued to hunt. We don't even have a way to find the victims they've already killed."

"I know." *It still makes me sick.*

He enveloped her in his arms, his fingers holding the cool cloth to her flesh, but Meera needed his skin. She brought his hand up to her temple and leaned into his palm, letting the quiet of his touch soothe her. Rhys tried to tug his hand away, but she held on tight.

"Don't," she whispered. "I need your skin. Just for a minute."

Rhys fell completely still. "Why?"

*Shit.* Meera dropped his hand and moved away, instantly raising her shields.

Rhys followed her. "Meera, why did you need my skin?"

*No no no no no.*

She couldn't deal with this. Not now. Maybe not ever.

She could see Roch from the corner of her eye. His eyes widened for a second before he walked to the truck and climbed inside, slamming the door behind him.

Rhys grabbed her hand and spun her around. "Stop." He forced their palms together, though Meera refused to look at him. "Is this what you need?"

*Heaven above, yes.* She pressed her eyes closed, refusing to meet his penetrating stare.

"Is it?" He pressed her palm to his rough cheek. "Do the voices go silent? Can you hear my soul?"

She said nothing.

"Is it like a bell in the morning?" His voice was thick with emotion. "Is it, Meera?"

"Rhys, it's not..." She opened her eyes and met his stare. She couldn't bring herself to lie, but she couldn't say the word.

"It's not what?" he asked, his eyes wild. "Are you denying... You're not denying it."

She said nothing. It was too much. He was too much.

*He is exactly what you need.*

"Do you know?" he insisted. "Do you hear it?"

She lifted her chin. "I'm not talking about this right now."

His lips twisted and he dropped her hand. "You selfish, self-centered, arrogant woman. I've been nothing but honest with you from the beginning. I've hidden nothing. *Nothing.*"

Rhys turned and walked back to the car, leaving Meera in the forest with the dust of the Grigori hanging in the air around her.

———

THEY RODE BACK to the hotel in silence, Meera sitting in the back seat, trying not to stare at the back of Rhys's head while Roch tried to catch her eye in the rearview mirror.

Awkward did not begin to describe it.

They stopped at the hotel and Rhys jumped out of the truck, not even looking back as he walked to his room. He said nothing to either of them.

Meera leaned against the truck and stared up at the moon as Roch came to stand beside her.

"I can guess what that's about, and I can't say I envy him."

"Thanks so much," Meera said. "Your support as a friend is noted."

"Hey," he said. "If I'm guessing correctly what Rhys was hollering about, then I have no sympathy. Singers hold all the cards when you're talking about finding your *reshon*."

"But how do you know?" she asked under her breath. "For sure? How do you know?"

"Meera..." He gave her a little smile. "You know."

She knew. After the sound of his voice in her most vulnerable state, she no longer had any doubt. But what did that change?

She said, "I have been told my whole life who and what I'm supposed to be. And now it feels like heaven above is conspiring to rob me of the one thing I'm supposed to be able to decide for myself."

Roch gave a hard laugh. "Me, myself, and I. Do you even hear it?"

Meera blinked. "What?"

"Meera, I love you, girl. You're a hell of a woman and a good friend. But you can be self-centered as shit sometimes. No one blames you. You carry an enormous burden, and your life has been prescribed down to the minute. But have you thought about his side? About what caring for you means for a scribe like Rhys? It's not gonna be rainbows and dancing. All people come with baggage, honey, but you come with a whole damn luggage store."

Meera was speechless.

"Maybe a luggage *museum*," Roch mused.

"Thanks."

"But he's still around. He knows who and what you are, and from what I can see, he hasn't backed off. That ought to tell you something right there. Now imagine, on top of all that, there's this one thing every scribe dreams of, and it's wrapped up in a person who is hell-bent on keeping her walls up, and she won't even give you a straight answer so you know which way is up."

Meera looked back up at the moon.

"He wants you for you," Roch said. "Look past your own fears and know that, because I can see it clear as day. Don't be a contrary little shit just because it's not something you thought up yourself."

She knew he was right, but Meera still bucked against the sense of inevitability. "It's not that I object to him. I just…" She frowned. "I wanted to choose."

"There's nothing stopping you from that," Roch said. "It's always gonna be your choice."

"It doesn't feel like a choice. It feels like a surrender."

"Oh, my girl." Roch smiled. "There's so much beauty in surrender when you have a fine place to fall." He pushed away from the truck. "You better get some sleep. Don't decide anything tonight. Your emotions are all torn up after whatever that was in the forest. Speaking of which"—he leveled a hard look at her —"we're gonna talk about that tomorrow, and you can count on that. I don't even know what was going on there, but I know that was some very big magic."

"Roch—"

"Not tonight. Get some sleep. I'm all outta wisdom for the day, and I need to go call my woman."

"Tell Sabine I said good night."

Roch gave her a short salute, then turned to walk inside.

# CHAPTER THIRTEEN

R hys called Malachi as soon as he closed the door. Before his friend could even say hello, Rhys blasted him with the question that had been plaguing him for days. "Why are women so completely bloody maddening?"

Malachi paused. "So I'm guessing you've come across some roadblocks in the mission."

"The mission is going fine, but this woman." Rhys had to pause and take a deep breath. "The arrogance, Malachi. The stubborn arrogance."

"Well, that seems completely foreign; I can't imagine having to deal with a person like that."

"Shut up and listen, you git." He took a deep breath. "I think she's my *reshon*."

Malachi was silent for a few moment. "Well... I'd say congratulations, but you don't sound very pleased about it. Is she a complete nightmare?"

"She's bloody perfect!"

"I thought you said she was arrogant, stubborn, and maddening."

"She is."

"And she's… perfect." Malachi laughed a little. "Okay. Fine then. Um… should I get Ava for this?"

"You're my best friend; you have to listen to me." Rhys sat on the edge of the bed and put his head in his hand. "She's the heir of Anamitra, Mal."

"You mentioned that suspicion. You're sure now?"

"Yes. And she's brilliant. She's powerful. Honorable. She cares deeply, even though I can tell it hurts her. She's… unflinching."

"She sounds like an incredible woman. How do you know she's your *reshon*?"

"I asked her. There was a confrontation tonight. Long story, but she reached for me. She'd been using some very powerful magic on Grigori and her shields were down. After… when it got to be too much, she pressed her head to my hand and—"

"You made the voices go away," Malachi said softly. "Yes, we can do that for them."

Rhys swallowed the lump in his throat. "I used to think fate was rubbish. What did it mean to us, after all, when most of our chosen mates were probably dead? Who should count on a *reshon* when she was probably killed during the Rending? It was a mad hope for a lucky few. Our mission was more important than finding happiness for ourselves."

"Happiness is important too," Malachi said. "If we're too weary to see joy, then we lose our sense of purpose. Everyone needs something to fight for."

"When I see her, I see my purpose." Rhys swallowed hard. "Finally I see it. All the places I've wandered. All the useless trails I've followed. They've all been leading to her. And she…"

"She's fighting it."

"Yes."

"Does she trust you?"

"No." He thought. "Some. More than at the beginning."

"That means she's cautious. There's nothing wrong with that; she has reason to be. Have you made your desires known?"

"Yes."

"Is she not attracted to you?"

Rhys scoffed, thinking about their kiss in the library. "That's not the problem."

"Is there anyone else?"

"I don't think so. She's dated human men in New Orleans."

"Humans," Malachi scoffed. "Ava did that too. They never last long; human men can't handle Irina."

Rhys rose and ran a hand through his hair. "I thought most singers want a *reshon* like scribes do."

"From what you've said, she doesn't sound like most singers."

"She's not."

Meera was the heir of Anamitra, heir of heaven's wisdom. The repository of Irina memory on earth. Raised by her elders. Taken from her parents as soon as her magic was made evident. Nothing about Meera's life had been normal. Everything had been prescribed...

"Everything was decided for her," Rhys murmured. "Where she lived. Whom she spent time with. What she ate and drank. Everyone around her is in her retinue."

"A very dutiful life," Malachi said softly. "She must value what little independence she has achieved."

"Yes." Rhys closed his eyes. "She doesn't want a mate chosen by her parents. She doesn't want a mate chosen by heaven either."

"No, I expect not."

"What do I do, brother?"

"If she were not your *reshon*, would you still want her?"

He'd wanted her almost from the moment he met her. He'd just been annoyed at the idea. "She is everything I want, even if I didn't know it before."

Malachi said, "That's beautiful, Rhys."

He squeezed his eyes closed. "Shut up and give me advice, Malachi."

"Okay, let me think." There was a silence on the line. "She's like you, isn't she?"

"What does that mean?"

"She's arrogant, impressed by her own intelligence, and likely to think her opinion is superior to everyone else's?"

"Well... yes."

"And she's a language geek as well?"

Rhys rolled his eyes. "What does that word even mean? It's a derogatory term for eighteenth-century circus performers."

"I'm going to assume that means she is." Malachi cleared his throat. "Excellent. Then all you need to do to convince her that you two belong together is to show her why falling in love with you is the most logical, sane, and productive path. If you show her that, continue to build trust, and practice patience, this will all work out. She needs to think this is her idea. Her choice. Not just another thing pushed on her from outside her own will. Persuade her, Rhys. Respectfully."

"I don't want to persuade her. And I don't want logical, sane, and patient," Rhys growled. "I want to rip her clothes off and run away with her."

"I'm just following my instincts here, but I wouldn't lead with that."

---

RHYS HUNG up the phone after fifteen more minutes of Malachi explaining to him why patience was a virtue. He was mostly convinced until he smelled Meera's scent on his shirt from earlier in the evening and his arousal raged again.

What was wrong with him? He was acting like a scribe barely out of the academy.

*She's your* reshon.

Everything in him pushed to go to her, find her, and make sure she was safe and protected. Logically he knew her own magic was formidable and she didn't need him to protect her. That didn't seem to matter.

Someone knocked on the door.

*Meera.*

Rhys opened it a second later. "Hello."

"I came to apologize for being self-centered."

He frowned. "That wasn't why I was mad. You have every reason to look out for yourself."

Two lines formed between her eyebrows. "Then I don't understand why you're so angry with me."

"I'm angry with you because…" He glanced behind her and saw two humans walking their direction. "Come inside. Please."

She did, and Rhys closed the door behind her.

The hotel was clean but not luxurious. He took a seat on the foot of the bed, allowing Meera to sit in the single available chair by the small table.

"I would appreciate a straight answer," he said. "Am I your *reshon?*"

She was silent.

"Understand," he continued, "I do not take anything for granted. I don't believe that entitles me to your affection or that it means our mating is inevitable. But each of us only has a single *reshon* in our lives, and I think I have a right to know if—"

"Yes." She said it simply with a deliberately blank expression on her face.

Rhys couldn't breathe for a moment.

*Yes.*

*Reshon.*

*There you are.*

Once his heart started again, he nodded. "Thank you for telling me."

"I didn't want to tell you in that field," she said quietly. "Not right after we'd killed three men."

"That makes complete sense."

"I didn't want to tell you at all," she said. "Not until I knew what I wanted to do with the knowledge."

"It is *not* all about you," he said through gritted teeth.

"I disagree." She folded her hands on her lap. "It's not my job to guard your interests. It's my job to guard my own." Her expression was solemn. "You've already said you want me. I assumed that you would consider it an opportunity."

"An opportunity?"

"Yes, for leverage."

"Leverage for what?"

"To secure me as a mate."

"To secure…" Rhys forced himself to remain calm. "A mate isn't something you *secure*, Meera."

She was silent.

"You really haven't spent much time around normal people, have you?"

"Define normal."

"Fair point." Rhys took a deep breath. "Do your parents love you?"

"Yes." Her expression softened. "I've always known that."

"And you love them?"

"Obviously."

"You're a woman with power and influence. Do they use your love to gain advantages? To *secure* anything?"

"No. They're my parents."

"And I am your *reshon*." He tried not to trip over the words. *I am your* reshon. He wanted to shout it. Wanted to whisper it against her lips. Wanted to write the words on her skin.

*Patience.*

He could tell she was discomfited by the words, but he said them again. "I am your *reshon*, Meera. I don't consider that an opportunity. I consider it a gift."

He couldn't interpret her expression. Surprise, maybe? The surprise angered him, but it also made him want to kiss her. He slid from the bed to kneel before her, taking her soft cheeks in his hands. His thumbs brushed across the flawless copper skin, and he stared at her lips, a deep pink fuller on the bottom than the top.

"I spend a lot of time thinking about your mouth," he murmured.

"It's just a mouth."

He angled his head and licked across her lower lip. "It's a delicious mouth." He bit her bottom lip softly, then drew back until she leaned forward.

Their lips met with no haste. Rhys eased into her kiss, tasting a hint of orange and vanilla as he drew the moment out.

*Reshon.*

His heart sang it, but he forced himself to be cautious, building Meera to a simmer until her arms went around his neck and her fingers played with the hair at his nape. She slid her hand into the back of his shirt, stroking soft fingers along his spine and tracing the raised *talesm* inked across his shoulders. He was drunk on her touch.

He scooted forward, easing his hands along her hips until he cupped her backside in his palms. She was round and soft and he loved it. Her bottom filled his hands, and a sigh came from her throat when he squeezed and pulled her closer. Her legs parted and she pressed herself against him.

Rhys groaned at the sweet ache. He could smell a hint of sweat on her skin. He released her mouth and kissed down her neck, tasting the salt and sucking on the soft skin. He ran his teeth along her collarbone, sliding his tongue into the soft dip at the base of her neck.

She was a feast. Teasing his neck and shoulders. Playing her fingers in his hair. Her thighs pressed against his hips.

The kiss turned from luxurious to heated. He could feel her pulse, rapid beneath her skin. Her fingers gripped his hair as something inside Meera unfurled. He could sense her magic reaching out to touch his.

He slid his fingers along the inside of her thigh. "Let me touch you."

She drew back, desire and caution battling in her eyes.

"Okay," he said, "not yet."

"I didn't say no."

Rhys smiled. "Yes, you did."

Meera frowned. "It's not… I want you."

"And I want you." He captured her mouth again, teasing her tongue until she softened under his hands, but he didn't press for more.

Patience.

"You don't trust me enough. Not yet," he whispered in her ear before he drew back. "We have time. I'm not going anywhere."

"Yes, you are," she whispered back. "You're going into the Atchafalaya Basin tomorrow. Roch got the boat this afternoon. But I *am* going with you." Her eyes sparkled. "Are you as excited as I am?"

"To find a source of lost Irina martial magic? Yes."

"*And* record a nearly extinct language."

Rhys smiled. "Malachi was right. You are such a geek."

"I still don't understand how a word originally used for eighteenth-century German circus performers came to be used for learning enthusiasts."

Heaven above, he adored her.

---

RHYS WALKED Meera back to her room, kissing her good night before he turned and saw Roch trying to disappear into a wall.

He cleared his throat. "My room is past hers, so…"

"Fine."

"Good." Roch nodded. "So you two…"

"Don't have any interest in discussing it."

"Fair enough."

Both men stood in the narrow hallway, nodding silently.

"Did you call Maarut?" Rhys asked. "About the Grigori?"

"Yes. He's going to check with his contacts about any unexplained disappearances, and he'll also get in formal contact with the New Orleans house."

"Good."

"Is Meera going to share what kind of magic she used on them?"

"That's up to her."

"She's like a damn Grigori magnet, isn't she? All that power. She keeps a tight rein on it, but when she lets it shine out…"

"Yes, I'm sure they're drawn to her." Heaven above, *everyone* was drawn to her. Humans, Irin, Grigori. Meera could probably have songbirds circling her like a cartoon princess if she wanted them.

"She spends a lot of time at the haven," Roch said.

"And?"

His expression was solemn. "They're drawn to her. You telling me they haven't been drawn to her this whole time? Why haven't they come to the haven?"

"The wards are powerful."

"So powerful they're not even attracted to the borders?" He shrugged. "Maybe. And maybe something else was keeping them away."

"What?"

"I don't know." Roch tapped his fingers against his leg. "It's worth thinking on. But what she did in the forest tonight… I've never seen anything like that. Have you?"

Rhys shook his head.

"That's why her parents let her live in New Orleans by herself, isn't it? Because they knew about… whatever that was."

"You'd have to ask them."

"Right," Roch said. "But you knew."

Rhys took a breath. "Whatever Meera has shared with me, she's done for her own reasons or out of necessity. I would not consider it an insult that she is cautious sharing things with you. She has cause to be private."

"True." Roch glanced at Meera's door. "I care about her."

"As do I."

"Yeah, I know you do."

Rhys truly hated feeling transparent. He hooked his thumbs in his belt loops. "What time tomorrow?"

"Early. I'm starting to feel like this is a wild-goose chase. I don't want to be stuck in that bayou any longer than necessary if something's coming for the haven. I'd like to be out of Lafayette by six in the morning."

"I'll set my alarm." He started back to his room.

"More are coming." Roch said. "That was the feeling I got from the Grigori today."

Rhys turned back to Roch. "I think Bozidar is getting reckless. Or brave. Maybe he knows about Meera and maybe he doesn't. But things are quiet in New Orleans—all that rich tourist traffic and hardly any Grigori. He probably sees an opportunity."

"That's what I told Maarut."

"Which makes finding the Wolf all the more important, don't you think?"

"Leave it to me, Englishman," Roch said. "I'll get you through the swamp. If you're lucky, you might even come out with all your fingers and toes."

---

HE WALKED through the damp field, the breeze rustling the cane in the moonlight. The rough ground made him stumble, and the smell of sugar filled the air. He heard someone in the distance, walking behind him, but when he turned and walked back, they had moved farther away.

Always at a distance. Always behind. He turned in every direction, but none led him toward the distant follower.

*"Matsah mashul."*

The whisper came from beyond the fields. It drifted in the wind, and he spun in full circle, hoping to find the source.

*Matsah mashul.*

"Find the path."

He searched for a path, but there was none. In the distance he heard the splash of a fountain, a cooing dove, and a child's laughter echoing off stone.

*"Matsah mashul, reshon."*

## CHAPTER FOURTEEN

M eera woke early the next morning with a sense of lightness she hadn't felt since she'd left her cozy home in New Orleans. She felt free. It didn't make any sense. She was embroiled in a critical search for an Irina elder. She was facing a grueling journey into the Atchafalaya wilderness. She'd just witnessed the deaths of three Grigori. And she had no idea how to feel about the scribe who was sneaking into her dreams.

*I am your* reshon.

The words should have felt binding, but they didn't.

She rose and showered, relishing the warm clear water she knew would be her last for days. She washed her thick hair and pressed it dry before she braided it carefully and coiled it around her head. Then she packed her linen trousers and tunics, knowing that her favorite dresses wouldn't be practical for traveling in the swamps. She might be a woman who enjoyed urban comforts, but she knew how to travel in the wild.

By the time she'd straightened her room and made it down to the truck, Roch was already there, waiting for her with the sweet black coffee she loved.

"Have you seen Rhys yet?"

Roch shook his head.

"Hmm." Meera walked back up the stairs and toward Rhys's motel room. She knocked and heard a crashing sound from inside. "Rhys?"

"I'm fine." He sounded very cross. "Fine. Just... Damn trousers."

Meera smiled. "Have you had your tea?"

"Don't—" He pulled open the door, his shirt half unbuttoned. "Don't yell through the door. I'm almost ready."

"You don't look like you slept well." She walked into the room to see neat piles of maps and notebooks next to a backpack and a duffel bag. The only thing in disorder was the bedsheets.

"I didn't," he growled. "Couldn't sleep."

*Did you dream too?*

She bit her lip and walked to the plastic coffeepot. "They don't have any tea."

"Yes, I discovered that at three a.m."

"Why don't I go to the diner next door and see if they have any while you finish getting ready?"

He grabbed her arm, pulled her to his chest, and brought his mouth down on hers in a hard and thorough kiss. He tasted like mint toothpaste and irritation.

"Hmm." Rhys buried his face in the curve of her neck and breathed deeply. "You're not a princess, you're a goddess," he said, his voice rough.

"A goddess for fetching tea?" She gently pulled back and placed a soft kiss on his lips before she headed for the door. "I hesitate to imagine the accolades when I make you breakfast someday."

---

THEY HEADED SOUTH FROM LAFAYETTE, crossing into smaller towns around New Iberia, and then drove to the small camp where Roch had secured a boat from a contact who didn't ask many questions. They would use the pontoon boat as a base as they explored Bayou

Chene and the area where Rhys was certain the Wolf had been hiding. Smaller kayaks would take them through the narrower channels of the swamp, but Meera was fairly sure the hip-high waders Roch threw onto the back of the truck were also going to come in handy.

They parked the truck off the road, securing most of Rhys and Meera's electronics in a waterproof toolbox—the exception being their basic recording equipment—and loaded their camping gear onto the pontoon. Then Roch hopped in the back, fired up the outboard engines, and they were on the water.

Meera sat next to Rhys as he nursed his second large cup of tea. She'd gotten him two just to be safe.

"Have you been on the bayous before?" she asked.

"No. Only seen pictures." He squinted into the morning light shining off the water. "They're primeval. We're only a few minutes from paved roads, but it feels very isolated."

"It is. We'll see a few fishermen, but this isn't a highly populated part of the swamp. The one village that used to exist around here was abandoned about seventy years ago."

"Why?"

"The water changed. Young people moved away." Meera spied the ruins of an old wooden home on cedar stilts crumbling on the edge of the water. "It's a hard life out here. The ecosystem is fragile. Rising sea levels will not be kind."

"But people still live here."

"A few." She put on her sunglasses as the boat changed direction and the sun grew brighter. "Not many."

"At first it seemed preposterous that a thousand-year-old singer could hide in the middle of a reasonably populated area and disappear until she became the equivalent of an urban legend. But once you come out here, it's not hard to imagine."

"No, you can get lost quite easily if you don't know your way around." She nodded at Roch. "I'd never come here without a guide."

"Please don't."

Meera's mood hadn't sunk, even when presented with a cranky British scribe who was apparently the mate heaven had chosen for her. She examined him in the morning light. His hair was thick and still damp from his shower. His skin was alarmingly pale. Was it genetic, or did he spend far too much time at a desk? She needed to make sure he didn't spend all his time inside. If they had children, she hoped—

*Moving that quickly, are we, Meera?*

Her mother would be delighted at her train of thought, but despite her continued reservations, Meera couldn't help but admire him. Rhys was a handsome man. He had a tall, lanky frame padded with lean muscle. His eyes were sharp and deep set, with a strong jaw that would grow a generous beard if he didn't keep his face shaved. She could see the dense black stubble already growing.

Meera reached across and brushed her thumb across his cheek. "Have you ever grown it?"

"Not for centuries. It's quite thick, and I always live in warm places. Do you like beards?"

"On some men."

"On me?"

She smiled. "I'd have to see it."

"Hmm." He sipped his tea, then offered it to her.

"No, thank you."

"You seem better today than you have been."

"I am." She frowned a little. "I don't deal well with uncertainty. I grew up with too much order to be comfortable with it. I choose disorder, but only planned disorder."

"Planned disorder?"

"Yes. I don't want my garden to fall in rows, but I do want to be the one who plants it. Does that make sense?"

"Yes. And life has been everything but certain since I showed up, hasn't it?"

"Putting it mildly." She leaned into his shoulder. "But now…"

He put his arm around her. "Now we know."

"Now we know what we are to each other. What we do from here is our choice."

Rhys's arm felt steady and secure. Familiar and still thrilling.

"Exactly," he said. "We focus on the mission. Anything that happens between us from here is up to us. And when the mission here is done, then who knows?"

"Won't you need to go back to Istanbul?"

He shrugged. "I've been their errand boy for several years now. If I asked Malachi for any kind of leave, he'd agree."

She nodded. "Then we can take our time."

"There's no rush." He stroked long, lazy fingers up and down her arm. "We'll take all the time we need."

"You're very confident that I'm going to choose to be with you, aren't you?"

"I can be quite charming to people who aren't idiots."

"Your generous nature continues to amaze me, Rhys of Glast."

---

THEY MOVED SLOWLY from large channels to smaller tributaries, Roch consulting the map that Rhys had brought with the listening stations marked, but they still got turned around more than once. Compasses were brought out once phone signals were lost. Meera tried to keep track of where they were, but every channel looked exactly the same to her.

Thousands of acres of flooded forest, streams, and marshes made up the terrain, and dense mounds of palmetto were the only indication of higher ground. Small birds perched like lazy sentinels in the bald cypress groves, egrets and herons hunted along the shores, and more than once Meera spotted eagles hunting overhead.

Alligators were their constant neighbors, lining the waterways and sliding in and out of the water as they passed. Meera watched for other residents of the bayou—beavers, otters, nutria, and even bear—but they hid from the sound of the motors.

"The first people who lived here," Rhys asked over the sound of the engine, "what kind of homes did they build?"

"Round houses from wood and mud, mostly."

"On stilts like the Cajun houses?"

"Not usually. They built on mounds."

Roch revved the engine.

"What?"

"Mounds. They were built up over years and years. Most used discarded shell as foundation. Eventually silt from the water deposited on them, creating mounds." Meera pointed to a rise of palmetto in the distance. "See that plant? It doesn't grow in the water. It needs solid land. So if you see stands of palmetto, you know that area is solid."

"That's where we'll camp once we leave the boat," Roch yelled. "Find high ground."

"The leaves also make good roofing material," Meera said. "Keep an eye out for palmetto. If you follow them, you won't sink. Probably."

"Probably?"

Meera shrugged. She didn't take anything for granted in the bayou. You could be walking on what you thought was solid ground only to have it give out beneath you.

"Good," Rhys said. "Excellent. And there are hurricanes here as well, yes?"

"Don't be silly." She smiled. "That's not for another few months."

He grumbled something under his breath.

"I'd make a joke," Meera said, "but they're not really a joking matter. The city has suffered too much, and the storms are only getting worse."

"Indeed."

Meera walked across the deck toward Roch. "How much farther are we going today?"

He gave her a lazy shrug. "Depends on how far you want to paddle."

Meera glanced at Rhys, who was slapping at a large bug on his arm. "I'm going to say as little as possible."

"Then we'll cut over and around a bit farther down," Roch said. "Maybe sleep on the boat tonight. Take the kayaks out in the morning."

She gave him a thumbs-up before she went back to Rhys. "Roch says we'll camp on the boat tonight."

"Good," Rhys said. "You can share my tent."

She knew he was teasing her for a reaction. But the offer was too tempting. "Sure," she said. "Why not?"

His teasing smile disappeared and a new and far more intense expression came to his eyes. "Not backing away anymore, princess?"

"Does it scare you?"

"Not in the least."

---

"Is the heat bothering you?" Meera had dressed in a thin shirt and a loose pair of pants to sleep, but lying next to Rhys, her temperature was soaring from far more than the muggy air. Was it the knowledge that he was different than others, or just the potent attraction between them?

Rhys rolled to his side, propping his head on his hand. "I can't say I'm accustomed to it. It's hotter than Istanbul. But I will say that I've adapted. Most of my assignments in the past hundred years have been in hot places. And it's not the hottest time of year yet. At least there's that."

He wore no shirt, and Meera tried not to stare at his chest. "Do you miss cool weather?"

"Constantly." He reached out and played with the end of her braid. "Tell me about the weather in Udaipur."

"There are a few months that are quite hot, but it is drier than here. The rains come in the middle of summer and cool everything off. I love the rain."

"I do too." He brushed her shoulder with the end of one braid. "Is it in the mountains? A valley? Plains?"

"It's lake country." Her heart was racing. "The city is surrounded by lakes, and there are hills."

He'd dropped her braid and was trailing a single finger up and down her arm.

"I want to kiss you." He leaned down and whispered, "Actually, I want to do far more than kiss you, but Roch isn't far away, and I don't care for an audience." He bit her earlobe and Meera smiled.

"So kiss me," she said. "Kissing is too often overlooked."

But though Meera was expecting a peck on the cheek, she got far more than that. Rhys braced himself over her, lowered himself down, and took her mouth fully with his.

Every time he'd kissed her, it had been different. Their first kiss was a test and a taste. Their second, a careful declaration. The third, hot and hungry.

But this...

He drank her in like a parched man in the desert. Meera lifted her arms and pulled him down until he was caging her body with his. Rhys's kiss was openmouthed, slow, and deep. His tongue tasted of mint with a hint of the whiskey he and Roch had shared after dinner.

Meera wanted his weight. Wanted the heavy feel of his body on hers. She hooked an ankle around his thighs and pulled him closer, only to have Rhys nudge her knees open so he could settle in the cradle of her body.

She sighed into his mouth.

It was so good.

Years had passed since Meera had taken any lover, and she hadn't felt the touch of an Irin male for over a century. His carefully contained power was stronger than any aphrodisiac.

His lips were firm and his hand rested carefully on her hip, but she wanted more. She ran her hands up his sides and along the ridges of muscle that framed his lower abdomen. She scraped her fingernails along his skin until his careful mouth lost its patience and nipped her jaw in rebuke.

Meera laughed. "Don't you like it?" She'd felt the quick shiver on his skin. The raised flesh against her thigh. She dipped her fingers beneath his waistband, teasing him for a second before she ran them up the center of his belly, playing with the fine black line of hair. She brushed her thumbs over his flat nipples and felt him groan against her neck.

"Princess, you're tempting me."

She arched her hips up. "Good."

His mouth took hers again, and she couldn't say a word. He kept their lips fused together as he began to move, pressing his arousal between her legs. She could feel her flesh heating, growing damp and hungry for him.

Meera reached for his pants, but Rhys grabbed her hand and knit their fingers together.

*He didn't mean to—*

"Oooh!"

Rhys covered Meera's lips with his own and swallowed her moan as the line of his erection stroked at a perfect angle between her thighs. The cloth between them was thin, and Meera felt *everything*. The act felt illicit. Forbidden. He was teasing her to orgasm fully clothed, only a few feet away from another scribe.

Meera arched up when she was close, but Rhys kept right on going, not stopping for a second until the tension gathering in her belly snapped and she came hard and long, shuddering beneath him. She felt a burst of magic release from her body and fill the tent, reaching for Rhys and surrounding him.

He lifted his mouth and arched up, red riding high on his cheekbones and his lips swollen from her kisses. He locked his eyes with hers and let out a long breath as he reached for her knee and angled it up until he pressed long and hard between her thighs.

Meera saw a flash of silver in the darkness, and Rhys swallowed a guttural groan of pleasure as he came. He released her knee and rested on top of her, pressing his cheek to hers. His breath was hot on her neck.

"Meera," he whispered, kissing her neck. "*Sha ne'ev reshon.*"

The tender words nearly brought her to tears.

*My beloved* reshon.

His skin was damp with sweat. He placed one more kiss on her mouth before he rolled to the side and stripped off the loose shorts he'd been wearing, cleaning himself before he rolled them into a ball he tucked into the corner of his duffel bag.

He glanced over his shoulder. "Enjoying the view?"

"Yes." She ran a hand down the intricate tattoos on his back. "Your family marks are long."

"That's not the compliment I was looking for."

Meera rolled her eyes. "I don't need to tell you things you already know."

Rhys laughed, pulled on a clean pair of shorts, then stretched out beside her, pushing up her shirt to place his hand over her abdomen.

Meera smiled and tried to move him. "I have a belly." It was the one part of her body she was a bit self-conscious about.

Rhys said not a word, but his hand slowed and he moved it deliberately over the soft rise. He pressed a kiss over her belly button and whispered, "Perfect."

The gesture was so unexpectedly tender her breath stopped for a moment. She reached down and traced the arch of his eyebrow and the line of his nose, wanting to explore every inch of him.

*Who are you, Rhys of Glast? Who is the man the Creator designed for me?*

He stretched out next to her, scooting his sleeping bag closer to hers, and tucked her into the curve of his arm.

"Tell me more about Udaipur," he said sleepily.

"Are you going to fall asleep?"

"Yes." He yawned. "But I want to hear your voice while I do."

"Okay."

---

SHE WOKE in the blue light before dawn. Something was waiting for her in the darkness. Meera untangled herself from Rhys's arms and crept out of the tent.

The pontoon rocked slightly on the gently moving water, and the moon was full, hanging low in the sky. Meera walked to the edge of the boat and looked out toward the forest. A flash of green eyes met hers before they disappeared.

*Come with me.*

It was an animal. Animals couldn't talk. But there was something out there, and it was calling her.

Meera opened every sense and searched in the night. She heard the souls of the two scribes resting peacefully on the boat. She felt the hum of plant and animal life verdant in the bayou.

But there was something else. Someone else.

*Anya niyah...*

The whisper of a children's song carried in the wind.

*Mashak tamak...*

"She's old." A voice came from the edge of the pontoon. Vasu was sitting in child form, swinging his legs back and forth from the railing of the pontoon.

"What are you doing here?"

"Did you miss me?"

"Not particularly."

He frowned. "She's old. Older than you. Older than Anamitra."

Meera frowned and slipped on the rubber boots Roch had set out for her, then she grabbed a headlamp and stuck it in her pocket.

She whispered a spell for night vision before she slid the wooden planks over the edge of the water and into the trees.

Vasu walked beside her, a child with ancient eyes. "Do you know who you seek, Meera Bai?"

"No." She glanced down. "And neither do you."

"That's true. She is an enigma. The singer who can slay an angel with her voice. So many others tried. She was the only Irina who won. Is that why you want her magic?"

"It's not about winning."

"It is for him."

Meera turned to reply, but Vasu had disappeared.

Annoying creature.

Walking carefully across the boards and balancing herself on the knees of bald cypress near the shore, Meera entered the forest. She picked each step with care but followed the memory of the green eyes and the whispered song.

Cicadas and crickets sang around her, adding to the wild cacophony of life that surrounded her. The magic of the bayou filled her up and spilled over. She could feel the threshold as she crossed it, a magical boundary redolent with moss and the earthy scent of pine.

A fox jumped on a log and perched there, watching Meera as she came closer. It was so intelligent-looking, she almost wondered if Vasu had shifted again. Perhaps it was some other creature.

"Do you understand me?" she asked, coming closer. She tried French. Did foxes speak French? "Are you a true animal or something else?"

"No."

Meera raised her shields and spun around to see a lean woman squatting next to a fallen cypress log. She was dark-skinned even in the moonlight, and intricate black tattoos covered most of her body. Her hair was knotted at the top of her head, and a thick necklace of shells hung around her neck. She wore no clothes save for a skirt made of animal skin wrapped around her waist.

"It's just a fox," the woman said in French, and the animal went to her. "My fox." It curled around her arm and settled next to the woman after an affectionate scratch behind the ears.

"Atawakabiche." Meera stepped toward her. This had to be the legendary Irina. There was no hint of evil around her, no sense of illusion or Fallen trickery. Though she was difficult to see in the darkness, there was a heady power that lay within her like a banked fire.

"I haven't heard that name in a long time."

"You found us." Meera fell to her knees before the legendary Irina. "We were looking for you, but you found us."

The Wolf cocked her head, not unlike the foxes that gathered around her. Two more had come and stood at attention as she spoke. "You called me."

"We did?"

"Something did." The Wolf brushed away the animals. "Is your mate with you?"

"My mate?"

"I felt mating magic," the woman said, standing to her full height. "I haven't felt that for a very long time." She was tall and lean with the muscles of an archer. She reminded Meera of her mother. "Stand up. Is your mate near?"

Meera rose. "I… I'm not mated."

"Are you sure?" She frowned. "Come closer."

Meera did, lowering the shields she'd thrown up at the first hint of danger.

Atawakabiche, legendary warrior of the Irina, breathed out a long string of words in a language Meera couldn't translate, then she fell to her knees.

"What are you doing?" Meera asked.

"*Somasikara.*" The Wolf breathed out the name with reverence. "*Sha somasikara.* You are a keeper."

Of all the things Meera had expected, this one hadn't even crossed her mind. "You remember the keepers?"

"I know the magic of a *somasikara* when I feel it."

"It's been a long time since anyone called me by that name." As always, Meera's heart was humbled by the use of her title in the Old Language. The *somasikara* were the keepers of memory, and it was rare for younger Irina to even know the word. "Please." Meera held out her hand. "Mother, I come to ask your wisdom."

"I thought I would never see another keeper on the earth. I thought they had all been taken." Atawakabiche looked up, weariness written on the planes of her face. "Surely Uriel has sent you so I can finally die."

# CHAPTER FIFTEEN

Rhys woke with the dawn and the knowledge that Meera was not beside him. He sat up, activated his *talesm,* and opened his senses.

Two powerful energies came to Rhys. One was Meera, familiar and intoxicating. The second was older. Far older. He rolled to the tent flap silently, grateful that the zipper was already undone.

Who was with Meera? Was it Vasu?

No, he'd felt Vasu before. This was an unfamiliar magic.

He moved on silent feet, tapping on the edge of Roch's tent before he walked across the planks leading to shore.

He didn't draw his knives.

He crossed the unsteady bridge and followed the muddy footprints to the clearing in the forest.

Meera. And a woman who could only be the ancient warrior they'd been seeking.

Her skin, from her chin to her toes, was intricately tattooed with signs and symbols he didn't recognize. They were not in the Old Language. This was some different magic. Her hair was pulled up into a topknot, and she had looped a crown of shells around her head. She wore no clothes save for a short leather skirt.

The warrior woman watched him from her seat on a fallen log. Meera had her back to him and did not turn.

"Meera?"

She turned. "Rhys, she found us."

*Yes, she did. Why?*

Meera was speaking French. The woman appeared to understand it. But then, a ruler of the Uwachi Toma would have easily spoken French to communicate with the Europeans who invaded their land.

"I can see she found us." But he couldn't see whether they were welcome or not. "Atawakabiche of the Uwachi Toma"—he spoke carefully in French—"I am Rhys of Glast, son of Angharad the Sage. Archivist of Istanbul—"

"Where?" she asked.

Rhys racked his brain for a name she might recognize. "I am the archivist of Byzas, the city between the seas, now called Istanbul." Some of the old scribes in Cappadocia used that name.

"You're from across the oceans," she said. "Like her."

"Yes."

"You are her mate."

Rhys paused. "I am her *reshon*."

Atawakabiche nodded. "Yes, I can sense that. You are welcome on my land."

"Thank you, mother."

"For now. When I have no more use for you, then you must leave."

"That's fair."

"I don't care if it's fair or not. That is what will be."

Rhys nodded carefully, but the Wolf was already ignoring him and speaking to Meera again.

"All my people are gone," she said. "I believe I am the last one living. You must take my memories so that I may join them."

"You could be correct," Meera said sadly. "And I am so sorry. But surely there are other people you might—"

"No." Atawakabiche made a dismissive motion with her hands. "I have made my peace with this. It is the way of ages and peoples and war. One group rises when another falls."

"I don't believe it has to be that way," Meera said. "The Creator has granted you life despite your loss. You and your brother brought five centuries of peace to this continent. Can't you teach us how? The Irin people desperately need peace."

"You have a beautiful spirit, *Somasikara*, but what you're asking for is more than you realize. When I have given my memories to your keeping, then I will be content to fade."

Rhys heard Roch coming down the forest path.

"Atawakabiche, there is another with us," Meera said. "He is my friend."

"Then he may be on my land as well." She looked up and narrowed her eyes. "I have seen this one before. He's a son of the Old Ones."

Rhys looked over his shoulder. Roch was standing with hastily-pulled-on pants and a half-buttoned shirt.

"Meera, you all right?" he asked.

"She's fine," Atawakabiche said. "Why are you here again?"

Meera started, "His mate—"

"No." She held up a hand. "I asked him. He visits this wilderness often. I recognize him. What do you want?"

"The woman I love…," Roch started. "My *mate* is sick in her mind. You helped her once. I think you can help her again."

"When was this?"

"Nearly two hundred years ago," Roch said.

"In the past." Atawakabiche frowned. "I help anyone who comes into the swamp if they are not of the Fallen."

"Her name is Sabine," Roch continued. "She was hurt and calling for you when you found her. *Anya niyah, mashak tamak.*"

The warrior closed her eyes. "Old magic. Child's magic. There have been many."

"Children?" Rhys asked.

"If they are lost, my foxes find them. If they mean harm, my wolves find them."

Apparently her canines had good instincts. The Grigori had said they'd been attacked by wolves.

"And what happens if they seek knowledge?" Rhys asked.

Atawakabiche examined him. "You have a seeker's face. And you are mated to the somasikara." She rose and three foxes circled her legs. "You may come with me."

Roch started. "Mother—"

"No." She raised her hand. "I know what you want, old son, but I've given her everything I can. It is up to you now. Wait here and think about what your mate needs."

Meera turned to Rhys and Roch with wide eyes. "Roch?"

Rhys turned to his brother. "If you want us to stay—"

"No," Roch said. His jaw was tense. "Go. I knew it was probably... Just go."

"I'll try to get more."

"Sure." He shrugged. "You can try."

Rhys frowned. "She said she'd given Sabine everything she needs."

"Don't make the mistake of equating age with virtue or wisdom," Roch said in a low voice. "Just because a singer is old doesn't mean she's kind. Doesn't mean she knows more than you do."

Rhys glanced at Meera and Atawakabiche, who were huddled together. The Wolf was hanging on everything Meera said. "Okay."

"You don't believe me." Roch nodded at the two women. "Watch. She wants something from Meera, otherwise she'd have stayed as hidden as she has before. You watch out for our girl, Rhys."

"I will."

Roch's eyes softened. "I know you will." He clasped Rhys's hand. "I'll get your packs ready and stay with the boat. You know how to mark a trail?"

"I'm not completely useless."

"Good."

---

"Do you have it?" Rhys held his hand for Meera as she jumped down from a fallen log.

"I'm good."

He grabbed her hand before she passed him. "This isn't how I'd planned to wake up this morning."

Meera raised her eyebrows and started to speak, but the Wolf interrupted.

"If you get lost, those marks you're making aren't likely to help you find your way back," she shouted.

"We better go," Meera whispered.

They had walked for what felt like miles, their packs strapped to their backs, while Atawakabiche seemed to dance through the forest. She stepped lightly on fallen logs and through shallow snakelike streams. She always seemed to know where the high ground lay, because following her, nothing but Rhys's feet got wet. She moved from mound to log to rock to log, never slowing, her fox companions following closely.

The Wolf had taken them on a circuitous route that Rhys suspected was designed to confuse and disorient.

The sun was high when the mound appeared before them. One moment they were walking along a narrow waterway, and the next they had ducked under a tilted cedar, and a massive earthen mound rose before them. The foxes ran ahead, clearly at home.

Atawakabiche turned and paused at the stone steps built into the mound. "You won't be able to find this place again, not without my help. So don't try to mark it in any way."

"Thank you for welcoming us to your home, mother," Meera said, still speaking French. "We will not intrude on your solitude."

"Does the fire still burn in this place?" Rhys asked in the Old Language.

The traditional greeting seemed to please the Wolf. She nodded at him. "It does burn, and you are welcome to its light. You and your own." Then she turned and walked up the steps.

Meera turned to Rhys. "Thank you."

"For what?"

"Coming with me."

"Did you honestly think I wouldn't?"

"A mysterious woman shows up in the middle of the night and drags you away from the boat and guide we so carefully planned? You'd be more than justified to think I was crazy for following her."

Rhys smiled. "Well, now you know. Even if I think you're crazy, I'll follow you."

The edge of a smile teased her lips. "She thinks we're mated. I tried to tell her otherwise, but—"

"We're *reshon*. She senses the bond between us. Don't you?"

Meera bit her lip, but she didn't say anything.

"Stop fighting it." Rhys bent down and kissed her lips. "And you'll feel it."

He took her hand and the path the Wolf had walked. The steps wrapped around the old earthwork, and Rhys saw bits of shell, bone, and rock sticking out of the soil. Moss and grasses grew from the sloped walls, and Rhys was surprised by how high the construction went.

How had they not seen this from their satellite maps?

When they reached the top, Rhys understood.

A dense canopy grew on all sides of the mound, which was built in a spiral pattern reminiscent of a snail's shell. Because of the spiral and the trees growing in the space between, there was little to no sun on the mound. Only a few scattered patches were cleared so vegetable patches could grow.

Three round houses were built along the edge of the widest part. They were made of straight poles and smooth mud with Spanish moss filling the cracks in the walls and stiff palmetto leaves thatching the roof.

The Wolf pointed to the first. "This is my home. The second is a bathhouse and ritual room. The third is in the distance. You may use that one to sleep."

"Thank you," Meera said.

"Yes, thank you." Rhys wondered just how long the Wolf planned for them to be there. He walked to the hut, surprised by the breeze that cooled the afternoon. Apparently even a slight elevation made a difference in the humidity and the temperature.

He brushed back the woven curtain hanging in front of the house to find a well-kept cottage with brushed earthen floors and high windows to let in the air and light. The breeze rustled the palmetto leaves covering the roof, and he set down his pack on a low bench.

There was a low wooden bed in the corner covered by a woven blanket, and grass mats covered the floor.

"This is quite nice," Meera said.

"Yes." An earthen water jar sat near the door with a wide metal bowl next to it for washing. "She was prepared for guests."

"Who? Us? How could she know?"

Rhys shrugged. "Maybe us. Maybe she's ready at all times. She said there were many. I wonder if she collects lost people in the bayou."

"It's possible." Meera sat on the edge of the bed and bounced a little. "Spanish moss," she said with a smile. "It'll be cool at night."

"Thank heavens, because I don't foresee any air-conditioning. Not even the magical variety."

"No, but look at the windows." Meera pointed up. "At night this place will be far cooler than our tent."

It gave Rhys a little thrill every time she said something like "our tent."

"Are you hungry?" he asked.

"Starving." She opened her backpack and took out a bag of peanuts. "Share?"

"Please."

He sat next to her on the bed, and they ate the small bag of roasted peanuts while sharing a bottle of water.

"Roch has most of the water," Meera said. "I only have this bottle and one more."

"She has to have a fresh water source here, or she'd never have built the mound."

"Do you think she built it on her own?" Meera shook her head. "I don't think she did. It's too old. I can feel the earth magic here."

"Then she has to have a water source. There was a vegetable garden and a ritual bathhouse."

"Hopefully it's not too far to walk."

"How are you feeling?" he asked. "This wasn't what we planned, but you must have imagined this meeting for years."

Meera's smile was bordering on giddy. "I feel good. She found us. She invited us here. She recognized my magic. That's more than I imagined."

"She called you a *somasikara*."

"Yes," Meera said. "That is what I am."

Even with everything he'd learned about her, it came as a surprise. Rhys hadn't put the heir of Anamitra together with the ancient magic of the memory keepers. Memory keepers were something out of stories and tales of the first children.

In Irina legend, the *somasikara* were the first daughters of heaven to receive the wisdom of the Forgiven. They were given the ability to remember all other magics the Irina would need on the earth to tame the soul voices of humanity, heal the sick, tend the earth.

All Irina magic was given to the *somasikara* who then taught it to the other singers. As new magic was found and developed, the memories were given to the singers with the ability to remember it. Mother passed the memory to daughter from generation to generation until the keepers became legends and the formal system of Irina library magic took over.

"So there are memory keepers still living," he said. "It's not just a legend."

"As far as I know, I am the only one left," Meera said. "That is why Anamitra was so closely guarded and so highly respected. Why my birth was such a long-awaited event. Anamitra was beginning to suspect another child wouldn't be born with the necessary magic. But unless others are hidden around the world, I am the last. Even before the Rending, we were rare. After it…"

"What makes your magic different?" He asked. "Why can you do what you do?"

"It's born in me. Hereditary magic." Meera toed off her shoes and crossed her legs on the bed. "But not entirely. It takes very intense study. The magic to keep the memories is part of me, but learning how to use it is not. When I was young, I couldn't understand what I was seeing and hearing. I tapped into ancient memory around my aunt, but I didn't know what it was. It took years of study to absorb what she was teaching me."

"So you are literally a walking library."

"No. A librarian only records the words and some of the feeling." Meera took his hand. "I carry the true memory."

"I'm afraid I still don't understand."

"It's the difference between Sabine telling you a memory and you magically seeing through her eyes. You sense what she sensed. Feel what she felt." Meera smiled. "It's hard to describe. If we ever… Well, you might see someday. I might be able to show you."

"If we ever what?"

Meera rose and walked to the door. "We shouldn't disappear for too long."

"If we ever what, Meera?"

Her smile teased him. "We don't want to be rude."

"Meera!"

She walked out the door.

Blasted woman. She was going to drive him mad, and he'd enjoy every minute.

THEY GATHERED around a fire where a stew of some kind bubbled, and Atawakabiche roasted long spears of meat that Rhys highly suspected came from a reptile. He didn't ask. She didn't say. It smelled good, and that was all he would think about.

"My people built this mound," she said. "A long time ago. There used to be more houses. Of course, there used to be more people."

"Our house is very comfortable, sister."

Rhys began, "Atawakabiche—"

"Heavens." She grimaced. "Your tongue sounds like it is tripping over itself. You can call me Ata."

"Thank you, Ata." Rhys smiled. "How have you remained hidden for so long? Is it all magic?"

"Look around." The darkness was already falling. "This place—this wilderness—will turn you around. It's bigger than most humans will admit. Once they're inside, most lose sense of direction. The magic helps, but it's almost unnecessary. The older ones, they came across me more often. But they were like me. They wanted to be left alone. Respected those who wanted the same." She waved a hand. "I had no quarrel with them."

"Modern people?"

"Magic," she said. "Strong magic. I use earth magic to keep them away."

"So you're an earth singer."

"My mother was an earth singer. She and her sisters made these mounds we're standing on."

"And you were a warrior," Rhys said. "Are you of Mikael's blood?"

Ata smiled. "You aren't a fool. You know that most of this land is filled with Uriel's children, even those who came from the south like me. Uriel's children are special. We can have many gifts."

Rhys desperately wanted to ask what hers were. Which blood made Irina warriors? Which lines should be trained in martial magic if not for Mikael's blood? Uriel's children were known in Irina tradition to be flexible in their gifts, often changing roles throughout their lives. Were Uriel's children the key?

"What was your first gift?" Meera asked. "Mine was memory. Were you always a warrior?"

"No," Ata said. "I wasn't." She turned the meat. "You are mated, but it is a new mating. I don't see deep ties of magic between you. Only the beginnings of them."

"We are not mated," Rhys said. "Though we are *reshon*."

"Rhys is correct," Meera said.

Ata waved her hand. "You are mates, whether you've sung the magic or not. I can see the soul-tie. It is one of my gifts, seeing ties that way. It was why my brother and I were such successful warriors. I could always tell who were the most influential soldiers in a group. I could see where loyalties lay and target those whose loss would affect our enemy most."

That was utterly fascinating and Rhys was dying to know more, but he didn't want to guide the conversation. Ata wanted to speak to Meera. Meera wanted to speak to Ata. He'd have to approach the martial magic in that context.

"Mother, you know I am a *somasikara*. I am hoping to record your language before you decide to fade. You may be the last speaker."

Ata sat up straight. "Why?"

Rhys blinked. "Why?"

"Yes, why? If the people are dead, the language isn't needed anymore, is it? What does it matter?"

Meera said, "To preserve a language is to preserve not only the memory of a people but a way of life. A way of thinking. A vision of the world. To lose all those things means your people would die twice."

Ata set the meat skewers down in a long basket and unhooked the cooking pot from over the fire. "I'll think about it." Then she left the food in front of them and walked away.

"But—"

"Don't." Rhys put a hand on her arm. "I think that's all you're getting tonight. Give her time, Meera. You have to be patient."

She huffed out a breath, and he could tell she was still considering chasing after the recalcitrant Irina.

"Does badgering work on your mother?" he asked.

"Badgering?"

"Pestering. Bothering. Asking for the same thing over and over again."

Meera laughed a little. "No. That doesn't work on Patiala."

"And it won't work on her. She's not part of your retinue. You have to build trust."

She propped her chin in her hand. "Like you slowly wore me down?"

"You love my persistence," he said, reaching for a spear of meat. "Don't lie."

"You do realize that's probably alligator, don't you?"

"I'm not thinking about that right now. I'm too hungry." He bit into the meat, which was juicy and smelled of peppers. "For now, princess, just eat."

# CHAPTER SIXTEEN

M eera watched Rhys as he climbed up the ladder and Ata handed him the palmetto leaves. Apparently if they were going to sleep in her village, she was happy to use their labor. Meera was grinding dried leaves in a round cypress mortar while Rhys was using his long reach to repair the roof of the bathhouse.

Like Ata, he was bare to the waist, and the dark lines of his *talesm* moved and flexed with his muscles. They labored in the filtered shade of the pines and cypress trees; she could hear short drifts of conversation pass between them as they worked.

A breeze floated over the mound, cooling Meera's skin like the sweet, fresh herb she was grinding cooled her senses. She found herself humming an old song her grandmother had sung, rocking back and forth with the grinding pestle.

She couldn't describe the sensation in her spirit. She felt settled. Rooted. Surrounded by old magic and verdant life.

Despite never having visited before, Meera felt connected to this place, to this foreign village so far from the centuries of tradition in her home country. There was magic here, familiar and old. The very ground beneath her was made with it. It was a place of immense power.

A shadow fell over her and she looked up.

"You've ground enough," Ata said. "Thank you. You can pour the powder into that jar."

Meera reached for the jar Ata had pointed to. "What is it?"

"The Creole call it filé—they use it for soups—but it was ours first. Sassafras leaf. I dry and cure it. It's good for eating and medicine. It's the fastest way to break a fever."

"I'll remember that."

"You'll remember everything when you agree to take my memories so I can die."

"Ata, I can't agree to that. Your magic is too necessary for our people. Though I can hold your memories, I cannot be your voice. And your voice is needed. Please come back with us. Just a visit would be a blessing."

"So you say." Ata sat beside her and took a carved wooden spoon hanging from a hook on the wall of the outdoor kitchen. She scooped the bright green powder from the mortar, using her hand as a funnel to pour the filé into the jar. "The soup last night had filé in it."

Meera knew the subject had been officially changed. "It was good. I was wondering—"

"What does your mate want from me?" Ata didn't look up as she asked. She kept methodically transferring the powder into the jar. "He is being very patient, but I can tell he wants something."

"Yes." Meera had decided to stop correcting Ata regarding the status and her and Rhys's relationship. Ata ignored any protestations about Rhys and Meera not being mated anyway. "I've told you I want to record your language, but he has a different goal."

"What is it?"

Meera debated whether to reveal Rhys's plans but decided that for the Wolf, frankness was a better tactic than subterfuge. "Rhys wants to know your martial magic."

"And you?"

"I want to know how you found peace."

Ata raised an eyebrow.

"You and your brother achieved peace in this land. Lasting peace for over five hundred years. At no other time in Irin history has that been accomplished. How did you do it?"

Ata shook her head. "You're not going to like the answer."

"Tell me anyway."

"We made them afraid," Ata said. "Very, very afraid."

The singer was right. Meera didn't like that answer. "How?"

Ata frowned and dragged her foot though the dust. "What happened to the Irina on the other side of the ocean? Why don't you have warriors anymore?"

"We do have warriors. My mother is a warrior. But… the Irina across the ocean—and the modern Irina here—don't have battle spells anymore. Most Irina warriors died out or were killed in the Rending. The majority are scholars and healers now. Scientists and businesswomen. But fighting has been taken over by the scribes."

Ata shrugged. "That makes sense since modern Irin are stupid."

Meera blinked. "I'd like to think not all of us are stupid."

"You are the *somasikara*, so of course you are not stupid. You carry the memories of our people, so you have their wisdom. But most modern scribes and singers?" She shrugged. "I have watched them. I think they are stupid."

Was that why she was determined to die? So she could avoid the stupidity of modern life? "Why do you think so?"

"Modern Irin have become like the humans, fighting for unimportant things. They create laws and rules to fight the sons of the Fallen, who are animals meant to be driven from the earth. Grigori don't deserve laws. They deserve death."

Meera's mouth fell open. "That's… I mean… Do you know that there are free Grigori—Grigori whose angelic fathers are dead— who are trying to live in peace with us? At peace with humans? That there are female Grigori who have no magic and no ability to shut out the voices of humanity? Some of their brothers have become our allies. Some of the women have actually mated with Irin scribes."

Ata's face was blank. She stared across the village, watching Rhys go up and down the ladder. Without another word, she stood and walked away.

Meera let out a long breath. "So I'm going to guess she *didn't* know that."

———

MEERA LAY in bed that night next to Rhys. They'd been exhausted the night before after finding Ata's mound, but now her mind was spinning. Ata's isolation. Her determination. The magic she held without any desire to share it.

"How do you speak to someone who withdrew from the world over two hundred years ago?" Rhys mused. "Closer to three hundred. She's completely disconnected from society. She feels no responsibility to it."

"I was thinking the same thing. The humans and then the Grigori took everything from her. No other Irin came to help her people."

"They were isolated. The council didn't even know—"

"She doesn't care about that." Meera rolled on her side. "She doesn't feel a larger responsibility except to the memory of her people. She's ready to die."

He shook his head. "I don't understand giving up like that."

"Maybe she doesn't see it as giving up. Maybe she sees it as simply following the path all her people have traveled ahead of her. How would you feel if you were the last of your people? If all that was left of your language was your own memories? Think about it, Rhys. That's a profound level of loneliness."

His eyes moved from the thatched roof to Meera. "Your empathy is staggering. Is that part of being *somasikara?*"

"I suppose. Carrying the memory of thousands will do that to you."

"I'm trying to wrap my mind around it, but I can't." Rhys put a hand on her cheek. "How do you bear that burden? How can one person carry a load like that?"

Meera smiled. "Um… magic?"

Rhys's cheeks dimpled. "Is that your polite way of telling me 'duh'?"

"Look at you smiling. It's almost like you have a sense of humor."

"Imp."

"I would never say duh to you." She lay down in the curve of his arm as he stretched it across the mattress and pulled her closer. "I have much more academic ways of telling you you're missing the obvious."

"Good to know you maintain academic standards in all things."

Warmth welled up in her breast. He was wonderful. He became more wonderful every day they spent together. A small, rebellious part of Meera kept trying to push back her growing feelings for him. She didn't *want* a mate chosen for her. She didn't want to be a servant of fate. She didn't want her love dictated by family or political obligations or the whims of heaven.

*But he is exactly what you want.*

"Rhys?"

He lay calmly beside her. "Yes?"

"Are you backing off?"

"From you?" His voice was deeper. "A little."

"Why?"

"You wanted to focus on the mission. You told me that. The last thing I want to do is pressure you. I want to be a help here, not a hindrance."

And he just became more wonderful. She turned her face up to his. "I do want to focus on the mission. But I am also very good at multitasking."

He didn't miss a beat. Before she could blink, Rhys's mouth was on hers and he'd reached down to cup her bottom and hook her leg over his hip.

Meera's mouth was invaded so skillfully her body surrendered without protest. She opened to Rhys and felt his tongue delicately trace the edge of her teeth and the tip of her tongue. He tasted of herbs, smoke, and the whiskey he'd shared with Ata after dinner.

Meera clutched his shoulder, her mind overwhelmed by a flood of sensation. His hand was warm and firm on her bottom, the other smoothed over her hip and over the curve of her waist, up her body until he was holding her breast and teasing the sensitive peak with his thumb.

"Your skin is so soft," he murmured against her lips. "I want to touch you."

"Yes." She rolled away and pulled off the thin cotton gown she wore to sleep, leaving her bare to his very appreciative gaze.

"Meera," he whispered, propping himself up with one arm and playing his fingers lightly over her skin. "I want to kiss you."

She pulled him down and met his hungry mouth with her own. She luxuriated in the rich taste of his lips and the rasp of hair on his jaw. His chest pressed against her own, and she relished the weight of him, the solid muscle of his body against the softness of her own.

He kissed down her neck. "I want to kiss *everywhere*."

Rhys kissed over her collarbone and down the valley between her breasts before he licked slowly up one mound and sucked the sensitive tip between his lips, teasing her nipple with his tongue and his teeth. Meera's back arched with pleasure, but Rhys took his time, sampling each breast before he continued moving down.

"What—?"

"I told you." He bit the soft skin under her belly button. "*Everywhere*."

She'd taken a bath in the basin, but she still had to ask. "Are you sure?"

"Very sure."

She smiled and spread her legs as Rhys slid off the edge of the bed, still in his boxers but sporting a very impressive tent. He knelt at the edge and tugged her toward him.

"While I'm down here," he said, "I need you to tell me about these scrolls of magical congress you were talking about."

She gasped as he nibbled the inside of one knee. "The scrolls?"

"Yes." He licked slowly up to the juncture of her thighs. "For research purposes, I'm going to need you to be very, very specific."

Heaven above, the man's mouth was magic.

"The first—ah!—scroll was written around… uh… four hundred Common Era by…" She gasped and lost her train of thought when his tongue teased the tip of her clitoris.

Rhys raised his head and Meera tried not to cry in disappointment. "Written by…?"

"The scribe Jargrav. He wrote it as an ode of joy to his mate, Kashvi."

Rhys went back to work, kissing the top of Meera's pubis as his hands massaged her breasts. "Please continue."

"The scroll describes their mating ritual in… ah, some detail."

"Details?" His tongue dipped down, then drew up with aching languor. "I'm going to need more than that."

*Yes, so am I.* "Um… Jargrav was a warrior as well as a poet, and he ahhhhh—"

Rhys picked his head up again, his lips red and wet, his cheeks flushed with pleasure. "He what?"

Meera blinked and tried to focus. "I just remember a lot of sword metaphors. Are you going to ask me to summarize all the scrolls?"

"How many are there?"

"Forty-seven."

He bent his head. "Research like this can't be rushed. Please continue."

---

HOURS LATER, he was kissing her slowly as he ran his fingers lightly over every inch of her skin. Meera had lost count of how many times he'd brought her to climax—with his mouth, his fingers—but she wanted more. She wanted *him*.

"Rhys."

"Yes." His eyes were closed. He had to be exhausted, but he wouldn't stop kissing her.

"Make love to me."

His tongue licked up the side of her neck. "I am."

She reached her hand down and grasped his erection as it pressed against her hip. He arched into her touch and groaned but made no other move.

"You know what I mean." She squeezed him lightly, and he released a hard breath against her neck. "I want you."

"I want to wait."

"Empirical evidence suggests otherwise."

He laughed against her skin. "There's the bold woman I met in Jackson Square. I was wondering where she'd run off to." He nipped her skin with his teeth. "I want to wait."

"Why?"

He took her mouth in another breath-stealing kiss. Brushing her hand away, he rolled on top of her, giving her the full weight of his frame. The pressure was delicious. Meera felt like she'd been enveloped in a full-body hug. Her skin was ultrasensitive; goose bumps rose over her legs and arms.

"Anticipation is a beautiful thing," he whispered. "Watching your pleasure was like seeing the sun rise."

"And rise. And rise." She smiled. "If you're determined to play the martyr, then we should sleep."

"No martyring for me." He rolled to her side and drew her to his chest, pulling her leg over his thigh. It left his erection nestled between her thighs, making Meera groan. "I'm going to make myself very comfortable."

"You're not playing fair."

"You've found me out." His voice dropped. "When it comes to you, I do not aim to be fair. I want you to be mine and mine alone."

His words cooled some of the heat in her blood. "Whoever becomes my mate will have to share me, Rhys. The heir of Anamitra belongs not only to herself but to the Irin world. I will never be able to ignore my duties. Have you thought about that?"

"I understand duty better than most. But I'm not talking about the heir, I'm talking about my *reshon*."

"We are one and the same."

"Tell me this, if the heir of Anamitra belongs to the world, does the world belong to her?"

*No. No one belongs to me.*

Rhys tilted her chin up. "Listen to me. The human poet Solomon spoke with the wisdom of heaven: 'I am my beloved's and my beloved is mine.' Part of you may always belong to the world, but the whole of me would belong to you, Meera. Who better to care for the woman in the role than a scribe who was created by heaven to love her?"

Meera blinked. "That's very logical."

"Your gift of memory was given by heaven, and the Creator must know it would be a burden. So wouldn't it make sense he would create for you a *reshon* capable of sharing that burden?"

Meera frowned. "Yes."

He smiled. "So we are agreed. Logically, I am the best mate for you."

"I'm not sure—"

"I do love reason." He closed his eyes and tucked Meera's head under his chin. "Makes decisions like this very simple."

Tricky, tricky scribe. She knew he was taking advantage of the oxytocin flooding her system, but she couldn't find it in her to protest. She was tired and all she wanted to do was cuddle.

"This is an ingenious debate strategy," she said before she yawned. "Bring a woman to multiple orgasms, tire her out, flood her brain with positive hormones, then make your argument. Have you used this strategy in the past?"

"No, but I plan on using it often in the future."

"Use it on anyone other than me, and I'll hurt you."

"*Sha ne'ev reshon,*" he murmured, "I would not even be tempted."

---

SHE DREAMED that night of walking through a forest flooded with silver water reflecting the sky above her. She waded through stars as the distant sound of night birds called. But the wind didn't carry the scent of salt and cypress to her nose. It carried the rustling sound of sugarcane and the wet, sweet scent of the fields beyond the haven.

*Why are you walking in the forest when you know where your love resides?*

The fox perched on the cypress stump, staring at her with bright green eyes.

"I don't know love." She knelt in front of it. "Show me your magic."

*I have no magic; I am merely a messenger.*

"For whom?"

*For you.*

"Whose message do you carry?"

*Your own.*

"You are talking in circles."

*Only because you are walking in them.* The fox leapt off the stump and splashed into the starry water. *You know of what I speak.* Matsah mashul. *Find the path and the answers will come to you.*

"Vasu?" She yelled after the fox. "Stop invading my dreams."

"I'm not." The dark angel stood beside her, looking down. "You invite me in. Look at the stars."

She looked. "They fill the sky."

"And the earth."

"No, it's only a reflection of heaven."

"Only to those who haven't yet seen the heavens." His voice came from all around her, filling the wind that cut through the flooded forest. "The balance you seek is an illusion."

"I don't believe you."

"Do you know more than I?"

"Maybe I do."

The bright smile cut across his beautiful face, illuminating it in the darkness. "Arrogance becomes you."

"You are the only one who says that."

"No." The rustle of the cane fields filled the wind. "I am not."

The forest sank into the stars, and rising before her, the green cane fields swept out toward the horizon. A tall figure stood in the distance, arms held out, long fingers brushing the top of the drifting grass.

"Who is it?"

*You know. You have always known. He was created for you when the stars were born. The keeper of memory and the seeker of truth.*

She walked toward him, but he was always in the distance, just past her reach.

*You know how to reach him.*

"I know."

She had always known.

---

MEERA WOKE to see the blue light of predawn shining around the woven curtain. A shadowed figure stood in the distance.

She rose and left Rhys's side, wrapped a light scarf around her shoulders, and stepped out into the cool morning as the stars faded above her.

Ata spoke in a low voice. "The magic of our first mothers was only passed from mother to daughter," she said. "That was how everyone was taught. That was how every person was valued. We were all pieces of one whole. Only the *somasikara* held the whole of our memories."

"I understand what you're saying."

The pain on Ata's face was brutal. "I never had a daughter. I never bore a child. All my sisters are gone. Unless you take my memories, the songs of our first mothers will die with me."

"I can hold your memories, Ata, but I cannot be your voice." The loneliness of the mound nearly ripped Meera in two. "Please don't choose this path. Walk a little farther if you can."

Ata said nothing for a long time. "Come with me." She turned and walked toward the edge of the mound. "I will sing you a song of rising."

Meera followed her and sat cross-legged on the edge of the mound facing east as Ata started to sing. Her voice was low and guttural, rough at first before her throat warmed to the chant. Meera knew she might be hearing words that hadn't crossed Ata's lips in years. Decades maybe. Longer?

She didn't want to pause for recording equipment, so Meera opened her senses and whispered her own spells of memory, tapping into the well of magic she'd spent a lifetime perfecting.

As Ata sang, Meera channeled the song and the memory directly, wrapping up the words Ata sang, the feel of the earth under her, the cool, humid air that surrounded her, and the song of morning birds. She took all of it into herself, capturing the memory in a crystal faceted by sound, scent, taste, and touch.

*This is why we need you*, her heart cried. *This is why you must not fade.*

In Meera, the memory of Ata's rising song entered the communal memory of the Irina, forever preserved in magic. The memory sank into her, a silken thread captured, unspooling into eternity before her eyes.

# CHAPTER SEVENTEEN

Rhys rose with the first morning song. He walked barefoot out of the hut and watched from the edge of the garden as Ata sang. Meera's eyes were fixed on the warrior singer, her body swaying with the sacred rhythm, and Rhys knew he was witnessing the true purpose of her power. He could feel the pull of it, even from a distance, the expansion as Ata's magic rose over the bayou.

It showered the mound in magic. He could feel it in the ground beneath his feet, feel the deep age of the earth and the water and the foundation that held this place above the forest floor.

His mind struggled to process what Meera's magic felt like. It was an opening. An unfurling. Like a flower soaking in the sun, taking the magic of the song into itself and sending that energy to the root of her soul.

The beauty of it brought tears to his eyes. He walked to the edge of the mound across from them and felt the sun rising at his back, but he could only stare at her. She was a star rising before his eyes.

*I am for her. She is for me. No other will love her the way I can.*

Rhys estimated that Ata's song lasted two hours. Approximately an hour before the sun rose through the hour after it broke over the horizon.

How did she know when to wake?

It was only one of the questions he had. What did the rising song do? What was the purpose of the magic? From the feeling beneath his feet, Rhys suspected the purpose was an establishment of the land the haven sat on. He would guess the song would be sung communally when more Irina lived on the mound. Now it was only Ata.

*"Maybe she sees it as simply following the path all her people have traveled ahead of her. How would you feel if you were the last of your people? If all that was left of your language was your own memories?"*

Meera was right. Rhys didn't understand that level of loneliness. The human half of his DNA had run rampant over the earth, filling the world with English language and customs. It was impossible to imagine ever being the last of his kind.

But here on the mound, as Ata sang her morning song, Rhys could empathize with her. She had guarded this place for centuries, all on her own. She'd sheltered the travelers and cared for the weak. She'd tended gardens that only fed herself and protected a place lost to the modern Irin world.

Her strength humbled him, but he also knew why she wanted to fade. Meera was resisting it with every breath in her body, but Rhys understood. He understood even if he didn't agree.

*Our world needs her. It needs them.*

Ata finished her song, but Rhys didn't move. Meera was still in the fullness of her power though she looked exhausted. Her eyes were closed as she sat planted in her spot on the bare ground. The morning sun touched her skin, turning the warm copper to gold before his eyes. He imagined gold written on her skin, gold mating marks he would write, a gold vow over her heart.

*Sha ne'ev reshon.*

Ata rose and walked over to him. "Water? I'm getting some for your woman. She'll be tired when she wakes."

"Please."

Ata went to the water jug and raised the wooden lid before she filled two drinking gourds. She set one next to a meditating Meera before she came back to Rhys. Meera was rocking slightly, her eyes closed, her energy effervescent but fading.

Rhys continued to watch her as Ata sat next to him. "Have you seen her kind before?"

"Yes." Ata's eyes were shadowed when she passed him the gourd. "We had a *somasikara* of our own once. She was killed before she could pass on her memories."

"I'm sorry."

Ata shrugged. "It is the way of history, scribe. I hope you understand your duty to protect this one."

"I do. Though she's pretty good at protecting herself."

Ata glanced at Meera, who had stretched prone on the ground, soaking up the earth magic that surrounded her. "I will teach her songs to use against the Fallen and the Grigori. I will give you both that. When she takes my memories, she'll be even more powerful, but she'll still need a keeper to make sure she protects herself from herself."

Rhys's heart beat faster. "Does that mean you've decided to share your martial magic with us?"

Ata gave him a crooked smile. "I don't think she's the one who wants it."

"She may not, but she needs it. You were the only Irina in legend able to slay a Fallen with only the sound of your voice."

She flinched. It was so minute, Rhys almost missed it.

"The only one?" she asked. "No one else figured out how to do it?"

He nodded.

"I told her modern Irin were stupid." Ata rose to fetch her own gourd of water. She came back and sat next to Rhys again. "Tell me, scribe, why do the Irina need this power? Aren't the scribes willing to protect them?"

"Of course we are, but we also respect balance. Right now the only way we know to kill the Fallen is with a heavenly blade. And only scribes can wield a heavenly blade."

"And there are only so many black blades in this world."

"Exactly."

"My brother held one, but it was taken by the French when they killed him."

"How was he killed?" A warrior like the Tattooed Serpent would not have been easy for a band of Grigori to kill, much less any human.

"He was killed by deception and dishonor," Ata said. "And that is all I'll say about that. My mate, praise the heavens, died honorably in battle as he would have wanted."

*Her mate?* Rhys blinked. "I didn't know you were mated."

Ata stared at him. "What?"

"We don't have a record of your taking a mate. The stories we have say that you and your brother fought together and that you'd chosen a warrior's life."

"So you assumed I'd never mated?"

Rhys was speechless. "I haven't really thought about it much, to be honest. In the stories—"

"The stories, the stories, the stories. I am not a story. I am a person. And my mate was the other part of me." Ata's eyes were fierce. "He was my *reshon*. How in Uriel's name did you think I sang the magic that slayed the angel?"

Rhys blinked. "What?"

"Who is stronger? Mated Irin or unmated?"

*Oh damn.* "Mated, of course."

"And strongest are those mated to their *reshon*. It has always been so for Irin, why would you assume it would be different for Irina?" Ata shook her head in disappointment. "Here's the truth, scribe. The martial magic that slayed Nalu died the day my mate did, because it was only together that we were strong enough to take down an angel, and he died in the effort."

"Did they know?" Rhys asked. "Did the Grigori—?"

"Of course they did. The Grigori have always known our weaknesses. That is all they have to study. While we work to build lives, they only think of death. They have no creation, only destruction. And it is far easier to destroy than to create."

"And yet you want to destroy your life instead of create new magic." Rhys set his drinking gourd down and held his hands out to her. "I know that is the way it has always been. I can't understand your loss, but I do feel it. I also know that we are trying to change the old ways. Meera is trying to change them. I am too. Otherwise, what do we have but endless war?"

"Life *is* war," Ata said. "Anyone who tells you otherwise is trying to lower your defenses." She rose and started to walk away.

"Wait," Rhys called. "What does this mean? Are you going to teach us the martial magic the Irina need? Ignore what we're asking of you for a minute. If you truly believe that life is war, if you're truly ready to die, don't you want to give your sisters every weapon possible so that they can take up the mantle of guardian when you are gone?"

Ata stopped and turned. "You speak with sense. That's a fair question."

"Is that a yes?"

She looked at Meera, then at Rhys. "I know you think I've been ignoring your words, but I haven't. Is she your mate?"

His heart sank. "I want her to be."

"Until she is your true mate, I can teach you nothing. The magic I know only works in tandem."

Ata walked away, leaving Rhys sitting on the edge of the mound, staring into the morning forest.

---

"SHE HAD A MATE?" Meera asked. "Everything makes so much more sense now. When was he lost? Was it during the battle with Nalu? Are you certain?"

"Are you hearing what I'm saying?" Rhys asked. "Do you understand what she said?"

"We have to mate and she'll teach us the Irina martial magic? I still don't like the idea of using it, Rhys—especially considering that it sounds like it might be very dangerous to you if her own mate was killed—but I am willing to concede that killing the Fallen may be the only path to true peace. Until we can free more of the Grigori, we can't effect fundamental, structural—"

"We have to be *mated* in order to learn this."

"I heard you."

Rhys paced back and forth in the small space the hut afforded. "Maybe there's some way to learn it without being mated. If she teaches you the Irina part, then perhaps I can use my empathy to access her memories. She'd have to be willing but—"

"Wait." Meera rubbed her eyes and took another drink of the tea Ata had brought her. "I'm confused. Didn't I just agree with you?"

"You really need to be resting right now. I know it's hot in the hut, but I can move a pallet into the shade outside. I can see how much that took out of you this morning." Rhys knelt down beside her and took both hands in his. "Does my touch help or is it draining? Tell me how to help."

"It helps, but what would really help is you explaining what the problem is." Meera frowned. "I mean… you're the one making the argument that I should be your mate."

His heart ricocheted between mad rejoicing and crushing disappointment. "Yes."

Her expression was resolute. "And Ata is saying that we need to be mated to learn this magic."

"Yes."

"This is a once-in-a-lifetime offer, Rhys."

He wanted this, but he didn't. Not this way. Not another obligation. He wanted to wipe away the infuriating mask that had fallen over her face. He gripped her hands and said nothing.

Meera continued, "While I have my issues with Irin tactics and council policy, we cannot ignore the opportunity this is. Being able to preserve this knowledge is—"

"Don't fucking say it," he bit out. "Don't tell me you'll agree to be my mate because it's logical or strategic or whatever fucking argument you were just going to make."

Meera's mouth dropped open. "You were the one telling me last night that reason dictated—"

"I was teasing," he bit out. "I was playing with you."

"You're not making any sense," she said. "Wanting me as a mate was a joke? A tease?"

"No, of course not. That's not what I'm saying."

"You're not making any sense. You say you want me as a mate, and Ata says we need to be mated to learn this magic. Don't you understand I'm agreeing with you, Rhys?"

"Don't *you* understand it would kill me if you chose me because of an obligation?" He stood and stepped away from her.

Her face was stricken. "Rhys—"

"I will *not* be another burden you take on your shoulders to fulfill a role you are duty bound to perform. When you become my mate, it will be because you want me so much you're mad with it. It will be because you love me as much as I love you. How can that be confusing?"

Her eyes were wide. "You say you love me, so you *don't* want to be my mate?"

Rhys had to get away from her. The temptation to just say, *"Yes, of course I'll be your mate! How about now?"* was too strong. "Not like this." He shook his head. "Not like this, Meera." He left the hut and walked across the mound and down the stone steps leading out to the bayou. He grabbed the closest boat he could find—a narrow dugout canoe of sorts—and he pushed off with the pole leaning against a cypress tree.

He needed to get away.

Far away.

Heaven and circumstance had just handed him everything he'd ever wanted.

What the hell was he going to do?

———

RHYS COASTED INTO THE BAYOU, keeping the mound in distant sight. He had no illusions about his navigation abilities. He'd be turned around in minutes if he wasn't careful.

He kept to the main channel and listened to the birds calling overhead. Alligators slid like silent sentries into the water as he passed, and fish jumped, lazily snacking on the bugs that circled.

"It's her training," a voice said behind him.

Rhys spun and nearly knocked the boat over reaching for his knives when he heard Vasu's voice. He turned, but there was no one behind him, not even in the distance.

"You'd be very foolish to try to hurt me," Vasu said from overhead.

Rhys spun again to see a young man who looked to be in his late teens perched on a cypress branch overhead. A line of crows alighted behind him. They were the only crows Rhys had seen in the bayou.

"Believe it or not," the fallen angel said, "I'm trying to help."

He resisted throwing a knife at the creature. Barely. "What are you doing here?"

Vasu shrugged. "I can't be on the mound. Not even I want to deal with that earth magic. It's very old." He rolled his shoulders. "Makes my skin itch."

Best not to question the Fallen too much about things like Irina earth magic. "But why are you here? And what were you saying about Meera?"

"I was saying that it's not her fault she doesn't see things like you do. You were raised with very common notions about love and family and your role in life. Meera had different lessons."

"Her parents are mated. They love each other. It's very obvious."

"Yes, but that love grew over time. They were arranged. They expected to arrange Meera's mating as well. For them, duty comes first. Always. It is the rule of the Tomir and of Udaipur. Patiala loves her daughter, but she gave her up when her gift became clear because that was what tradition demanded. Yet she does not love her daughter any less than your mother loves you. That sense of honor is quite beautiful really. Very rare in Irin society these days."

"I don't want Meera to take me as a mate from duty."

"She won't be able to see past it now. The duty will always come first. If she sees a mating with you as something necessary for the greater good, she will not hesitate."

Rhys's heart sank.

Vasu cocked his head. "Why does that distress you?"

"I wanted her to choose me."

"She will choose you."

"But not because she wants me for me," Rhys said. "Why am I even talking to you about this? It's not like you'd even understand."

"I understand selfishness very well." Vasu swung his legs. "I am mostly a very selfish creature. I only have very brief moments of generosity. And most of those are because I get bored unless something distracts me."

"There is nothing selfish about wanting Meera to choose to be my mate instead of doing so out of obligation." Rhys started to pole away from Vasu, but the damned angel only disappeared and reappeared on another branch in front of him.

"Of course it's selfish. The outcome is the same, only your ego feels the wound. You will be mated. She will love you as deeply as you love her. You are *reshon* after all—which is the only reason I am trying to help you at all. I don't care about you. Only Meera."

"Why?" Rhys propped his arm against a tree. "Why do you care about Meera?"

Vasu frowned. "Because she's interesting. Anamitra was interesting, but Meera is... more. I like the way her mind works. Her vision amuses me."

"Selfish."

"Yes." Vasu stood and hopped to another branch. "I told you that already."

Why was he arguing with the Fallen? He hated to admit it, but Vasu was right. The outcome would be the same. He had no doubt that he could make Meera fall as deeply in love with him as he was with her, especially once their magics were linked.

Why did it matter?

*It just did.*

Was he being selfish? If he was, it wasn't for himself. Or was it? He didn't want that shadow hanging over their relationship. Didn't want Meera to ever question why she had chosen him.

But did it matter to Meera or just to him?

*She won't be able to see past it now.*

Rhys was very afraid that the angel was right.

# CHAPTER EIGHTEEN

M eera was stripping palmetto leaves with Ata. "Men are infuriatingly emotional."

"I agree." Ata split the palmetto leaves with her teeth and wove them into the sturdy basket between her legs. "I often told Akune that he needed to cool his temper."

"He has been the one pushing to be mated ever since he found out we were *reshon*. And I wasn't averse to mating, I just wanted to be sure he was certain of his feelings and not purely operating on fate."

"Being *reshon* doesn't guarantee a happy mating," Ata said.

"Exactly!"

"It merely guarantees you are mating the person heaven designed for you. But if you're a miserable person by nature, you still might be unhappy with that."

Meera paused. "I'm not a miserable person."

"You don't seem to be. If Rhys is resisting the mating now, perhaps he avoids happiness."

Meera frowned. "Rhys doesn't avoid happiness. That's not what this is about."

Ata curled her lip. "He likes to complain."

"But in a teasing fashion," Meera said defensively. "He's not a negative person. It's just his sense of humor."

Ata shrugged. "Perhaps."

"He's a very generous person. Miserable people aren't generous."

"You know him better than I do, so I will leave you to judge that. Perhaps he's fickle and his feelings have changed." Ata reached for another strip of palmetto. "You definitely want to avoid a fickle mate. His feelings would be changing all the time. You'd never be able to depend on him."

"Rhys is very dependable," Meera said. "He's not fickle."

"Odd for his feelings to change like that then."

"It's not about his feelings," Meera said. Or was it?

*"Don't you understand it would kill me if you chose me because of an obligation?"*

Did Rhys fear that Meera would regret their mating? That she would come to resent him? That he would someday be an obligation?

"He would never be an obligation to me," Meera said.

Ata looked up. "Who said that? A mate is a gift. Especially a *reshon.*"

"Yes, Rhys said the same thing." Her fingers felt frozen. He'd said *exactly* the same thing.

*"I am your* reshon, *Meera. I don't consider that an opportunity. I consider it a gift."*

She'd been surprised. Taken aback. No one but her parents had ever cared for her without obligation. The Tomir guarded her. The singers of Udaipur served her and learned from her. But Rhys... he didn't owe her anything. Nothing at all. He wanted Meera for herself. He said he loved her for herself.

Meera didn't know what to do with that love.

Ata reached for another palmetto strip. "Perhaps he is simply brooding. My mate did that occasionally. Men need to brood."

"Maybe." Meera picked up another palmetto frond. "That must be it."

"Finish that frond," Ata said. "And I'll teach you another song."

"Can I record it this time with my digital recorder?"

"I don't care what you do," Ata said. "But make those strips narrower."

---

HOURS LATER, Meera was loading the digital file of Ata's weaving song into her computer, and Rhys still wasn't back. She had asked Ata if she could sense him close by, and Ata had told her not to worry, so she tried not to.

She did more weaving.

She weeded the garden.

She made preliminary notes about the grammatical structure of Ata's language, as much as she could discern from its relation to the Natchez language and the way the Uwachi Toma had tied their language and the Old Language together in spells.

She washed clothes.

She tried not to think about Rhys.

It was impossible.

He came back to the mound before sunset with a long string of fish held in his hand.

"Good work," Ata said. "You stink."

"I know. Is there water in the bathhouse?"

"Yes, and it's already heated." Ata held up the fish. "I have a stew going for dinner, but I can smoke and dry these."

"Whatever you think best," Rhys said. "I just needed some quiet."

"And now you need a bath." Ata glanced across toward Meera. "I'll send your mate in with some drinking water."

Rhys heaved a sigh. "Meera is not my—"

"Don't care." Ata turned and walked away, leaving Meera standing at the door of their hut, watching Rhys.

He looked at her. Opened his mouth as if to speak, closed it, then walked into the bathhouse without a word.

Meera went back into their hut and sat on the bed, unsure of what she should do. She hated feeling unsure. Hated it. From the time she was a child, she'd always known what to do and where to go. She'd always known her role and her duties.

Rhys didn't want to be a duty to her. So what was she supposed to do with him?

Ata stuck her head through the curtain of their hut. "What are you doing?"

"I don't know."

"Go bring the man some drinking water. He's been out in the heat all day. I'm shocked he isn't unconscious."

Meera jumped up. "Okay." Bring the man some water. She could do that.

She walked to the drinking-water barrel and dipped a large gourd in. Then she walked to the bathhouse rehearsing what she could say to Rhys to make him understand her confusion.

*I want to be your mate and I know I will not regret it.*

*You could never be an obligation.*

*Just because a mating is logical doesn't mean it's unwanted.*

*I think I love you, but I'm not sure what that means.*

*You make me feel alive and reckless and a little crazy, and I want to feel that way for the rest of my life.*

"Rhys?" She stepped into the damp air of the bathhouse where a fire burned in a potbellied stove in the corner, heating the stones that Rhys poured water over to fill the room with steam. He was naked to the waist, scrubbed clean, dressed only in ceremonial linen and his black-inked skin.

He was so beautiful Meera was struck dumb.

Rhys turned and saw her in the doorway. "Is that water for me?"

She nodded and held out the gourd.

He walked over, took it from her, and tipped it up to his lips, drinking so deeply it spilled from the corner of his mouth and dripped down his neck and chest.

He held out the cup. "Are you thirsty?"

Meera nodded, but her eyes were locked on his chest, following the drips of water that trailed down his neck, over his heart—bare skin waiting for a mating mark—and followed the ridges of his abdomen to disappear beneath the linen.

He put the cup down and reached for her, hooking his arm around her waist. "Meera?"

"Yes?" Her voice was thick with wanting him.

"Are you thinking about our argument this morning?"

She finally lifted her eyes. "Yes. And no."

Meera couldn't decipher the expression he wore. Sexual hunger. Tenderness. But with an edge of anger. Or was it frustration?

"Rhys, I think—"

"Don't tell me what you think," he said quietly. "Tell me how you feel. Right now. This moment. Tell me how you feel."

"Greedy," she whispered. "Rebellious. More than a little unwise."

He didn't say anything at first. Then he nodded and muttered, "That will do."

Rhys took her mouth before she could speak another word, and Meera was glad for it. She didn't want to talk or debate or reason with him. She wanted his body. Wanted his mouth. His hunger and desire. The longing was elemental in nature. She bit down on his lower lip, and Rhys's hand came down on her backside in a hard slap.

He pulled away and cleared his throat. "Sorry." Then he smoothed his palm over her buttock. "Actually, not sorry."

Meera blinked in surprise. "Um... not sorry either."

"Good." His mouth took hers again, and he tugged at the buttons on her shorts until Meera unbuttoned them and shoved them down her legs. Her shirt was already off, and Rhys made quick work of her bra and underwear. He picked her up by the waist and walked her over to the warm basin of clear water where he dunked a washcloth in and squeezed the water over her shoulder, following with his mouth.

Rhys licked from her shoulder down to the tip of her breast, sucking hard and catching her as her knees buckled. His mouth and hand worked in tandem. Clean, kiss. Clean, bite. Clean, suck. He covered every inch of her skin with warm water and his lips before he stripped off the linen he wore at his waist and rubbed her from shoulder to toes, drying her off before he nudged her toward a low pile of furs and linen cloth in the corner.

"Remember how I said I enjoyed anticipation?" He pulled the hair at the nape of her neck, tilting her head back so he could kiss her throat.

"Yes."

Her back hit linen, and Rhys came to rest between her legs, kneeling on the furs heaped on the floor of the bathhouse. Her body was ready for him. The hard line of his erection pressed against her inner thigh.

"That may go out the window this first time." He leaned down and bit the side of her breast, his teeth scraping up the valley between her breasts as she pulled him closer and tilted her pelvis up.

"Please."

Rhys braced one arm at her side, cupped her bottom in the other, and angled her hips before he drove into her in a long, steady slide.

Meera let out an aching breath. Heaven above. So good. So full. She'd been aching for this ever since he'd kissed her the first time.

His mouth came down on hers as he pulled out, then drove in deeper than the first time.

"Gabriel's fist," he muttered against her lips. "So good."

"Yes." She wrapped her legs around him and arched up, driving Rhys into her at the perfect angle. She saw stars behind her eyes. She felt raw, uncontrolled. There was no thought, only feeling and hunger and pleasure.

Rhys thrust into her with a steady rhythm, his mouth sealed over hers, stealing her breath and her groans of pleasure.

Meera's magic rose up and embraced its mate. Her body and soul recognized him. She was heady with magic, drunk on his touch. She saw his *talesm* glow silver in the rising steam of the bath-house, lighting the room and the gleaming drops of water that coated her body.

Her magic rose with her pleasure, cresting a moment before the climax clutched her body and she threw her head back. The vision of the cane field and the starry forest rose in her, and she threw it instinctively toward Rhys, sharing the vision with him as he began to come.

"Meera!" He sank his teeth into her shoulder and groaned when he spilled his pleasure into her. "I knew it was you."

She wrapped her arms around his shoulders, pulling him close as his body came to rest in hers, the profound peace of his touch melting her bones until she felt weightless. Ephemeral. Her mind floated to the rustling cane fields where she felt a hand reach out and touch hers before it drifted away.

"It was you," she whispered. "It was always you."

Rhys turned his cheek, scraping the rough stubble of his beard over her cheek until their mouths met. "It will only ever be me."

Meera closed her eyes and nodded, her legs still wrapped tight around his hips. "Good." She didn't want to let him go. Maybe ever. He felt like he was hers. The only thing that had ever been hers before.

He arched into her, still hard. "Our mating ceremony will be tomorrow. Is that enough time for you to write your vow?"

She nodded. "And you?"

"I've had my vow written since the night you told me we were *reshon.*"

She opened her eyes. "But you didn't take anything for granted?"

"It wasn't presumption." Rhys smiled. "It was hope."

SHE SAT on the edge of the mound at sunset, shaking the satellite phone. It was freshly charged—they had a solar charger that worked well—but nothing was getting through. Nothing. Was it Ata's earth magic? That was the only explanation.

An explanation that her mother would be wholly unsympathetic toward.

*Shit.*

Rhys sat next to her and grabbed the phone. "Shaking it isn't going to do anything."

"Logically I do know that, but since I don't have a hammer, shaking it seemed like the best course of action."

He smiled. "Still no signal?"

"Nothing." She tried to ignore the flutter of panic in her chest. "Rhys, if we mate—"

"When we mate."

She nodded. "*When* we mate…"

He frowned. "What are you worried about?"

"There are so many traditions we are ignoring," she said in a rush. "I can't even tell you how upset my mother and father are going to be. It's not that I don't want this mating. I do. But they won't just be upset, they'll be hurt. Mating celebrations in Udaipur…"

He grimaced. "Are elaborate?"

"So elaborate," she whispered. "There are feasts and dances for days. Formal blessings that should be given to both of us. There are songs my mother has been preparing since my birth to sing over me before I bind myself to a mate. There are spells my father has written…."

"These are important to you."

"No. Yes. But this mission is more important. I just don't know how to make them understand that we have to—"

"Meera." He gripped her hand. "We don't *have* to do anything. I was being high-handed earlier because I want this. But there is no disaster. Yes, we suspect Bozidar is making a move to New Orleans, but there is no imminent threat. His Grigori aren't waiting at the outskirts of the city."

"Do we know that?"

Rhys said nothing because they didn't know. They were isolated on the mound. New Orleans might be crumbling from Grigori attack, but they would have no idea while they stayed with Ata.

"We need Ata's magic," Rhys said quietly.

"I know that. I need to record more of her language and culture. I'll even concede we need her to teach us the angel-slaying spell, and she can't do that unless we're mated."

"I don't want you to give up your traditions," Rhys said, his voice still quiet. "This is important to you. I can tell."

"Are you saying we should go back to Havre Hélène, have our mating ceremony there, then try to come back here? I don't think we'd be able to find our way back."

"And if we leave, it's unlikely she'll cooperate in the future."

"I think…" Her heart sank. "We have to be here. We just have to have a simple mating here and my parents will have to understand. They'll be disappointed"—*disappointed wasn't the word for it*—"but they will understand."

"Because they understand duty."

"Yes."

"So we could do that." Rhys leaned back on his hands, squinting into the setting sun. "Or… I can give you everything you want."

"That's not possible." She smiled sadly. "But thank you, Rhys."

"These traditions? They are *formal* mating ceremonies of your people?"

"Yes. I have attended many mating celebrations. When Anamitra was alive, it was our responsibility to preside over any festival in the fortress."

In her mind's eye, Meera could see the yellow path of chrysanthemum petals her sisters walked upon as they sang the

Anthem of Uriel joined by the elder singers. She could see the crimson-painted banners of the Tomir flying from the fortress ramparts, scribed with spells of safety and prosperity for the new couple.

Meera said, "Both the Tomir and the singers of Udaipur have very elaborate traditions. If we were having our mating ceremony at the fortress, the preliminary dinners alone would take days."

"Days?"

"Maybe it's better we're not doing all that. It can be taxing." She'd seen the stress those ceremonies put on the mated couple. She'd never envied the fancy clothes or being the center of attention—she'd always been the center of attention—but the idea of entering mated life without her mother's song or her father's blessing hurt Meera's heart.

"They're formal events though." Rhys's face was a study in concentration. "If we were in Udaipur, would political leaders and elders come to the ceremony?"

"Without a doubt. When Anamitra and Firoz mated, even human kings attended the feast. They were lavished with gifts, speeches, toasts. Over two thousand singers and scribes were invited."

Rhys was nodding. "Yes. *Formally* invited."

"Yes, it's all quite formal. I don't understand why—"

"And I'm sure it would have been a huge insult for any of them to refuse, correct? For a leader or an elder to be invited to the mating feast of the heir of Anamitra and then not to show up...?"

"If they had a very good excuse, I'm sure— Oh." Meera's eyes went wide when she realized the devious direction Rhys's thoughts had turned. "Oh, Rhys. No. That can't be a good idea."

He turned to her and his grin was wicked. "She's a leader. A *chief*. Even if her people are gone. She understands honor, formality, and tradition."

"She is going to hate you," Meera said. "*So much.*"

"Probably. But I don't think she'll say no."

Meera shook her head. "No, Rhys. She's found refuge here. I don't want to disturb—"

"This is not a refuge," he whispered. "She's hiding. She's not a wounded bird. She's a warrior who has given up because her army was defeated and now she doesn't have a battle to fight. She needs to come face-to-face with the world as it is now, because we need her. We need her knowledge and her skills. And she needs to stop hiding."

"You may not get the answer you want," she said. "I just want you to prepare yourself. She may kick us out, and then what will we have?"

"We'll have ourselves. And a very strange angel who's oddly attached to you. But you know I'm right about Ata. If this will force her out of this swamp, it's the right thing to do."

Meera was silent.

"*Sha ne'ev reshon,*" Rhys whispered. "I would deny you nothing. Pissing off cranky old warriors is something I do on a near-daily basis in the course of my duties."

"The formalities aren't necessary, Rhys. We can be mated without them. We can have a simple ceremony—"

"And have you leave your parents' home without the blessings and songs they have waited your whole life to give you?" He leaned over and kissed her forehead. "Never. I would never take that from you."

She looked up and met his steady gaze. "I am a very wise woman who does many wise things."

He smiled. "I agree with you."

"But to take you, Rhys of Glast, as my mate," she said, "might be the wisest choice I have ever made."

What was that in his eyes? Was it love? Rhys folded her in his arms and pressed her cheek over his heart.

"Come to bed," he whispered. "Tomorrow we can piss off an ancient warrior, but tonight you're mine."

# CHAPTER NINETEEN

Rhys woke with a naked Meera in his arms and the unflinching certainty that Atawakabiche, the Painted Wolf, last and most feared warrior of the Uwachi Toma, was going to make him pay dearly for this day. She would do what he wanted in the end, but sometime in the future he would pay. He glanced down at the woman lying across his chest, her hair spreading out in rippling feathers across his skin.

*Worth it.*

He kissed her shoulder and stroked a hand through her hair, tucking a strand behind her ear before he traced the perfect shell decorated with delicate gold rings.

*Creator, how have I pleased you? Show me, that I may always be so blessed.*

"Meera," he whispered.

"Hmph." She wrinkled her nose and rubbed her eyes. "What?"

"We need to wake up and make ourselves as fancy as we possibly can under the circumstances."

She grimaced, her eyes still pressed shut. "I left my fancy back in New Orleans."

He smiled. "I left mine back in England. But we still need to make an effort."

"Fine." She rolled over and stretched across the moss-filled mattress. "How are we doing this?"

"As formally as possible. She's a military leader and a chief. She'll respond to formality and a sense of honor, even though it's going to piss her off to high heaven that we're making her do this."

"And pissing off an ally we need and a source of invaluable magic is a task you want to take on?"

"I told you, pissing people off is practically my job description." He slapped her bottom and spent a few pleasurable seconds watching it bounce. "I am becoming immeasurably fond of your bottom."

She laughed, which only made it shake more.

*Hmmm. Lovely.*

Meera said, "I'm glad you're fond of it, because it's unlikely to be leaving anytime soon."

"I find that reassuring." He stood. "Let's move. If you want me to do the talking, that wouldn't be a bad idea. Most of the magic she needs to teach is to you, so make me the bad guy."

Meera sat up and shook her head. "This could go so very wrong."

"All the best ideas can," Rhys said. "No point in dragging it out."

Rhys dressed in his last pair of clean trousers and a linen shirt he'd washed and hung up two nights before. It was still damp, but it would have to do. They'd only been in the swamp four days, but it was remarkable how much dirt a body could attract.

He anointed his hair with the sweet oil he'd found in the bathhouse the night before and combed it back before he rubbed some oil on the dark beard that had begun to cover his face. He glanced at Meera, who was watching him groom himself.

"I think you like beards."

She smiled. "I do. Most of the men in my life have worn them. It's traditional for the Tomir to leave their hair uncut."

He walked over to her and bent down, sliding his mouth over hers. "But do you like *mine, sha ne'ev reshon?*"

"I love it when you call me that." She brushed her hand over his cheek. "I do like your beard. And I like you without. Whatever you prefer."

"I prefer you." He kissed her once more before he turned back to the small mirror he'd hung on the wall of the hut. "For now the beard stays since I can't find my razor."

"It looks very nice." Meera stood and began unfolding a long linen cloth from her backpack. "Let us begin rudimentary fancy preparations."

"Is that a sari?" He smiled.

"It is, though quite a plain one. Just ceremonial robes. In my defense, I didn't know I would be greeting anyone formally."

"I've never seen you wear one."

"I like sundresses." She began folding the sari in hand-wide pleats. "But I always bring a sari for ritual occasions. Most of the time in Udaipur"—she tucked the pleats in the pants she wore before wrapping the length of linen around her waist—"I wear linen pants and a tunic because it's the most comfortable and people are very, very traditional there. But saris are nicer for formal occasions, and they're quite easy to travel with."

Rhys watched in amazement as yards and yards of fabric methodically became a garment. "Yes," he said. "Easy. That was the first word that came to mind."

Meera finished the wrap quickly, folding the fabric over her shoulder before she deftly arranged the remaining cloth around her waist and secured the garment with thick gold pins she pulled from her bag. She affixed two large gold hoops to her ears and coiled her hair onto her head with braids. In minutes she had gone from rustic traveler to elegant diplomat.

"Stunning." Rhys blinked. "Heaven above, that's quite impressive."

She smiled. "I'm no stranger to formal events."

No, he could see she wasn't. Her bearing had changed completely. She was regal. Arresting in her carriage.

*A queen.*

He'd teased her about being a princess, but in that moment, she was his queen. Rhys cocked his elbow out. "Shall we?"

"We'll both formally introduce ourselves," Meera said. "Then you offer the invitation. As the scribe to be mated, it would be your role."

"Very well."

They left the hut and walked across the mound to the garden where Ata was weeding corn. She looked up, frowned at them, but immediately came to attention.

Rhys stopped a few yards from the warrior and bowed. "Atawakabiche, elder singer and last chief of the Uwachi Toma, guardians of the Western lands and keeper of Uriel's fire, I am Rhys of Glast, son of Angharad the Sage and Edmund of Glast, heir of Gabriel's library, archivist and warrior of Istanbul."

Meera mirrored his bow, pressing her hands together in respect. "Great Atawakabiche, I am Meera Bai, heir of Anamitra, *somasikara* of Udaipur, daughter of Patiala, guardian singer of Udaipur, and Maarut, commander of the Tomir warriors."

When Rhys rose, he could see their formal introduction had accomplished its goal. Ata was standing straight, her carriage formal even if her eyes were suspicious.

"Honored brother and sister," she said cautiously, "how does heaven greet you, and how can my people be of service?"

Rhys glanced at Meera. Her eyes spoke to him although she remained silent.

*Do it.*

He turned to Ata. "Through heaven's blessing, we have found our *reshon* in each other and choose to honor the Creator through our mating ceremony."

Ata nodded. "I am pleased for both of you. I also believe you

236

honor the Creator, the Forgiven, and the first mothers by this union."

"Further, honored sister, we request the blessing of the Uwachi Toma at the ritual ceremonies to celebrate the union of our bloodlines and families. We will be traveling to Havre Hélène to formalize our mating and receive our family blessings, and we invite the chief of the Uwachi Toma to be the guest of honor at our mating celebration. Your presence would bring honor and blessing to our union as the Uwachi Toma were the first Irin to inhabit this land, granting it protection and Uriel's light."

Ata's eyes spoke volumes. She was furious. Confused. Furious. Impressed. But mostly furious. She hadn't even seen the attack coming.

"I was not expecting this… generosity," Ata said through gritted teeth.

Rhys and Meera both remained silent. Any argument at this point would only give Ata an avenue for refusal. The invitation had been made. It was up to the Wolf to refuse or accept it.

Refusal would be a formal insult to two prominent Irin clans who had never offered her any offense. Acceptance was the honorable answer, especially considering she was their host.

"It is my honor," she finally said, "to accept the blessing of your invitation." Her eyes locked on Rhys. "I only hope someday I can repay this consideration in kind."

Translation: *I will make you pay, and it will be painful.*

Rhys nodded. "We are honored, Atawakabiche. Would you grant us the distinction of escorting you to the haven?"

"I know where that old place is," she said, turning back to her fields. "Pack your things. I will lead you to your boat at tomorrow's first light. Then I will follow in four days' time. That should give you enough time to prepare for me and my retinue."

Rhys had absolutely no idea what her retinue would be. Alligators? Birds? He didn't question it. He bowed and turned to leave.

Meera stepped forward. "Thank you, Ata."

The old warrior turned and her eyes softened a fraction.

"Thank you," Meera said again. "It will mean so much to me and my family that you will be our guest. I hope you will feel welcome."

"The honor is mine, *Somasikara*. And as you honor me, I hope I will honor you by the favor I ask." Ata stepped forward and straightened her shoulders. "Three days after your mating, when your magic has been replenished, I ask that you take my memories —the whole of them—so that I may die and rejoin my mate. I want nothing more to do with this world. I want to rejoin my people."

Damn. Rhys watched Meera. It was a reasonable request—a favor for a favor—but everything in him rebelled at the thought. The Irina needed the Wolf. She could be a hugely valuable asset, a political force, a voice no one could ignore.

"Five days," Meera said quietly. "Five days after our mating—if you still feel this way—I will take your memories from you. All of them."

"Agreed." Ata turned back to her fields. Meera grasped Rhys's hand and walked back to the hut. Then she sat on the edge of the bed, and tears rolled down her cheeks.

---

THE NEXT MORNING Rhys and Meera had packed all their clothes and equipment along with some of the smoked fish Ata had dried and two large jugs of water. They pushed off through the bayou in Ata's boat, poling through the narrow channels until they reached a larger waterway.

It was not the way they had come, but Rhys found it just as confusing. If Ata's aim was to make her territory impenetrable, she was very, very successful.

She approached the pontoon boat from the far end of the river, but Roch had spotted them long before Rhys could see clearly through the mist. He was waiting on the edge of the boat.

"Welcome back," he said.

"I'm bringing your friends to you, old son. Have you discovered what you need to do?"

Roch shook his head. "I don't do well with riddles."

Ata said nothing. She reached for the edge of the pontoon and began tossing bags and supplies into Roch's boat.

"I don't speak in riddles," she said. "There is no hidden meaning. You know already what it is she needs. You do it already. Just... do more."

Roch's eyes reflected the grey clouds overhead. He shook his head and muttered under his breath, but he said nothing more. Without another word, Ata handed Rhys and Meera off to Roch like so much luggage. Then she turned and poled off into the misty swamp.

"And that was that," Roch said. "How was your trip, kids?"

"Interesting," Meera said. "And that is not that."

Roch looked Rhys. "What did I miss?"

"She's coming to Havre Hélène in four days," he said.

Meera pulled out the sat phone. "And my parents need to arrange a mating celebration before that happens."

Roch blinked. "Well, I do miss things when I stay on the boat." He started up the engine. "Let's get home. You can fill me in on the way, and I'll let you know what Bozidar and his little bastards have been up to."

---

"You want us to arrange a formal mating celebration in four days because you've invited the chief of the Uwachi Toma to be a guest in our haven?" Patiala rose to her feet and loosed her tongue on her daughter in a language Rhys did not understand.

But... he understood.

Maarut sat silently beside his mate, grimacing and trading uncomfortable looks with Rhys as Meera and Patiala argued.

The angry interchange stopped when Maarut stood up and

stepped between his daughter and his mate. "Enough," he said. "My love"—he turned to Patiala—"she's not asking for the pageantry of Udaipur. We both know she would never want that anyway. She is only asking for our blessing and song over her mating to this scribe whom, I will remind you, we selected for her."

Rhys frowned. "Selected?"

Maarut turned to Meera. "My beloved daughter, I am so happy you have found your *reshon*. I hope you understand that the facilities here are more rustic than those of Udaipur and thus the celebration will be more modest."

"That's fine," Meera said. "I'm not asking for anything elaborate."

"But you invited Atawakabiche here!" Patiala said. "A legend among Irina is the guest of honor at my daughter's mating celebration, and we have *no* retinue, *no* chefs, *no* staff, *no* guard—"

"We have all those things," Meera said. "Just not in the quantities we have at home. Think of this as a…" Meera turned to Rhys with wide eyes. "Destination wedding?"

"Yes. Excellent way of putting it." Rhys stood and put his arm around Meera. "And to be fair, the woman has been living on a very nice shell mound in the middle of the Atchafalaya Swamp for several hundred years. I don't think she'll be scrutinizing the menu."

Well, that wasn't a popular opinion with his new mother. "Is there anything I can do to help?" he added quickly. "I am at your service, Mother."

Calling her mother softened the hard-eyed look Patiala was giving him, but only for a moment. The next one, he was kicked out of the library with Maarut.

"Clean yourself up!" Patiala said. "And then clean this place up. We're having a banquet in four days."

Maarut turned to him. "I'm pleased my daughter has chosen you to be her mate. You should consider keeping the beard."

"I'm thinking about it. What kind of clothes am I going to need for this?"

"Since this is short notice, I'm sure Patiala will do a simple ceremony. Only three outfits for two feasts."

"That's the short ceremony?"

Maarut chuckled. "Talk to Chanak. He came with us from Udaipur. He and his mate are magic with needle and cloth. They will take care of you. I need to get to work on the property."

Rhys frowned and looked over the sweep of lawn, the green cane fields in the distance, and the graceful alley of oak trees that framed the house. "Honestly, this place is beautiful. What do you really need to do?"

Maarut gave Rhys a smile and a hard pat on the shoulder. Then, without another word, he walked around the corner of the porch and disappeared.

———

RHYS SAT on his small porch with Roch, watching the haven rouse into action. "This is mind-boggling."

"You should see the place at cane harvesttime. These women are demons of efficiency. I just shut up and do what they say."

Rhys turned away from the action. "Tell me what we know."

"More Grigori. They're quiet, but they're there. My contacts here called their contacts up north. Once we put it all together, it's pretty clear. We just weren't making the connections before. Bastard is making his way down the river. It's possible he's had people in place for years, lying low."

"Why now?"

"I don't know. Something changed. Maybe a new enemy? Maybe another angel has shown up in the area and he's feeling like he needs to flex his muscles or something?"

Rhys glanced across the lawn to Meera, who was walking with Sabine as they surveyed the sloping back lawn. "Is it her?"

"She's been here four, five years almost? I don't think it's her."

"But it's something." *A new Fallen in the area.*

*Vasu?*

Could the mere presence of the angel have put them all at risk? Meera said he'd just managed to find her. That he'd only recently shown up. Could that have tipped Bozidar off to an increased magical threat?

"What do we do?"

Roch leaned back and crossed his arms over his chest. "Right now? Nothing. Y'all decided to have a mating production that's gonna rival Mardi Gras. I got nothin'."

Rhys smirked. "Not your cup of tea, is it?"

"When I convince Sabine to take my mark, I want to sneak away and leave everyone behind. No company needed, thank you very much."

"Have you tried? Have you asked her to take your mark?"

Roch shook his head. "Man, I been trying for years."

---

OVER THE NEXT TWO DAYS, Rhys learned just what an effective military commander Patiala could be. She rallied her army of scribes and singers to create a paradise of flowers, draped tents, and colorful banners across the lawn.

Further construction on the guest house was halted, and finished rooms were cleaned and furnished to make room for Atawakabiche's retinue, whatever that ended up being. Simple cottages were decorated lavishly. The kitchen garden was roped off, and a fountain was erected at the base of the stairs leading off the back of the big house.

Rhys watched, gobsmacked, as Havre Hélène changed from a functional, beautiful home to something out of a movie set.

He walked hand in hand with Meera under the oaks where crimson banners hung in the trees. "How is this even possible?

Where are all these things coming from? How much more are they going to do?"

"To answer in order, money makes most things possible when you have a lot of it, which I do. Most of these things are coming from New Orleans." Meera looked up. "Though the banners are from the Tomir. One of my father's brothers flew in last night from Ahmedabad. And I have no idea how much more my mother has planned. For a woman of simple tastes, she also takes her responsibilities as guardian of the heir of Anamitra very seriously."

Rhys could tell she was moved and a little overwhelmed. "Everything is beautiful, Meera. I'm honored everyone is going to this trouble for us."

"It's not trouble to them, you know." Meera squeezed his hand. "It's a celebration. A continuance of Anamitra's line. The history of Udaipur's singers will continue for another generation, and the fortress will gain a new scribe and a new family alliance dedicated to its protection."

"It's because they love you." He kissed the top of her head. "It is all those things you mentioned, but it's also because of love."

She stopped and turned to him, closing her eyes and taking both his hands in her own. "Are you sure about this, Rhys? Are you *sure*? This is me. All of this is me. The ritual and the ceremony. The obligations and the responsibilities. Your life as you know it ends when you take me as a mate. We will be able to travel, but we will ultimately be bound to Udaipur, a place you have never even visited."

"It sounds beautiful. I hear there are lakes."

"Please, be serious. You need to know—"

"I know everything I need to," Rhys said. "I will be your partner, Meera. In all things. This is what we were created for."

She threw her arms around him and held him tightly. Rhys gripped her with both hands.

*Sha ne'ev reshon.*

*My beloved.*

He didn't want to lie to her. The ceremony and weight of responsibility were intimidating even if the celebration was a joyful one. The guest list had been the first surprise.

Rhys had been expecting only the scribes and singers already at the haven. After all, secrecy was still essential even if the chief of the Uwachi Toma was going to attend. But his mother and father were being flown in, which would make for an awkward family reunion considering they'd never heard their son mention Meera's name and they hadn't seen him in decades. Damien and Sari were flying in from Europe. Malachi and Ava had been invited, but since Rhys was gone, Malachi couldn't leave the Istanbul house unattended.

Rhys had no idea how many people were flying in from Udaipur. He'd stopped asking questions when the third massive tent went up behind the house.

Despite his nerves, he felt the love and joy permeating Havre Hélène even as he worried about the darkness spreading closer to the haven.

Rhys had called Zep that morning to check on Grigori activity at the scribe house in New Orleans. The news wasn't reassuring. Zep's information seemed to back up Roch. Attacks in the city had picked up, and nests of Grigori seemed to spring into existence fully formed. The human news called it a crime wave.

They had no idea what was really going on.

The scribe house in Houston had sent reinforcements, but no one seemed to be looking for the source of the problem. They were tamping down sparks without looking for the source of the fire.

The Fallen was on the move. Bozidar and his sons were pushing their way to the sea, eager to flex their power for some unknown reason.

And where the hell had Vasu disappeared to?

Rhys just hoped he and Meera would be able to finish their mating ceremony and learn and practice the magic they would need before danger reached their door.

# CHAPTER TWENTY

M eera stood for the fitting, her arms spread out, the shell of the silk tunic folded and fitted around her as singers fluttered like cheerful birds in her room. Despite the happy buzz of energy, she longed for the quiet peace of her garden off Frenchmen Street, longed for a morning cup of coffee and conversation with the old man on the corner playing a harmonica.

It felt like the beginning of the end.

She didn't blame Rhys. She didn't blame anyone really. Her job —the whole reason she had come to North America—had been to research the magic and language of the Uwachi Toma and record as much as possible. She had recorded many of Ata's songs, studied her language, and agreed to take Ata's memories after her mating ceremony. After that, her mission would be complete.

She'd been frivolous in New Orleans, spinning out her days of enjoyment and neglecting her duties. Vacation was over.

"Sisters," Patiala said, entering the room. "May I have a word with my daughter?"

Cora, the seamstress making her dress under the direction of Chanak, their tailor from Udaipur, stepped away from her and removed the remaining pin in her mouth. "I have all the measurements I need, young lady. This is going to be fun. I haven't worked in silk for centuries."

The American singer had been an accomplished seamstress and literally worked magic with a needle back in the golden years of New Orleans's Irin elite. She'd been delighted to create formal gowns and outfits with Chanak and his mate, Bhama. The three artists had been working around the clock to outfit the haven with dresses, suits, and other finery.

Meera adored Cora and had insisted that the haven seamstress make her dress instead of taking Patiala's offer to have mating clothes and jewelry flown in from the treasury in Udaipur.

All the singers who had been hovering left Meera's room, leaving Patiala alone with her daughter.

"You're not happy," her mother said.

"I'm just a little tired."

"Is it Rhys?"

"No," Meera said with a smile. "I am so pleased with Rhys. You were right about him, and I was being stubborn. He is truly a wonderful man."

"He is your *reshon*." Patiala's eyes were shining. "Daughter, I would never have even dreamed of this blessing. So why are you still unhappy?"

"I told you—"

"I know you." Patiala walked over and kissed both of Meera's cheeks. "I know my daughter."

"I'm worried about the threat to the haven. Bozidar may be coming. We don't need to be having a party right now."

"Do you think we're any less ready for an attack because we're throwing a party?" Patiala looked offended. "Daughter, you know me better than that. What's really going on?"

"Are we going back to Udaipur after this ceremony?"

Her mother's expression smoothed into practiced calm. "Do you want to do that?"

"Ata has agreed to share her memories with me. All of them."

Patiala's eyes went wide. "Has she? Does she know—?"

"She knows I am *somasikara*. She sensed it immediately. She wants to give me the whole of her memories. Everything. She wants to be released from this life so she can die and join her people."

Patiala let out a long breath. "Have you agreed to this?"

"I have."

"You'll need to wait until after your mating. Magic like she is asking—"

"Will be exhausting. I know. But I'll be mated to Rhys when it happens. I'll be able to draw from his magic too."

"This time line concerns me, Meera. A mating ceremony while there is a threat against the haven is… troubling. Asking you to do a memory spell while we're still under threat—"

"Maybe Ata knows something we don't."

"That's possible."

Meera could tell her mother wasn't convinced. "She has martial magic, Mata. Powerful spells I'll be able to teach to other singers. While I don't anticipate using that magic, I do see the necessity of it for now."

Patiala smiled. "So the storehouse of Irina martial knowledge will reside in the memories of a staunch pacifist? Surely the Creator laughs."

"I would never withhold knowledge my sisters needed."

"No, but you'll be cautious distributing it, won't you?" Patiala took a deep breath. "Perhaps that is as heaven would want. We don't know what kind of magic she wields. Whatever it was led to five hundred years of peace on this continent, the longest stretch any of our people have gone without war. So perhaps it is wise to hold this knowledge close."

"Five hundred years of peace," Meera mused. "I can't imagine such a gift."

"But every gift has a price, doesn't it?" Patiala tucked a long lock of Meera's hair behind her ear. "We don't know what the price of that peace was. Has she spoken about the Fallen-slaying magic the legends talk about?"

"She said only that peace was achieved by making the Fallen very afraid."

Patiala's gaze turned inward. "What do the Fallen fear?"

"Nothing. Not as far as we know. But I do not doubt her magic."

"And only a mated pair can perform this magic?"

"I only know Ata's mate was a part of whatever spell killed Nalu. Akune, her mate, is dead, though Ata says she'll be able to teach Rhys what magic he needs to perform just like she can teach me."

Her mother's eyes shone. "So my daughter would become an angel-slayer with the heavenly blade of her voice."

Meera kept her shoulders straight. "Yes."

"Another burden."

"Knowledge is never a burden."

"What an incredibly stupid thing to say." Patiala spoke sharply. "Of course it can be a burden. Knowledge is the greatest burden there is, and you've been loaded down with it since before you could speak."

"Mata—"

"This is why you are unhappy, isn't it? It isn't the responsibilities of mating or the man you've chosen. It's the weight of more knowledge. More magic."

Meera said nothing. What could she say? It was arrogance to say a gift was too heavy. It felt ungrateful.

"I wish I could bear some of this for you," Patiala said. "But I am not you. I cannot keep the knowledge as you can. I wish I could."

"Hopefully Rhys and I can teach the magic to you and father. After all, mated warriors would be the natural practitioners of magic like this."

"We would be grateful. We would use it wisely." Patiala squeezed

Meera's shoulders. "Speaking of mated warriors, when do Damien and Sari arrive in New Orleans?"

"Tomorrow morning."

Patiala smiled. "You and Rhys should go into the city tonight. Stay at your house. Rest and spend some time away from here."

Meera frowned. "There is still so much to do."

"Nothing we can't handle. Go. Enjoy your house. Have some fun. Go dancing."

Meera hugged her mother. "Thank you."

"And to answer your earlier question, we go back to Udaipur when you want to return, *Somasikara*. Your retinue follows you, not the other way round. Being Anamitra's heir has enough responsibilities. You need to take advantage of the privileges when you can."

---

RHYS DROVE her car back to New Orleans, and Meera tilted the passenger seat back, left the windows down, and reveled in the feeling of the soft breeze threading through her hair. Not even the creepy smile and wave from the old man by the river could spoil her mood. That morning he was wearing a red baseball cap. Was it her imagination, or had he looked younger than the previous week?

She was imagining things. She had to be. They had checked the old man. He was human. Just a human. She closed her eyes as she turned her face to the sun and breathed deeply.

"I love to see you like this," Rhys said.

"Lazy?"

"Relaxed." He reached for her hand. "I don't think anyone would ever call you lazy."

"I feel like I'm going on holiday."

"Sometimes going home can feel like that. I spend plenty of time for my work traveling. I know what you mean."

She turned to him. "Where is home for you?"

"Ah…" He scratched his beard. "England for a long time, even though I didn't like it much. Now Istanbul mostly feels like home. And once we're mated, you'll be my home."

"A person can't be a home, Rhys."

"Of course they can."

"We all need roots, and you—"

"You're worried about me living in Udaipur because I've never been there. I'm telling you it won't be a problem."

"It's very formal. And the level of ceremony is oppressive. And the history—"

"I know all that." He reached for her hand again. "I know it. And when it gets oppressive, we'll run away for a bit."

"Are you going to be bored?"

His eyes went wide. "Heaven above, of course not. I've heard about the library there. I can't even imagine being bored. What are you talking about?"

Meera smiled and brought his hand up to kiss his knuckles. "You're perfect for me. I'd be irritated that my mother was so right, but I'm too pleased."

"I just want the stress of all this to pass so we can get back to focusing on what we're both after." He steered the car toward the highway.

"Memorizing the other forty scrolls of magical congress?"

Rhys nearly swerved off the road. "You blasted woman."

She took off her sunglasses and blinked innocently. "What? That wasn't what you were thinking?"

"I was thinking about finding more biscuits and gravy, but I like your suggestion more."

———

THEY WALKED DOWN FRENCHMEN STREET, hand in hand, enjoying the spill of music in the night air and the buzzing crowd that had drifted over from the French Quarter. It was Wednesday night in the Faubourg Marigny. Not too busy. Not too quiet.

Meera loved the energy. She always had. She felt buoyant. Light.

She almost overlooked the shadowed presence on the edge of Washington Square.

She stopped in the middle of the street and turned.

Rhys, who'd been listening to a brass band on the corner, came to attention. "What is it?"

"Vasu."

He grimaced. "Won't that damn angel—"

"Stop." She held up her hand. "Something is different." She dropped Rhys's hand and walked toward the sidewalk surrounding the park. Artists were packing up their canvases for the day and tourists walked hand in hand, but Meera's eyes were locked on two huddled figures on the sidewalk.

She walked over to them.

Vasu looked up, his face swathed in rags and his appearance changed to the face of a grizzled old man. "Did you forget me?"

"Of course not. Vasu—"

"What power have you been tempting, Meera Bai?" His voice was guttural and harsh. His elbow nudged the old homeless man sitting next to him. The man toppled over sideways, and the hat fell from his head, revealing grey skin and a blank, dead stare.

Vasu became a shadow when a pedestrian noticed the dead man and screamed. Rhys grabbed Meera's hand and melted back into the gathering crowd. Meera heard the squawk of a police radio and two dogs barking.

She felt them before she saw them. Four Grigori making their way through the crowd, cold eyes locked on Meera and Rhys.

*What power have you been tempting?*

"Grigori," Rhys said, taking Meera by the elbow. "I think Bozidar is in the city."

"But why? Why now?"

"Maybe you should ask your friend Vasu!" He hustled her up Elysian Fields and cut through the neighborhood, taking the back way to her house. "Maybe it has nothing to do with him. But maybe it does."

"The Grigori are still behind us," Meera said.

"I know. Dammit, I don't want them following us home."

"Find me an alley," she said, nearly running to keep up with his strides. "An alley, a warehouse. Somewhere deserted. We need to question them."

"Fine, but my pacifist tendencies died with the human in the square. These aren't lost souls looking for redemption. These are Bozidar's soldiers, and that was a Grigori kill."

"I know." She'd seen the look of twisted ecstasy on the human's face. Only Grigori could make a human happy to hand over their soul. "Find me an alley, Rhys."

They turned to the right on Burgundy Street, walking against traffic as they passed newly renovated shotgun houses on the right and boarding houses on the left. There was little traffic, but lights were on in most of the homes, and Meera could hear televisions and phone calls in the residences around them. She could also feel two more Grigori join the four that had been following them.

They passed an old church on the left, its doors boarded up. Rhys ran past, then stopped and ran back.

"Here?"

"A church?"

"It's empty."

He reached up and tore off the boards covering the front door, tossing them to the side before he grabbed Meera's hand.

"Once we aren't running from Grigori, I'm going to swoon properly over that manly show of strength," Meera said.

Rhys shot her a smile over his shoulder. "And I will properly appreciate your swoon."

They ran into the shadowed church, and Meera nearly tripped over a curled-up edge of carpet.

She muttered a quiet curse.

"Don't Irina have spells for night vision?" Rhys asked.

"Yes, but it's not something I'm very good at." She whispered a different spell, and six sconces down the center aisle sprang to life and glowed with a steady gold light. "I'm quite good at that one though."

Rhys's eyebrows went up. "Handy in libraries."

"Exactly. No flame, just light."

The church had been the target of vandals, and spray paint was scrawled over many of the walls, but the pews and the altar seemed to be in good repair. Meera hoped someone was caring for it, but she didn't sense any humans nearby.

The Grigori, on the other hand, had surrounded them.

Two entered by the front door, and Meera heard two coming from a back door she couldn't see.

"Four," Rhys muttered. "What happened to the other two?"

"Never a good feeling."

The Grigori had surrounded them now. The four circled Rhys and Meera along the edges of the sanctuary.

"I'm going to have to let these bastards get close to you, aren't I?"

"If you want me to find out what they want? Yes."

A long string of curses in the Old Language was the only response Meera got.

The men came closer, and Meera whispered a spell and allowed her magic to flood out. She spotted the first Grigori who felt it.

The knife he'd been holding dropped from his hand, and he cocked his head and locked his eyes on Meera, ignoring Rhys entirely.

"Rob, what's your problem?" one of the Grigori asked a second before he felt Meera's power too. Meera heard his knife clatter to the floor.

Rhys, on the other hand, seemed unaffected by the spell. Since it was a spell to entrance an enemy, it shouldn't have had an effect on him, but nevertheless, Meera was grateful he remained on guard. Sometimes magic like this unintentionally leaked over.

Four Grigori were walking toward her like she was a magnet. Meera forced herself not to panic. She knew Rhys had his daggers out. His control was impeccable.

"I'm here," he murmured as they drew closer. "Relax."

"Okay." It was difficult, even knowing she was in control. "Stop," she told the men.

They stopped.

"Kneel."

They knelt.

There. That was better. Meera let out a long breath. She hadn't forgotten about the other two Grigori, but she had confidence Rhys was keeping an eye out for them. She couldn't sense them when her magic was this high, though she knew every Grigori in the neighborhood was going to be drawn to it.

"Who do you belong to?" she asked.

"Bozidar," they said in unison. The chorus of voices made Meera's skin crawl. Their audible voices were vibrant and smooth, at horrible odds with their soul voices, which scraped against her mind like nails on slate.

"Why are you here?"

"The city is ours," one said.

"The city is ours," another echoed.

"Fresh hunting."

"Rich with souls."

"We will drive out the other."

*Who was the other? Was Rhys right? Was this about Vasu?*

Rhys spoke when Meera lost her voice. "When is Bozidar coming?"

"Our father is here," they said together.

One of them added, "Our father will take what the great Nalu lost."

"Bozidar wants to take over North America," Meera said. "He wants to control it the way Nalu did."

"Nalu?" one of the Grigori asked.

"The archangel killed by the Wolf."

"The Wolf no longer hunts," one of the kneeling Grigori said. "We are the hunters now."

Rhys stepped toward one. "Tell me where your father hides."

The Grigori looked up at Meera. His face was pained. She knew he was fighting a strong compulsion.

"Tell me where your father hides," Meera repeated, reaching for the man's outstretched hand. "Tell me and I will give you some of my power."

The man let out a long breath. "He hides on the river where the water bends to—"

A shot rang out and a spray of blood puffed near the Grigori's eye a moment before he fell to the ground.

Meera turned to the left to see Rhys already lunging toward the fifth Grigori on the edge of the room. She was distracted and almost didn't hear the metallic cocking of the gun to her right.

She turned, dropped to the ground, and shouted, *"Ya fasham!"*

Meera heard the Grigori and the gun clatter to the ground, but the spell holding the three remaining Grigori around her had been broken. The men shook their heads and blinked as if coming out of a dream.

Meera crawled between the pews toward the Grigori with the gun. She'd unbalanced him, but the spell only lasted so long. She needed to get the gun.

She heard quiet scuffling on the other side of the church and a strangled cry before the scuffling went quiet. Meera didn't stop to think or look. Rhys was a skilled warrior. Four Grigori were probably very little trouble for him, but Meera wasn't accustomed to so many surrounding her at once without guards. She could hear one scrambling along the pew next to her. She spotted the gun sitting on the tattered carpet just as she saw a hand reaching down toward her.

She rolled to her back, grabbed the arm and pulled it toward her, slamming the Grigori's nose into the back of the pew before she sank her teeth into the man's forearm.

"You bitch!"

She reached for the handgun, and the cool metal touched her fingertips. She hooked her finger around the trigger guard and spun the gun into her hand, sweeping her arm up and pointing it at the Grigori whose blood was spraying over her from a broken nose.

Without hesitation, Meera aimed the gun at the center of the man's chest and pulled the trigger. The shot hit her target and he fell forward, his shoulders hanging over the back of the old wooden bench.

Meera scooted under the pew, rolling toward the incapacitated Grigori before she pushed herself up and peeked over the benches.

Rhys was in the center aisle, a Grigori clutched by the hair, his dagger flashing down as golden dust rose around him in the flickering light.

She saw a movement to her right. It was the first Grigori she'd knocked over.

"*Domem man!*" The man froze.

Rhys ran to her, leaping over the pews and reaching for the man she'd shot. He was already beginning to rouse himself. Gunshots couldn't kill Grigori unless they pierced the spine. Rhys grabbed the Grigori by the shoulder, flipped him over, and slammed his silver knife into the back of the man's neck, releasing his soul for judgment.

"You all right?" he shouted.

"One more." Meera didn't have knives and she didn't particularly want any. Violence, even necessary violence, made her ill. But she was profoundly glad when Rhys walked over and finished off the Grigori who'd almost shot her.

Rhys reached out and took the gun from her hand. "Are there wards around your house?"

Meera nodded.

"Then let's go." He hooked an arm around her neck and kissed her forehead. "Let's go before more come. We need to call Roch. This is far worse than we thought."

# CHAPTER TWENTY-ONE

"*He hides on the river where the water bends to—*"
The Grigori had died seconds before he could reveal anything important. Rhys wondered if that was the exact reason two of the soldiers had hung back. Did Bozidar know what Meera could do? It was an unnerving thought.

*Vasu knew.*

Suspicion licked at Rhys's mind, but he didn't want to accuse the angel. Not unless he was sure.

He knew Meera was always going to be a target, but he felt wholly unprepared to guard her on his own, even in her cozy house with all the wards refreshed. He'd called the New Orleans scribes and asked them to patrol the neighborhood for the night, though he'd avoided telling them exactly where Meera's house was.

He was becoming nearly as paranoid as Damien and Gabriel. He trusted no one but his brothers. He wished he could spirit Meera away to Istanbul or pack her off back to Udaipur.

Something very big and very bad was coming, and it wasn't paranoia if they were really after you.

"Rhys." Meera slid a hand along his shoulders. "Calm down. No one is going to get through mine and my father's wards. I don't even feel anyone close."

*What about Vasu?*

"It was too close in the church," he said quietly.

She sat across from him at the small kitchen table while a pot of soup simmered on the stove. "Don't do this."

He wiped a hand across his forehead. "Then tell me how I'm supposed to react."

"You're supposed to have confidence that I can defend myself." Her voice was low and steady. "You're supposed to remember I'm a very powerful singer with defensive spells I'm well practiced with. That I was born of and trained by two warriors and have good situational awareness."

"He almost shot you. I didn't even sense them."

"That's partly a consequence of the spell I was using, and I should have warned you about that," Meera said, rising to check the soup. "It's geared toward Grigori, but it can have a muddling effect on Irin as well. You'll be more aware next time."

"Next time?"

She turned to him with a grave expression. "You won't lock me in that fortress. I won't allow it."

Twin instincts battled in his heart. He wanted to protect her desperately. For the first time he truly understood scribes who had wanted to lock their mates up in retreats before the Rending.

*If she was guarded.*

*If she was away from danger.*

*If if if...*

"I would give you anything," he began. "But Meera—"

"Stop before you make a very big mistake." She turned off the stove and stepped toward him. "I have agreed to take you as my mate, not my keeper. I have no keeper. I have no master." Her voice vibrated with barely controlled anger. "And I will never take one. Not even one designed by heaven. So stop that train of thought before it even starts, Rhys."

"You've been a target your entire life. You're going to be an even bigger target once you become the librarian of Irina martial magic." He stared at her. "Don't you have any fear at all?"

"Of course I do, but if you're wondering about tonight, no. I wasn't afraid in the church. I don't operate like that. I would be afraid if I didn't know what to do, but I did know what to do." She turned back to the stove. "Also, Vasu didn't even show up, so you know I wasn't in any real danger."

The angel suddenly appeared, sitting on the counter and swinging his legs. He looked like a teenager again. "That's true."

"You." Rhys gritted his teeth. "Is he going to just show up like that everywhere we go now? Like an annoying stray cat? What do you know about this angel, Vasu?"

Vasu slid off the counter and shifted into a large gold-and-black striped tiger before he padded to Rhys and bared his teeth.

Meera kicked her foot back, making the tiger grunt and turn. "Stop. Don't be annoying, Vasu. This house is too small for that form."

The angel shifted into a medium-sized cat with grey and ochre markings Rhys thought might have been a clouded leopard. The leopard sat on the table in front of him, flicking an ear and staring.

Meera shoved him. "Go away. You're just trying to annoy him now."

Vasu bared his teeth. Rhys bared his right back. Petulant? Perhaps. The angel was acting like a child, and Rhys had suspicions.

"What do you know about Bozidar?" he asked the cat under his breath. "Is this you? Why is he showing up now?"

The leopard said nothing.

"What are we going to do about Damien and Sari?" Meera asked.

"Pick them up in the morning and take them back to the haven," Rhys said. "At this point I'm relieved they're coming. They've fought more angels than anyone else I've known, and Damien wields a black blade."

Meera nodded. "Good. That's good."

Rhys could feel her sorrow like it was sitting under his skin. "Meera, I know you hated what happened back at the church. I know you're not eager for conflict. But think of it this way—if we can kill Bozidar, we free his children."

The tension in her forehead relaxed. "I hadn't thought about it that way."

"This angel has thousands of children scattered across this part of the world. Free from his influence, many of them might choose to live peaceful lives. Fighting and killing this angel could free thousands." And rid the world of one of the most vicious angels in history.

"Vasu?" Meera called.

The angel appeared in his teenage form on the counter again. "Yes?"

"Do you know this angel, this Bozidar?"

The young man swung his legs. "A little."

*Liar.* Rhys could see it in his face. The angel was hiding something. *What a surprise.*

Meera asked, "And? What do you know? Is he an ally of yours?"

"No." Vasu shrugged. "Kill him. I have no loyalty to him or any other Fallen."

"He's not an ally?"

Vasu laughed. "Bozidar doesn't have allies. He has minions. He only aligns himself with others until they're not useful to him anymore. Then he usually kills them." The angel watched Meera from the corner of his eye. "His death would sorrow no one, not even his human consorts."

Rhys narrowed his eyes on Vasu. "For once I agree with him." *But why do you want this angel dead?*

"Fine." She reached up to a shelf where she grabbed three bowls. "Then we're all in agreement. We must kill this angel."

Rhys saw the look of triumph in Vasu's eyes, but Meera's back was turned.

*What are you about, troublemaker?*

Not that he objected to killing Bozidar. Rhys had been telling the truth. Killing the angel would free thousands of Grigori and *kareshta.* That was purely good.

But there was nothing pure about the expression on Vasu's face in that moment.

"Vasu," Meera asked, "are you staying for dinner?"

Rhys glared at the Fallen and shook his head.

Vasu turned to him and smiled. "I would be delighted, Meera Bai."

---

DAMIEN AND SARI were standing on the edge of the sidewalk at the airport in the morning, two tall and lethal sentinels in a river of unsuspecting humans. Damien's long hair was twisted at the back of his head, and Sari's blond hair flowed around her shoulders. They were both wearing sunglasses and had a foot on their luggage, watching the cars that drove past.

Rhys pulled up in Meera's compact and crawled out of the driver's seat. "You two look like European rock musicians."

Damien frowned. "I don't know what that's supposed to mean." He put his hand on the small of Sari's back. "We tried to pack light, but it is a formal mating celebration, so we brought more than usual."

Sari hooked an arm around Rhys's neck. "Congratulations, brother. I'm so pleased for you. Meera is an incredible woman."

He opened the trunk of the car and loaded Sari's suitcase. "Slight change of plans for your visit. Still doing a mating ceremony with all the formalities and rather epic food, but we're also hunting and killing an archangel while you're here."

Damien looked up from his phone. Sari visibly perked up.

"Interesting," she said. "That's much better than formal dinners."

"Oh, I'm quite certain we're not getting out of the formal dinners," Rhys said. "We'll just be wearing weapons while we eat."

"Bozidar?" Damien threw his suitcase in the trunk and climbed in the back seat. "Malachi mentioned growing activity in your reports, but there wasn't any mention of the angel himself."

Rhys got in the driver's seat while Sari sat across from him. They quickly merged into the exiting traffic from the airport. "Meera and I were followed last night. The Grigori who attacked us said Bozidar was already in the city."

"Anything more than that?" Sari asked.

"I think Vasu has orchestrated all this, but I'm not sure why."

"Him again?" Damien muttered. "That angel needs a hobby."

"He's oddly attached to my mate," Rhys grumbled. "Future mate. And she doesn't hate him, so I'm making an effort not to throw daggers at him when he shows up."

Sari smiled sweetly. "Rhys, I never thought I'd see the day you were mated. I was quite certain you were too cranky for any woman, but I can see Meera has softened you."

"Do be quiet, or I'll sic Meera's annoying angel on you."

"Yes," Damien said. "I see the glow of love around him. An almost Zen-like peace. It's extraordinary."

"Listen," Rhys said. "You both just came off a plane, so I know you're not armed. I've been itching to stab something since last night. Please, *please* give me an excuse."

Sari looked over her shoulder. "He's really got that diplomatic mindset now, doesn't he? He's going to do so well in Udaipur."

"Almost as well as you do in Rěkaves, my dove."

Rhys smiled. "And how is your mother-in-law, Sari?"

"Probably as well-armed as yours." She scratched his cheek. "You should keep the beard. I hear they're all the rage in Udaipur."

"Tell us more about Bozidar," Damien said. "What has prompted this move?"

"I don't know anything for certain, but Roch—one of the scribes in the haven—has been getting reports from various scribes scattered around this area. There are quite a few brothers not attached to either the Houston or the New Orleans house, and they've been noticing growing activity for a few weeks. Which, according to Meera, was right around the time Vasu found her here in the US."

"If this is some conflict between two Fallen, why are we getting involved?" Damien asked.

"Because we don't know for certain if that's the reason," Rhys said. "Bozidar might simply see an opportunity. A city with no real watcher and a rich hunting ground of tourists. It's to the New Orleans scribes' credit that the city has been peaceful so far. They don't get many attacks."

"Or do they and they're simply not noticed?" Sari asked. "New Orleans has had several natural disasters in the past twenty years, has it not?"

"That's a good point. The city has a large tourist and transient population."

"So this problem may have been growing for some time, just going unnoticed by human authorities."

"Anything is possible, but activity has definitely ratcheted up in the past few weeks, and I don't think it's a coincidence."

"You always were a suspicious one." Damien tapped him on the shoulder. "Causing problems wherever you go."

"If my watchers would give me more peaceable assignments, I might take a vacation." Rhys glanced in the rearview mirror. "Why did you send me here, Damien? Was it to find the Wolf, or was this an elaborate matchmaking scheme?"

"Are you complaining about the results of either?" Sari asked. "As far as I can tell, you've found a legendary warrior with a trove of Irina martial magic, discovered your *reshon*, and will probably kill an angel before this is all finished." She clapped his shoulder in a friendly pat worthy of a heavyweight wrestler. "All in all, one of the most successful missions we've ever orchestrated."

"That did not answer my question." Rhys glanced in the

rearview mirror, but Damien had his eyes on Sari, watching her with a smile.

"Take us to meet your woman," he said. "We'll plan for battle in the morning, but tonight we should celebrate."

———

MAARUT HAD DRIVEN into the city to take Meera out to the haven, so Rhys drove Damien and Sari to the edges of the wards, passing the old house at the bend of the river. The old man was gone, but a dog perched on the edge of the porch. His tongue hung down and his tail wagged as Rhys's car drove past.

Patiala greeted them at the edge of the wards with a wave from the back of a small four-wheeled vehicle they used on the farm.

"Sari." She dismounted from the four-wheeler and walked over to embrace the taller woman. "Gabriel's fist, it's so good to finally meet you in person."

"My friend, I am full of joy for you and Maarut."

Patiala smiled at Rhys. "It was a good recommendation. I knew they would be suited from what you said, but to be her *reshon*... It was far more than we could hope for."

"Well, that settles that." Damien nodded. "You and Meera were definitely set up."

"So you're feigning ignorance of this?" The corner of Rhys's mouth turned up. "I can't be angry. Could you?"

"Considering how many matings my mother tried to arrange for me, I want to say yes, but she's your *reshon*, brother. There is no greater happiness on this earth."

Sari climbed back in the car after a quiet exchange with Patiala, then with a softly whispered spell, they drove into the haven, Rhys shrugging off the now-familiar feel of old earth magic that guarded the property.

They drove under the oak trees, now even more decorated with colorful banners and flowers. Someone had created a spell that made tiny gold petals fall from the trees on either side of the alley.

"What joyful magic," Sari said with a smile. "Rhys, this is stunning."

"Are you regretting our quiet mating in Norway, my love? It was nothing like this." Damien chuckled. "Had we gone back to Rěkaves—"

"There would have been ceremonies for days," Sari said. "Rhys, one of the *sabetes* found her mate last fall. She was the eldest instructor and Katalin insisted on a full mating celebration for her."

"The castle and village were partying for a week," Damien said.

"Over a week," Sari added. "Nine days for the formal celebration."

"It was fun."

"It was a lot of work," Sari said. "And all the children had special dances during the feast."

When Sari or Damien talked about the Grigori children they were fostering at Rěkaves, their manner changed completely. They *doted*. That was the only word for it.

"Well, I have a feeling that pomp and ceremony will be my good friends going into the future," Rhys said. "My mother will find all this most amusing."

"Are they here yet?"

"They arrive tonight."

He pulled the car up to a field that had been designated for vehicles and got out, searching for the woman at the center of the maelstrom. He saw Meera on the back porch of the house, talking with her father.

Heaven above, he adored her.

"And when does the Wolf arrive?" Sari asked.

"She said four days, which would be tomorrow morning," Rhys said. "But how she's arriving is a mystery to everyone but her." He glanced at the two scribes hustling toward them with a wave. "I think these gentlemen will take your luggage to the cottage Patiala set up for you. Let's go meet Meera."

He walked across the lawn, marveling at all the decorations. Flowers and fountains seemed to have sprung up like magic—they probably *had* sprung up by magic—and the heady scent of freesia filled the air.

"Rhys!" Meera spotted him and broke into a huge smile. "You're earlier than I thought you'd be." She ran down the steps and into his embrace. "Traffic must have been easy."

There. Safe. Surrounded. He let out a huge breath, not failing to notice the three new Tomir warriors who had joined Maarut on the porch. They had come for the mating celebration and decided to stay at Maarut's request.

Rhys was decidedly in favor of that. Meera, less so.

"*Sha ne'ev reshon*." Rhys kept his arm around Meera. "This is my former watcher, Damien, and his mate, Sari."

"We are also his friends," Damien said, taking Meera's outstretched hand and bowing over it. At the first touch of his hand to Meera's, Damien looked up with wide eyes. "*Soma...?* Does he know?" Damien glanced at Rhys.

Meera nodded. "He does."

Damien looked at Sari. "Did *you* know?"

She smiled softly. "Some secrets are not mine to tell, my love. You know this."

Damien let out a long breath and fell to his knees before Meera. Tears filled his eyes. "Forgive me. It has been over seven hundred years since I have been in the presence of a keeper."

"Rise, brother. I am just a woman."

"No. You are much more than that." Damien rose and wiped his eyes unashamedly. "Does the light still burn in this house, sister?"

"It does, and you are welcome to its light, you and your own."

Damien bent and kissed both Meera's cheeks reverently. "I am honored to be here, both for my friend and to meet you."

"As I am honored to meet you." Meera smiled up at Rhys. "My *reshon* speaks very highly of you."

"I find that hard to believe considering how headstrong he's always been. Rhys of Glast is the absolute worst kind of scribe to command. Stubborn. Arrogant. Filled with a vast well of self-importance—"

"I think you mean confident in my own opinions." Rhys pulled Damien away from Meera. "I'm almost sure that's what you meant to say."

Sari pursed her lips. "No, I'm fairly sure I've also heard him say—"

"Aren't you tired and needing to freshen up?" Rhys asked. "Let's go feed you. Maybe then you'll stop talking."

"Oh no." Meera linked her arm with Damien's. "Please, tell me more."

---

RHYS WAS SLEEPING that night when he heard the knock on his cottage door. He rose and rubbed his eyes as he opened it.

Maarut was standing at the door. "Dress in your linen clothes. Patiala says the Wolf is at the border of the wards."

Without another word, Rhys nodded and combed his fingers through his hair. He dressed hastily in the ceremonial linen tunic and trousers, walking barefoot out of the cottage and onto the grass. He followed the line of torches, not to the formal alley that led to the river, but back to the vast sugarcane fields at the back of the property. He could hear drums beating in the distance and the sound of foxes howling.

Ata's retinue?

Rhys found Meera in the predawn light and took her hand as the sound of drums grew closer. They knelt on the grass with Patiala and Maarut on one side, Rhys's parents standing quietly on the other.

Angharad and Edmund had arrived late in the night, only a few hours before, and he'd barely greeted them before they'd begged for sleep, but seeing his mother and father that morning, dressed in the linen robes he remembered from his childhood, he was utterly grateful they were there. They were meeting a legend of Irina history, a warrior come back from the dead.

Scribes and singers filled the lawn, many holding torches to light up the pathways. Others held heavy ropes of flowers to greet their guests. Roch and Sabine were standing to the side, hand in hand, and Rhys was pleased to see Sabine's expression was serene.

Meera squeezed his hand. "Are you ready?"

"Are you?"

"Yes." She smiled at him, and he saw a bright blue stone sparkling at the crease of her nose.

"That's new."

"Not new, I just don't wear it often. Do you like it?"

Rhys smiled. "I love it."

"I do too."

They turned back to the cane fields where the sound of drums was growing louder. Rhys's heart pounded with them, with the power he felt permeating the ground.

*Such strong magic.*

The wolves emerged first, their silver-grey coats glowing in the moonlight. Five of them leapt out of the fields, circling before the gathered scribes and singers before the largest wolf lifted its head and howled. They sat in a semicircle at the edge of the fields, wild sentries waiting for their commander.

The foxes came next, their bright red fur vivid against the green of the fields and the grass. Their green eyes shone in the darkness as they ran back and forth, sniffing the ground and the people gathered.

A few moments later, two drummers emerged from the fields, one male and one female, holding wide drums they beat with bone clappers. Their tattoos were different than Ata's and reached from their toes to their forehead. The sides of their heads were shaved and tattooed, and the rest of their hair fell down their back in a fountain of long black braids.

Their clothing was made of linen, as all Irin ceremonial clothing was, but instead of white, it was a vivid purple styled into long-sleeved tunics secured by elaborate, inlaid belts.

"Dene Ghal," Meera whispered. "Native Irin from the north and the west."

Two singers crossed to the drummers and scattered red flower petals at their feet.

"She invited guests." Rhys was thrilled and a little intimidated by the power he felt from the man and the woman. "Where did they come from?"

Meera shook her head. "I know a large community of Dene Ghal still lives in the Pacific Northwest and Canada, but it's a very spread-out group."

The drums kept on, unceasing, and Rhys heard more footsteps coming through the fields. The Irin who emerged next would have stopped the fiercest Grigori in their tracks. Four spear bearers, three male and one female, stepped forward. The scribes were tattooed with familiar-looking *talesm,* but the woman bore no tattoos. Her rich brown skin glowed in the torchlight.

Both the men and the woman wore crimson linen, their robes pinned at the shoulders with elaborate gold brooches. More gold was threaded through their hair, which was twisted in intricate coils and ropes around their heads. The spears were also gold and the handles were carved and painted brightly.

"Koconah Citlal," Meera whispered. "Irin from the south. Related to the Uwachi Toma. You could think of them as distant cousins."

Four scribes stepped forward and held out necklaces of red flowers. The Koconah Citlal warriors inclined their heads and allowed the flowers to be placed around their necks.

Finally, flanked by the four spear bearers and the two drummers, Ata emerged, but she barely resembled the simple woman they'd met in the bayou.

She was still bare from the waist up, but paint had been added to her tattoos to create a stunning pattern of color. The linen she wore around her waist was bright yellow and secured with a gold belt. And on her head was a tall crown of gold feathers radiating in a half circle reminiscent of the rising sun.

Atawakabiche, last of the Uwachi Toma and Painted Wolf of the Western Lands, was in every inch of her bearing a queen and a warrior.

She walked with a gold spear in her hand, and elaborate ceremonial armor wrapped around her lower legs. Her foxes circled her, yipping excitedly, and the drummers and spear bearers beside her bowed their heads as she passed.

As she approached them, Rhys and Meera rose. Her eyes still held the edge of fury, but her voice was utter politeness.

"Does the fire still burn in this place?" Ata asked in the Old Language.

Meera answered, "It does, and you are welcome to its light. You and your own."

Patiala stepped forward, handed Ata a rope of flowers, and bowed. "Atawakabiche, sister of Uriel's blood, you honor my family with your presence. We have prepared the guest house for you, or a comfortable tent if you would prefer."

Ata looked around at the warriors and animals who followed her. "I think whichever option is closer to the outdoors for my animals."

"We will prepare the tent."

"Thank you."

Ata spotted Sabine and Roch on the edge of the lamplight. She walked over without a word and stood in front of Sabine. Then the fearsome woman leaned forward and whispered something in Sabine's ear before she turned back to Patiala and Maarut.

Rhys exchanged a glance with Meera, but he had no idea what

might have been said. Sabine's expression was frozen. Roch only looked confused.

Patiala and Maarut grabbed torches and led the visitors to the largest of the tents, an elaborate structure lavishly decorated with silk cushions, large mattresses, and rugs Patiala had pulled out of storage.

"Damn," Rhys muttered. "I was hoping they would choose the house."

"So you could move into the tent?" Meera asked.

"Have you seen inside? It's smashing."

The guests of honor departed before the sun breached the horizon, and the scribes and singers of Havre Hélène retreated to their beds. Roch and Sabine drifted away before Rhys could find them and ask what had passed between them and Ata.

He took Meera's hand in his, eyeing her Tomir guards. "Come to my cottage, just for a few hours. I have a feeling today is going to be hectic, and I'd love some time for just the two of us."

She melted into his chest. "That sounds amazing." She waved her guards away and slipped her arm around Rhys. "We're going to have to steal the time when we can."

"Don't worry. I've spent several hundred years perfecting the ability to be sneaky."

"I know. Damien and Sari spilled all your secrets."

"All of them?"

"A badger, Rhys?" She shook her head. "Honestly, what were you thinking?"

# CHAPTER TWENTY-TWO

M eera sat in the library with Roch, Damien, Sari, and Rhys. "Go over what we know," she said. "And tell us what Ata said to Sabine, if that's within your rights to tell."

"What passed between Ata and Sabine doesn't relate to any of you," Roch said. "But I need tonight to myself. I'll make our excuses to Patiala."

"It's the welcome feast," Meera said. "The whole haven will be there. We'll miss you, but if you need time, take time."

"Thank you."

Sari said, "Why has killing Bozidar become a priority? He's existed in North America for centuries. Irin have had their skirmishes, but by and large, he's kept a lower profile than most Fallen."

"The lower profile has also allowed him to grow in numbers and strength," Rhys said. "We were talking with Zephirin—one of the New Orleans scribes and a friend of Meera's—about what they know and what kind of resistance is in place."

"Is there anything?" Damien asked. "If he's alive, his sons are still under his control."

"If he even knows they exist," Meera said. "Zep says there is already a contingent of Bozidar's sons who aren't free of him, but they aren't loyal either. They're rebels who've escaped his attention. Flying under the radar, so to speak. They don't make trouble. He forgets they exist."

Roch said, "He does have a *lot* of children."

"Daughters?" Damien asked.

"A few," Rhys said. "But there is no organized protection for *kareshta* like Kostas has developed or what's happening in Thailand. It seems that most of Bozidar's female offspring are simply abandoned. They wouldn't have any idea who they are."

Sari shook her head in disgust. "Those poor girls."

Meera continued. "These rebels have been tracking Bozidar's movements for the past decade. He's increased his numbers, spread his influence. He's been slowly working his way down the center of the country from Chicago."

Roch said, "He's counting on infighting between eastern and western Irin communities, and he won't be disappointed. There's no love lost there." Roch stared across the room. "He's moving down the river. Splitting the continent in two. I bet he's got his eye on Houston."

Sari asked, "If he wants Houston, why would he be in New Orleans?"

"A flank attack," Roch murmured. "The Fallen would see New Orleans as the soft belly of Houston. Less guarded. More lazy."

"The scribe house in New Orleans isn't lazy," Meera said.

Rhys said, "Maybe not. But I wouldn't call them vigilant."

"They haven't had to be." Meera spoke up in their defense. "They try to keep the peace. If a Grigori isn't causing problems, live and let live."

"Except," Roch said, "this angel is using that peace-loving attitude to lull them into complacency." The scribe rolled out a map on the library table. "I've identified as many new nests of Grigori with Zep and his Grigori associate as I possibly can."

Meera had to admit she was shocked. There were far more red markers on the map than she'd expected. Like the New Orleans scribes, she'd been lulled into thinking lack of deaths meant lack of Grigori. It clearly wasn't the case.

Nearly two dozen red areas were highlighted, most in the industrial zones of the city. Warehouses, abandoned apartment complexes, and condemned houses.

Sari asked, "Have you looked into unremarkable deaths?"

Meera asked, "Unremarkable deaths?"

Sari said, "Grigori trying to remain hidden often feed from the homeless and the poor, who usually don't have good medical care. Particularly the homeless. Humans might die unexpectedly, but their deaths will be attributed to liver failure, heart attack, or some other consequence of poor health, not anything unnatural."

"I've checked into it," Rhys said. "Higher than normal, but not enough to raise any human alarm."

"There could be an epidemic of Grigori," Damien muttered, "and it wouldn't raise human alarm."

"Right now we can't do anything about the human deaths except to recommend upping patrols," Roch said. "Which the scribe house is already doing. I don't know how much further we want to drag them into your plans, but if you want to keep the haven hidden—"

"We want to keep the haven hidden." Meera didn't even want to think about telling her mother she'd revealed the location of Havre Hélène to Zep and his brothers, who would immediately report it to their watcher in New Orleans. "We can do this on our own."

Rhys nodded. "Fine. We have resources."

Meera leaned over the map. "So what do we do? What is the plan?"

"He knows you're here." Vasu appeared in the corner of the room.

In unison, Damien and Rhys muttered curses and flung silver daggers in the direction of the voice. The Fallen disappeared and the daggers embedded in the toile-covered wall.

Roch shouted, "What was that?"

"Will you stop?" Meera asked. "My mother is going to murder you all if you ruin her library. Vasu, what are you doing here?"

Roch pointed at the angel. "Is that what I think it is?"

Vasu appeared behind the scribe. "Yes," he whispered. Then he disappeared again and reformed standing behind Sari.

"Don't"—she raised her staff when the daggers pointed her direction—"even think about it. Vasu, you pain in the ass, don't make me hurt you."

All weapons were lowered, though the temper of the room remained high.

"Explain yourself," Meera said.

"No," Rhys added, "explain what you mean about Bozidar knowing we're here. Explain why this is all happening *now*, Vasu! What have you done?"

"Me? Nothing. What makes you think this is my fault?" He turned to Meera. "Bozidar knows about Havre Hélène. He's known for years."

"So why—"

"He can't be bothered." Vasu waved a careless hand. "Or… the wards are too strong. Or he knows you'd kill too many of his sons before he could do anything. Something like that." The angel sat on the library table and swung his legs back and forth. "This table is sturdy."

"He knows the haven is here?" Meera felt her stomach drop. The singers. The children. The hidden ones.

"Why now, Vasu?" Rhys wouldn't let up. "If he couldn't be bothered before, why now?"

"Maybe… he likes parties." The angel grinned.

Meera's mind was spinning. "Rhys, what are we going to do? He knows we're here."

Rhys didn't answer, but Meera saw him having a wordless conversation with Damien and Sari. There were raised eyebrows, frowns, and head shakes.

"You have a veritable army coming to your mating ceremony," Damien muttered. "It could work."

Rhys said, "If he's coming anyway—"

"He wouldn't be able to resist." Damien shook his head. "I see your point, but I can't be a part of this decision. It's not my haven to protect. What you're thinking carries a lot of risk."

Meera tried not to lose her temper. She hated being left out of the conversation. "Tell me what you're talking about."

"There are warriors in this haven," Rhys said quietly. "Legendary heroes."

Sari let out a long breath. "Wow. That is... bold."

Meera knew enough about how Rhys's mind worked to imagine what he was thinking. "You're suggesting we somehow tell Bozidar that the Painted Wolf—the last warrior of the Uwachi Toma—is here and... what? Use her as bait?"

"I could tell him," Vasu said. "I'd be happy to tell him."

Meera rounded on Vasu. "Is this why you've been poking your nose in all this? Because you've been wanting to draw Bozidar into a fight?"

"Bozidar is a vile, ugly creature with a self-inflated sense of his own importance," Vasu said. "He engenders no love anywhere, not even among his allies. They are squabbling, petty, power-hungry sycophants with no higher purpose than the satisfaction of their own squalid appetites."

Roch said, "So... he's an angel."

The Fallen grew several feet, his presence filling the room as power poured off him. "Are you comparing *me* to Bozidar? My people once worshipped me as a *god*. Do you know who I am?"

*Well*, Meera thought, *this has the potential to get very ugly.*

"I know who you are," Rhys said. "You're a Fallen with vendettas and no army. How did Bozidar offend you, Vasu? What made you decide to use Meera and her family for your own twisted purposes?"

"She was mine before she was yours, scribe."

"I don't *belong* to either of you, so stop fighting." Meera stepped between Rhys and Vasu. "It doesn't matter anymore."

The room was silent. Not even the angel spoke.

It didn't matter. Meera looked at Vasu with no illusions. She knew he wasn't her ally or protector. That role belonged to the man at her back who was fighting for her at that very moment. Rhys was her ally. Rhys was her protector.

Vasu was... Vasu. It was entirely probable that her *reshon* was correct. Vasu had drawn this attention. Vasu had caused this conflict.

"It doesn't matter," she whispered. The angel was coming and he had Havre Hélène in his sights. "Vasu, am I correct that you think you can draw Bozidar to the haven? You and he are clearly not friends."

"I'd hardly have to crook my finger." Vasu smirked. "Bozidar will do anything if you flatter him. He lives for it. He was voted Most Easy to Manipulate in the heavenly realm."

Meera blinked. "Was that... a joke? Did you make a joke on purpose?"

"Are you saying I make jokes accidentally?"

Meera couldn't think of a single thing to say to him that wouldn't lead to far more conversation than she wanted. She turned to Sari. "What do you think?"

The other singer raised her eyebrows. "I think nothing. It's not my haven. But if you're asking what I would do, I'd speak to your mother first. She's the one tasked with guarding this place. I wouldn't even dream of revealing its location to one of the Fallen—"

"He already knows," Vasu said. "I told you."

"—without full knowledge and permission of the elders here," Sari continued as if Vasu hadn't spoken. "If Patiala is in favor of this plan, then talk to Ata. She's not alone anymore. She has allies. The Wolf might want the chance to slay Bozidar herself. She's done it before."

Damien said, "And if you decide to go forward, you have both of us with you. You know that. What I don't have is my black blade."

Rhys asked, "You came here unarmed?"

"I came for your mating feast, dammit! Some vacation this is turning out to be."

---

MEERA TOOK a deep breath and clutched Rhys's hands. "So I'm going to go in there, tell my mother and father that one of the Fallen has been my... associate—"

"Friend seems too generous."

"—for most of my life, that he knows our location has been compromised to another one of the Fallen, and that we could potentially draw said Fallen to the haven by revealing the location of a legendary warrior, who is staying in my parents' house as a guest at our mating celebration."

"When you string it all together like that, it does seem like an incredibly bad idea," Rhys muttered. "Maybe lead with having discovered a way to kill an angel and free hundreds of Grigori and unknown numbers of *kareshta* from the influence of the Fallen."

Meera nodded. "Good. I like that."

"But they're going to be upset about the Vasu thing," he said. "There's no getting around that. You should probably leave out our suspicions that he goaded Bozidar into this fight."

"This is Anamitra's fault!" Meera said. "It's not like I found Vasu on my own. I... inherited him."

"Maybe mention that too."

She squeezed his hand again, then entered the tent where her mother was directing the cooks for the dinner that night. The scribes and singers of the haven had been gathering food for days. Though the guest list wasn't large, the feasts would still be elaborate.

"Mother," Meera called.

Patiala looked up and smiled. "Hello."

"Can Rhys and I speak to you and Father for a moment?"

"Is everything all right?" She frowned and glanced at their joined hands.

"We're fine," Rhys said. "It's about the larger issue we've been talking to Roch about."

With a businesslike nod, she followed them out of the cooking tent. "Your father is in the fields." She pulled out her phone. "I'll call him and tell him to meet us."

Rhys led them to his cottage and cleared off two chairs so Patiala and Meera could sit. Maarut joined them a few minutes later, and Meera gathered her courage.

"So," she began. "Rhys and I are fine and very happy with our mating celebration so far. We're looking forward to everything. But talking with Roch and the scribe house in New Orleans has clarified some of the problems the city is facing, which might explain what happened the other night in New Orleans."

Maarut nodded gravely. "I have a few questions."

"That's understandable," Rhys said. "You might have more before this conversation is over."

---

MEERA HAD SEEN her mother angry. She'd thought she'd seen her shocked. It was nothing compared to the utter and complete silence that greeted her after she'd outlined the problem the haven was facing.

"And how long," Patiala said, her voice measured, "has this... creature been known to you?"

"When did I go to live with Anamitra?" she asked.

"When you were three."

"Since then," Meera said in a quiet voice. "You have to understand, Anamitra told me that Vasu was a secret only the two of us could know. That he was useful and he would not harm me."

Maarut nearly choked on his anger. "And you trusted him?"

"When I was young? Yes. To a degree. As I grew older, I saw what Anamitra did. Vasu was odd, but also oddly loyal to those who entertained him. Anamitra and I entertained him. We were interesting to him. And he offered information and perspective at times. I wouldn't call him a friend—"

Patiala let out a very loud expression of disbelief.

"—but he was useful. And he seemed to be able to find me wherever I was. He found me here, even with the wards. But it would be years sometimes between visits. Often he'd come and tell me stories for an afternoon, then be gone for a year. Other times it seemed he was living in my pocket."

"Kind of like now," Rhys muttered.

"And when did you learn of this?" Maarut asked Rhys.

"Not long after Meera and I began working together. But Vasu was known to me before. He was an ally of Jaron, who was the grandsire of my watcher's mate. He feels a certain... proprietary interest in Ava. So far it's an interest that has served her. But I'm always watchful."

"Rhys throws daggers at Vasu nearly every time he shows up. Don't blame Rhys for this."

"Good," Patiala said. "It's good this... *thing* isn't too comfortable with you. He shouldn't be, no matter how long you've been familiar with him."

"I understand your concern," Rhys said. "Trust me, I share it. But so far Vasu *has* given us valuable information. And he hates Bozidar, which is why we've come to you. If he says Bozidar knows the location of the haven—"

"He won't be able to enter it," Patiala said. "The wards here have been built for centuries. Sabine renewed them just before our guests arrived. Despite her mental state, her earth magic is very strong, and we've been able to channel it into the land here."

"He isn't able to enter it," Meera said. "Vasu confirmed that. Not unless..."

"Unless what?" Maarut said.

"Not unless we let him in."

Maarut and Patiala looked at Meera with twin expressions of incredulity.

"Hundreds of Grigori," Meera said. "Possibly hundreds of *kareshta*. All those souls locked to his power. If he were dead—"

"You're assuming we can kill him." Patiala said. "But though he is an enemy of your Vasu, he's still an archangel. Who here has slain an archangel?"

"Damien has," Rhys said quietly. "I have experience fighting one. And don't forget Atawakabiche. She, more than any of us, would know how to slay this monster. She killed Nalu. She could help us kill Bozidar."

"You said her magic only worked with her mate."

"But she still holds knowledge."

"Rhys and I," Meera said. "Rhys and I will be mated soon."

"But you're not mated yet," Maarut said. "And you won't be at full strength after you mate. The bond needs time to develop and mature. You don't understand what it's like."

*But don't you realize...?* Meera thought about interrupting, but she wasn't sure how much she could actually explain to her father. No one beside Anamitra understood her power.

Maarut shook his head. "This is a ridiculous conversation. We didn't invite Atawakabiche to our home in order to ask her to fight a battle. It's the height of arrogance to even speak of this. I will call for my brothers and the Tomir—"

"They could take weeks to gather," Meera said. "Ata is here now. We could draw him out now. How many more humans have to die before we act? We have a gathering of warriors unlike this haven has ever seen."

"Is this my daughter?" Patiala stood. "The pacifist? The singer who wants to find a peaceful way? Are you searching for war on the eve of your mating? I don't even recognize you."

"Even I acknowledge the better way cannot happen without

freedom from the Fallen," Meera said. "There can be no hope of negotiation or change until Bozidar is dead."

"I suppose I should thank you." Patiala turned to Rhys. "She's finally being realistic about our enemies. The day before her mating feast!"

Rhys raised his hands. "I'm only—"

"Don't blame Rhys for this," Meera said. "And don't blame Vasu. We are coming to you because you're the guardians of this haven and I see an opportunity to rid the world of one of the Fallen. One of the most dangerous. Bozidar has grown quietly in power and now presses into the territory where this haven sits. If we succeed, we could usher in a new golden age, like the one Ata started when she and her mate killed Nalu. But ignoring Bozidar, even for our mating ceremony, accomplishes nothing."

Patiala stormed out of the cottage and Meera started to follow her, but Maarut put a hand on her arm. "Don't. Give her some time. Let her think. She's angry right now."

Meera looked at her father. "You know we're right about this."

"I also need time to think." Maarut stroked his beard. "If we try this thing, the Tomir would still be useful. You know our reputation for secrecy."

"How fast could they get here?" Rhys asked.

"Two days," Maarut said. "A group of the guard are always ready to be summoned."

"Call them."

Meera glared at him, but Rhys only shrugged. "Call. It's never a bad thing to have backup, and I trust your father's men to be discreet."

"I'll call." Maarut rose and kissed Meera on the cheek. "And I'll talk to your mother. Just so you know, the welcome feast will still go on tonight and you'll still be expected to attend. I do not want any mention of this to get to Atawakabiche until your mother decides. She's the haven guardian. In the end, it's her call."

"And I'm the heir," Meera said quietly. "I'm sorry, Father, but in the end, it's actually my call."

"Careful." He gave her a half smile. "This isn't Udaipur. The hierarchy here isn't quite so settled. You push and you might find yourself facing a not-so-minor rebellion."

———

THE FEAST that night began with much ceremony and little conflict. Meera watched, her heart full, as the singers of Havre Hélène joined Patiala to sing a blessing over Meera and Rhys. They sat at low tables under the oak alley where the Tomir banners—written with her father's spells of protection—fluttered in the breeze coming off the river.

Rhys's mother rose and gave a formal blessing from the library of Glast, praising their hosts and the legacy of Atawakabiche. Meera hadn't had much time to spend with her quiet mother-to-be, and she got the feeling that, outside of formal duties, Angharad would be someone she needed to meet in a smaller setting.

"Do you think we'll have time to visit Glast soon?" Rhys asked quietly during a break in the speeches. "My parents tend to be very stiff at events like this, but I promise they're not completely without senses of humor."

"I'll have to take your word for it. Your father looks like a meter stick has been glued to his back," Meera said. "I've never seen posture so straight."

"A stick glued to his back... Yes, that's a much more diplomatic expression than the one I usually use."

Meera elbowed him in the side.

"Ow. You're small and mean, future mate."

"You love it."

Atawakabiche, the guest of honor, was quiet throughout the evening, though the various members of her retinue talked and socialized with the other singers and scribes of the haven. The

Koconah Citlal from the South were decided fans of the spicy North Indian and Creole dishes. The Dene Ghal—a brother and sister from Washington State—were wonderful storytellers.

The wolves and foxes stayed back in the tent.

Meera noticed a large raven sitting on a low branch of the oak tree nearest the river.

*Vasu.*

It hopped and croaked every now and then. Meera wasn't the only one who noticed. The woman from the Koconah Citlal leaned over to Ata, who was already watching the bird. They exchanged quiet words before the Koconah Citlal singer wandered over to Meera.

She greeted Meera and Rhys formally before she leaned in close. "I do not mean to alarm you, but do you know an angel watches you?"

"Yes," Meera said simply. "It's… complicated."

"It can enter the haven?"

"He can."

The woman nodded silently before she departed and went back to Ata's side. They exchanged a few more words before Ata turned to them. Her eyes were narrowed and thoughtful.

"She knows something is brewing," Rhys said.

"She does."

Rhys leaned over and plucked half an apricot from Meera's plate, feeding her as he whispered in her ear. "Wake tomorrow morning, go out to the cane fields, and sing the rising song she taught you. I'll come with you. If she wants to talk to us without all the formality, that will give her a chance."

"Good idea." Meera took a piece of melon from Rhys's plate and took a turn feeding him. "What a smart scribe my *reshon* is."

"The very smartest," he said around the bite. "Heaven above, Meera Bai, how *did* you get so lucky?"

"I love you," she blurted.

The teasing light fell from his eyes. "Meera—"

"I mean, I *think* I love you. I…" She looked down, ignoring the festivities going on around them. "This moment was chosen poorly. I have been feeling… this *feeling* since the night we were first together in the bayou. I was resisting it because I didn't want my emotions dictated by fate. Or my parents. Or… anything really."

"You don't love me because of fate," he said roughly.

"No, I love you because you're the one man who is a match for my mind, my body, and my heart. And I am the same for you."

He fought against a smile. "Must you be *such* a know-it-all? Even now?"

"I'm only telling you things you already know."

"Exactly."

Meera asked, "So why are you arguing with me?"

The smile broke through. "Because you're infuriating."

"I am infuriating because I'm right."

He slipped an arm around her back. "I love you."

"I love you too."

"Blasted woman."

"Heaven picked me. Blame heaven."

"Never." He leaned over nipped her earlobe. "You are my mate, Meera Bai. Tomorrow and for the rest of time."

# CHAPTER TWENTY-THREE

Rhys rose before dawn. The land around him was silent save for a few night birds calling.

What had woken him?

*Meera.*

He felt her before he heard her. He rose and walked to the door, opening it just as she crossed from the kitchen garden to the cottage path.

Though he made no sound, she looked up.

*Reshon.*

It was a piercing joy every time he saw her. He wanted her so much it nearly made him resentful. He'd never experienced anything like it. It was far more than lust. Far more than affection. It was need wrapped in adoration with a healthy dose of possessiveness.

*She loves me. She is mine.* And the aching sweetness of the complementary realization. *I am hers.*

She ran the last few steps to the cottage, a pale pink nightdress clinging to her ankles, its edges soaked from the grass.

"Meera." He whispered her name and she put a finger across his lips.

*Shhhh.*

He didn't hear her voice in his mind. It was nothing audible. But the hair on his arms stood as he touched the edge of her magic, and her thoughts became his own.

*I want to show you. Before we see her, you need to know.*

Rhys drew her into the cottage and shut the door. He wrapped an arm around her waist and lifted Meera up, pressing his mouth to her forehead, her cheek, her lips.

*You should know.* She kissed him again before she pressed her forehead to his. *I think I can show you.*

"I'm not imagining it. How do you do that?"

*Later.*

He closed his eyes as their lips met over and over again. Raw need gripped him, but he tuned every sense to Meera. Her scent. Her touch. The gentle brush of her thoughts against his.

Without thinking, he touched his *talesm prim* and felt his magic come to life. It wasn't a conscious thought, but he knew she needed him to be open.

*I can show you.*

*Show me,* reshon.

Rhys felt his magic wake, like the slow stretch of a sunbeam crawling across the floor. Each spell woke with a hum, the oldest first.

Long life.

Understanding.

Perception.

Concentration.

The *talesm* he'd inked during his training to help him focus.

Meera slid to the floor in front of him, gently guiding Rhys to the small sofa in the corner. She pressed him back into the seat and straddled him, never letting their lips break apart. His magic grew and grew.

Vision.

Strength.

Speed.

His training as a warrior.

The spells had reached his right shoulder when they became more intricate. More personal.

The rising spell of Chamuel's blood, the spell his mother taught him, woke in him with a jolt. He spread his palms wide, and Meera pressed their hands together, palm to palm. But instead of the murky sense of knowing and glimpses of memory he usually received from this magic, a door broke open in his mind and Rhys stepped through.

*This is what I can show you.*

A memory. It was one of Meera's memories.

An old woman sat on a cushioned stool near a trickling fountain as a child with flushed round cheeks chased a pair of peacocks around a flower-strewn garden. The little girl ran after the birds only to turn and let the birds chase her. There were peals of laughter, and the old woman sang a soft song.

*Guide them with your mind,* the woman sang in the Old Language. *Let them play and dance. Teach them to follow you and they won't stand a chance.*

It was a game. Meera's mind was joined with his. He could feel her utter joy as the birds chased her around the garden. He could also feel a shadow in the magic the little girl didn't sense.

It was more than a game, it was training.

> *Let them play and dance.*
> *Teach them to follow you.*
> *They won't stand a chance.*

Rhys didn't hear the old woman's thoughts, but he knew she was Anamitra, *somasikara* of the Eastern Irina, keeper of memories and Sage of Udaipur. And Anamitra was teaching the little girl to control the minds of the birds with her song.

He didn't just see or hear the memory. He felt like he was there.

It was hot, far hotter than his cottage in Havre Hélène. The air wasn't misty and soft, it was dry and tinged with the earthy smell of baking bread. He could feel the sun toasting his skin. He wasn't just seeing or hearing the memory. He was living it.

*I have brought your mind with me.*

*What does this mean?*

Meera's lips broke from his and Rhys blinked slowly. The dawn was still breaking and Meera straddled his lap, her soft hands playing with the fine hair at the back of his neck. A gentle smile played across her lips.

"What does it mean?" he asked.

Meera whispered, "This is what I can do. With my magic and your blood—"

"We can be in a memory together."

"Yes."

Rhys's mind went wild with the possibilities. "And after we're mated?"

Meera's gaze turned inward. "Anamitra once told me that Firoz walked with her through memories that were too painful for her to bear alone. Perhaps he had Chamuel's blood too."

"The Tomir are Uriel's children."

"So…" Meera shrugged. "I don't know, Rhys. We'll only find out after we mate."

Would Rhys be able to see the treasury of Irina memory as Meera did? Experiencing that memory with her was like touching the edge of the sea. He knew a vast depth stretched beyond her, but he could only see ripples on the surface.

Meera climbed off Rhys's lap, straightening the gown he'd shoved up to the juncture of her thighs. Rhys watched with displeasure as her legs were hidden behind the thin cotton fabric.

"I haven't had you in days," he said bluntly. "It's been too long since your taste was in my mouth."

"You'll have me tonight," she said. "And the next night. And the next."

Their mating feast was tonight. After that, Rhys and Meera would be left in solitude to perform their mating ritual, tattoo their magic, and cement their bond while her parents' guests continued to celebrate without them.

Rhys was profoundly ready to have Meera to himself.

"Is it wise," she asked, "to continue with this while Bozidar approaches?"

"We're stronger together."

"But not at first."

"That's the common wisdom. Judging by what I just saw, I'm not certain the common wisdom holds for us."

She held her hand out. "Come with me. I have a rising song to sing."

---

He watched her from the edge of the field as Meera sang facing east, the rising sun just below the horizon. The song that Ata had taught her was simple and beautiful, a quiet melody that blessed the morning and welcomed the Creator's magic onto the land and into the hearts of those who dwelled in it.

It was completely beside the point of her magic, but Meera's voice was lovely. It soothed Rhys's mind and soul.

It wasn't long before Ata was standing next to him. Gone was the ceremonial dressing. She was the simple, powerful presence he'd come to know in the bayou.

"She remembers." Ata's eyes were on Meera.

"She remembers everything." And he was just beginning to grasp the weight of that burden.

"Why did you call me here?"

Rhys turned to her. Ata was a direct woman, and he'd offended her with his machinations to draw her from her sanctuary. The least he could do was honor her directness with his own. "We needed to be mated to learn the magic used to kill the Fallen, but I didn't want Meera to miss the blessings of her family so that I could accomplish my goal. Bringing you here—"

"Forcing me here."

"—blesses our union. We'll also be able to learn the magic we need. That's why we brought you here, and I'm sorry I wasn't more forthright from the beginning. We could have asked you."

Ata shrugged. "I would have refused."

"I know. That's why we didn't ask."

The edge of a smile touched her lips. "I don't want to like either of you."

"But you do."

"I like you a little. Her?" Ata motioned to Meera and shook her head. "I cannot. I honor her. I admire her. I need her. I cannot like her."

Rhys's heart broke a little, wondering how many times and in how many ways that same sentiment had been expressed to Meera. "I don't know if I understand that."

"She is the living embodiment of our victories and our failures," Ata continued. "Our lives and our deaths. She holds all memories, scribe, not just the good ones. The *somasikara* exist in a direct line from the first singers. They are our mirrors and our reminders." Ata turned to him. "No one can be friends with their true reflection. It is too painful."

Rhys couldn't take his eyes off her. "The Irin have nothing like this, so I can only understand a little. I just want to protect her. Love her."

"The scribes have no such thing because you write your memories into stone and onto skin, etching them into strict control. But the Irina?" Ata shook her head. "Our memories live and breathe like our magic. We are our memories."

"Which is why we need yours. Now more than ever."

She frowned. "Tell me bluntly. Does it have to do with the Fallen?"

"Not the one you saw." Rhys took a deep breath. "Bozidar approaches. Meera and I want to kill him."

"Bozidar is an archangel."

"Yes, like Nalu."

"And he's in the city?"

"We think so, but he knows where this haven is. We need to draw him here and kill him."

Ata lifted her chin and pointed it east. "Why not hunt him in the city?"

"Among the humans? We can't count on a shield of protection around us like we had in the Battle of Vienna. No angel fights with us in New Orleans."

"What about that one posing as a raven?"

"He's... unreliable," Rhys said. "At best."

"He's an angel." Ata said nothing for a long while. "How would you draw Bozidar to the haven?"

Rhys smiled. "We have something he wants."

Ata's nostrils flared. "You cannot use the *somasikara* as bait."

"I wasn't thinking about Meera."

The warrior understood immediately. "Me?" Ata nodded. "Yes, Bozidar has likely wanted me dead for a very long time. He might hope I am dead, but in his heart he knows I am not."

"Have you fought him before?"

"Yes. He was there when my mate was killed. He didn't kill him, but he was there."

Meera finished the rising song, lowering her arms and relaxing into a lotus pose, her fingers lightly skimming the drying grass.

"Her parents would be shocked and horrified I'm even bringing this up to you. You're a guest here."

"I'm a warrior. I understand using the resources at hand, and I am a resource. Still, I don't know how you think you're going to kill him. As far as I know, you don't have an army wielding black blades, and that's likely what you'd need."

"Or just a singer who knows what she's doing."

293

Ata's face hardened. "I told you. That magic can only be performed by—"

"A mated scribe and singer." He reached out his hand as Meera walked toward them. "After tonight, we will be."

Meera smiled and tucked herself under Rhys's arm. "We are your willing students, Ata. We want to learn."

Ata cocked her head. "You think the two of you can perform your mating ritual tonight and learn my magic the next morning? That's not the way this works."

"Why not?"

"You can't learn magic that quickly. It needs time. Connection."

Meera asked, "Even for me?"

Ata nodded deeply. "Even for you. I mean no disrespect. I speak nothing but the truth."

"I can learn it. I'm telling you. Rhys can learn it too."

"Eventually."

"Immediately. Other singers can't. I can."

"No." Ata shook her head. "The other pair perhaps. The warriors from across the sea. The tall blond woman and her mate. I might be able to teach them."

"Fine." Rhys put a hand on Meera's arm when she began to protest. "That's fine. But you can teach us at the same time."

"You won't be able to learn."

Rhys said, "Maybe not, but we are willing to try."

Ata's expression was blank for a long time. "Fine," she said. "I will teach you. Then you will take these memories from me, *Somasikara*, so that I may die."

"Ata—"

"You have already agreed to this." Ata turned and started to walk away. "I expect you to honor our agreement."

———

"IT'S TIME." Maarut and Damien held the veil in front of Rhys's face as they stepped barefoot across the flower-strewn path leading to the banquet.

The unveiling was last of the formal rituals he had to perform before he could claim his mate. The linen veil represented division between singer and scribe. Letting it fall when his mate stood before him was not only symbolic of union between male and female but led to many a foolish-looking scribe. Everyone loved taking pictures of the tongue-tied man in awe of a beautiful woman.

Rhys refused to be that scribe.

He had seen Meera looking sultry in a jazz club, sweaty and bug-covered in the middle of the bayou, and just plain naked more than once. As beautiful as he found the woman, he wasn't mating with her for her looks. He wasn't a scribe to be struck dumb by beauty.

They came to stop on the gold-petaled path. He could hear whispers and laughter beyond the veil.

"Brother, are you ready to behold heaven's beauty?" Damien asked quietly.

"Of course." Rhys smiled indulgently as the veil Maarut and Damien held before his face fell away.

And he froze.

*Heaven above, I am not worthy.*

Rhys ignored the chuckles and whispers. They no longer existed in his world. Meera did, and she had rendered him speechless.

She was adorned in rich red silk that hugged her curves and fell to her toes. Her hair was twisted in an intricate halo and threaded with gold. Gold dusted the lids of her eyes and painted intricate patterns over her hands, arms, and shoulders.

And her eyes.

Heaven above, he was not worthy of the emotion he saw in them. She watched him with dark, kohl-lined eyes, a soft smile on her lips.

*She loves me. She loves me.*

"*Reshon.*" Meera reached up and touched the corner of his eye. "There is only joy tonight."

Rhys blinked away the tears, too happy to be embarrassed. "I am in awe, *sha ne'ev reshon.*"

"Take my hand, Rhys," she whispered. "We have a banquet to attend."

"And then you're mine," he said. "For three days, you are mine alone."

A dark blush touched Meera's cheeks. "For three days, you are mine."

He bent down and whispered, "But there are at least forty more scrolls. We have our research cut out for us."

"In only three days? Are you sure you're up for the task?"

"I am. Uncomfortably so."

Meera threw back her head, and her joyful laughter led them into the banqueting tent.

---

"You're staring at me again."

"Yes." He would stare at her forever. Nothing in the pageantry before them even remotely competed with a single fold of his beloved's dress.

Meera's cheeks warmed with color. "You have to watch, Rhys. They went to so much trouble for this."

A line of a dozen singers danced lightly over a carpet of bright yellow flower petals as Patiala sang a soaring anthem praising Uriel for long and blessed life. Patiala's own mating marks glowed with power as she sang the traditional song woven with personal touches only a mother would add for her daughter. A few moments were funny. A few were sad. All were unique, and Rhys couldn't help but be thankful that Meera had pressed him to wait for this.

He would remember this night for eternity.

They sat on a platform covered with flowers while singers

played beautiful music and scribes danced. The contingent of Tomir warriors Maarut had called bowed to them before performing a dangerously beautiful spear dance that set Rhys's warrior heart racing.

There were speeches and songs, toasts and dances. The meal started with delicate bites that Meera and Rhys fed each other while guests came up to the platform to visit and bring gifts.

Damien draped around their shoulders a long silk scarf embroidered with blessings from the scribes at Rĕkaves. Sari brought an intricately carved wood and mother-of-pearl chest from Istanbul filled with a dozen different teas and another similar chest filled with spices.

Rhys's parents, clearly anticipating future grandchildren, brought a richly illuminated copy of the *Hokman Abat*, the Irin manual for fatherhood.

"Read it before you need it," his father advised. "There are many wisdoms about caring for a mate in the *Hokman Abat*. It's not only about children."

"Is this the Salman translation?" Rhys asked.

"It is."

He frowned. "Do you think it's more accurate than the Gen'ez? I've never asked, but I've read varying opinions on which holds most closely to the—"

"Rhys." His father smiled. "Not the time."

Rhys glanced at Meera. "I imagine she's curious too."

"The Gen'ez version is what's used most widely in Udaipur," Meera said, reaching for the book. "So I'm curious to compare the two for discrepancies."

"Heaven above." Angharad sighed. "She really is perfect for him."

"I told you," Edmund said. "The Creator makes no mistakes, my love."

Meera slid the book over to a silk-covered table with other gifts. "Thank you. We'll enjoy examining it later."

Gift after gift. Song after song. Eventually Rhys wanted all of them to just go.

And then Ata came forward.

As the honored guest, she wasn't required to give a gift. Her presence was deemed to be more than enough. But dressed in her finery, Ata reached into a beaded leather bag and withdrew a small, leather-wrapped package.

"Open it later," she said. "When you are alone. Rhys will understand what it is."

"Not me?" Meera asked.

"No."

Then she turned and walked away.

Ata's departure was like a bell being struck. The singers making music walked toward Rhys and Meera to sing and lead them to the tent that had been prepared. Rhys rose and held his hand out for his mate. She took it and followed him.

They walked down a torch-lit path strewn with purple and red flower petals, then turned at the door and watched as the singers walked back, extinguishing the torches as they went.

And at last they were alone.

# CHAPTER TWENTY-FOUR

R hys let out a long breath. "I thought this day would never come."

Meera turned to him with a smile. "I told you the formal feast was a marathon. And that wasn't even the long feast, that was the short—"

"No." Rhys took her hand in both of his and brought her knuckles to his lips. "I'm not talking about this week."

He led her inside the tent, which had been outfitted like something out of a fantasy novel. Rugs and pillows covered the grass, tapestries hung on the walls, and banners covered the ceiling. A bed was raised on a platform near the center of the tent, and a washroom and bath had been built and partitioned off the back. There was no electric light, but skylights would illuminate the interior during the day and lamps glowed at night.

Meera had never seen anything like it, not even during her luxurious upbringing in Udaipur. "This is amazing."

"Beautiful." Rhys wasn't looking around the tent. He was looking at her.

"Rhys—"

"I want to say something to you," he said softly. He led her to the center of a tent where a round stove sat with a small glowing flame. It wasn't cold, but Meera knew the fire was from the sacred flame burning in the ritual room of the haven. Rhys would need ashes from the fire to tattoo his *talesm* after their mating.

Meera sat on a low cushion near the stove. She couldn't take her eyes off the tall man who was quickly becoming the steady center of her world. She held out her hands for Rhys's as he sat across from her.

He took them and gripped them tightly. "I never thought this day would come for me. I wasn't talking about the formalities this week. Those were... an honor. Truly, I consider all these guests, everything your parents have done, to be an enormous honor." He stared at their joined hands but didn't look at her.

"What are you trying to say, Rhys?"

"I remember those months. That horrible summer. I remember the Rending. The heartbreak and the terror. Though much of my family survived, not all did. More than that, I saw singers I'd grown up with, ones I'd cared for, killed during that time." He looked up, raw emotion clear on his face. "I have been a cynic for most of my life because I didn't think I had any reason to hope. I did my duty, but in my heart I thought our people were too broken to survive. Even as I watched my brothers find mates in the past few years, I doubted. And I honestly did not think I would ever have that same privilege."

Meera squeezed his hands. "Why not?"

"I don't know." He smiled a little. "Maybe the Creator thought I was too contrary. Too much of a doubter."

"It doesn't work that way."

"I know that now." He cleared his throat. "What I'm saying, Meera Bai, is that you are the most unexpected and perfect gift I didn't have the hope to imagine. I could not have imagined you. I wasn't capable of it." He finally looked up and met her eyes. "It has nothing to do with your role or your magic or your status in our world. None of those things matter to me. You are *sha ne'ev reshon*.

My beloved. Your brilliant mind. Your open heart. Your wit and your optimism."

*Thank you, Uriel, for the gift of this man.* Meera's heart was too full to speak.

"You could have been anyone," he continued. "A farmer or a healer or a tradeswoman, and you would still have been the most perfect gift I wasn't capable of imagining."

Meera leaned forward and captured his lips. She couldn't take any more. Tears filled her eyes. Her heart overflowed with the desire to touch him, possess him, make him hers. She pulled away, tears wetting her cheeks. "Put your mark on me, Rhys of Glast, because you are my own perfect gift, a man who sees *me*. Not the role I have been given or the gifts I bear. I already love you. I wasn't expecting that. I never could have imagined it. Thank the heavens the universe is wiser than we are."

Rhys kissed her again, pressed his lips to her throat, and lifted his hands to the back of her neck where he began to unbutton the silk tunic she wore. His dexterous fingers made quick work of the fastening; he stood, drawing her up, and Meera let the tunic fall to the ground. Rhys knelt before her and pulled down the silk that covered her legs. He reached up and untied the linen undergarments that veiled her until she was bare before him.

"Goddess," he murmured, kissing the top of her pubis.

She smiled. "I am no divinity."

"You are to me." He stayed on his knees, running his hands from her knees up to her hips and along the curve of her waist until he cupped her breasts in his hands.

"Mark me, Rhys."

"I have to taste you first." He lifted her leg and draped it over his shoulder. "I'm too hungry to think."

Meera braced her hand and closed her eyes as Rhys feasted on her. He held her breast in one hand, teasing the nipple, and he gripped her bottom with his other hand, pressing her flesh to his mouth.

"Gabriel's fist!" She gasped. The swiftly building climax was so intense she nearly lost her balance. "Rhys!" Her knees buckled, but he caught her around the waist.

"There." He nibbled the inside of her thigh. "Now I can think."

"I can't." Meera carefully lowered herself to the cushion before the fire. "Sorry. My brain has completely abandoned me, so we'll have to finish this mating another time. I can't remember my song."

He chuckled and swatted her bottom playfully. "Turn around."

"Are you staying clothed?" She turned on the pillow. "That seems very unfair."

"If I don't keep these clothes on, I'll never finish your mating marks. If I don't finish, I don't get to hear your song." He pulled her closer, his chest to her back, and whispered, "And I have been waiting hundreds of years to hear your song."

She saw the henna pigment and brushes laid out by the fire. Rhys chose the finest sable brush and dipped it in the ink. Then he kissed the nape of her neck. "Are you ready?"

Meera closed her eyes. "Yes."

As the brush slipped over her skin, she entered a meditative trance. She could feel the fine curls and intricate twists of his hand. The magic touched her skin and grew. She could smell it rising. Taste it in the air. Incense had been lit, and the heady fragrance mixed with the scent of magic.

Rhys hummed as he wrote, old songs and whispered melodies as ancient as the people whose line he continued. In her mind's eye, Meera saw rolling green fields and dark crags of rock rising from cold seas. Grey skies and damp earth that smelled of salt and sea grass.

The brush slid down the center of her back and swept up to her left shoulder. She could feel the fine hairs lifting to follow Rhys's hand. His lips touched her shoulder, a featherlight brush of fingertips on her arm. Meera lost all sense of time, staring intently into the blue and red flame as Rhys marked her.

The trappings of ceremony and pomp had been stripped away.

They were male and female, two beings of angelic blood binding their magic in a ritual as old as time.

Meera felt Rhys's magic lock hands with her own, a simple moment of clarity and understanding as the veil of self ripped in two. A surge of power lifted her mind to a new plane.

Complete.

Her magic flexed and flooded spaces previously unseen. She felt full. Redolent with power.

Rhys was whispering to her. *"Sha ne'ev reshon. Eos ni danya. Sha nahiya. Ya le disha silaam."*

Meera's head spun with his fervent demands. "Please," she whispered.

"Almost, my love." His teeth sank into her shoulder a second before he started writing on it. Rhys spun her around and captured her lips, his brush never leaving her skin. He pulled back and continued writing, his lips full and flushed red, his green eyes intent, his fingers quick and clever as they held the brush. The spells written in henna trailed down her arms then up, dipping across her breasts and over her heart. He marked her collar, her belly, her pubis and her thighs.

His spells were a delicate bouquet of potent magic, as beautiful as they were powerful. Spells for binding their magic. Spells for health and healing. Strength and longevity. As he wrote, Meera felt his magic wrap around her like an embrace. Tears welled up in Meera's eyes. The need for him grew with every inch he marked.

"Rhys, please."

"Breathe, my love." He kissed her. "I'm writing my vow."

"Before time was counted," he whispered.

> *"Your soul was meant for mine.*
> *Sha ne'ev reshon, anchor your heart in me*
> *And I will be your calm port,*
> *Your steady pillar.*
> *Your truth.*

*Hide your heart in mine*
*For I will be your refuge.*
*I will be the sword guarding you*
*And the proverb in your ear.*
*Rest, sha reshon.*
*Your scribe stands near."*

The ink was still wet on her skin when Rhys finished. Kneeling before her, he curled over her feet and gripped her ankles. Meera could tell he was both exhausted and exhilarated. His spells covered her in glowing gold *talesm*. After the henna faded, they would remain within her, bound to Meera through her life.

In that moment she was a living vessel of Rhys's magic, and he was at his most vulnerable. In this state, loaning power to a ready and willing singer, a scribe bared his soul. It was the ultimate moment of trust.

Meera waited motionless for the last mating spell to dry on her skin. The air smelled of fire, incense, and living magic.

"My love." She rose and held out her hand. He lifted his head and looked up. Vivid green eyes held hers, and Meera's heart flipped in her chest.

Even in his weakness, he captured her.

Rhys rose and took her hand. She led him to the bed and he sat. She took her time unbuttoning his tunic and opening it, baring his tattooed skin to her eyes. The intricacy of his familiar *talesm* was now echoed on her skin.

"We match," she whispered.

"We always did." He watched her, never taking his eyes from her face. "You undo me."

Meera paused, then pushed the tunic from his shoulders. "And you have captured me. Like a fox tamed to eat from your hand."

His hand hovered over her breast, but it did not touch. "Are you hungry now?"

She could feel the heat of his palm. "Yes."

Rhys lifted his hips, and she slid silk trousers down his legs. She unwrapped his linen undergarment as he leaned back, watching as she undressed him.

His skin was pale, flecked with dark hair that lightly covered his chest and trailed down his belly. His musculature was firm and lean, not bulky like so many of the warriors she'd known in the past.

"When I first met you," she said, "you reminded me of a leopard."

"A leopard?"

"Powerful and lean." She pushed him back on the bed. "Watchful. Dangerous."

Rhys swung his legs over to lie flat, his erection jutting upward, drawing her touch. He hissed when she gripped him, then let out a long sigh of relief. "You reminded me of an imp, sent to torment me."

Meera smiled. "Do you want me to torment you?"

"In any way you like."

"Like this?"

"Heaven above." He groaned when she squeezed him. "Yes and yes and yes again."

She wanted to kiss over his whole body, but that pleasure could wait. He was vulnerable in this moment, and she found herself uncomfortable with the loan of his power. She was uneasy with it, her body shaking with magic.

Rhys scooted over to the center of the bed. "Come here."

Meera went gratefully, the magic so full within her that her jaw clenched. "I need to sing."

"I know." The playful teasing was gone from his expression. "Meera, come here."

Her skin ached all over. "I need—"

"I know what you need." Rhys took hold of her hips and urged her to straddle him. He lifted her up and reached between her thighs.

"I'm ready." Meera ached with need. "Rhys, please."

He arched up as she slid down, and Meera nearly cried in relief. He filled her, body and soul. Rhys knit their hands together as Meera rocked over him. He urged her down and captured her lips.

"Sing," he murmured against her mouth. "Sing to me."

Meera began the *S'adrasa Kasham*, the ancient mating song of the Irina that would bind Meera's magic to Rhys. As she began, she felt the mating marks Rhys had written come to life as his magic rose and the marks glowed silver in the dim light.

The torches had flickered out, and the only lights illuminating the tent were the low light of the sacred fire and the silver-and-gold radiance of their magic.

Meera sang verses composed by the Forgiven that bound Irin and Irina magic into one, completing the circular power of the heavens. Feminine and masculine. Spoken and written. The language of the heavens alive in perfect harmony. As she sang, Meera saw the fullness of Rhys's soul and her own merge. Dark and light. Night and day. They were necessary to each other, incomplete alone, only perfect in union. He was the body, she the breath.

Meera's song lasted for over an hour; their conjoined magic gave her strength. Rhys held her over him, their bodies linked, potent with magic.

Coming to the end of the song, Meera finally felt the effects of borrowing Rhys's power. She was hungry and exhausted all at once.

He urged her on. "Only a little more." Rhys had been revived as Meera gave him her magic. His skin was ruddy and his *talesm* shone vivid in the darkness. He sat up and wrapped his arms around her, their bodies locked together. "*Sha ne'ev reshon.*" He wiped the tears that fell down her cheeks. "Give me just a little more."

Rhys began to rock gently, the length of him filling her up as her body grew needy and focused on pleasure. Love and desire burned in her breast.

"Just a little more," he whispered. "Give me your song, *reshon.*"

Meera opened her heart and sang the last of her song, the vow that would rest over Rhys's heart, the *talesm* that would shine every time they made love.

> *"Joy of my heart, you have found me.*
> *Others see your wisdom, but I see your light*
> *Hidden within, the burning hope of my reshon*
> *Lights my path. He is the lamp in my hand.*
> *My love.*
> *To him, I will give my ear. His wisdom is my gift.*
> *His counsel guides me, his hand protects me.*
> *His heart is my treasure; I guard it with my voice.*
> *Though my reshon grows weary, I will refresh him*
> *With a song on my lips, I will lift him high."*

Meera gave in to the magic. It wrapped itself around them and bound them. Rhys gripped her hips, lifting her as the power of her voice and his touch grew more potent. Fire chased fire. Gold chased silver. The light grew and built until power rose and spilled over, cresting with her climax and pouring from Meera into Rhys. Rhys into Meera.

She cried out as their souls rose and merged. She did not know whose pleasure she felt. Theirs was only one pleasure. One heart. One soul together.

Rhys held her head in his hands, angling her mouth to his, swallowing their harsh cry of release. The climax was soul deep, holding them in a timeless place. Meera felt her mind's eye open, and she wasn't looking from her own perspective but from Rhys's. In his vision she saw herself, head thrown back, body marked with magic, dark eyes gleaming with gold light behind them. Her hair was tangled around her body, the intricate halo taken apart by her mate's hands. Her cheeks were red and flushed. Her lips swollen from his bite.

She felt him in that moment, felt his heart and his desire. Aching tenderness combined with a need so powerful it nearly destroyed her.

*Goddess*, his mind said.

*Do not call me a goddess*, her mind whispered back. *A goddess cannot love you as I can. Here between us, we leave all roles behind. Call me a woman. Just a woman.*

*You* are *a woman. And you are mine.*

*Come with me*, the voice of memory whispered to them. *And I will show you what we can do.* Meera recognized the power of the *somasikara* rise within her, flooding into Rhys as their bodies and souls remained linked.

---

THEY LOUNGED ON A SILKEN PILLOW, Anamitra's body swollen with child. Firoz held her hand.

"This child is not the keeper," she whispered. "I can feel his mind."

"Are you certain?"

"She must come from another of my blood." Sorrow overwhelmed Anamitra. This son would be beloved, but he would not survive to adulthood, and she would have no other children. Vasu had whispered the news to her as she wept, but she could not tell Firoz. Her mate's fierce heart would be broken. She would treasure every day of her child's life, each one more precious for knowing the end before the beginning.

Meera felt the familiar weight of a newly revealed memory, because each one showed itself only at the time it was needed. She was expecting that. What she wasn't expecting was the already-familiar touch of Rhys's soul settled next to hers. He was Firoz. He was Rhys. He was within and of the memory just as she was.

She fell back into the plane of memory, taking him with her.

---

Kashvi arched her back, the sweet release Jargrav offered her a symphony of pleasure and sharp pain. The tiny bites he'd made with his teeth crossed her belly in an intricate geometric pattern designed to please his eyes as he drank his pleasure from between her thighs.

"Are you going to write this down?" she asked him with a panting laugh.

Jargrav stood from kneeling by the bed. "Of course I am."

Her serious warrior looked grave; only she could see the teasing light he showed no other. As he scribbled notes on a scroll, she drew his erection toward her lips. "Shall I add to your new poem?"

His hand came down on her shoulder and held her in place. "You'll have me singing my own song, lover mine."

Meera pulled away from the intimate moment and felt Rhys with her, his hunger echoing the dark glint in Jargrav's eyes. She forced herself to the surface of her mind, holding her hand out for her mate to come with her.

---

They woke together, their bodies still locked in place. He was erect within her, aroused from the stolen memory of Jargrav and Kashvi.

"What was that?" he asked with a gasp.

"I'll explain later." She pushed him back and braced herself over him, moving with an urgency born of magic and memory. "Again. I need you again."

"Yes." Rhys rose up, wrapped his arms around her shoulders, and rolled them over, landing hard on top of Meera. He rose on his knees, hooking his hands around her thighs and dragging her closer.

"More!"

"This is me," he said, his teeth clenched. "This is you."

"Rhys." She made sure to say his name. He stroked her with expert fingers, the pleasure of it forcing a cry to her lips.

"Come with me," he said. "Meera—"

"Yes!" She came again, her mating marks bright gold in the darkness. He shouted her name when he climaxed. They reached their pleasure together, then Rhys fell to her side, gasping for breath.

Meera gave him a few moments, then she rolled toward him, ready to answer the inevitable questions.

She didn't get far. "Rhys—"

"Quiet." Rhys hooked her leg over his hip. "Jargrav wrote thirteen scrolls of magical congress." His chest was heaving, but he had a familiar glint in his eye.

"I probably should have warned you that— Wait, thirteen? Most of them are anonymous. How do you know—"

"We can both explain later." He entered her with aching slowness. "But trust me. Jargrav wrote thirteen scrolls of magical congress, and I remember them all."

# CHAPTER TWENTY-FIVE

"Adelina."

She turned to the potent voice of her lover and felt her heart rip in two. "What have you done?"

"It was necessary."

"No!" The ground fell from beneath her feet and her mind spun. The faint hope she'd harbored was as dead as her child.

The Fallen gripped her wrists, holding her effortlessly as she tried to beat his chest. Damn him! Damn his angelic brothers! Damn them all to the depths of hell! How could he?

"He was an abomination," the Fallen said coldly. "He was not meant to exist. The havoc he would have wrought—"

"You don't know that!"

"I have seen it." A hint of emotion cracked the angel's voice. "I saw what he would become."

"You're a monster." She fell to the ground and ripped at her hair. "Leave me before I kill you. Like you *killed our son*."

The monster stood like a statue before her.

"Leave me!" she screamed. "You are dead to me. Go back to your brothers and your sycophants. Leave me to die alone."

Adelina wanted to die. Wanted to rip the earth with her fingers and tear the stars from the sky. And she wanted his comfort, which made her rage harder. She screamed at the angel, hurling spells at him that did nothing.

"We are bound," he said simply. "Your magic does not work against me."

She spit on him. "I curse the day I gave you my song."

"I know."

The keening cry tore loose from her throat as angry magic gave way to unrelenting agony.

*My child. My child. My child.*

The angel spoke softly to her. "Meera."

"Why won't you leave?"

He stepped closer, his cold expression never changing. "Meera, you must wake."

---

SHE WOKE from the memory with a gasp.

Rhys gripped her wrists. She was gasping for breath, her eyes darting around the tent.

"Rhys?" She folded into herself when she realized where they were.

Rhys and Meera were still in the mating tent. They had been there two nights, and today was their last day in seclusion. Rhys had tattooed his mating mark the day before, then made love within the heady rush of magic tattooing brought. Meera had fallen asleep, peaceful in his arms, only to step into the deepest well of memory, pulling him with her.

"That was Adelina," Rhys said softly. "*The* Adelina."

Meera nodded. "She was one of the first keepers."

"Have you shared her memories before?" *Do you know what that was?*

She sat up, drawing the silk sheets with her. "Adelina's memories are some of the few that come like that. Usually—like I explained yesterday—they only come when I seek them. They are… intense. And engrossing."

Yesterday had been the host of more than one very complicated conversation. Rhys was still confused how he could share Irina memory as a scribe, but Meera could only explain so much. As far as she knew, no other of Anamitra's line had ever been mated to her *reshon*, especially a *reshon* rich in Chamuel's empathetic blood. So while other bonded mates like Firoz would have experienced memories as Rhys did, none of them were as intimately involved.

For the time Meera and Rhys had been in Anamitra's memory, Rhys had *been* Firoz. He'd had no knowledge of Anamitra's memories that Meera shared later. No idea what their child's fate would be. He had experienced that moment as Firoz had. No more and no less.

And he'd *been* Jargrav, enamored of his mate, dedicated to discovering the sacred and numerous ways of bringing pleasure to the mating bed. Knowledge that had led to more than one very arousing episode once Rhys managed to conquer the creeping sense of voyeurism.

Rhys stroked Meera's hair. "You told me you had to open up for the memories to come. That your shields protected you from being taken over by the past." The idea of Meera locked in some memory with no control over it terrified him. Would there come a time or a memory where he could not reach her?

"That is what happens." She glanced at him. "Most of the time."

"But not with Adelina."

"She was one of the first *somasikara*," Meera said. "I carry her blood. There is a very deep connection."

"I didn't know any of her children lived."

"They did."

"But not the one in that memory," Rhys said softly.

Meera looked up suddenly. "You were there. You joined his mind like you did with Firoz and Jargrav the first night."

Rhys nodded slowly.

"Rhys…" She blinked. "Heaven above, you know what that angel saw. You know why he did it."

His heart sank. "Do you need to know?"

"What?"

"What I saw in his mind…" Rhys shook his head. "Ask me later, Meera."

"How can you say—"

"It's not important now. I'm still processing what being in that creature's head means."

He could tell Meera didn't want to leave it, but she nodded. She'd put it to the side.

For now.

"There's one more thing we need to do today," Rhys said. "Before we rejoin the others tomorrow."

"Only one? That's not very ambitious."

Rhys smiled. "We'll be doing that for the rest of our very long lives. But right now …" He ducked down and kissed her neck. "I am very curious what it was that Ata gave you."

She perked up. "The present. I'd almost forgotten that. And I love presents."

Meera climbed out of bed wrapped in a sheet and walked over to the table by the tent doorway. Rhys watched her walk, delighted by the sway of her backside. He'd explored every inch of her body over the previous two days and nights.

He still couldn't get enough of her.

"I really am extremely fond of your bottom," he said. "I'm considering an ode."

She looked over her shoulder. "An ode to my bottom?"

"A song perhaps. Poetry of some kind."

Meera shook her head. "You're ridiculous."

"No, I'm quite serious. If an ode to that bottom doesn't exist somewhere in Irin memory, it's a glaring omission in the historical record."

She bent over—*yes, please, and thank you*—and retrieved the small leather-wrapped package Ata had given them. She wasn't wearing any undergarments, and the sway of her full breasts as she walked back to him had Rhys transfixed.

"You're staring." Meera climbed back onto the bed.

"I'm newly mated." Rhys tugged the sheet away and bent his head to kiss her belly and her breasts. "I'm allowed such indulgence. I only get you to myself for another day."

She ran a finger through his tangled dark hair. "We'll make the time. Even if life gets busy, we need time for ourselves."

"For ourselves. For our families. For our children." He looked up. "Please tell me you want children."

Her eyebrows rose. "You, the cynic? Don't tell me you harbor a soft spot for little ones. I assumed you enjoyed the role of cranky uncle."

"I adore children," he said quietly. "Before you, they were the only thing that gave me any kind of hope."

"Rhys." She drew him to her shoulder and he rested his head over her heart. The quiet, steady beat that had become the siren song of his life. "I love children and have always imagined becoming a mother when I mated, though I have no idea what I'll do with them. The singers of Udaipur would be charged with raising them, I imagine."

"*We* will raise our children," he said. "The two of us. Others can help, but they'll not be reared by nannies or guards."

"Do you know about babies?"

"I am a very accomplished uncle," he said, trailing a finger around her belly button. "I'll teach you everything you need to know."

"Very well." She played with his hair. "The heir of Anamitra, changing diapers and cleaning spit-up. Udaipur won't know what to think."

He looked up and smiled. "We'll enjoy turning them on their heads. Now, where is Ata's package?"

She handed him a leather-wrapped parcel no larger than a deck of cards. Rhys unwrapped the ties holding the bag together and unrolled it.

A plain, chalk-colored stone fell into his hand. It was worn smooth by magic, its seemingly plain surface pulsing with power.

"Uriel's light," he said softly.

"Rhys, what is it?"

"A memory stone."

He'd never held one in his hand. They were an object for textbooks, the magic so old it was considered too inefficient for modern scribes. Rhys touched his *talesm prim*, felt his newly charged magic wake. The words etched under the surface of the stone came to life before his eyes, each line glowing silver for a few moments before it faded and the next one came to life.

*I, Akune, eldest son of Uriel's blood and chosen mate of the Sun Singer, Atawakabiche, the Painted Wolf of the Uwachi Toma, do write this record before our battle against Nalu, tormenter of the lakes and archangel of the heavens. If we succeed, our sons will know how to kill these Fallen and free the minds of their children, that they may rejoin our race as the Creator intended.*

"Ata's mate knew that Grigori could have free will," Rhys said quietly. "He wrote that it was the Creator's intention that the Grigori rejoin the Irin."

*If we fail, let this record be my lesson to our people, for I will kill Nalu, the murderer, or I will die in the attempt.*

Meera scooted closer. "What is this, Rhys?"

"This is the magic they used to kill Nalu." His fingers traced the edges of the stone. "This is the scribe's role, the part Ata can't tell us. Get me a paper, a scroll. Anything." He looked up. "This is going to hurt."

Her eyes went wide. "For me?"

"For both of us."

———

THE NEXT MORNING his new mate, splendid and glowing in the morning sun, sang a rising song passed down by Anamitra. They greeted the dawn hand in hand, family and friends gathered behind them. They were joyful and refreshed, full of newly shared power and knowledge Rhys knew would give them victory. Akune's memory stone was safely stored with his most precious possessions and would stay hidden from everyone except Damien until he could place it in the most secure library he could find.

Until then, the magic Akune had written was hidden in his mind.

It was an ingenious spell. Wickedly simple and elegant in execution. It was a spell that turned an angel's intrinsic nature against itself and used an Irin warrior's humanity as a strength instead of a weakness.

Rhys held Meera's hand, but his eyes were on Ata across the meadow. Ata watched Meera, not even glancing at Rhys. Her expression was nearly impossible to decipher. Why had she changed her mind about teaching Rhys and Meera? What had she seen between them? Or was she simply divesting herself of everything so she could die as she'd stated?

The breakfast served after the rising song was a simple one. Low tables had been placed under the oak alley with cushions and pillows scattered on the grass. The previous days had been filled with games, sport, and celebrations as Meera and Rhys had been in seclusion, and the easy familiarity of the guests was evident in the mixed company and lively conversation of everyone attending.

Even Ata looked more relaxed. She was speaking with Sabine and Roch, smiling at a trio of children who were tossing a ball over their heads while adults chased them farther onto the grass.

"Everyone is getting along," Meera said.

"Which is exactly the point of leaving them all alone to socialize while we have copious amounts of sex." Rhys sipped the glorious dark tea Patiala had served him. "Excellent tradition."

She smiled and shook her head. "Something happened with Roch and Sabine."

"I saw Ata talking to them."

"She looks steady," Meera said. "More so than she usually is."

"She's clutching Roch's hand like he's her lifeline."

"But she's not hiding. Normally with this many people, she would."

Rhys raised his eyebrows. "Curious."

"Very."

The meal was winding down, and baskets of fruit were being passed around the tables when Ata stood. Though she didn't step forward or make any loud noise, the entire gathering came to attention.

"I was reluctant to come here," she said simply. "Not for any reason other than my own desire for solitude."

Rhys glanced at Maarut and Patiala, whose faces were frozen in polite smiles.

"But I was wrong to be reluctant," Ata continued. "This mating was ordained by the Creator. For this time. In this place. And I was meant to be here as well."

Had Rhys imagined a collective sigh of relief or was that simply a breeze passing from the river?

"The singer and scribe we gather to celebrate come from two honorable lines and families"—Ata nodded toward Patiala and Maarut, then Angharad and Edmund—"but they have made their own powerful connections as well." She nodded to Damien and Sari, Sabine and Roch, who was blushing furiously. "We honor those connections and marvel at the wisdom of a Creator who brings all these strands of fate together in this exact place." Ata turned to Rhys and Meera. "Weaving them together for this precise time."

What was she doing?

"I have spoken to my retinue," Ata said, glancing at the Irin and Irina scattered at tables around her. "And we agree that a gathering of warriors such as this could only have been brought together to fulfill heaven's purpose on earth."

*Gabriel's bloody fist*, she really was a direct one.

Rhys squeezed Meera's hand. "She's going for it."

"Apparently." Meera cleared her throat. "Damn."

"We haven't had time to practice."

"She hasn't even taught me my part," Meera hissed.

Ata lifted her head. "Servant of heaven, come to me." A black raven landed on the oak tree over Ata's head. "Send whispers among the Fallen," she said to Vasu. "Tell Bozidar the Uwachi Toma are rising to rid the world of his presence. In three days' time, the wards will fall. Atawakabiche, the Painted Wolf, waits for his challenge."

The raven flew off with a caw that sounded very much like a chuckle to Rhys's ears. Ata looked at Rhys, nodded, and sat.

The entire party broke into frenzied conversation. Patiala and Maarut rose and rushed to Ata's table where a small crowd was gathering. Damien and Sari appeared at Rhys and Meera's table only seconds later.

"Well," Damien said with a grin. "You two certainly know how to end a mating celebration."

# CHAPTER TWENTY-SIX

D*on't panic, don't panic, don't panic.*
   "You're panicking."

"I am not!"

Sari raised her eyebrows. "And very bad at hiding it. You've had body piercing, haven't you?"

"Not many."

Sari shrugged. "Tattoos don't hurt that much."

"You've marked your skin before?"

"I have always wanted to do this. From the time I was a singer in training."

"I've never even considered one."

Sari offered her a wry smile. "We've got two days to master this magic before the hordes descend. Embrace the ink, sister."

The haven had roused to Ata's call. The most vulnerable singers and children had been taken to safe houses around the country the day after Ata had made her announcement while the haven prepared for battle. Sabine, though she still appeared frail, insisted on staying to bolster the wards and build new boundaries to protect the humans once the Grigori came.

And the Grigori *were* coming.

Ata's call had triggered something. Zep said the attacks in the city stopped that very night, and the Grigori had abandoned New Orleans. He was worried, but Patiala still insisted that Meera could not tell the scribe house anything about them battling the Fallen.

Weapons had come out of hiding. Drills long forgotten in the peaceful, bucolic home had been revived. Meera had seen Nanette cooking meals with her short staff on her back, and Sabine was practicing with silver daggers.

And Sari and Meera would be tattooed by their scribes.

Necessary. It was necessary. And at least she wouldn't be covered in tattoos like Ata was. The singer had explained that part of her tattoos were magically given and part were simply tradition among the Uwachi Toma.

Though Irina song was the core of the magic that would defeat the Fallen, the scribe's role in the spell was to tattoo their singer. It was the most basic blood magic the Irin possessed and not usually necessary. In most cases, Irina mating marks held magic equally as well as Irin *talesm*.

But this magic was blood magic meant to tap into the essential human nature of the Irin race. Humanity was what set the Irin apart from the Fallen. It was their human blood that gave them conscience.

Human blood was the key. Human blood needed to be spilled, and Irina were half human.

Damien and Rhys were preparing their needles by the sacred fire in Rhys and Meera's tent. Ata stood over them, watching while Damien referenced the memory stone.

"Do you think we'll all be necessary?" Rhys asked. "Two mated pairs almost seems like overkill."

Damien said, "Overkill is never a bad idea when you're dealing with an angel."

Ata said, "It would work with only one of the singers. But Nalu killed many of our people before the spell overwhelmed him. I'm hoping that with both Sari and Meera performing it, the magic will work more quickly."

Damien looked up from his needle. "And you?"

"A scribe's magic is never as potent after death. Akune's magic is more memory than power to me now."

Meera felt the words in her chest in a way she couldn't have before. Even in their nascent mating, she felt profoundly tied to Rhys. She tried to imagine losing him, and it took her to such a dark, rage-filled place she needed to back away.

*No. Never. It could not be.*

But that loss, that rending, was exactly what Ata had lived with for hundreds of years.

*And she wants to die. She is doing all this so she can die to be with her mate.*

It was a desire Meera felt more keenly now.

"Why did you change your mind?" Meera asked.

Ata looked up. "Why do you care? Do you want to learn or not?"

"I want to learn."

"Then be quiet and wait for your mate's mark."

Rhys and Damien walked over. Meera and Sari had bared their backs, leaning forward on cushions so their mates would have an easier time giving them tattoos.

"Are you ready?" Rhys asked quietly.

Meera nodded, but she couldn't speak.

*Don't panic, don't panic, don't panic.*

The *talesm* would start on her left side near her waist. It would rise up to her heart, over her shoulder, and across her back before it trailed down the right side. It was a single line. A single spell, and not one mistake could be made.

Damien settled behind Sari, his touch easy and sure. *"Milá?"*

"I'm ready." Sari closed her eyes, and Damien kissed her spine a second before he began to write. "I've been waiting my whole life for this."

"Are you sure?" Rhys asked Meera more hesitantly.

Meera thought about the dark lines marking Ata's body and knew from that moment forward she would wear magic on her skin. Martial magic. Violent magic.

*Blessed are the peacemakers.*

The old human proverb sprang to her mind. Could one be a peacemaker when she was fundamentally marked by violence?

Meera would just have to see.

"I'm sure." She gripped the edge of the pillow. "Go."

---

HER SKIN QUIVERED beneath his needle, but Rhys began the intricate spell and did not stop. He could not stop. He murmured the words under his breath as the magic came to life beneath his hand, marking the perfect skin of his mate.

As he tattooed, Meera and Sari began the song that Ata had spent the past two days teaching them.

The old spell depended on compounding magic. A singer using her voice to bolster a scribe's strength while the scribe tattooed an intricate spell to strengthen the singer. Voice and writing working in harmony to build and build power.

Rhys could feel it coming like a trickle of water turning into a flood.

He had reached Meera's shoulder when her mating marks came alive.

---

THE PAIN WAS EXCRUCIATING. The needle tapped over and over in rapid rhythm, but no endorphin rush came. No sense of calmness or peace stole over her. She felt a knotting in her belly like a twisting sickness. She concentrated on the magic she was chanting, ignoring everything but the building power.

The magic pierced her skin. Her voice reached up. The power was circular. Exponential. It built and built.

The needle had reached her shoulder when the knot in her belly loosed a flood of magic that threw her head back and opened her throat. What had been a whisper turned into a guttural shout.

The magic unleashed a dam inside her. The still sea of memory rose up and crashed over her.

She was Adelina, slaying the sons of her lover until his line was stricken from the earth.

She was Jaleh, who sang for the rain and drowned the army of Zarab where they stood.

She was Kokab, her song so painful it paralyzed the Grigori and stopped their hearts.

She was full to the brim. She no longer felt the needle. Didn't feel her mate's soft lips when he finished the tattoo and pressed his forehead to her spine.

*Meera*. His magic was within her; his voice was in her mind. *Let me walk with you.* He took her hand in the torrent and steadied her until she could channel the minds of other singers into steady streams.

*There are so many.* His mental voice was awestruck.

When Meera spoke, her voice was a chorus. *I hold multitudes.*

*Warriors.*

*Peacemakers.*

*Healers.*

*Destroyers.*

*Irina are no strangers to vengeance.*

*NO.*

She felt herself swimming to the surface. *We must be better.* When she opened her eyes, Meera was staring into Ata's face and her voice came from the depths. "Sun Singer. Painted Wolf. Are you a healer or a destroyer?"

"Do I have to choose?" Ata asked. "All of us are more than one."

Meera closed her eyes and saw the multitudes in her mind, felt the truth brimming inside her. Healer and destroyer. Mother and killer. To create was to destroy. Destroy the past to create the future. Birth a child destined to die. Bind up the wound and fight again.

*There is no end to this.*

"*Somasikara*," Ata said. "You will take my memories now."

Still overwhelmed by the churning consciousness within her, Meera only shook her head.

"You must," Ata said. "I know what I am asking, but I challenge an angel tomorrow. I may not have another chance, and then my people will be lost. Take my memories now while you are flush with power."

"Your people will never be lost," Meera said, her senses renewed by the surging memory magic. "Their blood runs through this land. The earth itself sings of them. Can't you hear it?"

"Please." Ata bowed her head. "Do not let their memories die."

"She's too tired," Rhys said. "Look at her."

Sari stepped toward Meera, visibly shaking and wrapped in Damien's linen robe. "She may be tired, but she's near-bursting with power." She put her hand on Meera's shoulder. "I can feel you. Do this now. Taking her memories will purge some of this magic, correct?"

Meera could only nod.

"Then do it. Or you'll be useless tomorrow."

Meera knew Sari was right. Even though she wanted to beg Ata for another day or two, they didn't have time. "Sit in front of me," she said. "Give me your hands."

Ata's shoulders slumped in relief. She sat on the cushion across from Meera, held out her hands, and closed her eyes.

Meera dragged herself from the edge of exhaustion and began chanting the spell she would need to take Ata's memory.

This time when she fell, the sea stretched into eternity.

"WHAT'S HAPPENING?" Rhys asked in a panic.

Meera had taken Ata's hands and started to sing the keeping spell, then her spine arched, her eyes rolled back, and the audible chant turned into inaudible whispers Rhys couldn't understand. Her lips were moving too fast for him to keep track. He reached for her, only to have Damien tug him away.

"Don't," he warned. "I know this seems strange, but she's entered the mind of a very old singer. She's accessing not only Ata's memory, but the ancestral memory passed from elder to child."

Sari put a hand on Rhys's arm. "The Uwachi Toma have spent thousands and thousands of years on this continent. The memories she's sharing—"

"I know." Rhys pulled up a low stool and positioned himself behind Meera. He shouldn't touch her, but he wanted to remain close. "I've walked with her through other memories."

"And when it's time, you'll walk through some of these with her too," Damien said. "But the *somasikara* are vessels. None of this will make sense until Meera needs it to. That's just the way her magic works."

*And tomorrow she fights an angel.*

His mate might have seemed playful and delicate, but she had to be the strongest woman Rhys had ever met.

He glanced at Sari and Damien. "Do you understand what has to happen tomorrow?"

"Yes," Damien said. "Do we have any idea what form this angel will take?"

"You'll be surprised and you won't." Vasu appeared, sitting next to Meera. For the first time since the angel had appeared to Rhys, he didn't feel like stabbing the creature. Vasu's eyes were intent on the two singers. "This is never easy," he murmured.

"How many times has she done this?"

"Five." Vasu glanced at him. "Two before Anamitra died, the transfer between them when Anamitra was fading—that was the worst—then two since. This makes six."

"And she just... takes all Ata's memories?"

"She doesn't take them away. Ata's memories will remain hers. But the knowledge she holds... To put it in terms you might understand, this is a download. She's adding the memories of the Uwachi Toma to the library that is her mind. You're mated now. You've seen it."

"It doesn't make sense to me," Rhys said softly. "I still don't understand."

Vasu's voice was the closest he'd ever heard an angel to awestruck. "Her mind is a sea that is only a tiny facet of the Creator's mind. Yet a glimpse of it might drive an angel mad because we long for it so much."

"You long for it?"

Vasu met his eyes. "We are creatures of service. Our truest nature longs only for the Creator's presence, even if we are exiled."

"And Meera's mind is a facet of that," Rhys said. "That is why you follow her. That is why you were Anamitra's friend."

Vasu said, "I don't have friends."

"So you say." Rhys turned back to Meera. "How much longer?"

"I cannot say. Every memory is different."

* * *

ATA'S MIND wasn't a sea but a river. Deep, wide, and swift. It flowed from cold mountains to warm shallow pools. It dipped and trickled over stones. It roared and launched itself in violent waterfalls of memory. Meera flowed with it, rolling in the tangled waters of a people born of light and earth.

She cried, a newborn at dawn, staring into the radiant face of heaven. Blood of heaven and earth, she rose from the ground and danced on mountains thrusting toward the sky. Her hair grew long and caught the wind, carried her from snow-capped mountain to swift-moving stream.

She grasped at stars and sang with them before she fell to the earth. Dancing at sunrise, male and female, scribe and singer. The magic was circular. Complete. She pierced her body with thorns and ash from the holy fire. Her legs grew long and swift.

Mother to mother. Magic passed in the blood. Blood of the daughter given to the moon. Moon and sun in eternal concert, circling like the people of the lakes and streams.

*We followed the sun,* old voices whispered. *It led us to the water. We followed the water; it led us to the sea.*

Mountains rose in the forest, built with ice and magic. The earth rising and flourishing. Green grass and the taste of honey on her tongue. Milk flowed from her breasts and fed the earth where vines curled and twisted. Seeds dropped in the furrows and bellies grew fat and fertile.

Children's laughter and women's tears. The cries of warriors, male and female. A dying gasp of the lover who rested on her breast, followed by a golden dawn that stretched on and on until the day was ruled by the sun and the night was no more.

But fire came with the new day of peace.

*And the serpent was slain by fire.*

Smoke rising over a flooded forest. Blood stained the water and turned the soil red.

Blood and smoke. Ash and gold.

The circle was broken.

Broken.

The womb that was waiting ran dry.

---

MEERA WOKE with a sharp pain in her belly, her womb seizing with loss. She lost her grip on Ata's hands and rolled to the side, curled in agony.

"Meera?" Rhys was there, his soft hands held her.

"You lost your child when your mate died." Meera's voice was a rasp. "It was the beginning of the end."

"The peace lasted for five hundred years." Ata was pale and shaking. "Singers' magic was passed from mother to daughter. My son would have taken my brother's place as leader, but we could have survived his loss. If I could not have a child, then it could have been a woman of my blood. Someone. Anyone. Uriel's line always found a way."

"But you hesitated. Found excuses. You hoped to take another mate someday and have more children in your line."

Ata nodded. "I was arrogant. Proud."

"Then after the Rending, the women were gone," Meera said. "Or scattered. You never shared your magic with anyone after that. The Uwachi Toma began to die."

"We died the day I withdrew from the world," Ata said. "There could have been others. I could have found them, gathered them. But I was stubborn and narrow-minded. Angry. I am the one who killed my people. And now you know." Her shoulders slumped. "I have confessed, and I can die."

"You're full of shit." Meera struggled to sitting. "The Grigori killed your people, but your stubbornness may bury them. There are others who would listen to you. Singers you can teach. You taught me. You taught Sari. You could teach the Koconah Citlal or the Dene Ghal. There are hundreds of others who are searching for wisdom, and you're still hoarding it." Rhys held her up, his arms bracing her. Meera felt different than she had after other transfers. Stronger. Healthier. And far more pissed off. She glanced to the left. "Vasu, what are you doing here?"

"Just watching."

Ata eyed him with disgust. "If I had my knives with me—"

"I would have to hide them so you didn't hurt yourself," Vasu said. "You're weak as a baby." He smiled. "Why am I smiling?"

Rhys said, "Because you're petty."

Vasu's eyes lit up. "Ah! Yes, that's probably it."

"Why are you here, Fallen?" Ata asked. "Do you have a message from Bozidar?"

Vasu lounged back on an embroidered cushion, looking like a lazy noble waiting to be served. "Yes. He's coming tomorrow. He said thank you ever so much for opening the wards and he looks forward to killing you all."

"Really?" Rhys asked.

Vasu shrugged. "Okay, he didn't say thank you, but he is looking forward to killing you all. You should expect his Grigori tonight."

Damien and Sari were still waiting by the fire. Damien rose and held out his hand for Sari. "We'll alert the haven," he said. "Meera, rest. I'll let your mother know you need some tea."

"With honey please." She felt like she would crumble at any moment. "Vasu, are you staying?"

"Of course. I can't let Bozidar do anything to you, can I? What would I do for fun?"

Rhys said, "I'm assuming you could just kill him yourself. Why don't you?"

"Could I?" Vasu cocked his head. "I don't know. Probably? Yes, I likely could. But I don't want to."

"Why not?"

Meera muttered, "He's still keeping a low profile. He has bigger targets in mind."

Vasu winked at her. "Clever girl."

"I hate him," Ata said with a grimace. "And I want to stab him."

"And yet you are too weak. How amusing." Vasu disappeared without another word.

"He'll be back," Rhys said. "For now, both of you need to rest and recuperate. And Ata, this will likely not make any difference in your plans, but I agree with my mate. You're full of shit, and there are many singers who would be your ready pupils should you choose to share your wisdom."

"I don't care what you think."

"I didn't think you would." He lifted Meera in his arms. "Now get out of our tent. My mate needs her rest, and you have to challenge an angel tomorrow."

# CHAPTER TWENTY-SEVEN

The morning dawned cold and foggy, unlike anything the humans in Saint James Parish had come to expect. But they shrugged and went about their day, blind to the supernatural conflict brewing around them. No one had noticed when the sons of the Fallen stole into the country. No one connected the old people who hadn't woken from their beds or the transients who had disappeared.

Humans could be so blind.

The old man sat on the dock at the bend of the river, watching the forest of trees that lined the old Delaure plantation. If he were only an old man, he would have seen nothing but an overgrown mess and a crumbling house fenced off from the road.

But he was not an old man, he was an ancient one.

The raven had come to him three days before, speaking in the Old Language of heaven's sons, tempting him and teasing him with the promise of a feast. He'd smelled the echoes of fragrant meat roasting beyond the wards, smelled the spices drifting on the breeze with the scent of river mud and bayou rot.

*They mock you,* the raven said. *They rise again, defiant in their cele-*

*bration. Who are they to think they own the earth? They were mongrel dogs;* he *was the glory of heaven.*

The old man plucked a twisting fish from the line and opened his mouth wide, swallowing the slithering creature whole. He coughed up the bones and flicked them to his hound.

His sons waited on the banks of the river, looking up at him in adoration, waiting for scraps.

"Go," he whispered to them. "The wards will not stop you now. Your feast is within."

---

THE FIRST GRIGORI came from the river. The Tomir sentry raised the alarms and the Koconah Citlal warriors descended on them, four warriors against two dozen. Even with those odds, it was no contest. The Koconah Citlal were an ancient clan who had never lived under a golden age. There was no peace between the Irin and the Fallen in the south. They swept down on Bozidar's Grigori with no mercy, their blades swift and silent in the morning fog.

The long, curving blades of the southern warriors took the heads of the Grigori. They thumped on the ground like falling rocks, and gold dust mixed with the cold, drifting fog.

Runners ran to other watch points.

*Grigori are here. The Fallen is coming.*

Singers and scribes spread through the haven, running along the boundaries and watching the footpaths.

"The fields," Patiala told her mate. "They will come through the cane fields where they can remain hidden."

"The river—"

"Watch the road." She spread her hands over the map of the property. "The Fallen might come from the road. But the Grigori are cowards. They'll come through the fields."

---

MEERA DRESSED IN LINEN, the loose pants and shirt the easiest wardrobe for practicing magic. She wore no weapons, though her mate had many. Her battle would not be fought with blades but with magic.

Sari sat next to her, meditating before the fire.

"Have you fought an angel before?" Meera asked.

"Not directly, but you have."

Meera frowned. "I haven't."

Sari turned to her. "*Somasikara*, you have. You have fought, and you have won."

She nodded, knowing what Sari was trying to say. "I only find that a little reassuring."

"The hardest part isn't going to be killing this angel. The hard part is going to be letting him hurt our mates."

"I know."

---

RHYS AND DAMIEN bound their weapons to their bodies, their *talesm* alive and pulsing with power. Both had shared magic with their mates that morning. Both were redolent with innate and shared magic.

"Missing your black blade?" Rhys asked.

Damien gave him a grim smile. "This will be quite unlike any other battle we've fought. I don't think a black blade would even work against him."

"Do we have any idea what Bozidar's power is?"

"Sight."

"So he might have seen this coming?"

"It's possible."

"We have to provoke him. None of this works unless he is provoked."

Damien slapped Rhys on the shoulder. "He's an arrogant

archangel who calls himself the gift of heaven. And you're you. Provoking him should be the easy part."

---

THE YOUNG GRIGORI stole through the cane fields, tripping over his own feet, rising, running. He gave no thought to snakes or the usual dangers in the dense cane. He only knew that it had been days since the prostitute had fed him, and he was voracious. His father had said there was a rich feasting waiting for all of them, but the Grigori knew Bozidar had been talking to him. Others were there, but his father loved him the most.

*The feast is waiting for you. The sweet souls of the Irina will fill you to the brim.*

It was all he thought of. All he wanted. He could see lights and trees in the distance. The haven was close. He could smell them.

They would be his.

The trip wire caught him unawares. He planted face-first in the mud, caught in the tangled net of tall grass. He didn't feel the pierce of the silver blade at the back of his neck.

His death came too quickly for him to feel anything.

---

ROCH KILLED THE GRIGORI, releasing his soul, only to find three more soldiers piling on top of him. They were running like rats through the wet, green fields.

He sent a sharp whistle up as he fought them off. Push, shove, kick, elbow. No one fought elegantly in the mud.

An arrow sang over his head. He ducked down and it punched through the chest of the Grigori riding his back. Roch kicked out and rolled over, his clothes caked with mud, hoping that none of his brothers or sisters mistook him for the enemy.

It was dark. It was muddy. The fog wasn't helping. In the thick of battle, the line between scribe and Grigori was harder than ever to discern.

"*Ya domem.*" His mate's whisper snaked through the cane fields, hitting its Grigori target without even touching him.

Sabine ran to the edge of the field. "Again?"

Roch struck out and pierced the spine of one Grigori, but two more still struggled. "Again!"

"*Domem man!*"

The stunning spell left both the Grigori reeling, and even Roch was a little woozy. He managed to kick both the men to their bellies and dispatched them before he ran out of the fields.

He grabbed Sabine by the waist and kissed her hard. "You gorgeous, vicious little thing."

"I try."

"You succeed." He grabbed her by the hand. "Let's check on the others. These bastards don't seem to have an end."

The wild expression in her eyes settled with her mate's touch. "Were we foolish? Are you weaker?"

"Your song makes me strong," he said. "A little wild, but strong."

Their mating had been done with no fanfare or ceremony. Sabine didn't want any, and neither did Roch. They hadn't even told Patiala they'd done it, though Roch suspected Rhys and Meera could tell.

No magic bullet had struck its target, but Roch could tell that whatever mating magic they'd shared had steadied her in ways he couldn't before. He was feeling more edgy, more erratic, giving him a better glimpse into her mind. It was a process and would continue to be a process, but in the middle of battle, he decided a bit of an edge wasn't a bad thing.

He caught movement beyond a stand of trees. Dark shadows hidden by the fog.

It was a young singer, a girl who worked in the kitchen, set upon by three Grigori. Roch couldn't tell if she was dead or alive, but she wasn't moving.

"No!" Sabine screamed.

Before Roch could catch what she was doing, Sabine had flicked a lighter from her pocket and grabbed a flame, hurling it toward the three men who fed from her sister.

"Sabine, no!"

The flames arrowed toward the Grigori and enveloped them. Roch ran over and dragged the singer from beneath the burning, screaming men.

She was dead. Her lips were blue and her gold eyes stared into the grey dawn sky.

Sabine screamed and laughed and screamed again. The Grigori curled and howled on the grass.

Roch glanced at the cane fields, hoping all the scribes and singers had run toward the house, because all hell was about to break loose.

---

"THE CANE FIELDS ARE ON FIRE." The sentry ran into the library, her eyes wild.

Patiala looked up. "Sabine."

The sentry nodded.

Patiala grabbed her bow and walked to the back porch overlooking the fields. "Bring me another quiver."

The sentry ran off as Patiala grabbed the first arrow. With the fields on fire, the rats would be fleeing their cover. "Get the scope," she barked at her assistant.

"It's foggy," her spotter said.

"I trust you."

Her angle wasn't perfect, but she hit the first Grigori in the shoulder, spinning him around so she had a clear angle on his back. The second arrow pierced his spine.

"Dust," her spotter said.

"Find me another one."

Where was the Fallen? Patiala bit back a curse and resisted the urge to abandon the house and find her daughter. She needed to trust Meera. She needed to trust Rhys.

"Dust," he spotter said again.

And again.

And again.

Patiala picked off the Grigori one by one, but she was no match for the Tomir warriors moving like shadows through the haven.

But still there was no sign of the Fallen.

---

THE OLD MAN patted the hound dog on the head and glanced at the laughing raven that perched on the top of his house.

"Are you afraid?" the bird asked.

"Who are you?" He was irritated he couldn't discern the raven's identity. This was a trickster. A dragon sent to mock him.

"I am your audience," the raven said. "I came here for a show, but you are boring me. Are you afraid of the Wolf?"

"I'm not afraid of a mongrel woman."

"She's old." The raven taunted him. "She killed Nalu, who was far more powerful than you. I think you're afraid. You probably should be."

The old man turned back to his fishing pole. "My sons can win this battle for me. That is why I made them." Soon he would rid himself of these vain Irina and turn his attention back to the real prize, a city filled with vulnerable humans ripe for the taking. And he would rid the city of the lurking power he'd sensed weeks ago.

This territory was his and his alone.

"Your sons will spill their blood and take your spoils." The raven's message was as annoying as his voice. "But why would you want your sons to enjoy the fruit of this battle?"

"The prize of an old warrior?" He picked his teeth. "I like softer flesh."

The raven transformed into a black cat, sliding between the old man's legs. "Don't you know who waits in that haven, Bozidar?"

"Of course I do."

"No you don't. If you did, you'd never let your sons enjoy this prize." The cat clawed up the old man's back and hissed. "*Somassssikara.*"

The old man rose to his feet. He hadn't known the haven guarded a keeper, not that he'd tell the annoying messenger taunting him.

*Somasikara?*

The lure of such a soul was too powerful to resist.

The old man flipped off his bright red hat, walked off the porch and across the road, passing through the wards with barely a hitch. He shrugged off the itch along his skin. Their wards were nothing to him. Not now. Not with his blood staining the ground. His sons had made their sacrifice, and he reaped the benefit.

Havre Hélène would be his.

# CHAPTER TWENTY-EIGHT

M eera felt him as soon as his step breached the wards. "He's here."

"Where?" Ata asked.

She frowned when she realized where the massive movement of power was coming from. "He's coming from the river. He's coming right through the front gate."

"Arrogant," Sari said.

"Yes." Ata's paint was washed away. She had returned to the hardened warrior they met in the swamps. The two Dene Ghal stood on either side of her, their jovial expressions absent as they watched the Wolf strap twin silver blades to her waist and pick up a silver-tipped spear. "We go."

*I'm not ready yet!*

Sari glanced at Meera as if reading her thoughts. "Come, sister. Go with me."

Their mates were already at the house, assisting Patiala and waiting for word of the Fallen.

"Send a runner," Sari said to the scribe by the door. "Bozidar approaches the house."

As soon as Meera reached the door of the tent she smelled it. "Smoke?"

"The cane fields are on fire," Ata said. "That's not our concern. Begin the spell as we walk. It takes time to build."

Ata sang with them as Sari and Meera walked hand in hand. The Dene Ghal siblings guarded their steps. Meera had heard the woman griping at her brother the night before, wishing her mate had come with her to fight instead of watching their young child.

Meera felt no such envy. She wished someone else had the burden of this magic because the spell, while she knew it would be effective, was also horrible.

They would have to wait until their mates were in agony, near death, before they unleashed its true power. Anything less than that meant the spell was unlikely to work.

---

*"Ashmala, the star that shines*
*Ma'alk, the first eternal mind*
*Baruk, who blesses us*
*Taraná, who feeds us—"*

MEERA AND SARI invoked various names of the Creator-Who-Was as they walked across the warded ground of Havre Hélène.

It was a binding spell, whispered over and over, the simple brilliance of it centered on building and focusing empathy, a human trait unknown to the Fallen. For as Vasu had said, the Fallen were created to be servants of the Creator-Who-Was. They were not relational. They were created with no need for empathy. For those who followed the will of their maker, it was their highest and most primal need.

But empathy was human. Empathy was vulnerability. Empathy required something angels were not capable of.

Empathy, in the end, could destroy them.

The spell repeated and built, drawing on the mating magic of the Irina, with the singer focused entirely on her mate who would be provoking the rage and violence of the angel he was battling. Meera and Sari had to stay connected to their mates, understand and measure the pain, then release at the very moment it was strongest in order to fling the agony back to the angel. The spell would bind the violence and rage inflicted by the angel into its own soul, creating a self-repeating magic that would eat the monster from within.

She could already see Sari's face tense with pain. Damien was being pummeled by something, but her voice never wavered.

Meera, on the other hand, felt nothing.

*Rhys, what are you doing?*

---

HE AMBLED THROUGH CENTURIES-OLD WARDS, a crooked old man who straightened as he grew closer. The swagger became pronounced halfway down the oak alley. His shoulders drew back. His chin jutted out at a petulant angle.

"The old man." Rhys had known something was off about that human. The fact that not a single one of them had picked up any hint of magic from Bozidar's disguise warned him that this evil could not be underestimated.

Damien stood next to Rhys, watching the man approach. "You know," Damien mused, "they choose their human form."

Rhys frowned. "And?"

"And this angel, somehow, decided that this form is attractive," Damien muttered. "Is that a fake tan? I wonder if his teeth are capped like those politicians you see on the television. He looks like a politician."

Rhys couldn't contain his smirk. It was a stark moment of levity in an otherwise tense situation. "I wonder if any of the Fallen have become politicians."

"It would not be a shocking revelation."

The angel approached, eyeing the gathering of Tomir warriors, Irin scribes, and singers. Every one of them was frozen, ready and waiting for the signal. Bozidar had grown from an average human height to somewhere around eight feet tall. His human form slowly burned away. Clothing dissolved, revealing flesh marked by raised *talesm* that radiated in the morning light. He was at once monstrous and beautiful in his heavenly visage.

He eyed the gathered warriors with disdain.

Rhys could still hear the cries and screams coming from the cane fields. Could feel the heady scent of magic flowing in the air as gold dust scattered in the breeze. Acrid smoke filled his nostrils.

But he, like all the warriors who lined the oak alley, was silent.

"Mongrel bitches," Bozidar muttered as he passed a group of singers.

An arrow flew through the shadows, striking Bozidar directly in the throat. The angel took a single step back, glanced down, and roared.

Damien muttered, "And here we go."

Arrows and spears flew through the air, bouncing off the angel and occasionally piercing his skin. He batted them away, pulled them out. They did nothing to him, nor did the warriors aiming them think they would. The goal was to kill time and allow Meera and Sari's magic to build. The goal was to antagonize him until he lost his temper and loosed his true rage on his tormenters.

Which was why Rhys and Damien stood directly in the angel's line of sight.

Damien lifted a shotgun and aimed it at the angel's face. He shot once. Twice. Bozidar turned from batting away a spear to snarl at Damien.

"Sorry, Bozo! Was trying to improve your face," Damien called.

Rhys aimed to be even more annoying. He grabbed a red laser pointer from his pocket and shone it directly in Bozidar's eyes.

"A laser pointer?" Damien reloaded his shotgun.

"Have you ever tried giving a presentation with someone using these? I hate them. Hopefully he will too."

The spears, arrows, and gunshots all came from the trees or from the front porch of the main house. Rhys and Damien were the only scribes in the path of the angel. Everyone else was attacking from the sides.

Bozidar narrowed his eyes on Rhys.

"Can I have the gun?" Rhys asked. "This laser pointer might have been a bad idea."

"Pissing him off *is* the idea."

Bozidar reached down and picked up a giant concrete urn, growling before he hurled it at Rhys's head.

He dived to the side and rolled. "Well, it's working!"

"*Somasikara.*" Bozidar's voice rumbled through the trees. "Where is she?"

"You're really not her type," Rhys shouted. "She generally prefers the nonmonstrous. Also, men with beards."

"She's picky that way," Damien shouted. "Quite the diva."

"Did you come for the Wolf?" Rhys shouted. "I win the bet, Damien. She said he'd be too afraid to come."

"Well, she did kill Nalu." Damien rolled closer to Bozidar and aimed up at the Fallen, shooting the monster in the groin. "And Bozidar is nothing to Nalu."

Bozidar didn't even pause. He reached down and grabbed Damien by the foot. He flipped the scribe over his head and tossed him to the ground, where Damien landed with a hard thud. "I do not fight dogs. Give me the *somasikara,* and she will come to no harm. I will keep her as my mongrel pet."

Red-hot rage rose in Rhys, along with a burning desire to kill the angel. Hate flooded through him, souring his mouth.

*You cannot.*

Ata had warned them. The key to fighting an angel was mental control, not physical. They could never be a match for an archangel. Their only hope was turning his own magic against him.

Bozidar started a low, guttural chant. The magic hit Rhys like a punch to the belly and he doubled over.

*Where is she?* he whispered in Rhys's mind. *Give her to me, and I will leave you. Give me the memory keeper, and I will leave you in peace.*

Rhys threw up. The vomit splashed into a flower bed and turned black, eating at the verdant green plants that had been blooming only minutes before and spreading toward the singer closest to him.

Rhys's eyes went wide. What was this? What had the angel put in him?

"It's not real!" Damien yelled.

All around him, singers and scribes were vomiting and crying. Staring at the ground or at their brothers and sisters in horror. The constant assault had stopped and Rhys heard crying in the background.

"He's making you see things," Damien yelled again over the sound of Bozidar's magic. "Wake up!"

Rhys clamped down on the feeling of terror and pushed it to the edges of his mind. He looked down. The vomit was only vomit. The plants weren't eaten away. The oily black stain was gone.

Rhys felt Meera reaching out, felt her touch the edge of his magic, searching for him. He resisted the connection. What if she felt the angel's influence in her mind? Everything would fall apart. If she could feel the angel, *would the angel feel her?*

*"Bozidar!"* A commanding shout cut through the air. "What dog enters the territory of the Wolf? I am the killer of Nalu, greatest of the archangels." Ata walked through smoke, the glowing fire of the fields at her back. "Have you come to beg for his scraps?"

The angel stopped chanting and lunged toward Ata. The warrior drew her sword, flipped head over heels, and launched herself at Bozidar's head.

Rhys searched the smoke, but he saw no sign of Meera. Where was she? Ata's job was to guard the singers as they built the spell. Only she knew when it would be ready. Only she knew what needed to happen. Now the scarred warrior was flinging herself into battle against an archangel of unspeakable power, and she had no mate to guard her back.

*Heaven above.* Rhys remembered too late. "She wants to die."

---

MEERA CLOSED HER EYES, ignoring the chaos outside the house, focusing only on the building magic in her breast. She could feel it growing like a black hole inside her. Dark magic. Blood magic. It drilled into her soul like a sickness. Every dreadful thought, every antagonism, every negative energy built and built, rolling over and over like an avalanche thundering down a mountainside.

"When?" Patiala said. "We're holding him off and shielding her presence, but we can't wait forever."

Ata's right hand, the Koconah Citlal woman, knelt between Sari and Meera, her face and arms covered in Grigori blood. "I was there when Nalu died and Akune was slain. They will know when it is time."

"Are you sure?"

The woman didn't say another word, and Patiala pressed her mouth shut and nodded.

"I can feel him," Sari said. "He's angry."

"Damien?"

"Bozidar." Her eyes were closed and she was in pain. "He's attacking their minds, creating horrors."

---

THE LITTLE ONES wailed at his feet, their eyes gone, nothing left but bloody sockets they covered with tiny, soft hands. "*Tatá, tatá!*" they sobbed. "Why did you leave us?"

The fear ripped through Damien's chest. *Lies. All lies.* But the little hands reached for his ankles and he could feel them, feel their terror and pain. He saw the fingers missing. The stumps where feet had been. They crawled in the mud, and the ground beneath them was pooled in blood.

*"Tatá, why did you leave?"*

Damien nearly lost himself to rage. The only thing holding him back was the tug of Sari's magic in his mind and the mating mark over his heart.

*Here,* her magic whispered. *My love, I am here.*

---

"I CAN'T FEEL RHYS," Meera said, tears dripping down her cheeks. "I'm completely blocked."

Sha ne'ev reshon, *what are you doing?*

---

RHYS ROCKED ON THE BATTLEFIELD, holding Meera's lifeless body in his arms. The cut ran from her breast down to her belly. Blood was everywhere and her eyes stared up at him, lifeless and accusing. Rain poured over them, drenching the ground in her endless blood.

*You didn't protect me. Why didn't you protect me?*

"No!" he screamed in rage. "Meera!"

*Rhys.*

He wept and clutched her to his chest, soaking his shirt with blood.

*Rhys.*

Her gentle voice accused him.

"I'm sorry," he cried. "Meera, I'm sorry."

*Look up, my love.*

He looked up and he was not on an empty field. It was not raining. No lifeless body was in his arms.

*He lies.*

Rhys narrowed his eyes on Bozidar who was whirling around,

trying to swat Ata off his back as if she were an annoying bug. Through all that, he'd still managed to send all the singers and scribes around him into wailing horrors.

"Wake up!" he screamed. "It's not real. *It's not real!*"

———

"I HAVE HIM," Meera said. "The field is in chaos. Bozidar is sending visions to everyone."

"That's different than Nalu's power," the Koconah warrior said. "Can we use that?"

Of course they could. "We throw it back on him. They need to let it take them over," Meera said. "Tell Damien and Rhys they need to lower their guard. Let Bozidar bring their fears to life."

"No." Sari's face was pale. "Damien will go mad."

"Not if we pull them out in time," Meera said.

"You don't understand what he's seen," Sari said with a protective snarl. "*He will go mad.*"

Meera turned to her mother. "Then it has to be Rhys."

Patiala turned and ran out the door.

———

RHYS THOUGHT he was imagining Patiala running through the smoke. He'd just banished the vision of Meera dying in his arms and was forcing himself to focus on the fight in front of him. The last remaining Grigori had reached the oak alley and gone after the scribes and singers Bozidar held in his grasp. The youngest members of the haven seemed the most immune to the horrors and were doing their best to fight them off. Ata and Damien were attacking the angel, striking each time they were able, only to be thrown off, batted back, or otherwise neutralized.

*He's playing with them.*

The giant had a smirk on his face watching the writhing Irin around him, but he scanned the grounds, still looking for the memory keeper.

"Rhys!" Patiala ran to him, her bow still clutched in her hand. "You have to give in to the visions."

He thought he was hearing things. "Are you a vision?" He reached out and grabbed her shoulder. She felt solid enough. "What lie is this?"

"No lie." Patiala grasped his hand. "Meera says you have to give in. Let the nightmare take you. She'll pull you out in time. You have to trust her."

Nausea spread in his belly. "No." It was one thing to have a vision of horrors attacking him. It was quite another to walk into it.

"It's the only way," she said. "If we can let the horrors build, then they can fling Bozidar's visions back on him. Turn the nightmares against him."

It was completely logical. Of course it was. It was a good plan.

All it needed was Rhys's complete surrender to a monster.

*Do you trust me?*

Falling to his knees, Rhys let his defenses fall.

---

He was walking through the great library of Glast, but there was no one inside. The stacks had been torn down and blood splattered everywhere. Gold dust layered the floor.

"You left."

He turned and Angharad stood at the end of the room. Blood ran down from her cut throat.

"You left."

"*Mam!*"

The floor fell away. He splashed in the sea. Unfurled scrolls and lifeless bodies sank with him. *You left.*

HE WOKE in his room in Istanbul. Rising from his bed, he stepped into the garden. Matti and Geron were playing near the roses, giggling while they told each other secrets.

Rhys smiled. "What mischief are you two making?"

Matti turned and raised a hand. "We're playing."

Rhys froze. "What are you doing?"

Matti began to whisper, and Rhys realized he was truly paralyzed. Locked within his own body by the baby he'd fed and cared for.

"We're playing," Geron said. He walked over and held his hands up. Bloody wounds rose on Rhys's skin. "Don't you think this is fun, Uncle Rhys?"

Their eyes had turned from warm gold and grey to pitch-black.

"No," Rhys whispered.

"Fallen blood," Matti sang. "Fallen magic."

"Blood will tell." Geron ran in circles around him. "Blood will tell."

"No." Rhys sank to his knees. "No!"

As he fell, he saw the rose vines twining around the familiar forms of Ava and Malachi. The vines twisted and squeezed, choking off their breath until they both disappeared in a cloud of gold dust.

"NO!"


HE LOOKED AWAY from the roses and saw Meera lying on the edge of a shell mound, surrounded by a forest flooded with blood. Her body was broken and the light in her eyes was extinguished. She turned her face to Rhys.

"You didn't love me."

"I did."

"If you loved me, why did you let me die?"

"I didn't." He began to cry. "You're not dead. You're not dead."

"I am."

"No," he sobbed. "Meera, no."

He felt his soul rip in two. This was the agony they sang of in laments. This was the true rending. Rhys fell on her, tried to straighten her broken limbs, and cried onto her bloody breast as bugs crawled out of the swamp and swarmed over his lover, hiding her from his sight.

"No!" He tried swatting them away. "Get away!"

It didn't matter what he did. He crushed them under his hand, but more came. They covered him. Covered his *reshon*. Covered the mound. The insects swarmed over everything before they began to eat Rhys alive. He screamed but he did not let go. They crawled into his eyes and mouth, devouring him from within.

---

MEERA OPENED HER EYES. "NOW!"

She gripped Sari's hand and ran to the front porch. Bozidar saw her and looked up.

"*Somasikara.*" He grinned.

Meera and Sari shouted the final lines of the spell.

> "*Ya kaza pure anán*
> *Atam sukha misran.*"

Return the rage given, bind darkness within. Meera ripped the vision of horror from the mind of her mate and flung it toward the fallen angel.

> "*Ya kidin ruta a briya*
> *Vash livah a suf ó silaam.*"

Yoke pride to the soul and bring on the end. She arrowed her magic directly into Bozidar's heart, using the black hole she'd woken in herself to tunnel into the light of his being. He was a star, but even stars could be swallowed.

*"Zimya dawan, Bozidar!"* she cried. *"Da'anamé!"*

She didn't plead for his submission, Meera demanded it.

Bozidar's eyes went wide. The arrogant grin fell from his face. He dropped Damien and Ata, who were both struggling to use their swords, and his shoulders hunched inward.

"What have you done?" His glorious countenance turned grey.

"Do you need to ask?" Meera watched in fascination and horror as a black mark bloomed on his chest and spread. It traced the lines of his *talesm* and slowly covered his body. Bozidar's eyes lost their focus and turned inward. The angel began to groan. Then he began to keen.

"Get away from him," Ata yelled.

Damien and Ata dragged away any singer or scribe near the angel. Rhys was on the ground, and he wasn't moving. Patiala knelt next to him. She looked up at Meera with tears in her eyes.

"He's not dead," Meera whispered. "He is not."

Now was not the time for fear. She opened her mouth and sang a song of victory as Bozidar fell to the earth. He writhed on the ground, curling into himself and wailing like a wounded animal. He gnashed his teeth and snapped at them, but he could not move.

"No!" he wailed. "What have you done?"

Damien limped up the stairs to Sari. "What do the Fallen dream of," he asked, "when they are locked in their own nightmares?"

"Whatever it is," Ata said, "they fear it."

Meera kept singing even when her father appeared behind her. Maarut laid a hand on her shoulder, and Meera reached up and squeezed his fingers, realizing too late he was missing one of them.

"Don't stop singing," he whispered. "I'll get Rhys."

Maarut walked down the stairs to his mate. With the gentle hands of a father, he lifted Rhys as Patiala held his head. They brought her mate up the stairs and disappeared into the house.

Bozidar lay curled and twisted on the ground. Meera descended the steps of the old house and walked over to the monster. Ata, Damien, and Sari walked with her.

His face was inhuman. Ugly and twisted. Frozen in nightmares. He didn't taunt or mock them. Black veins marked his skin, and his eyes stared into nothing.

Meera turned to the bloody warrior at her side. "Ata?"

"You can kill him with your voice, but not without killing your mate. That was the sacrifice Akune and I didn't know that heaven demanded. Even knowing that, Akune wouldn't have hesitated," Ata said. "Not if it meant killing the Fallen and freeing their children. He believed, even when I didn't. That was how we found peace, *Somasikara*. We made the Fallen fear humanity. Even the humanity of their own children."

"So how do we finish him?" Damien asked.

The Wolf reached into her belt and pulled out a small black blade. "The French did steal it. I just stole it back." She handed it to Damien. "A singer cannot wield a black blade."

"No, but she can ruin an angel with her voice." Damien looked at Meera. "Well done, sister."

Meera felt bruised all over. She felt sick. She wanted to vomit. Wanted fresh, clean water in her stomach. She wanted to lay next to Rhys and sleep. Wanted to wake next to him and banish his nightmares.

"Finish it."

Damien plunged the knife into the back of Bozidar's neck. The earth rocked beneath them and the angel rose to heaven, dissolving to dust in the air.

# CHAPTER TWENTY-NINE

R hys knelt in the burned cane field; the bitter smoke stung his eyes and nose. The ground was muddy beneath him, and black ruin stretched to the horizon.

"Gone."

It was all gone. Hope. The future. He'd grasped for beauty beyond his reach, and it had been taken from him. His pride had led to this. His greed. His dishonor.

A soft hand touched his shoulder. "It's not gone."

His shoulders began to shake. "I'm dreaming."

"Yes." She wrapped her arms around his shoulders, and the sweet scent of her skin brought a flood of new tears. "You're dream-walking. With me."

"I'm sorry," he whispered.

"For what?"

"For letting you die." The wound bled fresh. Every night would be this way. Every night he would relive her life. Her death. It was what he deserved. He'd known hope wasn't for him. He'd known it wasn't what he deserved.

"*Reshon*, wake up."

"No." He clutched her arm. Reliving her loss was worth it if he remained in her presence for even a few more moments. "Stay with me."

"I'm here." She bent to his cheek and kissed it. "Do you understand?" She sang in his ear, and green shoots speared through the mud. She sang and the sun rose over the horizon. "The nightmare cannot have you," she whispered, "because you are mine."

Soft grass grew beneath his knees. He bent down and touched his lips to the earth. The stink of death was gone and the air smelled sweet.

"Open your eyes, my love."

---

RHYS OPENED HIS EYES, and Meera was lying next to him. Her cheek was stained with ash and her eyes were bloodshot, but she was there.

She was alive.

A hoarse groan ripped from his throat. He reached for her and clutched her to his chest. Raw cries ripped his chest. He coughed and wept, holding her and touching every part of her.

Her arms. Her precious hands and fingers. He kissed her knuckles and felt down her body. Her legs were strong and whole. No gash marked her belly. No blood stained her skin.

He kissed every inch of her face and rocked her back and forth.

Alive. Alive. Alive.

The terror hadn't been real. The visions were lies.

"My mother?" he asked roughly. "My father? Your parents?"

"Safe. They're all safe and mostly whole."

"We need to call Istanbul and check on the children."

She nodded. "We can do that."

"Damien and Sari?"

"Alive and conscious. You were the one who bore the brunt of Bozidar's attack." She was crying too, wiping the tears from his face. "You were the one who let him in."

"He's dead." The angel must be dead, or his courageous mate would still be fighting.

"He's dust," Meera said. "Facing judgment before the Creator now."

It was over.

Rhys coughed and looked around the room, not recognizing where they were. "What is this?"

"My old room at the house. Unfortunately, our tent and most of the outbuildings were burned. The house is okay though."

Rhys tried to sort through his muddled memories of the battle. "What started the fire?"

"Sabine." Meera pulled away, and her expression was stricken. "The Grigori killed a girl. Sabine saw them, lost control, and…"

"Is everything gone?" He pulled Meera back to his chest; even a little distance between them felt unbearable.

"Of course not." She wrapped her arms around him. "We're here. We lost five of our people, and many more were injured, but far more survived. We killed an archangel. We protected our home."

"We let him in," Rhys murmured. "What were we thinking?"

"He felt safe." Meera took a deep breath. "That *thing* lived across the road from us, knowing who and what we were for decades. Taunting us right under our noses even though we couldn't see him. Watching and waiting for a moment of weakness."

"They can't feel safe," Rhys said.

"If they feel safe, then no one—not Irin or Grigori, and definitely not human—can feel safe. We have to change the rules. In a fair fight, any Irin warrior can stop any Grigori. We've played fair and we've mastered them."

"But we're battling a hydra, chopping off heads that only regrow."

She nodded. "We have to aim for the heart."

"Aim for the Fallen."

"And have mercy on the sons."

It was a difficult thing to wrap his mind around, especially after waking from a nightmare. "Ask me tomorrow for mercy. Right now I need to remember you're alive."

---

RHYS AND MEERA washed together in the bathhouse, which had only taken a little bit of fire damage, and hid in Meera's room. After a short visit from his parents and hers—along with a call to Istanbul—he locked the door and took her to bed.

The first time they made love was urgent and necessary. The second time was tender. The third sent them both into dreams.

---

THEY WALKED hand in hand through a path in the fields. Rustling cane whispered around them and night birds sang overhead.

"I saw you here before."

He turned to her. "Before?"

"Before I knew you."

"How did you see me?"

She kissed his knuckled. "I loved you then as I love you now. I just hadn't met you yet."

At the end of the path lay a sea of memory that stretched into the distance as stars danced overhead. The stars touched the water and the water touched the stars.

She walked up and touched her toes to the edge. The water danced before them, and the waves whispered secrets.

"Do you swim?" she asked.

"I can."

"Will you swim with me?"

"Always."

She slipped off her shoes, but he held her back. "Why?"

"Not tonight."

The whispers became louder; waves rose along the shore.

He turned to the sea. "You are not her master."

The whispers grew quiet and the waves calmed.

"Tonight we'll walk," he said. "You need to rest."

She took a cleansing breath. "I do need to rest."

"I know you." He bent down and kissed her softly. "I've always known you."

"Did you?" A smile bloomed on her face. "That's right. You did."

# CHAPTER THIRTY

S abine met Meera on the edge of the blackened cane fields.

"How is it so muddy?" Meera asked.

"I called the rain." Sabine turned to her, speaking in English. "I remember how to do that now."

"Handy."

"For a farmer? Yes."

Meera stood next to her sister, charred fields before them and a ruined haven in the back.

"Roch and I are mated," Sabine said. "I imagine you probably guessed that. We didn't tell anyone because... We didn't know if it would make any difference." The singer's face was solemn. "I thought it had, but it turns out he's just officially bound to a crazy woman now."

"It has made a difference." Meera glanced at her from the corner of her eye. "I can see it. You will too when you're not so upset. And Roch has always been bound to a crazy woman. Now it's just official."

Sabine's smile was sad. "I thought I was going to get better. I really did. And then I did this."

"You had a moment of madness and lost control in your grief."

Meera shrugged. "It happens. Just think of it as a jump on the harvest this year."

Sabine grimaced.

Meera softened her voice. "You were trying to protect us. You'll rebuild."

"I don't know—"

"I'm going back to Udaipur with Rhys."

Sabine's jaw dropped. "What?"

"We need to be there. I need to make this training available to mated pairs who want to learn. The Tomir have already secured Akune's memory stone and are taking it to the treasury. Rhys is ready to be settled for a while, though I think we may go to Istanbul for a long visit soon."

Sabine blinked. "Your parents?"

"My retinue comes with me."

Sabine's eyes grew panicked. "And the haven?"

"Is yours," Meera said softly. "Yours and Roch's. My parents agree with me. This land is tied to you and your blood. Your wards deterred an archangel for decades, even when you were unstable. You're the best possible guardian for Havre Hélène."

"You're leaving me in charge of the haven?" Sabine's laugh was manic. "I'm still half-crazy!"

Meera pursed her lips. "You're a work in progress. Aren't we all?"

"Meera, I appreciate what you're trying to do, but—"

"I trust you." She put a hand on her sister's shoulder. "I trust you, Sabine. Roch trusts you. My parents trust you." She leaned forward and kissed the singer's cheek. "You need to trust yourself."

Sabine's expression was still riddled with doubt.

"And Ata has agreed to stay close," Meera added softly. "She will not fade. At least not right away. Some of the Koconah Citlal will be moving north to rebuild the Atchafalaya mound with her. You'll have another haven close by. A new place of learning. An elder able to guide you."

"Meera…" Sabine's lip trembled. "I want to succeed. I want to be a guardian. I just… don't know what you expect me to do."

"I expect you to rebuild. I expect you to be you. Bright and brilliant and protective and strong. And when the madness threatens to come and overwhelm you"—she gripped Sabine's hand tightly—"I expect you to grab it with both hands, find a safe place, and dance."

---

MEERA FOLLOWED the sound of shouting men to the old guest house, partially renovated and now partially burned. Rhys stood on the roof, tossing down charred shingles to waiting scribes on the ground. His shirt was stripped off and sweat ran down his chest.

His body was whole. The only wounds left in her mate were those on his psyche. And those, like any wound, would take time to heal.

He was even starting to get a tan. Meera hadn't thought that was possible.

Rhys spotted her, whistled for a break, and climbed down the ladder. "Hello." His smile was still held an edge of arrogance, but it was softened by the love in his eyes. "Did you talk to Sabine?"

She nodded before he kissed her. "How much water have you drunk today?"

"Enough." He gave her bottom a friendly smack and nudged her toward a towering magnolia tree that shaded what was left of the back porch. "And they insisted on pouring that hideous tea down my throat."

"It's cold and sweet and delicious."

"It's cold tea." He grimaced. "It ought to be illegal."

She handed him a bandana to wipe his forehead.

"Tell me again"—he stretched out on the grass and put his head in her lap—"about the weather in Udaipur."

"Um… not as humid as here?" *Most of the time.* "And don't forget the large, air-conditioned fortress. It's been completely modernized."

He smiled and closed his eyes. "Right now that's good enough."

They lay in the shade of the magnolia, listening to the hammering and labor of the scribes and singers repairing the guest house. In the distance, Sabine started her old gramophone and pointed the horn toward the workers.

The breeze smelled of burned sugar, but it was soft and cool. The fire had burned the chaff away from the cane, but it had not destroyed everything. The ground was raw and exposed, but the roots remained. The cane would grow back, healthier than it had ever been.

"I love this place," Rhys said. "Quite surprised by that, but I do. I want to come back."

"But you don't want to stay."

He reached up and twisted a lock of her hair around his finger. "Now is the time to let others build. You came to record a dying language only to revive it. Ata's traditions were dying. Now they're growing. You helped with that."

"And you came to learn martial magic, only to dread its use."

"I've always dreaded its use," Rhys said. "But I understand its necessity."

"What do you do with a weapon too terrible to use?"

"Use it on the terrible." He drew her down for a kiss. "And then hope you can rebuild."

"One day, when the Fallen are gone, there will be peace."

"I believe that now," Rhys said. "I can see it, thanks to you."

She smiled. "I'm glad."

"And thanks to me." Vasu appeared next to them, stretching out on the grass like a lazy cat. "You're not going to get rid of me, are you? How boring would that be?"

Rhys closed his eyes. "If I don't look at him, can I pretend he's a figment of my imagination?"

"Then you'd have a disturbing imagination," Vasu said. "Did I hear that you're returning to Udaipur?"

"Yes, Vasu."

"Good, I'll see you there." And he disappeared.

Rhys stared at her. "Please?"

"No. And you have to stop throwing daggers at him. I don't need holes in the walls."

"They're stone walls, aren't they? They can take a few holes. Gives them character."

"Try to restrain yourself."

He grumbled, "You like it when I'm unrestrained."

Meera laughed and Rhys pinched the back of her thigh. Then he rolled over and bit her leg while she yelped and scrambled away. They played in the grass like children, drawing disapproving glances and rolled eyes from the scribes and singers trying to work.

Meera's whole life had been bound by duty. She'd been born to it, nursed on it, and resigned to its call. She'd traveled to the other side of the world to escape its clutches, only to find her heart's desire in the soul of a rebellious scholar.

Rhys had remembered how to teach mischief.

And Meera was more than happy to learn.

# CHAPTER THIRTY-ONE

*Five years later...*

Vasu showed up when Rhys was changing the diaper of his only son. Quick as a wink, a dagger escaped its sheath and flew through the room, lodging in a chink in the wall just as the angel darted away.

"I'm telling her you did that."

"It makes the baby laugh," Rhys said.

Bodhi Anil, tiny scribe of Udaipur, did laugh. He grabbed his chubby feet and rolled to the side, watching the angel who'd taken the form of a bird and hopped up and down on the window ledge in Bodhi's room. The bird seemed completely content to play the clown for the little round baby whose belly shook at the bird's antics.

And that, more than any strategic reasoning, was the reason Rhys put up with Vasu.

"Why are you here, Vasu?"

The bird transformed into a slim young man in his early teens. It was the most common disguise Vasu used in Udaipur. Rhys had been surprised to see the angel running among the gardens and walkways of the fortress with little to no notice from anyone other than Meera and himself.

"I just wanted to visit the baby," he murmured, leaning over Bodhi's crib. "His dreams are beautiful."

The fear never left him. No matter how many times Vasu visited their household, Rhys felt the clutch of it in his throat. It was the instinct of a father, fierce in his love for his mate and his child. He knew Vasu was more powerful. No matter how many of the Fallen Rhys and Meera had slain, Vasu was more powerful than the others. And Vasu had aims none of them could predict. If he chose to harm Meera or Bodhi, it was out of Rhys's control.

It was a hard and humbling reality.

And yet... Vasu didn't. Instead, he'd appeared the night of the baby's naming ceremony and stood over his cradle with the closest expression to tenderness Rhys had ever witnessed from the inhuman creature. There was something about the little boy that drew the angel, just like he was drawn to Matti and Geron in Istanbul.

Rhys picked up his son and bounced him on his hip. The boy was eight months old and the star of Udaipur. The light of his grandparents' lives and the favorite of every scribe and singer in the fortress.

"He's hungry," Rhys said with an obligatory scowl. "I'm taking him to Meera. Come along if you want."

"Fine." The young man followed Rhys from the room.

All the way to Meera's teaching quarters, Rhys did his best to avoid the curious scholars and warriors who populated the castle. Every single one of them would want to hold the baby. Everyone would offer to take him to Meera. If Rhys and Meera weren't careful, their child would have been raised by everyone in the fortress except his parents.

"I think I'm beginning to like you," Vasu said. "You're the only being on the planet who dislikes people as much as I do."

"I don't dislike people." He looked down at Bodhi. "I don't dislike you, do I, little man? I like you and your mama the best."

"Meera and Bodhi don't count."

Rhys glanced at Vasu. "I don't dislike most people."

"You just don't have any patience with their foolishness."

"If you're referring to that emissary from Jerome's staff, he had it coming. He interrupted her five times during an audience that *he'd* requested. If you're not going to let the Sage of Udaipur speak, then why waste her time?"

"Do you want me to kill him?"

Rhys took a deep breath. *And this is why my guard is never down.* "No, Vasu, you cannot kill him. He had a political disagreement with Meera, he wasn't threatening her."

"But he was still annoying."

"Yes. Annoying is not a threat."

"It's a threat to my sanity."

Rhys wondered if it was a bad sign that he was beginning to agree with Vasu more than he disagreed. Bodhi reached for the angel, and Rhys reluctantly let him go.

Vasu brightened immediately. "Hello, little wisdom."

The baby began babbling to the angel, who answered back with just as much sincerity as the child was exhibiting. Rhys was beginning to wonder if Vasu was playing along with Bodhi or honestly understood something his parents didn't.

"I know."

"Bah!"

"I'm saying I agree with you, child."

"Guh ish pfffffft."

"That's not part of our agreement. You'll have to speak to your parents about that."

*What agreement?* Rhys shook his head. Having an infant had clearly been a strain on his sanity because he was starting to feel left out of a conversation between an angel and an eight-month-old. "I need more sleep," he muttered.

But as he turned the corner, he was reminded why he didn't waste time with sleeping.

His mate, the love and joy of his life, sat on a low chair under an arching fig tree with three young singers on mats before her. She was singing the weaving song Ata had taught her so many years before and instructing the young women in weaving while they discussed the instrumental magic being developed by *kareshta* in Southeast Asia.

Meera looked up when she heard Bodhi's laugh, and the smile that lit her face nearly stopped Rhys's heart in his chest.

Rhys took the baby from Vasu and walked to Meera's side. "*Sha ne'ev reshon.*" He leaned over as if he were bussing her cheek, but instead he ducked down and pressed his mouth to her neck in a lingering kiss. "We missed you."

"I missed you too." Her pulse fluttered against his lips. "Sisters, would you excuse us?"

The young singers giggled and picked up their books, leaving Rhys and Meera alone with Bodhi.

And Vasu.

"Depart, heavenly creature." Rhys pulled a large cushion to his wife's feet and lounged against it with the baby in his lap. "I want privacy with my mate."

"Fine, but I'm taking Bodhi with me."

Meera's eyes didn't leave Rhys's. "Unless you're going to feed the ravenous little man, I wouldn't suggest it."

Vasu grumbled and disappeared.

"It's like having an infant and a teenager at the same time," he said.

"I talked to Ava today. I'm not looking forward to the teen years."

"The twins are only nine."

"They're precocious."

Rhys frowned and kissed the mop of sable hair that covered his son's head. "Our child will never be as unruly as the twins."

Her eyebrows went up. "Yes, because his father was such a mild-mannered and calm child."

"I have no idea what you are talking about. I was an angel." *And we all know how much trouble they can cause.* As if Bodhi were reading his father's thoughts, the little boy let loose a peal of laughter and reached for his mother's breasts. "Yes, I suppose he does take after me a bit."

"Give me my boy." Meera reached for the baby, her face alight with joy. "Hello, my darling. Have you been a good baby today?"

She'd been an unsure mother at the beginning, reluctant to make any mistakes or missteps. She'd never been around children and didn't know their quirks and moods. She wanted to do everything perfectly and was often very hard on herself.

Luckily, Rhys was as accomplished at soothing the mother as he was the child. Over the early months of Bodhi's life, Meera's insecurity in her new role faded away, and she became a delighted and easy parent. She brushed away the offer of nurses and nannies, insisting that she and Rhys were more than capable of caring for their son with a little help from Patiala and Maarut.

Like so many other things in Udaipur, it was a change and not always a welcome one.

But under Meera's leadership, many of the more formal aspects of life in the fortress had been quietly retired. Though a deep vein of tradition still flowed through the fortress and the library, new ways of life were blooming.

The first *kareshta* came to train at Udaipur a year after Meera and Rhys returned. In fact, it was his own brother's mate, Kyra, who became Udaipur's first *kareshta* pupil. Meera reasoned that if the library in Udaipur exhibited a willingness to train the daughters of the Fallen, soon other houses would follow suit, for who would question the wisdom of Anamitra's heir?

Meera opened her tunic and brought her son to her breast. The little boy gave a sigh of contentment and settled his chubby palm on Meera's chest, blinking up at her with dark, adoring eyes as he began to nurse.

And Rhys said the prayer he'd repeated every day since Meera had chosen him.

*Creator, how have I pleased you? Show me, that I may always be so blessed.*

Their world was changing rapidly. And while evolution was necessary, the history and memory of the Irina had become an even more important anchor for their world. Dozens of emissaries arrived in Udaipur every week, and it was Rhys's job to sort through those who truly needed council and those simply looking for the tacit approval of a respected authority.

Rhys of Glast had no problem being the arbiter. In fact, on most days he quite enjoyed it. Meera's role in Udaipur was complicated enough. Rhys was more than happy to be the bad guy.

After all, if he was the bad guy it was only in service to the woman who was the center of his world. Other people had their own interests. Politics. War. Rivalries.

Rhys had Meera.

He would always guard her. Always be her most honest counselor, her truest lover, and her most loyal friend.

It was worth it. Every trial and tradition, every formality and constraint. He would give her anything—the blood from his body should she ask—because she was still the most perfect gift he hadn't been capable of imagining.

And she gave him hope.

THE END

# SIGN UP FOR A FREE SHORT STORY

Thank you for taking the time to read this book! If you enjoy a book, one of the best things you can do to support an author is to leave an honest review wherever you bought your copy. Thank you for taking the time to let others know what you thought.

Sign up for my newsletter today and receive a bonus short story "Too Many Cooks" FREE in your inbox! Subscribers receive monthly updates, new book alerts, exclusive contests, and original short fiction featuring favorite characters from my books.

# ACKNOWLEDGMENTS

This book had quite a journey.

I want to steal a few lines here at the end to thank those on (and off!) my writing team who helped Rhys and Meera come to life.

---

I want to send a special acknowledgment to the staff at the Lamothe House in New Orleans, who were so helpful guiding my introduction to the Faubourg neighborhood. It was our home away from home and a treat to stay with you.

I also want to thank our wonderful guide, Ginnie, the very knowledgeable staff at the Laura Plantation, and the Torres family of Bayou Boeuf. Your collective knowledge of Saint James Parish and Creole Louisiana was invaluable to making this book as authentic as possible. Any missteps are mine and mine alone.

---

Thanks to my family for slogging through this book with me, even when I lost my notes and had to reconstruct so much. I wasn't always the most pleasant person to be around, but my husband and son persevered, fed me coffee when I needed it most, and shoved me onto a bike and out of the office when things got too hairy.

My hat is off to you, gentlemen.

———

To my readers, you will always and forever have my most sincere thanks, but this year in particular, you've been champions. Thanks for supporting me through all the ups and downs. Thanks for your patience and understanding when life doesn't go according to plan.

I am the luckiest writer in the world, and you're a big part of that.

To Damonza, who designed the beautiful cover for THE SEEKER, I thank you. To Anne and everyone at Victory Editing who are always such professionals, I am forever in your debt. And to my agents at Dystel, Goderich, & Bourret, thanks for smoothing the way.

> *Two are better than one, because they have a good reward*
> *for their toil. For if they fall, one will lift up his fellow.*
> *But woe to him who is alone when he falls and has not*
> *another to lift him up.*
> *Ecclesiastes 4:9-10*

# ABOUT THE AUTHOR

ELIZABETH HUNTER is a *USA Today* and international best-selling author of romance, contemporary fantasy, and paranormal mystery. Based in Central California, she travels extensively to write fantasy fiction exploring world mythologies, history, and the universal bonds of love, friendship, and family. She has published over thirty works of fiction and sold over a million books worldwide. She is the author of Love Stories on 7th and Main, the Elemental Legacy series, the Irin Chronicles, the Cambio Springs Mysteries, and other works of fiction.

ElizabethHunterWrites.com

ALSO BY ELIZABETH HUNTER